ADEPT OF FORGOTTEN MYSTERIES

SORCERESS OF THE CELESTIAL NADIR

USUSI

It's not the dark—it's what the darkness hides.

Qari reached out from the glow into the darkness where Ususi trod and said, "Take my hand, Sister. You shouldn't be so afraid of the dark, you know. Darkness is my constant companion. It doesn't terrify me. I've learned to make a friend of it."

Ususi strained toward the hand. She struggled to rediscover her missing limbs. Or should she just will herself forward? She yelled, "Qari, where are we? What's going on?"

Qari swiveled her head so that the shocking emptiness of her missing eyes was indisputable. Qari said, "You need to embrace the darkness, as I have." So saying, she reached up with her other hand and pointed at the sunken, cavernous pits where eyes should have looked out.

WILL SHE SEE WHAT DARKNESS HIDES?

THE WIZARDS

Blackstaff
Steven Schend

Bloodwalk
James P. Davis

Darkvision
Bruce R. Cordell

Frostfell
Mark Sehestedt

December 2006

FORGOTTEN REALMS

THE
WIZARDS

DARKVISION

Bruce R. Cordell

The Wizards
DARKVISION

©2006 Wizards of the Coast, Inc.

Cover art by Duane O. Myers
First Printing: September 2006
Library of Congress Catalog Card Number: 2005935522

9 8 7 6 5 4 3 2 1

ISBN-10: 0-7869-4017-4
ISBN-13: 978-0-7869-4017-2
620-95545740-001-EN

U.S., CANADA,
ASIA, PACIFIC, & LATIN AMERICA
Wizards of the Coast, Inc.
P.O. Box 707
Renton, WA 98057-0707
+1-800-324-6496

EUROPEAN HEADQUARTERS
Hasbro UK Ltd
Caswell Way
Newport, Gwent NP9 0YH
GREAT BRITAIN
Save this address for your records.

Visit our web site at www.wizards.com

Dedication
For Dee

Acknowledgments
Rob Heinsoo's development suggestion
is much appreciated, as it lays the groundwork
for Kiril Duskmourn's emergence
as an important character.

Martial arts instruction provided
by John Staab gave the author firsthand
knowledge of the effectiveness of several
techniques, such as choke-outs,
which make appearances in this story.

PROLOGUE

A barren land smoldered beneath a cover of ash.

The desert was still, grim in its isolation, and decorated with bleaching bones and drifts of snow white sand. Ripples across the dunes traced meandering lines under a merciless sun.

The roar of a storm shattered the deathly quiet. The chalky stillness rose up to become a howling waste of breathless suffocation. Lightning etched jagged trails through clouds of airborne grit. Wind scrabbled over blasted stone.

When the wind screamed, the desolation recalled the ancient mistake that birthed it, a mistake of such scope it doomed its perpetrators, burying their memory beneath centuries of sand.

A blot above the storm twisted, strained, and ripped. Ruinous dark lay behind the dust-hazed sky, littered with debris.

The aperture over the desert widened, and something moved within the newborn gap. Something terrible.

A splinter of darkness slipped through the opening and fell—a shard of stone almost a mile in length—like a hungry predator bounding into unguarded territory.

It slammed into the desert floor, and nearly three hundred feet of its razor-sharp length punched into the bedrock beneath the shifting dunes.

Shock waves pounded out from the point of contact, clearing the air and overpowering the dust storm's constant shriek. Moments later, the storm settled back, cloaking the waste in a roaring haze of stinging sand. The splinter remained upright, its head rising above the storm's roil as a lighthouse rises over a wave-racked coast. In the full light of reality, the structure bore a faint purple translucence along its edges, though its core remained black.

The time of imprisonment was finished.

The time for sweet retribution was at hand.

CHAPTER ONE

Spring, 1374 DR

The vengeance taker walked steadily, not hurrying, not lazing.

He ambled across a scrubland of long dead grass, his boots crunching brown blades, and his steps carrying him past stony outcrops. Sparse foliage, cactus, and an occasional squat, thorny tree dotted the endless miles. Waterless gullies sometimes splintered the terrain. The only limit to his vision was the next distant rise. Unless he counted the mountains.

To the taker's left was a rugged, desolate barrier of stone. The crags of those distant heights promised no mercy on any who attempted passage. But Iahn Qoyllor traveled a path parallel to the mountains, not toward them. The Giant's Belt would not try his strength, at least not this journey.

His unwavering stride ate the miles.

He had been on the trail just over two months. When he received the order to find the fugitive, he accepted the task, despite its seeming impossibility. Within a few tendays, his considerable skill unearthed a trace nearly ten years cold. Until recently, his target had lived in the city of Two Stars. He wondered again why she'd left after such a long residence. Had she sensed his eventual arrival? Iahn didn't like to dwell on uncertainties. Among his brethren, he was known for his preference for action over supposition, and proof over faith.

The vengeance taker was close. He no longer sustained himself by imagining the day he would finally catch her. The need for such a crutch had passed. He knew with certainty he was just days behind the woman. Maybe only one day, if she paused in her route, as she sometimes did.

Iahn was a creature out of place in this too-bright wasteland. A masterwork crossbow, its arms folded against the barrel, was strapped to his left calf. His hide leggings were the color of volcanic stone, and the leather vambraces that wrapped his arms from elbow to wrist were blood red. His eyes were flecks of winter ice.

In his right hand Iahn carried his dragonfly blade with its long hilt carved of lyrwood, a tree of the ancient world that now grew only behind the Great Seal. The hilt concealed a slender dagger, needle sharp, that few living creatures had ever seen. Many foes, now dead, had glimpsed its silvery line as it ended their days. He called it a thinblade. Others of his order called it a stiletto.

A shriek jerked Iahn's attention to his side. His left hand was instantly in motion, anticipating trouble, before he recognized the scrub falcon perched on red-leafed chaparral. He nodded at the small predator and lowered his arm, the object affixed to his hand unused.

Oiled straps secured a pitted metallic relic—his *damos*—to the palm of Iahn's left hand. Every vengeance taker was issued one. A damos was the only badge of vengeance taker rank. Their most feared weapon, a damos contained the baleful fuel for vengeance taker sorcery that doubled as a uniquely potent venom.

Iahn topped another rise and saw telltale wheel ruts and hoofprints. Those ruts had become like a friend—obvious markers to hearten him. He no longer needed to ask the Voice for directions to stay on the fugitive's trail. In fact, the tracks revealed she traveled at a modest pace, unaware she was sought, neither speeding up to evade Iahn nor slowing down to intercept him.

Something in a rut caught Iahn's notice. He approached and squatted. Unfamiliar spoor stared back. The vengeance taker frowned.

Malformed hoofprints, smaller than the equine prints that drew the fugitive's wagon, partly obscured the wheel ruts. These prints were new to his quarry's path. A greenish film glistened in a few of the smaller prints. Had the woman summoned allies to patrol her back trail? Perhaps his earlier assessment of her foreknowledge was wrong. Perhaps the wizard knew fully that her heritage sought her, despite her attempt to discard all connections with her homeland. She possessed ability enough, but what clue had she found that tipped her off? Did she know a vengeance taker was after her?

He continued to squint at the intruding spoor. These prints seemed somehow . . . ominous. Even as he studied the glistening mucous, it dissipated, leaving the prints dry. He was lucky to have noticed it at all.

Perhaps the intruding sign was unrelated to his quarry, but Iahn didn't approve of assumptions. He retained life where many lesser people walked into traps because of too much imagination.

His desire was enough to cajole his damos open, like an eye dilating, revealing a dark cavity filled with oily fluid. Only a vengeance taker could hope to survive contact with the poison within a damos. The fabled magic of his ancestors assured that the reservoir would never run dry. The secrets of its fabrication were lost to time. In this day, vengeance takers counted but twenty-one, a number that equaled the remaining number of relics.

With a smooth and practiced glide, he flicked two drops of venom from the reservoir onto his fingertip. The damos closed immediately of its own accord. Each bead was so potent that if introduced into his waterskin, he'd have poison enough to kill twenty people. He considered the droplets for a moment, then licked the glistening globules from his finger.

His cheeks warmed and sweat broke on his brow. The desert was blotted out by a roar of light and a flare of sound. His eyes fluttered, momentarily beyond his conscious control. He collapsed to one knee as weakness clawed his viscera. The poison was loosed in his blood, scrabbling to find some small chink in his hard-won resistance.

A whisper broke from the cacophony. Iahn concentrated his senses, straining to hear the words spoken. Distinguishing the Voice from phantom noise generated by a poisoned brain was tricky. The prophetic spirit spoke to anyone who succumbed—or nearly succumbed—to the venom, but most survivors and victims failed to understand the words. It didn't matter to the victims, because hearing the Voice meant an ugly death was only a few heartbeats away.

Hopeful apprentices built up immunity by imbibing minute doses of diluted poison, then stronger and stronger droplets over time, gradually and painfully, to acquire resistance to damos venom. The final test was the ingestion of a full, concentrated dose.

Failure was obvious, if unsightly.

Honor was accorded to those who lived. Apprentices who spoke a true prophecy graduated as vengeance takers and took up their badge of office after swearing fealty to the Lord Apprehender of Deep Imaskar.

Nausea stirred, and Iahn's muscles loosened as the cacophony intensified. Then the Voice broke through dissonance into clarity.

"More than vengeance tracks the fugitive. An entity foretold . . . "

The message dissolved into inchoate syllables that poured into a river of relief from the damos's venom-induced pain. Iahn's body was throwing off the lethal effects of the dose. With the return of his senses, the Voice fled. Until next time.

Still on one knee, he considered the insight bequeathed him. No doubt Iahn himself was vengeance. It was the title of his rank and profession. Simple. So the fugitive was sought by someone other than himself. Which probably meant the strange marks along the wheel ruts were not the fugitive's doing, but instead were traces left by this "other."

Iahn sighed. The damos's messages were always brief and usually truncated. A longer message required a greater dose, and to hear all that might be foretold would be the listener's first sermon of the afterlife, even for a vengeance taker.

Iahn straightened. It wouldn't do to lose the fugitive at the last moment. He was accustomed to achieving his goals, no matter the difficulty.

He would find Ususi Manaallin and kill any force or creature that stood in his way.

CHAPTER TWO

Spring, 1374 DR

Darkness. Blowing, howling, damp gloom. Shadows reaching like fingers . . . grasping. Stretching closer. Screaming. . . .

Ususi woke, sitting upright, a cry on her lips. Where, what. . . ?

The dream.

The same damned dream that pursued her up the years.

She focused and slowed her too-rapid breathing. Just three days had passed since the dream last visited, but it had lost none of its immediacy, none of its mystery, and none of its enveloping terror.

Calm down, she thought. It's over—it's done, it can't hurt you. Nothing has changed. It was just a dream. Wasn't it?

The excuses were familiar. She and her sister

Qari made the same excuses to reassure each other when they were children. When they'd shared the same nightmare. But Qari had never known light—for her, darkness was natural. Her poor sister, already cursed to a sightless existence, had lost all remaining shreds of her reason when their parents died in the accident. After that tragedy, Qari was hidden away from even the enclosed world of Deep Imaskar, sightless and speechless. For all Ususi knew, the same terrible dream replayed through her sister's mind day after day after day, its terror unrelenting.

Ususi slammed her fist down on the nightstand. "What are you?" she screamed. "What do you want from me? Leave me alone!" She pushed all thoughts of Qari from her mind. Thinking about her sister was something she did only by accident.

The echoes of her yell died to nothing, and the darkness, the natural darkness of the night, pressed close.

And yet something about that darkness was unnatural, too. The lantern on the wall beside her bed, a lantern whose wick earlier burned with heatless flame and promised enough light for years, was dead.

Beyond its ability to terrify, the dream had the unsettling ability to reach beyond her closed eyelids. She'd awakened from the nightmare on other occasions to discover candle flames, lanterns, torches, and even campfires doused. Not even magical lights escaped being snuffed by her nightmare vision.

That allowed her to recognize the dream's malevolence. It was Darkbringer. Lightquencher. Dreamstalker. Something that craved darkness couldn't be good. She never managed to free herself from the curse of her personal nightmare, or flee far enough from its reach, despite all her abilities and the miles she'd put between herself and the hidden place of her birth.

Ususi rose. She was done with sleep for the night.

Time for some tea. She set the wick of the doused lantern

freshly alight with a word of kindling.

The interior of her traveling wagon was small but tidy. Everything was stowed just so. The cunningly designed interior of the coach was a marvel of carpentry, blending wood, metal, and glass, offering a surplus of storage that didn't sacrifice living area. Its elegance and grace was like the cabin of a small yacht designed by a noble who knew the value of precious space, but her coach was a craft that traveled upon land.

She folded the bed into the wall, forming a bench, and pulled an inlaid board from its slot, producing a sturdy table. From a cupboard, Ususi gathered the kettle, a crock of loose green tea, a silver spoon, and sugar cubes. The motions of preparation, almost ritualized, calmed her. Soon enough, she'd prepared an aromatic beverage in a delicate fired-clay cup.

Sipping, Ususi thought back to the day she had commissioned the master carpenter of Two Stars to build the traveling wagon. It had been, what . . . a year ago? A year since she'd decided to give up her decade-long residence in Two Stars. A year since she had parted ways with Marrec and the others. Marrec had his own quest, and she had hers. She'd lived in Two Stars almost since she defied the lord apprehender and slipped past the Great Seal. . . .

But that was long ago. What mattered now was her self-imposed mission of discovery. She would locate and map every site of power of her godlike ancestors, the Imaskari. Years of study had led her to the very first site of her obsession, the Mucklestones. That ancient ring of standing stones was one of the few known portals that connected to the famous Celestial Nadir—famous to Deep Imaskari wizards, anyway.

The Celestial Nadir was an artificial demiplane created by the original Imaskari Empire. It could be accessed only from certain locations, and only if one possessed a keystone. All the keystones were thought to be lost.

Then, just a short year ago, a surviving keystone was given into her keeping by its former custodian in the Forest of Lethyr. She wasn't sure if the previous guardian knew or understood the keystone's significance, or Ususi's heritage. She'd assumed the Nentyarch of Yeshelmaar had not known. On the other hand, the Nentyarch was a wise elf, and perhaps had understood what the gift meant to Ususi. Certainly no other person could have used the keystone better than she—at least no other person in a position to investigate the Nadir.

Ususi set down the cup. She plucked the keystone from its chain around her neck and gazed into its amethyst depths. The keystone was critical to opening the Mucklestones. More than that, it could open any portal created by the Imaskari to gain entry into the Celestial Nadir. With the stone's aid, she might well discover all of the famed twenty gates.

Each gate led into the Celestial Nadir, but each gate opened onto a different portion of that primeval space. So far, she had found only a single entry into the Celestial Nadir—the Mucklestones—and she had already plumbed those depths. Nineteen more gates to go.

The Mucklestone Gate opened onto great voids of cool darkness. Narrow, unsupported stone roads wound through that void. The paths sometimes connected enigmatic islands of stone, collections of debris, free-floating lakes, and stranger detritus of a vanished time. Most of the paths led to innocuous or crumbled ruins.

Unfortunately, her exploration revealed the Mucklestones opened onto an unimportant edge of the Celestial Nadir, far from the core that would shelter important Imaskaran relics. She was certain that other paths, closer to the core of the Celestial Nadir, would lead to secrets of fabulous power. Such as one or more of the fabled Imaskarcana.

While walking the paths of the Celestial Nadir connecting to the Mucklestones, she'd found nodes of translucent, purplish crystal. They formed almost like natural geodes within the artificial demiplane; they were manifestations of the Celestial Nadir itself. Her keystone was carved from the very same crystal, which could be found only in the Celestial Nadir.

She recalled again her surprise upon seeing raw Celestial Nadir crystal trading across the gem counters in the city of Two Stars.

She pulled from her purse a chunk of rough crystal whose hue matched that of the keystone, though unfinished. When she'd seen it in the gem shop in Two Stars, purely by accident, she'd purchased it immediately. According to the shop owner, the gem went by the ungainly name "Datharathi crystal." A small lot of it had come up from the far south, from somewhere in the Durpar region.

Her discovery of the fragment was the final impetus she'd required to continue her quest. The fragment was clear evidence that at least one other of the twenty gates, besides the Mucklestones, still operated. Moreover, someone was entering the Celestial Nadir and mining its substance for profit! Celestial Nadir crystal was a natural sediment of the artificial plane her ancestors had created, and could be found nowhere else.

But . . . here was something odd. Both the rough Celestial Nadir crystal and her keystone seemed . . . murky. Usually, she could see right through the crystal, but tendrils of darkness seemed to cloud the center of both pieces—only very slightly in her keystone, but noticeably in the raw chunk of Celestial Nadir crystal. It reminded her suddenly and uncomfortably of her nightmare.

"Bastard dream," she murmured. "You'd better not be responsible, or . . ." Or what, she didn't know, but her blood was hot with anger. Far better, though, than the fear that sang through her when she'd woken. She was more familiar with emotions of anger and annoyance than fear and uncertainty. But more than anything else, she was tired. Fear and anger both fell away, leaving a dull ache. And truth be told, the creeping warmth on her face and hands galled her. The day before had been a long day of travel, and she'd gotten too much sun.

She usually sat on the exterior of the wagon, coach style, driving the horses from beneath a protective sunshade. The Giant's Belt mountains rising to the left had drawn her gaze like a magnet. Beyond its towering peaks lay Raurin. Now a desert, the once fertile land had been ruled by Imaskar. Raurin was certain to be rich in ruins, but the desert sands were lethal. Her decision had been to first locate every portal she could outside Raurin. Despite her resolve, the barrier peaks still captured her imagination, and in her day-dreamy contemplation of what lay beyond, she failed to stay safely in the shade. The sun was something those of Deep Imaskar had forgotten. A sunburn was an affliction she had packed no balm or magical ointment to soothe.

Ususi finished the tea. She stood, rinsed her utensils with water from a hanging jug, and put everything back in its place. Morning's light was close enough. She might as well get a start on the day since sleep had left her behind.

Dawn chased away the night's obscurring haze. Morning's first light found Ususi standing outside her coach, putting together her expeditioner's pack. Ususi's great-jacket was cinched by a service belt to which were strapped all manner of needed things, including six leather scroll cases, three on each hip, written with utilitarian magic. The keystone dangled on its chain around her neck, and a slender leather satchel hung at her side, holding her purse filled with personal oddments, including the Celestial Nadir crystal from Two Stars. About her head revolved a free-floating delver's orb of her own design—a tiny piece of white granite wrapped in silvery wire.

The expeditioner's pack lay at Ususi's feet. It paid to be prepared when entering an unknown ruin for the first time.

Extra food, slender tools for jiggling old locks or deactivating traps, rope, water, lantern oil. . . . The pack, with all its pockets and storage straps, was like her travel coach in miniature. She hefted it, estimating its weight. It would be a burden to her, but not to her *uskura*.

She whistled, and an unseen presence ruffled her hair as it moved past.

"Carry this," Ususi said. Obediently, hidden hands lifted the pack and waited patiently for further instruction.

Back in Deep Imaskar, nearly every citizen could craft or purchase a minor uskura to act as a general, all-purpose bearer of burdens, opener of doors, and retriever of objects. For a wizard of Ususi's talent, an uskura was considered a necessity, though she'd gone long years without one since she'd left the refuge behind the Great Seal. That time was past. During her days of coach travel over the last year, she'd fashioned an invisible companion using the methods of her people. Each uskura was something like an enchantment and required a physical object to serve as its focus. Ususi had bound her uskura to her delver's orb. As long as she had her delver's orb, the uskura would never stray far.

Not unlike the simple, horselike entities she'd bonded to the travel coach's yoke, she mused. She didn't have the time, talent, or patience to see to the needs of actual living draft animals.

"Follow," said Ususi. The wizard turned and set out for the jumble of ruins visible within the cluster of brown hills. The uskura obeyed.

The edge of the first knoll was less than a hundred yards from where she'd stopped the coach last night, though the ruins were probably a half mile farther. The mounting sun touched the hilltops with gold, giving the brown grass a luster it probably didn't deserve. Many of the broad hills were crowned with dark slabs of stone, some standing lonely vigil, others clustered in small groups, and several fallen, as if lying exhausted from centuries of labor.

Ususi ascended the nearest hill. The grade was hardly noticeable—a lucky break. The rising sun and cloudless sky promised another overly warm day. She hoped the ruins would reveal structures with roofs, or perhaps subterranean pockets. She'd had enough sun for a while.

So far, so good—she saw no trails, animal or otherwise, among the hills. With even more luck, she might find the site undisturbed, though she knew that to be unlikely. In all the centuries since the outpost had been abandoned, numerous intrusions could have occurred. Looters were common, and were trained to expect ancient treasure in the bones of fallen civilizations. But no looter before her had a keystone.

She crowned the first hillock and looked down the gentle slope into a curved valley bounded by two adjacent ridges. Besides the occasional dolmen, scrub brush erupted from the earth in scattered dots. A warm breeze blew across the hilltop, and the scent of a jasmine reached the wizard's nose.

There. A central dome of faded stone. Another outpost promised by the ancient map she kept safely in her travel coach. The outpost looked like a hill itself, or perhaps a large boulder exposed by years of erosion. It was bald, cratered, and home to a colony of opportunistic lichen. In the few places where the stone of the station was visible through the covering detritus, Ususi astutely noted the faintest purplish tinge.

The wizard hastened down the slope toward the structure, a smile ghosting across her lips. Still no evidence of any recent disturbances.

When she reached the dome, the illusion of its solidity broke. Great cracks meandered across its surface, and large holes gaped where portions of the wall had collapsed. What had been the entrance—two dolmens surmounted by a third to form an arch—was similarly collapsed, and the passage was filled with solid earth, the runoff of ages.

Since taking up her quest, Ususi had investigated twelve or so lost sites of the ancient Imaskari. While only the first had harbored one of the twenty gates, she was becoming something of an expert on the styles favored by her vanished ancestors. To Ususi's eye, this dome promised a larger subterranean structure, if she could penetrate the stony cap.

She circled the dome once, slowly, taking note of every possibility. Every so often, she gave a quick glance at the tops of the surrounding hills. She'd run into few travelers and fewer tenants in this empty borderland between Veldorn and Estagund, but keeping a lookout was smart. The hilltops remained reassuringly clear of intruding silhouettes.

Ususi completed her circumnavigation of the structure. No paths or clear entrances presented themselves. On the other hand, several of the larger cracks revealed tufts of animal hair caught in rough edges. Evidence that beasts of the grassland used the cavity to shelter from the day's heat, the night's cold, or the rainy season's torrential downpour. Or so she supposed.

The wizard debated calling on one of her many prepared spells, which, like obedient soldiers, waited patiently, even eagerly, to be called into existence. A brief existence, but long enough to enact a startling change upon the world of the real.

Better to exhaust mundane approaches first, Ususi decided. Each prepared spell represented an expenditure of time, and in some cases, expensive resources. She approached the largest fracture that split the dome. The morning sun rose from the other side, and the cavity was dark. She reached up and brushed her finger against her circling delver's orb. Steady white light woke in the stone and poured forth in a concentrated, directed beam. The illumination shone in whatever direction she willed. Crouching down on elbows and knees, she wormed her way into the side of the dome.

No mud—Ususi was grateful for that. With the light of her orb, she easily crawled forward. The space remained wide enough, and she made her way into a large pocket, where she could stand.

A flurry of tiny wings sent her reaching involuntarily for a spell, even though Ususi had expected to disturb wildlife. The dome made a perfect place for the large southern bats to roost during the hot days. She was sorry to bother them. The sharp smell of guano was all they left behind.

The dome's central feature was a five-sided obelisk of rough, puce-colored stone. The obelisk's significance was enhanced by the elaborate symbology inscribed on every surface. Runes; pictograms; and depictions of idealized emperors, gods, and demons—typical images for the ancient Imaskari. The wizard had spent years learning the language of the ancients and automatically interpreted the meaning behind this elaborate façade: "Entrance restricted to authorized agents of the empire. Intruders will be punished by automatic safeguards. Expect no mercy."

"Bring me my pack," Ususi murmured, and the uskura silently offered her its burden. Ususi opened and rummaged through it.

"Here we go." The wizard produced a lilac-tinged stone shard that was a little shorter than her hand in its diameter, and about the width of her thumb in thickness. The shard was a fragment of a larger, heavily inscribed tablet, though many symbols remained on the broken piece. Ususi checked the fragment, then started searching the obelisk for matching symbols. The tablet chip, which Ususi thought of as a reference list, was something she'd unearthed about six months earlier in a crumbling spire in southern Mulhorand. Since then, it had proved invaluable.

The wizard located the runes she sought, the ones matching those on her list. She pressed each one on the obelisk, hoping the order was correct.

The ground shuddered and the dust of centuries rained down from the ceiling. The inscribed runes she'd activated lit up with brilliant blue light. Ususi stepped back, poised to flee in case she'd guessed incorrectly. Another shudder accompanied a familiar grating sound of stone on stone, and the obelisk slowly slid upward. A hiss of equalizing air blew a spray of milky dust in all directions. When it settled, a smooth-sided shaft angling steeply into the earth was revealed. A narrow stairway was chiseled into the side of the shaft, descending in tight loops out of the reach of Ususi's light. Demonic sculptures squatted at the head of the stair, one on each side of the shaft, their claws raised threateningly but immovably.

Ususi stood her ground for a hundred heartbeats, waiting to see if any summoned guardians or ancient countermeasures against intrusion would be deployed. Time trickled past and, as far as she could sense, her way remained clear. After another similar span of time, she stuffed the pale purple shard back into her pack, handed the pack to her uskura, and started down the newly revealed stairs.

CHAPTER THREE

Warian Datharathi studied his hand. With just three cards, his choices were few—a three of silver, an eight of silver, and a Bahamut. A six of silver he'd just revealed lay on the table; a three of black and a four of white, which his two remaining opponents had simultaneously played, lay next to his card.

The hand had gone around the table once, and one card lay before each player. Everyone would have two more chances to lay down a card, until each showed three cards.

Shem said, "I'll take this," and pulled a couple of coins from the pile at the center of the table.

Warian frowned. He'd forfeited the activation of his first card by playing a higher value card than either of his opponents. Shem, who'd played the lowest card, a three-point black dragon, was able to take money out of the stakes. Black dragons were thieves in cards as well as in life.

Warian's turn again. Warian slapped his eight of silver down on the table. Since he got to play first this time, his card was automatically the lowest value; its ability activated. Everyone with a good dragon in their flight got to draw another card. He grinned and drew a card from the shuffle deck. Silvers were moral paragons, after all.

Next came Shem, who played seven of black. Shem got to steal a couple more coins from the stakes. Warian stifled a groan. He was already possessive over the pile of coins—he was certain he'd win them and didn't want to see their value leak away.

Yasha played a ten of red. The card was too high to use, but Yasha's total score of fourteen between his two cards was respectable.

But the hand would be won by whomever showed the highest total after each had played three cards. Such were the rules of the tavern game Three Dragon Ante.

It was one of Warian's favorite games. Like many such games, Three Dragon Ante required a financial contribution to the stakes before each hand was played. Warian found that he could win the stakes more often than not, even when pitted against experienced players, as long as he didn't overdo it. If he stayed at a table, a tavern, or even in a particular town for too long, stories of his "luck" tended to spread, and the locals started taking a dislike to his winning ways.

"Hey, Glass-arm! Did you bathe today? You smell like an outhouse!" Tentative snickers bloomed around the bar. Warian glanced away from his game, even though he recognized that grating voice: his local nemesis, Bui the Hog. The big woman was a sore loser who'd gone too far into debt to continue playing for the evening. "Too long in one place" may have already snuck up on him, Warian realized.

Warian's right hand, his glass arm, tightened its grip on his cards. Not glass—crystal. His prosthesis was a wonder, no argument there. It almost accorded him the mobility and agility of his natural limb. But it also marked him as different. The arm and his gambling prowess were a combination that sometimes worked to his disadvantage among strangers.

Warian waited for Yasha to play a third card. Warian knew that his smartest move would be to make a joke, fold, and leave. The signs were all present—the bantering could easily turn ugly—ugly, as in physical. Bui was a lot of things, but "opposed to violence" was not on that list.

But Warian wanted to play his Bahamut. Since he'd played a middle-value card for his opener and second card, letting the advantage temporarily shift away from him, he knew he would win this hand with his last card, unless one of his opponents was holding a thirteen-point dragon scion, just like Warian. The stakes stood at one hundred sixty gold. That amount would go a long way toward seeing him to the next town along the trade road—maybe all the way to the city of Delzimmer, which bordered Eastern Shaar. He wouldn't mind leaving Crinti-controlled Dambrath behind.

"I asked you a question," Bui's voice blared. More laughter, less restrained this time, chased the heels of the woman's taunt.

Studiously ignoring the provocation, Warian merely looked at Shem and Yasha, saying, "Let's finish this hand and call it. What do you say?"

Shem nodded, but Yasha the Weasel folded his cards and put them down.

"No," said Yasha. "Why don't you answer Bui's question first? I can't concentrate with her yelling." Yasha smiled a knowing smile.

Warian tensed. He had one chance to deflect the gathering attention onto Bui. If he could make her look a fool, perhaps the rest would just laugh her down.

"She's loud, isn't she?" Warian asked. "Not so loud as when

she lost her stake to me a little while ago. But . . . "

"Hey!" boomed Bui, closer now. Too close.

"Guess she had enough copper wedges in her pockets to pickle herself in ale. By what I can smell," continued Warian, "she forgot how to find the outhouse to let it back out." While he spoke, he scooped his stake into an open pouch, wistfully eyeing the unclaimed pot. "She must be smelling herself."

A few patrons laughed . . . but not enough. Warian understood he'd miscalculated.

"Why, I'll. . . !"

The sound of something breaking heralded Bui's furious approach. That woman must have some orc blood in her, Warian mused ruefully. That, or she was a berserker from the north. Either way, time to run.

Warian put his cards down on the table, stood, and whirled. He'd left his sword up in his room, peace-tied in its sheath. It looked like he'd be kissing that, and whatever else he'd left up there, good-bye.

Rough hands grabbed him from behind before he could make good his escape. Yasha's voice purred in his ear. "Stand still, outlander. This'll go easier if you don't make a fuss." Yasha's laugh revealed his words for the lies they were.

Catcalls and more laughter answered from the room at large. Just over a dozen customers patronized the inn, none of whom seemed the least bit concerned about Warian's situation. That he'd failed to gauge the growing dislike for himself was a surprise. Warian fancied himself a skilled diviner of others' intentions—after all, he relied on the same skill to excel at his games.

Bui reached him, her face red with anger, and her right hand gripping a broken chair leg. Things had gone much further than they should have. Warian regretted his jibes all the more—they had spectacularly backfired.

"Bui, I'm prepared to return everything I won from you," stammered Warian, fear threatening to break his normally cool demeanor.

"Damn right you will . . . after I smash that glass arm into splinters!" Bui screamed in his face. She was drunk on beer and fury.

Reasonable talk died a whimpering death, a casualty of the dire situation. He shifted his weight and ground his heel on Yasha's toe, simultaneously shrugging his arms free of the man's ungentle grip.

Bui brought down the chair leg in a brutal snap.

Despite his arm's imperfect control and slow response to his desires, he managed to wrench his prosthesis up to block her blow. His artificial arm was crystal, far tougher than glass—Datharathi crystal, mined by his own family and enchanted to move almost like a regular arm. Datharathi crystal, so enchanted, was stronger than bone and sinew. The chair leg struck the translucent, violet-tinged crystal with a sick thud. The painful jolt traveled up Warian's crystalline arm into his living flesh.

His mind noticed a haze of darkness spiraling through the center of his artificial limb. He'd never seen that before. . . .

One of Yasha's arms snaked from behind, encircling Warian's neck, the man's elbow crooked below Warian's chin. With the counter pressure applied from Yasha's other arm on the back of Warian's head, the supply of blood to his head was instantly restricted. Yasha was trying to choke Warian out. At the very moment Yasha began to exert pressure, Warian's eyes bulged, and his head felt as if it had swelled to half again its normal size in only two or three heartbeats. Black spots swam before him. The effect shocked him as much from its suddenness as its unpleasantness.

Alarm skirled through Warian. He struggled in Yasha's grip. His flesh-and-blood arm, quicker, more precise, and stronger than his prosthesis, flailed ineffectually. He tried to claw at Yasha, but he could barely think. Yasha's deadly threat was more than a bluff. He must have had considerable practice choking people to apply the hold so quickly. If Warian didn't pass out first, he was in for the beating of his life. Darkness beat in on all sides as his vision began to fail. Blackness crept into the edges of his vision—dark and swirling, like that he'd just seen tendriling through the interior of his arm.

He concentrated all of his faltering will on pushing the darkness away.

Warian's crystal arm flared with amethyst brilliance. Warmth shot from his shoulder to his crystalline fingertips, a blaze of sensation where before he had felt only vague dullness. The arm fused more fully to him, spiking with sensation as never before, transmitting the sense of touch in a way he had not felt in all the seven years he'd worn it, since the mining accident. But he was still blacking out.

Warian reached up with his artificial limb, grabbed Yasha's forearm that held his neck in a vice, and pulled.

A shape flew through the air and smashed into the far wall. It took Warian a moment to realize that the shape, now crumpled and unmoving on the floor, was Yasha. Lavender luminance lit the faces of stunned tavern patrons as they stared at him with wide eyes. The light in their eyes reflected the glow that pulsed and rippled out of Warian's crystal arm.

"What the . . . ?" said Warian, looking at his prosthesis with eyes as wide as any of those in the bar.

Bui the Hog, still in the grasp of her drunken belligerence, and still holding her improvised club, struck at Warian again. Her swing was strong but lacked its former deadly speed. In fact, Warian realized, everyone in the bar seemed to be slowed, as if the light from his arm had encased them all in a syrupy dimension of sluggishness. Or was the light propelling him forward into a faster plane of perception?

Warian swayed his body to be just outside the arc of Bui's swing.

Bui moved in, assayed another brutal swing. Instead of stepping out of the way this time, Warian backhanded the oncoming wooden club with his prosthesis. The impact splintered the chair leg as it blasted out of Bui's hand. The woman remained fully in the clutch of her rage. She lunged forward, trying to catch Warian in her reddened, vein-popped hands.

Warian ducked beneath her lunge. Again. And again. Wishing to end it, Warian stood his ground for Bui's next lunge. As she rushed him, he reached out to tap her on the forehead—he was coming to understand that the strength and speed in his arm could be a deadly combination. Still, the impact was enough to tumble Bui to the ground, her head reeling.

Surveying the remainder of the tavern customers, Warian saw the dislike directed at him from the bar had transformed into fear.

"Don't worry . . ." he began as the light in his prosthesis guttered out. The dull nothingness of the last seven years flooded back into the crystal, and his supernatural perception evaporated.

He sagged against a table but caught himself before falling to the floor. He didn't want to advertise that the freak display of energy had dissipated, draining away as inexplicably as it had energized him.

More than that—weariness enveloped him as if he'd just run full out for a great distance. He couldn't get enough air, his legs and arms wanted to cramp, and exhaustion made him tremble. Warian had to get out of the tavern while the onlookers remained cowed.

He stumbled back to the table where his card game had been interrupted. Shem backed away. With careful nonchalance, Warian slid the contents of the pot to his pouch. He looked at Shem. "I would have won anyway, if not for the distraction. I had a Bahamut in my hand." So saying, Warian revealed the stern visage of the dragon and its thirteen points. With a shrug, he threw the card in with the rest of the coins. "It seems like a reasonable recompense for the transgression against my person. No harm done, I say."

Shem nodded quickly, fearfully. "Right, right—no harm done!"

Warian turned toward the exit. A few patrons gathered around Yasha. One crouched, saying, "Yasha? You still with us?"

Warian's feet propelled him from the tavern before he could discover Yasha's fate. He didn't want to know, especially if . . . well, he didn't want to know.

Warian Datharathi rode east down the trade road on a newly purchased and outfitted horse the stableman had called Majeed. He rode south, rather than north toward Delzimmer. He traveled toward the port city of Cathyr, where he could catch a courier ship up the coast all the way to the Golden Water. Then, on to Vaelan.

The answers to his questions lay in Vaelan.

Despite his past vows, the time had come to return to the family business. Datharathi Minerals stood for all the rules and family expectations he'd left behind when he'd fled five years ago. He didn't have a head for business, or a desire to acquire one. All the scheming between businesses to get the absolute best price on every wooden nail; the constant worry about whether Datharathi Minerals could retain its high standing from year to year; the making of less-than-honest deals with other businesses, trade guilds, and private regulatory councils, in pursuit of the almighty coin . . . it all turned Warian's stomach.

He had his own way of making a living—gambling. Well, he supposed that some folk might see a parallel. But everyone knew the risks when they sat down at a table for a game of chance. In business, the risks were mostly those raised by underhanded dealings.

Warian sighed and patted Majeed. He didn't want to return home, but something terrifyingly strange had happened with his artificial arm, the arm that had been a gift from his family. The prosthesis was carved from crystal mined from a secret lode that Datharathi Minerals jealously guarded. The proprietary crystal had an affinity for taking enchantment. The family business had made a handsome profit by selling small quantities of the substance to powerful and rich nobles and merchants in Vaelan and beyond. To Warian's knowledge, no piece of so-called Datharathi crystal had ever before exhibited as startling a transformation as what had happened to him in the tavern.

Warian sighed as he weighed his decision. After he had lost his arm in a rock fall while inspecting one of the family mines, his will to fly in the face of family demands temporarily crumbled. The trauma of losing a limb shattered his confidence. Against his better judgment, he allowed Grandfather Shaddon to give him an experimental prosthesis. To Warian's surprise, the false limb, the first of its kind, served him well, almost as well as a real arm.

Accepting the prosthesis was the only time he'd done as his family asked and found that the result was good.

Warian had been so overcome with relief after receiving the arm that he almost changed his mind about the business, and nearly accepted a position under his Uncle Xaemar, who sat at the head of the family council. If not for his sister Eined, who talked sense into him, Warian might have been sitting on the family council at that very moment.

After conferring with Eined late into many nights, Warian had skipped town. Eined had convinced her kid brother that he needed to see what the world was all about before becoming another cog in the Datharathi empire, however highly placed.

Thank the gods for Eined's counsel. Free of Uncle Xaemar's decrees, Grandfather Shaddon's schemes, Uncle Zel's unscrupulous deals, and Aunt Sevaera's crazy impositions, Warian realized life was a far more wonderful and wide stage than he'd previously imagined. Eventually, he cut his ties with the family permanently. He never returned to Vaelan. In all the time since, the only thing he'd missed was Eined.

Warian shuddered. And now someone lay hurt, maybe even dead, because of his arm. Had he killed Yasha? He'd never before taken a life. For a moment, he comforted himself with something his old sword instructor had told him: To kill a person is far more difficult than is commonly believed.

But what about when mortal strength was overcome by crazy bursts of potency and perception?

"Why did you wake up?" Warian addressed his arm, as he had done before. His prosthesis remained dull and barely responsive, offering no clues. He tried to will it back to life, yet nothing happened, as if nothing had ever happened. All his attempts to elicit a response from his arm since he'd fled the tavern had proven equally fruitless.

"It must be something they're experimenting with back in Vaelan," Warian murmured. Something he needed to know about, and soon. If he accidentally hurt Yasha, who might he inadvertently harm next? Or worse, kill?

Was Xaemar pushing Shaddon to empower the crystal lode with power in some mad scheme to propel Datharathi Minerals to the top of the trade empire in Durpar? Or was Shaddon, always a sneaky bastard in Warian's estimation, pursuing some crazy plot of his own? A plot that had momentarily woken a dangerous strength in Warian's prosthesis.

A strength, truth to tell, Warian wished to wield again.

CHAPTER FOUR

Thormud Horn used his moon white selenite rod to scribe a circle in the fine gravel. His grimy hands, thick with the soil of the world he so cherished, guided the rod with supernatural grace and accuracy. So it was when the dwarf geomancer immersed himself in the medium of his expertise. Thormud's constant companion, a tiny replica of a dragon carved in opal, roosted on the dwarf's right shoulder. Its name was Xet.

Kiril Duskmourn took a pull from her hip flask. The whisky hit the back of her throat like smoke, cleared her nostrils, and trickled down to warm her stomach. She watched the dwarf continue his methodical inscription in the loose soil atop the mesa. Kiril had watched Thormud inscribe similar circles nearly every day for the last ten years, or so it sometimes seemed.

Kiril's sword was rarely required to protect her employer, thank all the gods of Sildëyuir. Yet she maintained her vigil. Thormud's coin was good, but more importantly, few of her own elf race (or any race, for that matter) would put up with her. Kiril's excessive cursing and bouts of near-alcoholism were traits elves generally shunned. As a rule, elves preferred the fruit of the vine, not the distilled products of root and fruit. But who could carry such a burden as hers without some comfort? Kiril's ill-famed blade was her strength and her curse, and the whisky helped her through. She doubted any of her hidden kin would last a hundred days, let alone a hundred years, with Angul strapped to a hip.

Kiril upended her flask, her eyesight threatening to blur and her hand shaking slightly. She'd reached an accommodation with her fate that suited her.

Thormud paused for a time, then he spoke. "Again, the prognostication fails." Thormud's voice was low and melodious, a voice that belonged to a trained performer on the streets of Gheldaneth, not to a crusty dwarf geomancer who lived alone in the Mulhorand scrublands. Alone but for his surly bodyguard and diminutive familiar.

"Again, you say," said Kiril in a lazy, I-don't-much-care tone.

Thormud looked at her, one hand rubbing the chin hidden below his black and gray beard. Xet loosed a call like a chime and launched from the dwarf's shoulder into the hazy sunshine. A few rags of white cloud fluttered in the otherwise vacuous blue sky.

Kiril watched the tiny construct fly toward the edge of the mesa, then dip below its rim, out of sight. "Good riddance," she muttered.

Thormud spoke. "Yes, Kiril. As you no doubt recall, all my recent prognostications have come to naught."

Kiril sighed, then said, "And you still don't know why? Maybe your wits are departing as age creeps up on you."

Thormud considered and nodded. "I checked that possibility. Fortunately for your continued commission, I find my faculties remain as sharp as ever. The trouble lies elsewhere."

"Trouble?" wondered Kiril, slightly interested despite her studied detachment.

"As you've heard me expound on more than one occasion, dear Kiril, the stone and mineral beneath the feet of all the quick green foliage enjoys an unhurried life all its own. Information flows through the earth in telluric currents and tides, but slowly."

Kiril said, "I've noticed the slowness."

Thormud shook off the elf's subtle provocation. He continued. "Something has disrupted those currents. Something far to the southeast."

"Disrupted currents of the earth? I've heard you yammer too much over the years not to learn a little—disrupting the flow would take a massive event, right? Another volcano? I hate those." Kiril fingered an ugly burn scar on the back of her left hand as she spoke.

"No." Thormud shook his head. "For all their fury, volcanoes are natural disturbances, and as such would only modify telluric currents, adding their voice to the flow of the earth. I'm experiencing outright interruption. Only something inherently unnatural, large, and powerful could disrupt my work."

Kiril grunted.

The dwarf gazed into the headpiece of his selenite rod, his mouth muttering in time to some internal debate. The elf studied her employer, reading signs she recognized. A trip was in the offing, no doubt about it.

Thormud loved sight-seeing, especially when strange rock formations, lost canyons, earthquakes, and volcanoes were part of the expedition. The dwarf didn't care for cities, or any of the artificial stonework or engineering of which his kin were so fond.

Neither did Kiril. Too damned many people.

The elf swordswoman glanced away, out over the wide lands visible from their lonely mesa top. Mulhorand was an empty land, especially east of the southern range of the Dragonsword Mountains. Kiril knew the dwarf had selected his stronghold, carved into the heart of a mesa, precisely for its isolation. Disruptions were few, and visitors unlikely. Thormud was able to devote all his time to his "delving meditations." On occasion, his findings spurred a trip to confirm some theory the geomancer had cooked up. Kiril rarely appreciated the reason behind the trip, but she had to admit she enjoyed resting her eyes on new horizons every so often.

Kiril asked, "When do we leave?"

The lonely mesa was much tunneled and hollowed from Thormud's long years of occupancy—the dwarf was a master geomancer. Libraries, halls, storerooms, galleries, and even balconies lay within the otherwise natural tower. Thormud hadn't named his home, referring to it simply as "the mesa," but soon after arriving, Kiril started calling the place "the Finger Defiant." In his philosophical way, Thormud picked up the name and used it himself.

Ensconced within her own personal suite in the Finger Defiant, Kiril pondered whether she should actually go to the trouble of making up a pack. It wasn't like her to err on the side of preparation. However, if they were headed toward Durpar, as Thormud hinted, not north or west across the Alamber Sea as in the past, they might be away long enough to require more than a single change of wardrobe.

She selected three outfits, all of which would fit comfortably over her mail of fine chain links. And an extra pair of gloves, of course. Not smart to be abroad without those. She always kept a pair folded into her belt. Midnight black and woven of fine Chessentan silk, her gloves were sometimes all that stood between her and folly.

Kiril had never been south of the Finger Defiant. She wondered what the wines, beers, meads, and harder varieties of spirit in Durpar might be like. Not that she was ever in danger of doing without. Kiril pulled forth her one constant friend during the last many years and heard the familiar sound of liquid sloshing within its metallic body.

The flask was forged of bronze, probably by elves outside her lineage. The greenish blue patina of verdigris obfuscated the deranged face carved into one side of the flask—some ancient god of the vine. She could never recall the god's name—had she ever known it? In all the years she'd carried it, it had never failed to produce its potent drink. A bottomless flask to assuage her infinite shame.

Kiril took a sip for the road and stowed the container. The vitriolic taste wasn't enough to deter her preparations, though, and she retrieved a well-handled skull from her shelf.

The skull was that of a child, delicate and elongated—an elf skull. Kiril kept it to remind herself of mortality, and as a remembrance of what stock should be put in ideology when reality intruded. It was incontrovertible evidence of the perils of wielding Angul. The peril, and the payment required—the cost of her own innocence. She would never forget.

A chime blared at the door. Startled, she nearly drew the Blade Cerulean, despite the fact that she recognized it. She fumbled the skull and it fell to the floor.

"Xet!" Kiril screamed. "You want to end up a pile of crushed sparkly dust? Surprise me one more time, I swear!"

The crystal dragonet chimed again and darted up the passage outside her door.

"Damned little shardling," Kiril cursed. She'd gone more than a few months without loosing Angul from his imprisoning sheath. She didn't want to start the trip by bringing out the sanctimonious blade. Angul was an unbending, saintly bastard in his steel incarnation—more so than he'd been in life, and far more powerful. Kiril swore again, but refrained from retrieving the nameless god from her hip. She'd blurred the edge enough for the moment. She could stand only so much unsteadiness and faded reality.

The elf warrior picked up the skull from the floor and looked at it closely. It had a few new cracks. Kiril growled and placed it back on the shelf. Reminders of mortality were not themselves immune to destruction. She gathered up her saddlebags and departed her chamber. The amber glow of the earthlamp sensed her absence, and after ten heartbeats, dimmed.

The sun warmed Kiril as she spiraled down the exposed staircase to meet Thormud, Xet, and a pile of bags at the Finger Defiant's base. The morning was well along, and the elf didn't have to worry about treacherous night winds blowing her off the side of the mesa.

By the time she reached Thormud, after first spying him from higher up, nothing had changed. The dwarf stood, eyes closed, holding the tip of his selenite rod to the ground.

"Daylight's burning, Thormud," Kiril said. "You can poke rocks later."

The dwarf's eyes opened, and he said, "The earth speaks, to those with the patience to hear it."

Kiril sighed and dropped her saddlebags on the pile. "I've heard that somewhere."

Thormud rubbed his chin. "The disturbance prohibits me from knowing exactly where or how far, or even the precise direction to go."

"But we're going to Durpar, right?"

"We are going southeast, yes. I think, although it is impossible to say for sure, all the way to Durpar. I must build up a picture of the topography from the echoes of the disturbance that reach me. A challenging task."

Kiril waved her hand at the technicalities. "Is it a task you're up to?"

"Yes, if left to it."

The dwarf was the soul of patience, Kiril knew all too well. He was . . .

"You made a joke!" Kiril exclaimed. "All the gods of Sildëyuir, I thank you I was here to witness it."

Thormud inclined his head a few degrees in agreement.

"All right. Think of me as one of your less-communicative stones," Kiril said. "I'll be over there, polishing my blade." The elf had no intention of drawing Angul. It didn't require sharpening or polishing—the Blade Cerulean was sufficient unto itself. Instead, she pulled a dirk out of her boot.

The hilt of the dagger was unblemished silver, and delicate green traceries graced the blade. The weapon was one of the few keepsakes of her home. She kept it for more than just its good elven steel, trusty in a fight—it was a reminder of her childhood in the enchanted Yuirwood. In truth, she used the dagger more often than her sword. Better to wield a minor piece of elven steel than a naked, bitter soul in the shape of a long sword.

She perched on one of Thormud's chests and wiped down the blade with kuevar oil. Not for the first time, she wondered about procuring another long sword—sometimes the dagger, despite its incredible edge, was insufficient. Perhaps something she could use instead of drawing Angul that was dangerous in its own right. A magical blade, perhaps.

The sun moved a full hand's span in the sky. Finally, Thormud said, "I have determined our route as best I can. I will try additional detailed divinations as we move along, but those must wait for proximity."

Kiril stood, sheathing her dirk and packing her oil kit. She had traveled with the dwarf long enough to know what came next.

Thormud went to his knees and lay down, facing the earth. He spread his arms and legs wide, as if seeking to embrace the land. His fingers clutched and he crooned a gravelly tune. The sound went right through Kiril. The noise was less acute in her ears than in the soles of her feet—the ground vibrated in harmony with the dwarf's call. Thormud beseeched the deep earth itself, and he was answered.

The earth convulsed beneath Thormud's spread-eagled body. As if soft mud instead of solid stone, a blister of rock grew, raising Thormud almost fifteen feet into the air. As the blister expanded, it took on a vague shape. From formlessness came a head, a torso, and six pillarlike legs. A granite destrier was revealed, a quickening of the living earth. Kiril recognized it—the dwarf called one each time travel beckoned. Nothing ate up the empty distance like a granite destrier.

Thormud perched immediately behind the destrier's vulpine head. A flat expanse of the creature's back, perfect for securing baggage or additional passengers, stretched behind the dwarf.

Xet chimed and flew up to alight on the destrier's hard snout. Thormud wiped sweat from his brow. Even for a geomancer of the dwarf's expertise, calling forth such a mighty servant was difficult.

"Are you going to sit up there taking in the view all day," queried Kiril, "or are you going to lower that thing so I can get our gear packed?"

Xet belled a protesting tone at her. The dragonet was always mindful of its master's feelings. Not that Thormud had ever risen to the bait Kiril was so fond of dishing out.

Thormud kept his position a moment longer, then patted the great head. The stone destrier grunted, almost like a living beast, and lowered itself to the ground.

Kiril loaded and secured the gear. Thormud silently rested from his exertion.

When every saddlebag, chest, and case was tied down to Kiril's satisfaction, she took her position behind the dwarf. Thormud's calling had specified the creation of two seatlike depressions in the stone of the destrier's back. They would be comfortable enough, Kiril recalled, though the conveyance took a little getting used to.

Thormud patted the head of the destrier once again, saying, "Run free, my friend, above the confines of your mother flesh."

Kiril rolled her eyes. The dwarf was fond of such purple prose. Another perk of her employment.

The destrier stretched to its full height in a surprisingly smooth motion and began to run.

As if it were a coyote after a jackrabbit, the granite destrier lit out across the open plain, dust streaming in its wake.

As fast as the fastest horse at full gallop, the six-legged earth elemental streaked southeast.

CHAPTER FIVE

Low hills, bumpy knolls, and rocky ridges broke up the afternoon light. Covered in scrub grass, the hills' color varied between brown and pale gold, while the barren ridges revealed dark purple striations of vanished centuries. Here and there, stone slabs thrust up from the earthen hilltops, sometimes singly, other times in groups forming ancient rings of debatable purpose.

Since Iahn had ascended to the sunlit lands outside the magically sealed Deep Imaskar, he'd undergone a slow change in attitude. He was beginning to suspect he was made for wide open lands, not closely proscribed walls and corridors.

It amused him to recall that prior to his recent travels, he hadn't had the breadth of experience to think of his home as "proscribed." Before, he'd never thought of the artificially illuminated city behind the Great Seal as confining—but he'd never known anything else.

The vengeance taker's gaze wandered across the wide open, sun-baked landscape. Despite the variation offered by the hills, he traveled through essentially empty terrain, free of obstacles to clutter his view. His eyes could wander without getting snagged on walls, trees, or mountains, as long as he didn't look east.

Without distractions to his vision, his mind had space to roam, too. The vacancy of the earth cried to be filled, and so he filled it with tumbling thoughts, ideas, and even aspirations he'd rarely pondered since his childhood. No thought was too big or too odd to entertain.

The emptiness was restful as much as liberating. The sameness of the plain and sky was a balm, and it calmed the constant anxiety that plagued him—what was the fate of Deep Imaskar in his absence? Would he find the fugitive soon enough? If he found her, what then?

So much for the balm of empty land.

Anyway, he was close to his target. He smelled a change in the air.

Iahn moved closer, altering the angle of the scene by cresting the intervening edge of a rocky bluff.

Not more than three hundred paces from the first swelling hillside stood the coach Iahn had trailed over the last months. It could be no other—its long shape and widely set wheels conformed to the ruts he'd come to know so well. From where he stood, surveying the site, he saw no horses or other beasts of burden capable of pulling the coach. As he had suspected—his quarry summoned steeds at need.

The coach's door crashed open, and several creatures tumbled out. Iahn blinked, startled.

Before he could focus on the emerging figures, his attention was snatched by a hulking form that stepped out from behind the coach. Half again as tall as a human, the massive beast had thick, gray skin with features not unlike those of a troll. Its hunched, apelike posture emphasized its substantial bulk and hinted at the power of its huge fists. Its lower torso and legs were wrapped in uncured hides, forming crude clothing. A leather thong around its neck bore a raw chunk of purplish crystal.

Unless more hid in the coach, the vengeance taker counted a total of four creatures, none of them the fugitive.

Of the trio that spilled out of the coach, Iahn identified two people in long white gowns, reminding him of the desert nomads he'd met when he'd skirted the Plains of Purple Dust. Except those folk had been humans, and their garments had been dark brown. These were some variety of elf. One elf dervish was female, the other male.

The last creature was humanoid, but of a race completely unfamiliar to Iahn. It was covered in a luxurious coat of ebony fur that complimented its black, pantherlike head. It had cloven hooves where Iahn expected feet or paws. Where it walked, a sheen lingered in its hoofprints before slowly evaporating. Iahn recognized it as the same glistening spoor he'd encountered a few days earlier.

The vengeance taker noted that each wore amulets similar to the troll's—the only visible clue that bound the entire group other than their proximity. Were these creatures servants of the fugitive, guarding her coach, or did they represent the force whispered to him by the Voice? Probably the latter, but the vengeance taker rarely reached conclusions without absorbing all possible information.

The panther-headed creature saw Iahn and pointed. Iahn stared back, wondering what they would do.

The two elf dervishes produced slender recurve bows from their garb, stringing them expertly in less than a heartbeat. The troll-thing swung its head around to regard Iahn, and screamed an incomprehensible battle cry. Then it charged.

Hostiles. He knew what to do about that. Iahn stepped back behind the edge of the bluff.

The vengeance taker muttered a few words of sorcery and

ran one hand down the length of his body. Where his hand passed, his form became hazy and uncertain. Using this extra advantage, he eased back into a crevice.

The gray troll barreled around the edge of the rise, easily and quickly covering ground using both knuckles and feet. The earth trembled with each bounding step. It did not see Iahn, but paused, snuffling. The vengeance taker, whose position was hidden by both skill and magic, studied the creature's anatomy, musculature, and bulging veins. It was certainly of troll blood, but larger than any he had seen in a bestiary.

Iahn had studied on occasion in the Purple Library, an ancient and sadly out-of-date collection of scrolls, text fragments, and books retained in the heart of Deep Imaskar. He was an expert on all the bestiaries there. Apparently, troll varieties had multiplied and diversified in the millennia since the collection was gathered.

The vengeance taker studied the way the troll's muscles moved over its bones, the way its great chest rose and fell with each breath. He gently twisted the hilt of his dragonfly blade, then pulled it apart along the revealed seam. Silently, the thinblade slipped free of its enclosing hilt, giving Iahn the advantage of two weapons—the wafer-thin stiletto, and the long dragonfly blade, shaped like the wing of a dragonfly. Iahn froze, concentrating on his pursuer.

The troll snuffed and snuffled, its eyes vainly searching for its quarry. For his part, the vengeance taker had finished taking the creature's measure. A hollow caught the vengeance taker's eye, high up on the creature's neck, right below its jaw. The monstrosity would be dead before it realized it was threatened. All he had to do was to step forward and plunge his thinblade up and in . . .

The troll's awful nose flared and the beast charged Iahn. The vengeance taker abandoned his plan, bobbing and weaving wide to the left instead. A great fist smashed into the rock, barely missing Iahn. The stone cracked like thunder and a spray of shards rained down, leaving a fist-sized crater behind.

The beast had smelled him!

The vengeance taker struck, driving the thinblade deep into the creature—but missed the spot where he could have spilled the creature's life blood instantly.

The troll screamed nonetheless, surprised at the pain in its chest. Its claws fell with lethal fury, and Iahn rolled to evade the fatal embrace. He slashed at the creature's ankles, hoping to pierce a major artery, but its skin resisted his jabs.

Then a gray, questing hand grabbed him.

The troll lifted Iahn clear off the ground. He had sorely underestimated the threat the creature posed. The troll raised him higher, its roar a clarion, nearly bursting Iahn's eardrums. Its breath was a quagmire of rot and past blood feasts.

Scissoring his body in the troll's rough grip, he managed to slip the tip of his thinblade into the corner of its left eye. He simultaneously swung the longer dragonfly blade around to connect with the other side of the creature's head. It roared and dropped Iahn. The vengeance taker knew the wounds he'd inflicted were only superficial; after all, his opponent was a troll. Its flesh would knit soon enough.

"I see him," a voice pronounced. A slender gray shaft plunged into the ground at Iahn's feet as the vengeance taker dodged away from the gray troll's reach.

An answering voice said, "So do I, but he's wearing a charm of some sort. I missed." The last was said with some incredulity. The second voice was speaking in Elvish, one of the many languages Iahn had studied to achieve his rank and damos.

The two elves in desert dress stood not more than thirty paces from him, their bows drawn and nocked. The troll wheeled around, its eyes fastening on Iahn despite the blurring around the vengeance taker.

"Hold, I have not come to fight!" Iahn yelled in Elvish. He had lost the upper hand. He didn't doubt he could slay the troll by calling on his damos, but he didn't want to be skewered by the elves' arrows in the meantime.

The hoofed one rounded the knoll's edge. Iahn had enough experience with sorcery to recognize its infernal taint. It held up a hand, not speaking. Its eyes gleamed as if lit by tiny lavender flames. An answering fire burned in the creature's crystal amulet.

It said, "Then you will die all the sooner." It spoke not in the language of the elves—it used the speech of Imaskar.

This surprised Iahn. Perhaps these were guardians placed by the fugitive after all?

"Who are you?" demanded the vengeance taker.

"I am Deamiel, but you'll have little enough chance to remember it."

"Wait," interrupted Iahn. "Answer me this—do you serve the one called Ususi Manaallin? Has she set you against me?"

Deamiel executed a tittering shriek. It said, "We serve a power greater than mortal flesh. We are its eyes, its hands, and its claws. Ususi Manaallin will fall to us by its command."

"This 'power' you serve—who is that?"

"The death of all that remains of Imaskar!" So saying, Deamiel pointed a finger at Iahn. "Slay this filth!"

The vengeance taker threw himself backward and tumbled expertly through the gap between the troll's legs. His enemy's slow-witted confusion provided him with temporary cover from the dervish archers. A quick motion married Iahn's thinblade back into the hilt of his dragon-fly blade, freeing one hand to gesticulate just so. His voice was unimpeded and able to verbalize, and residual power sang in his blood from his last sip from the damos. These, too, were his weapons and his defense, just as surely as his thinblade.

Iahn assayed a quickslide, pushing his talent to the brink. The light dimmed. He skipped through space as far as he could. Two hundred paces, perhaps three hundred . . .

The broad side of the travel coach stood directly in front of him, occluding the sun's glare. The vengeance taker leaned his weight against the side of the coach with his free hand, breathing hard but quietly. He was drained. He knew the creatures would not give him up quickly if Deamiel spoke the truth about slaying all from Deep Imaskar. One thing was clear—the creatures did not serve the fugitive.

They must be a further materialization of the troubles that had erupted in Deep Imaskar, Iahn mused. All the more reason for him to catch the fugitive, and quickly.

Iahn peered into the side window of the coach and saw it was empty. Cabinet doors stood ajar, and cups, food canisters, a shattered tea pot, an overturned lamp, and other items littered the floor and surfaces of the interior.

The creatures had been inside the coach when he'd first come upon them. They didn't know where Ususi was, either. But she had to be close. She wouldn't abandon her travel coach—it contained all her provisions. Of course, she could summon a mount at a moment's notice to bear her—but Iahn suspected she had invested too much in the coach to leave it behind.

The vengeance taker studied the nearest dolmen up the slope and the unfolding hills beyond. He decided that the best place to look for the fugitive would be somewhere in those downs.

On the other hand, he knew the cat-headed thing and its minions would find him quickly enough—he hadn't shifted more than a few hundred yards—unless he put more distance between them and himself.

He was already moving forward in a low, quick dash, ascending the slope, making for the first dolmen. If he could keep the coach between him and his pursuers' eyes just long enough . . .

"There! There!" Cries of discovery chased Iahn up the hill. The vengeance taker's posture changed—staying low no longer served any purpose. He lengthened his stride and pumped his legs, calling upon all his reserves.

He reached the first dolmen without catching an arrow or magical blast in the back, ducked behind it, and peered back carefully.

The four pursuers had crested the knoll where he'd first attempted to waylay the gray troll, and were running toward the coach. They had already covered half the distance. The vengeance taker had to even the odds and give himself more time to hide among the folds in the hills. The troll would have to wait, and Deamiel was an unknown quantity, but the two archers . . .

Iahn leaned his dragonfly blade against the dolmen, then unbuckled the Imaskaran crossbow from its holster on his thigh with practiced ease. He unfolded the two arms and locked them into place, then strung the crossbow's wire. Six slender bolts were ingeniously clipped to the underside of the crossbow barrel. He plucked one, opened his damos, and dipped the bolt's tip into the swirling venom. The bolt's tip steamed.

The vengeance taker fitted the bolt to the crossbow and sighted down the hillside, careful to stay under the dolmen's cover.

The elf archers reached the coach and took up positions with a view of the hillside. The great troll lumbered after them, but hadn't reached the coach. Iahn couldn't see the panther-headed creature—a problem, but one that would have to wait.

Iahn's bolt sailed down the slope and buried itself in the chest of an archer. The elf cried out, then yelled, "I can hear you! I can . . ." The elf crumpled onto the brown grass beneath the coach.

The other archer loosed a shaft in return, but it cracked ineffectually on the dolmen pillar to Iahn's left. The archer, seeing her arrow fall, ducked behind the coach. She yelled out in Common, "Beware, poison bolts! Mohmafel is dead!"

The troll reached the shelter of the coach and hunkered down before Iahn could fire a second venomous bolt. The vengeance taker scanned for Deamiel. Was the creature already sheltering behind the coach? No matter.

Iahn yelled down the hill in Common. "Stand still, or prepare to hear your doom. If the Voice is the last word to enter your ears before death, your soul is consigned to wander forever." He doubted the creatures understood his implication, but Iahn believed the threat might give them pause.

The vengeance taker watched the coach. He saw no movement, heard no sounds. Like his adversaries, he didn't want to risk leaving the sanctuary of his dolmen. The blurring enchantment the taker had employed had dissipated. Iahn's quickslide to the coach had exhausted his small reservoir of arcane ability. Until he could renew it, the vengeance taker could rely only on his guile and skill.

A hundred breaths passed without any movement. The sun reached its zenith in the empty sky. Heat blistered the bare scrublands. Iahn was like the rock he sheltered behind; how patient were his adversaries? In the vengeance taker's experience, his tolerance for boredom was rarely bested.

Half-heard mutters from below preceded a sudden river of fog that streamed around, over, and past the coach, completely obscuring it. With the mist came cries and dreamy exhortations. Slender tendrils of mist extended from the mass, as if patting and feeling for sustenance. The diameter of the fog bank swelled.

The vengeance taker envenomed another bolt from his damos. Deamiel, presumably, had manufactured a cloak of concealing vapor, a perfect blind from which to launch an attack. Iahn's eyes narrowed—from which portion of the mist would it come? Did the . . .

The troll emerged from the mist, running up the slope with the speed of a bounding boulder.

Iahn took a bead on the fast-approaching troll, but an arrow scorched his left arm, ruining his aim. The elf archer had gotten off a shot from just inside the fog's boundary!

Iahn snatched a third bolt, taking the time to envenom it. The damos, too, was nearly spent this day. But the troll had to be dealt with, first and foremost.

The charging troll reached the crown of Iahn's hill. A great gray hand grasped the dolmen pillar Iahn sheltered behind. The hand was followed by an enormous head that blotted out the sun.

Iahn shot the bolt straight into the creature's left eye. It gasped out a word in a language the taker didn't know, then collapsed back down the slope. Iahn knew that the venom was more potent than the troll's ability to renew itself.

He dropped the crossbow and snatched up his dragonfly blade. Not a moment too soon—black-furred Deamiel had run up the slope in the troll's wake. The creature, roaring, sprang on the vengeance taker from the other side of the dolmen. The crystal amulet on its breast suddenly blazed with a wavering, violet light. Moving with a speed Iahn could scarcely fathom, Deamiel struck him. The violent blow hurled the vengeance taker back ten paces.

The world spun around Iahn as he tried to regain his feet. He kept his grip on the hilt of his dragonfly blade and used it to lever himself upright. Blood streamed from his cheek, and his left arm and shoulder were partly numb. The vengeance taker had assumed the troll was the greatest threat, but . . .

Deamiel was on him, hiccupping horrid laughter. It picked him up in both hands, so swiftly that Iahn failed to resist, and as easily as if the vengeance taker were but a child. Deamiel screamed. "Pandorym's blessing sings in my blood! Its will is mine, but . . . It . . . I . . . Pandorym! I am not . . ."

Deamiel's arms shook with some sort of inner struggle. Despite the creature's difficulty speaking, its grip was slowly tightening on Iahn's suspended body. More importantly, Iahn saw the crystal on Deamiel's breast pulse in tempo with its speech, word for word.

One arm still free, Iahn brought the steel hilt of his dragonfly blade down on Deamiel's amulet.

The crystal exploded.

The midnight blaze that blossomed from the amulet transfixed Deamiel, but Iahn was blown clear. The vengeance taker fell painfully for the second time in about as many heartbeats.

Iahn did not stir when his senses returned. Instead, he studied the scene with slitted eyes. Deamiel lay near, still burning, its chest cavity an exploded, gory ruin. Not a pleasant sight, but he'd seen worse. Farther down the slope lay the crumpled form of the gray troll. Farther still, the mist-shrouded coach.

Apparently, only an instant had elapsed since the amulet's destruction.

As Iahn watched, the fog bank swirled, thinned, and blew away in ragged, evaporating streamers. The remaining elf archer was revealed, showing little concern. She moved cautiously, studied her elf comrade, then hiked up the slope to the troll. The crystal on her breast did not glow or flare.

When she was close enough to Iahn, he sprang to his feet, catching one of her arms and twisting it painfully behind her back. Not all his skills brought death to his foes—some just delivered debilitating agony. Sometimes, final justice was not for a taker to dispense. Sometimes.

"Submit," Iahn demanded. The elf said nothing, but stopped struggling in his grip.

The vengeance taker jerked the elf closer. With his teeth, he grabbed the leather strand holding her amulet. He jerked his head back and stripped the amulet from the archer's neck. He didn't want to see a repeat of Deamiel's performance.

As the amulet dropped to the earth, the elf convulsed violently in the vengeance taker's grip. Then, as if she'd been slipped an overpoweringly lethal dose from the damos, she slumped, her life departed. Iahn was too familiar with death's onset to wonder if it could be anything else.

The vengeance taker lay the limp body on the ground and studied the scene.

"Strange."

The noonday light imparted brutal clarity, but no understanding.

CHAPTER SIX

Give me that," Ususi said, motioning the uskura
closer. Obediently, her expeditioner's pack settled
into her outstretched hands.

The wizard undid the ties and rummaged
through the bag. She pushed aside silver spikes;
a length of strong, lean rope; various vials whose
contents ranged from acid to healing magic; and
finally drew forth a tiny cylinder, just shorter than
the length of her hand.

She stared down the narrow hallway, and the
white light of her delver's orb flooded the ancient
darkness, revealing intricately carved walls.
Fanciful demons—or perhaps not so fanciful—gave
obeisance to a great emperor on the wall to her
left, while slender humanoids, too fey to represent
the mortal elves Ususi was familiar with, stood in

elegant congress around a kingly figure on the right.

The images fascinated Ususi, and she thought perhaps the image on the left represented Umyatin, the first Imaskari emperor. Umyatin had taken for himself the title "Lord Artificer." The demon on the lord artificer's left had a lion's head and a dragon's body. The demon to Umyatin's right was a midnight black centaur with an ebony unicorn horn emerging from its forehead. Its eyes burned with hellish glee. The lord artificer was reaching out to this one. Below the midnight centauricorn was a name, inscribed in Low Imaskari. "Mizar," it read. The wizard didn't recognize the name.

The image on the right was more interesting yet. Each of the elegant, elfin humanoids who stood with the central figure carried a magnificent tome, seven in all. She wondered if the likeness represented Emperor Omanond. According to legend, Omanond was ultimately responsible for the creation of the seven items of Imaskaran arcane lore, the Imaskarcana. These were commonly described as tomes, though Ususi had read accounts indicating that the Imaskarcana took many forms. According to *The Lore of Omanond,* a history Ususi had perused within the exclusive stacks of the Purple Library, the creation of the Imaskarcana had been made possible through connivance with a devious extraplanar race. A more-than-mortal race. She had always assumed this referred to demons, but the creatures in the art before her possessed no demonic traits. The name inscribed below the creatures was "leShay." Again, Ususi couldn't place the name.

Bother that. The identity and accuracy of the designs were secondary to the magical trap she sensed lurking in the flooring.

Behind and above her stretched the winding, stair-strewn path she'd traveled throughout the Imaskaran ruin.

The complex beneath the earth was in surprisingly good condition, which was both good and bad. Finding a well-preserved outpost of the Imaskari was good because it meant surviving enchantments might still power a functional gate into the Celestial Nadir. Finding a well-preserved ruin was bad because it meant a higher number of guardian enchantments and traps remained lethal.

So progress was slow. For safety, Ususi checked each new section of flooring, walls, and ceiling with a sluggish, low-grade magical charm. Was it a waste of time when going swiftly might spell sudden death? The uskura certainly didn't complain. Ususi nearly smiled at the idea.

She unscrewed the tiny cap of the cylinder she'd retrieved from her pack, and let a tiny dollop of red liquid fall onto the hallway floor. It was the last of the dye, and the drop was hardly visible.

Ususi eyed the diminutive red dot. Perhaps she'd been too liberal with the dye on the first several traps she'd encountered.

By comparison, wide stripes of warning dye painted all the previous traps she'd found in the complex.

Sometimes, avoiding a mechanical or magical ambush merely required knowing where not to step. Once a trap's trigger was identified, remembering its precise location was as important as its discovery. She'd developed her warning dye as the perfect visual signal. Ususi had the ingredients to make more dye back in her coach, but she preferred to press forward as long as possible before returning topside.

The wizard studied the tiny droplet and judged it a large enough reminder. Its location, coupled with the frieze of Emperors Umyatin and Omanond, would give her warning enough on her way back.

On the other hand, if she came upon just one more trap, she'd have to decide whether to return to the coach to make another batch of red dye, or try her hand at deactivating it.

Ususi had some experience in the deactivation of nefarious devices, but it was a dangerous business—far better to simply steer clear of the trigger. But some devices couldn't be avoided. For these, deactivation was the only sure method of getting past them. Because of her wizardly talents, ensnaring spells and blasting enchantments were far easier to eliminate than unthinking springs, levers, weights, and winches. Unfortunately, many traps dispensed with arcana and relied on simple mechanical principles.

Confident the hallway before her held no further surprises, Ususi put the empty cylinder back in her pack. She remanded the pack to the invisible uskura and walked down the passage, deftly avoiding the trigger point.

The radius of her magical light preceded her, bringing illumination where dark centuries brooded. Ususi held out her right hand, concentrating on her trap-finding charm. She supposed far more powerful spells might lay bare all the dangers in a large radius, but she didn't know them. She hadn't gone out of her way to find such spells—she preferred to save her greatest strength for potent spells of blasting. If she roused some guardian demon, she was ready, she hoped, to send it back to whatever netherworld had spawned it.

A few more paces, and the carvings on either side opened up to reveal a great, rounded chamber. Like the hallway, its periphery was heavily inscribed with images, words, and symbols. Even the ceiling was carved with thick clusters of sigils.

Ususi's breath caught when she spied the central feature of the chamber—a great stone annulus hovering unsupported in the air, measuring some ten paces in diameter. The ring slowly rotated, flipping end over end about once every two or three heartbeats.

But the ring was not intact. A section of the hoop lay cracked and shattered on the floor. Two parallel creases appeared on the wizard's brow as she studied the debris. This could be a portal, perhaps leading into the Celestial Nadir, but it was damaged.

First things first. Ususi renewed her concentration and

scanned the room for traps. She hadn't come this far so cautiously only to rush into the arms of a slicing blade or to be crushed beneath a ceiling block. The annulus itself could be a devious deception . . . but no. The room was clear. Other than the rotating ring, one other exit presented itself. A flight of stairs led upward, the first upward set she'd discovered since entering the outpost. She wondered if it was an exit to the hills outside. It would wait.

Ususi stood before the annulus. Inscriptions crowded the stone circle, many unreadable. One symbol was clear immediately—a ring within a ring, the interior circle slightly off center—one of the symbols associated with the Celestial Nadir!

The wizard drew the keystone from beneath her jacket. She held it forth, presenting it to the annulus. As Ususi handled it, the stone flickered and brightened, giving off a glow all its own. Ususi paused. Again, she noticed the hazed darkness at the stone's core. She shook her head slightly, deciding to worry about that later.

Ususi let her mind touch the stone, and through its interface, sought contact with the ring. She sought referents, points of synchronicity, answering reflections—even the smallest connection would be enough for her to try to gain control of the ring and force it open. Assuming it led to the Celestial Nadir. And if it was not broken beyond repair.

But no. "Four dooms and damnation!" she yelled. The annulus was dead. If it had ever been a portal, its functions were stripped. Only residual magic elevated it above the floor.

A sudden thud shook her from her anger.

Ususi whirled and stared. The light of her delver's orb sent feral shadows fleeing across the chamber. The sound had come from somewhere back along the way she'd traveled. She'd either missed a guardian, and it had roused from age-long quiescence to chase her down, or something or someone else had entered the buried outpost from the exterior. The wizard cursed herself for not securing the entry.

Either way . . .

Ususi touched the orb that hovered at her brow and its light died. The radiance of the keystone trickled away, too, as she hung it around her neck, under her jacket. The wizard didn't need light to trace her steps back over her course. She closed her eyes in the darkness and invoked a spell of clairvoyant vision. Beginning with the hallway where the two ancient emperors locked eyes for lost ages, Ususi's wizard sight bloomed, a window of seeing. Through her dark window, everything was blurred and colorless. Details faded and distances were hard to discern.

She traced her path, pushing her vision down the inscribed hall and into the square room with the pool of iridescent liquid—water with an enchantment against evaporation. The chamber was as empty as she'd left it.

Farther yet, beyond the pool room, she found a bright red band of warning dye painted at neck height along the narrow passage.

Something moved down that passage.

It was . . . what was it? Identification was difficult because the image was blurred—it degraded the farther she forced it along.

Whatever it was, it kept low, beneath the warning red stripe she'd placed on the wall. The figure used Ususi's system to its own benefit! She realized she'd marked a trail leading directly to her location.

The wizard tensed but concentrated all her faculties on sharpening the clairvoyant image. A human? A man, definitely, but his skin was pale and marbled, not unlike her own. His outfit was familiar.

Ususi let out an involuntary hiss and abandoned the vision.

A vengeance taker.

After all this time, Deep Imaskar had finally tracked her down.

Ususi brushed her orb and light flooded the chamber. The vengeance taker was too close—he would see it! But her wizard vision was too slow and unreliable in an emergency. She had to see in order to escape.

"Get up those stairs," she whispered to the uskura. Ususi pointed to the other exit in the chamber. She dashed after her retreating pack. How had they tracked her into this ruin? They must have been looking for her for a long, long time.

Ususi reached the archway and had one foot on the lowest step.

"Hold, fugitive!" The voice was strong and authoritative. It was the voice of a vengeance taker. It was a voice accustomed to its commands being followed, and for good reason.

Ususi darted up the narrow stairwell. The steps were high, shallow, and dusty. She gasped for breath, but the air seemed to have fled the stairway. She slipped and fell on the steps, catching herself with one hand but taking half her weight on the other shoulder. A cry of pain escaped her lips, like a sob. Her mind twirled, images of vengeance takers she had known and stories she had heard of their retribution causing tumult in her mind. She was panicking!

This was not her. Ususi Manaallin did not panic.

Ususi grasped the edges of her fear, wrenched it into halves, and cast its husks aside.

She was a wizard, trained by the Cabal of Purple. A single taker would not bring her down, she vowed. She scrambled to her feet and turned to face down the staircase. Better to confront your enemies than to suffer their attacks at your back, she knew. She counted herself lucky his attack hadn't already sprung.

Then she heard a strange, reverberating pulse. It was a sound like—yet unlike—the noise of some of her own spells when she cast them—a hum like a rushing torrent heard in the rainy season, mixed with the high-pitched harmony of forlorn, tolling bells. The noise halted as instantly as it had begun, leaving behind silence, the smell of ozone, and a glow of glittering, white reflections that patted at the bottom of the stairs.

The vengeance taker must be casting preparatory spells, readying his advance, she thought. Takers were moderate-ability sorcerers, after all—magic was part of the deadly training they received.

Yet it was no spell she recognized.

"Fugitive . . . Manaallin!" It was the voice of her pursuer. Yet his tone had shifted slightly. Ususi maintained her silence, waiting for the attack. Her hands were poised to release a torrent of destructive curses.

"Ususi Manaallin—if you can hear me, I pray you pause. I haven't come so far to lose you now." The voice sounded strained, and its authoritative blare was dulled—by what? Ususi couldn't tell.

He was crafty enough not to poke his head through the arch and look up the stairs—he must have sensed Ususi's spells ready to strip her flesh and worse. So instead, he seemed to be trying to draw her into the arms of his attack.

Ususi yelled down the corridor. "It's a standoff, Vengeance Taker! I will not walk into your trap, and if you follow me up these stairs, it'll be the last act you ever take!"

A chuckle answered her threat. The voice said, "Will you pretend you did not leave this painful blaze to catch me?" Another chuckle, somehow self-deprecating.

Ususi didn't have the first clue what the taker was talking about.

"Explain," she said.

"Your ploy succeeded—you were clever in identifying every dormant trap in this molding ruin with your red dye—but even cleverer in failing to mark the very last one."

Ususi recalled running low on dye when she entered the hallway of the two emperors.

The wizard cocked her head, wondering. Could it be? Ususi carefully descended twelve or so steps to reach the arch that connected into the room of the annulus.

The inscribed hallway was a blaze of white, syrupy light. Floating in its midst, like a fish in a bowl, was the vengeance taker. His arms struggled to reach a purchase they were not long enough to find, and his legs kicked ineffectually, failing to propel him in any direction at all. The vengeance taker was caught.

Ususi nearly turned and dashed back up the stairs. Now was the time to make good her escape, before the man figured out how to free himself. If he could do so. Or, she could strike him while he was helpless.

But how often would the opportunity to question a vengeance taker present itself? It couldn't hurt to discover how angry Deep Imaskar was with her for weakening the Great Seal enough so she could take her leave. Or why they'd waited so many years to send someone after her.

Better to ask the vengeance taker. Ususi pasted a conciliatory smile on her face and approached the ensconced agent of those who wished her harm.

"There are questions I'd like to ask you, Vengeance Taker."

CHAPTER SEVEN

Warian Datharathi disembarked from the sleek watercraft in the city of Vaelan.

The dissolute son returns, he mused.

He turned and watched the small crew as they opened the hold of the courier ship. First out was his horse, Majeed. Despite being on the outs with his family, being a Datharathi had its benefits anywhere Trade Authority offices or embassies operated. As one of the eleven most influential families in Durpar, Datharathi Minerals was partly responsible for paying Trade Authority upkeep. On the other hand, members of the Datharathi family enjoyed free passage on Trade Authority couriers.

Previously known as Vaelantar, and like its sister cities of Ompre and Assur, the city was overrun by monsters flooding out of the Curna Mountains. But Durpar finally expelled the invaders in 1096 DR. In the three hundred years since those tumultuous times, the name Vaelantar was shortened to Vaelan. More importantly, Vaelan grew into the crown jewel of Durpar's trading empire, and enjoyed status as one of the most preeminent destinations on the Golden Water, or indeed, in all the Shining Lands.

The Dolphin Pier was one of nine piers exclusively reserved for merchant traffic. Of course, many smaller and larger piers filled the coast in either direction: the private piers reserved for the personal yachts of the very wealthy, as well as piers set aside for the highly profitable ship-building businesses. Datharathi Minerals had, like many of the most influential merchant families, maintained interest in the ship-building trade.

Beyond those were the ramshackle piers used by the fishers.

Warian walked down the Dolphin Pier holding Majeed's reins. Beyond a press of warehouses, innumerable offices, and nearly as many wharfside taverns, the towers of Vaelan pointed proudly at the sky. The towers housed the most influential "chakas," as trading families were sometimes called. Any family with aspirations to challenge the predominance of the eleven greatest chakas that made up the Trade Authority first built a tower—or purchased the tower of another family whose fortunes were declining. Over a hundred pale towers pushed into the sky, some new since Warian had left the city behind.

Chaka towers were generally confined to the Gold District, and enjoyed the protection of delicate-looking yet strong whitewashed stone walls. Beyond the ordered towers and their well-patrolled boundaries, the larger bulk of Vaelan hummed and buzzed, nearly as loud and well-lit at midnight as at midday.

Aside from the towers, distinguishing discrete buildings

amid the mass was a fool's game in Vaelan. Great connected complexes of white-plastered walls, balconies, stairs, galleries, promenades, and open courts stretched in all directions. Wide streets separated one press of mazelike architecture from the next, but high bridges, held up as much by minor enchantments as engineering, arched over the streets to connect rooftop bazaars.

And the crowd! Everywhere Warian looked, people talked (in diverse dialects and languages), bartered (from countless windows, booths, wagons, and permanent storefronts), sought hard-to-find goods (such as philters guaranteed to bring the buyer true love, or cockroaches whose shells turned blue in the presence of magic), gossiped (about the future of Durpar if Veldorn's aggression wasn't checked), and enjoyed themselves (drinking from great glass vessels filled with weak but tasty beer—consumed nearly as fast as it was brewed).

Warian was one of thousands of people thronging the streets, pushing his way forward as quickly and economically as possible. The trick of moving with the ebb and flow of the crowd came back to him with hardly any effort. He was elbowed in the side once, but ignoring such slights was part of getting where you wanted to go in a reasonable amount of time. He quickly found a public stable on the outskirts of the wharf district and paid a small sum to put Majeed up for several days. He hoped he wouldn't be around that long, but better to pay ahead than risk the stablemaster selling his horse.

Freed of worry about Majeed's well-being, Warian waved over a rickshaw pulled by a surprisingly short man with hair as red as fire.

"Where to?" asked the redhead, as Warian settled into the seat.

"West Gardens," Warian told the rickshaw driver. "It's a tenement district near Kazrim's Plunge." The Plunge was a statue commemorating a Kazrim, whose heroics three hundred years prior were considered instrumental in freeing Vaelantar from the monsters.

The driver nodded at Warian and pulled the transport out into the throng. Warian was a little surprised that the driver did not give his crystalline arm a second glance. He was accustomed, at the very least, to eyebrows raised in surprise, if not outright amazement, and often enough, hostility.

Whoever had ridden the rickshaw before had left behind the redolent perfume of cherry tobacco. Smoking tobacco from a water-cooled pipe was a vice Warian tried to cultivate when he still lived in Vaelan—his family had a long-standing taboo against smoking for some traditional reason, and he'd wanted to prove his independence—but he'd never managed to enjoy the sensation. Probably just as well.

Moving through Vaelan's busy streets was enjoyable when someone else's worry and effort forged the path. Sitting back in his seat allowed Warian a chance to absorb the ambience and study the various city dwellers and visitors who strode to and fro, each intent on his own unknowable business. Many were from outside Durpar, having traveled from countries like the Shaar, Dambrath, or Halruaa. Others hailed from even farther shores, such as the nearly mythical Sembia or Cormyr. Warian had never personally met anyone from places so distant, but he'd heard stories.

The sharp, glinting light of sun through crystal caught Warian's eye. A woman walking out of a stylish saloon on the high balcony to his left carried a prism . . . no . . .

The woman's hand was clear, as if made of glass! More than that, delicate traceries of crystal writhed across her whole arm, and marked her face, too, with an elaborate embroidery. Warian gaped. As he pulled closer, there was no doubt—the woman sported a crystal prosthesis, and then some, just as he did!

Her body art reminded Warian of an intricate tattoo, but never had he seen one laid down in glass. He didn't doubt the glass of her prosthesis and decoration was Datharathi crystal.

Warian waved to catch the woman's attention, but she turned and moved down an elevated path, and a bridge intervened as the rickshaw continued to move forward.

"Say," Warian called to the driver who plodded along ahead of him. "Do you see many people who have crystal like mine?" Warian tapped his arm even though the driver didn't turn. "Like my crystal arm?"

The driver shrugged without turning, and said, "Sure. Plangents. Too rich for my blood."

"Plangents?"

"Yeah." The driver craned his neck to fix Warian with an assessing eye. "Like you." The driver turned his attention back to his path.

Warian searched his memory, but came up blank.

"I'm sorry, I've been gone from Vaelan for most of the last five years. When I left, I was the only one who had such a . . . um, crystal prosthesis."

"Hmph," the driver snorted, and turned down a high but narrow alley. "You're in good company now, eh? Datharathi's got the goods. They'll make you 'stronger, faster, smarter— better!' if you got the gold."

Warian shook his head and said, "But this prosthesis is worse than a real arm. It's slow, weak, and I can't feel a thing through it! I have this arm because I lost my real one in an accident. Who'd want that?" But, indeed, what of the flash of potency, the reason he'd returned to Vaelan in the first place?

"Well," the driver responded, chuckling. "You got a bad deal. The plangents I've seen are none of that—you put a plangent against me in a pulling contest, and even though I've pulled this rickshaw every day for thirteen years, a plangent'd beat me every time, if he had a brand new overhaul."

"What's this word you keep saying—plangent? Anyone

who gets a prosthesis is a plangent?"

"Well, yeah, that's what we call 'em. But from what I heard, you can't just replace an arm, a leg, or an eye. They replace stuff on the inside, too, stuff we can't see. The plangents—they're supposed to live longer—they're their own thing now. A new thing. A plangent." The driver snorted, then yelled at another porter who edged in front of him at an intersection.

Warian sat back. Uncle Xaemar and Grandfather Shaddon had been busy. Warian was confident that the crystal of his arm stopped at his shoulder. Since he'd been given his fake arm, they must have refined and expanded the technique. And improved it—no one would give up the limb they were born with for something worse, like Warian's. Well, it was usually worse. Did all the plangents enjoy the strength and speed he'd accidentally discovered? A scary thought! He didn't know enough, clearly.

All the more reason to seek out Eined first and get an unadulterated account from her before being propagandized by his elders.

Eined Datharathi lived in a quiet tenement in the upscale West Gardens district. Those who lived in West Gardens paid into a fund that employed spellcasting and sword-bearing sentries to make certain that things stayed quiet and safe. Thus, Warian was doubly surprised when he arrived to find Eined's door open, and her abode in the process of being robbed.

The awful crash of breaking glass and the gruff sound of men's voices echoed from within, confounding Warian for only a moment. He dashed through the entry passage yelling, "Eined!"

The entry parlor contained a single intruder, who whirled as Warian came upon him. The intruder, dressed all in gray and sporting greasy hair, held a metal prying bar clutched in one hand. All around the man, evidence of ransacking littered the room. Mirrors that once graced the walls were shattered on the floor. Carpets were pulled up, drapes were torn down, and chairs lay broken.

"Where is Eined?"

"She ain't here, and if you know what's good for you, you'll shove off, too," said the man with the metal rod.

Warian didn't know what was good for him. He willed his prosthesis, "Go!" but it remained as dull as ever. So he punched the intruder with his flesh-and-blood hand. The man's head rocked back.

"Who are you? Where's my sister?" demanded Warian.

The man shook his head, rubbing the back of his hand across the cut on his lip. He said, "That was a mistake. Now I got to feed you this!"

The intruder smacked the iron bar into his open palm, leering at Warian. But he didn't attack. Instead, he glanced down the hallway to the sitting room and yelled, "Hey! Get your butts up front! We got a visitor."

A voice called from farther in the house—a man's voice, not Eined's. "What you talkin' about, Revi?"

The man facing Warian, apparently named Revi, yelled back. "Just get your ugly mugs out here, will ya? We got trouble—a plangent."

"I'm not . . ." Warian trailed off. If they thought he was a plangent, maybe he could frighten them away.

In a more assertive tone, Warian told the man, "Put that bar down if you don't want to be the one who chokes on it." Warian raised his prosthesis and pointed it directly at his foe.

Revi's eyes widened slightly and he backed up a step, but then the man's friends rushed into the room. One yelled, "Plangents are tough, but not tough enough for one to stand against five!"

"I'm warning you . . ." proclaimed Warian, feeling foolish.

Greasy-haired Revi swung the pry bar like a sword at Warian's head. Warian's arm was still extended from his failed threat, and he needed only to raise and angle it just slightly to deflect the blow, which he felt only dully through his shoulder.

One of Revi's friends simultaneously kicked Warian in the stomach, something Warian wasn't prepared for. He stumbled back, and two more rushed up and easily grabbed his arms, one on each.

"Hold him!" directed Revi. "Watch his implant!"

Warian struggled, but as always, his prosthesis was about half as strong as a real arm. Another two goons grabbed him, three on his crystal arm.

"We got 'im," one grunted. "He don't seem so tough."

Warian desperately tried to recall—what had he done to trigger the arm the first time? He'd been in that tavern, and what's-his-name had gotten him around the throat . . . he had started to black out. Darkness had threaded his vision, and he was reminded of the dark tendrils he'd noticed within his prosthesis.

"Look at me!" yelled Revi. The man's lip was swelling and blood trickled a red streak down his chin.

Instead, Warian concentrated on his memory. If he didn't figure it out, the lights might go out for good . . .

Wait—light! What was it about light? As he'd been choked, darkness had pushed in on all sides—he'd mentally tried to push the darkness back, to illuminate it. He'd been pretty muddled as his brain starved for air, and had gotten a little confused on which darkness to illuminate—his tunneling vision or the black hazing in his prosthesis.

Revi wound up with the iron bar. Warian concentrated on the threads of darkness in his arm, willing them to shrivel away, to light up, to be revealed in the clarifying light of the sun.

The prosthesis flashed into bonfire brilliance, lilac in hue. Sensation shot from his shoulder to his crystalline fingertips, as if transformed from an inert sculpture to a live arm, or something that felt even more vital than flesh.

It was alive again, as it had been at the tavern in Dambrath.

His captors' grip on his arm suddenly seemed as light as tissue paper around a name day present. Lavender luminance lit their faces as they stared at him, alarm slowly overtaking what had been naked glee and the anticipation of a beating. They seemed caught and slowed in the syrupy radiance.

Warian laughed and gave his artificial arm an experimental shake.

He was free. The three on his left arm, his crystal prosthesis, scattered a few paces, yelling warnings with strangely deep, distorted voices. Warian lifted his left arm high, triumphant. He made a fist, thinking to scare those who'd grabbed him with an impressive threat.

The iron bar clipped him on the forehead and pain sawed through his brain. All the quickness in the world couldn't protect him from inattention. He'd seen the brutal end of the bar at the last instant and managed to flinch away, just enough so his head hadn't shattered like an egg . . . he hoped. It sure hurt, though.

Dazed, Warian went down on one knee. He cradled his throbbing head with his right hand. His aggressors moved in, thinking to fall on him, Revi in the vanguard, the bloodied metal bar raised high to finish the job.

Without standing, Warian reached with his left hand and grabbed Revi's lead leg just below the knee. He could feel Revi's muscles and bones through the crystal. He squeezed. The muscles and bones pulped in his hand like rotten fruit.

Revi dropped sluggishly to the floor, screaming and clutching at his ruined leg. The iron bar spun free, then clattered dully to the floor.

The downed man's friends failed to grasp Warian's

strength and speed—they continued to move forward. Or perhaps they didn't have a chance to react in the brief interval Warian allowed them.

He stood up, still rubbing his head with his right hand. The eyes of his attackers had trouble following Warian's movements. Good.

Warian strode to the fellow who stood nearest the entry hall, grabbed him, and threw him out the doorway. Ditto for the man's nearest friend, who had just enough time to scream and try to run, though it did him no good. He sailed, flailing, through the air, and was gone.

The other two, seeing their plan going horribly awry, turned to dash back the way they'd come, farther within the tenement. A few quick strides let Warian catch the hindmost. He plucked the man right off his feet. The weight of Warian's quarry was astonishingly little. The man's legs kicked, and he yelled in protest. As if he held a doll, he bumped the man's head against the ceiling. The man went limp, and Warian dropped him.

Who's next? he wondered.

Fatigue ambushed him.

The light in his prosthesis guttered out. Dullness flooded the crystal, and the world jittered back to its natural timeframe.

Warian stumbled and nearly fell flat on his face. Exhaustion hammered him. He sucked breath like he'd just finished a marathon race. His living arm trembled as he used it to support himself against the wall. Now that he'd returned to normal perception, he understood what the men were yelling. "He's killing us! Gods, he's killing us!"

Warian didn't have the strength to protest. Hurting badly, yes. Killing? No. At least, he hadn't tried to kill anyone. He looked at his left arm again. It looked as it always had, save for the dark tendrils at its core. Were they growing? Hard to tell. But one thing was certain—he'd managed to consciously activate the extraordinary new strength his prosthesis harbored. If he could consciously trigger it once, he was confident he could do it again. But should he? The way nausea struggled against his exhaustion, twice as bad as the first time. . . . If he called on the arm's strength a third time, would the aftermath multiply again? The wall was no longer enough to support him. He slid down to a squat, still leaning on the wall, and studied his feet. They seemed strangely far away.

A man appeared from down the inner passage—not one of the toughs who'd failed to overcome Warian. The newcomer wore the tailored black and gray robe of a businessman. His assertive posture, wiry frame, and dark but thinning hair were all too familiar to Warian.

It was Uncle Zel.

Zeltaebar Datharathi, who sat with his uncles on the family council, was a schemer, a dealmaker, a master of disguise, and a self-proclaimed scoundrel. Warian and Zel never had much to do with each other.

"Nephew, is that you?" asked Zel, squinting in disbelief. "What in the name of the Ten Dark Gods are you doing back in town? And why are you killing my men?"

CHAPTER EIGHT

The destrier flitted across moonlit hills, its stone feet
pounding out a tempo that mimicked the world's
heartbeat.

Kiril roused from her dozing trance when
Thormud called a halt. Blinking, she gazed around
at the monotonous plain, at low hills and rocky
ridges silhouetted in the silvery distance. Nothing
seemed amiss.

"Why are we stopping?"

"I am uneasy," Thormud responded. "Another
prognostication is in order."

"Really? In the middle of the night? I thought we
traveled by night to avoid the heat of the day and
unfortunate observation."

"The same principle holds for conducting arduous
prognostications, Kiril. I prefer to undertake such

exertions during night's cool and shrouding darkness."

Kiril looked around again. The destrier had stopped atop a low, smooth bluff.

"I'll tell you where to put your 'shrouding darkness,' " she murmured as she slipped off the stone destrier's back. The wait while Thormud performed his ritual promised to be excruciatingly boring.

Thormud let the elemental mount bend low before he dismounted. As soon as the dwarf's feet touched down, he moved to the center of the bluff and began scrawling in the earth with his rod. Kiril recognized the preliminary chicken scratches as standard geomancer preparations for "magical surveillance and interrogation of the mineral bones of the world," as the dwarf had once described it. Bah.

Kiril sighed and paced out a perimeter. She always hated waking from trance—her thoughts were too clear and connected. At those times, the temptation to draw Angul was worst—she wanted to drown her questions and uncertainties in the blade's overwhelming certitude. It was nearly a compulsion.

Nothing the verdigris god couldn't fix. She gulped down a burning shot and gasped. As the fire settled into her stomach, Angul's lure faded into low background noise, as always. The trick was to desensitize her mind. His call couldn't penetrate her alcohol haze.

She finished her circuit around the periphery of the bluff. A gauzy film of cloud partially obscured the moon, but her eyes were sharp in the dark. She spied nothing to threaten the dwarf's impromptu magical rite. Kiril found a likely rock and sat, gazing at Thormud.

The geomancer pulled a chest from the destrier's back. From it he produced various vials filled with mineral salts and viscous oils. These ingredients, along with his selenite rod, were familiar implements of high geomancy. Kiril barely paid attention—if a branch of magic existed that was slower and less exciting than geomancy, she hadn't seen it or heard of its disrepute.

❧ ❧ ❧ ❧ ❧

Thormud created a circle on the bluff top by pouring out measured quantities of multicolored dusts. He quartered the circle with his moon-white rod. When he finished, an invisible spark of connection passed up from the ground and into the dwarf, jolting him as if it were an electrical charge.

The dwarf stumbled and managed a controlled fall into the circle's center. He closed his eyes, not to see darkness, but a vision bequeathed him by the soil.

The world was composed of the four primary elements: air, earth, fire, and water. But earth held Thormud's attraction, and earth responded to his fervent attention. And more often than not, earth gave up its secrets to the dwarf.

Earth accepted all and tolerated all; earth observed all that occurred on or within its embrace. To those who knew the language of stone, earth poured out its knowledge in a slow, steady stream. Because so few had the patience to bother learning the deliberate arts of geomancy, Thormud often found his solicitations were answered energetically, almost eagerly, as if stone relished its rare opportunity to communicate.

The geomancer saw lines of connection running below the ground, lines of attraction and correlation, currents that passed telluric energy to all points of the world-sphere. He followed the lines south and east, and was slightly surprised when his trace pushed far beyond his past attempts. The disturbances which had turned to gibberish all his previous attempts to understand the earth's vision remained, but this time, he managed to slide between the disruptive waves and push forward.

An image flashed behind Thormud's eyes—a body of water shining like molten gold. The golden water ran up to a rocky coast. Inland from the coast, the ramparts of mountains unfamiliar to the dwarf darkened the sky, but these were not the focus of the insight. The vision concentrated onto a single, lonely feature close to the shore, like a lone tooth of a predator, a vicious animal's incisor cast in stone. The slender peak towered several miles above the surrounding lands. Thormud's expertise identified the peak as natural, but as the vision narrowed further, bringing him closer and closer, he spied signs of occupation: a narrow road winding up the peak, tailing beds in haphazard order, and pools of murky, tainted water.

The peak housed a mine—one that had been in use for years, by the size of the tailing beds . . .

Thormud's vision plunged into the side of the peak. A moment of jagged dislocation suffused him, as if he pierced a void far greater than the mountain could contain. He was overcome by white lights, threads of connection between vast spaces, and an empty feeling in his stomach as he flailed madly for purchase and understanding.

Then another jerk of true dislocation—he could not tell in which direction his sight was wrenched. When his vision steadied, the geomancer glimpsed a plain that shimmered under harsh sunlight. Vast dunes of sand rolled in paralyzed majesty to every horizon. All was silent and unmoving, bright and glaring, and empty. Then Thormud saw something lurking on the horizon. Something slender as a tower, something dark—something unnatural. Was it the spire of some great fortress unglimpsed by history? Or was it a shard of some alien reality standing unnaturally tall and narrow, a splinter in the world's flesh?

His vision closed on the spire. Its edges shimmered and flashed every color in the sunlight, but at the center, there was no color—it was black, a pure darkness whose paucity of light was a presence unto itself. The earth whispered a name into Thormud's mind: Pandorym.

With the name, Thormud understood that the splinter sapped the earth and pained it. The splinter was the source of the geomancer's discomfiture.

But where was it? His knowledge of place and location had

scrambled during the last dislocation. If he wanted . . .

Something in the dark splinter looked back at Thormud.

Kiril idly flipped stones down the side of the bluff. Most of the stones bounced and slid into a gully. The elf pondered the stars above, those that weren't drowned out by the vast light of the moon. They were like—yet unlike—the constellations from her childhood. And as a young adult, when she took the Cerulean Oath and met her soul mate in the citadel called Stardeep, her home was situated in an enchanted forest above which yet another wholly different set of constellations wheeled.

Not even the positions of the stars were a constant in her life, she mused.

She picked up another stone and paused. She hadn't heard the dwarf speak for a suspiciously long time.

Xet cawed out in alarm, an amazingly lifelike yowl.

Kiril whirled and looked for Thormud. He lay in his circle, thrashing. Moonlight revealed blood oozing from the dwarf's wide but unseeing eyes. Kiril's stream of invectives propelled her toward her prone employer. Xet fluttered ineffectually from its perch on a boulder, squeaking and chiming.

Thormud routinely impressed upon her the importance of not interrupting him while he remained in earthen communion within one of his circles. He'd noted that breaking the periphery could be dangerous.

Stuff that.

The elf, running hard, dived into the circle, hands stretched wide. Luminescence, violet and violent, stabbed at her eyes, and a scream of fury—not her own nor the dwarf's—broke upon her ears. Undeterred, she tucked and tumbled, grabbed Thormud's limp form in mid-roll, and allowed her momentum to carry them both out of the circle.

The moment she passed the boundary, the escalating scream ceased. The quiet of the night was like a balm, and a cool breeze caressed Kiril's face. She rolled Thormud over. The dwarf still breathed, and his eyes were coming back into focus. He groaned.

The elf yelled into his face, "What in the name of the nine were you doing?"

The dwarf shook his head and mumbled something inaudible.

"What was that scream?" Kiril demanded.

"Something . . . followed me," the dwarf croaked. He raised a trembling hand and pointed.

The swordswoman snapped her gaze back to the circle, or where the circle had been. Darkness cloaked the bluff top, too deep even for her elf eyes to pierce.

Kiril scrambled to her feet. "Great. Things keep coming up roses," she murmured, palming her dagger.

Two fiery violet eyes blinked open from within the unnatural night. The darkness coalesced, and a presence was revealed—a shrouded, half-real visage roughly human in outline. Kiril couldn't tell whether it was dressed in white robes or if its flesh was just naturally loose and flowing. Free-floating sigils pulsed a pale, dangerous light, slowly orbiting the creature. The glyphs seemed to promise death and severance, but severance of what, Kiril didn't want to pursue.

She flung her dagger. It flew with deadly accuracy, transfixing the creature between the eyes.

Or it would have, if the creature's flesh hadn't parted like mist and completely ignored the blade of elven steel. The dagger clattered on the rocks somewhere on the other side of the bluff.

"Blood!" spat Kiril.

The dwarf staggered to his feet, one white, bloodless hand still tightly gripping his selenite rod. Thormud pointed the rod at the earth where the creature stood. The ground trembled, but one of the free-floating glyphs surrounding the creature flashed like a shooting star. Thormud screamed, dropped his rod, and clutched his head. The temblor faded.

"My earth sense!" wailed the dwarf. "I can't hear the earth! Where is it?"

The half-material newcomer advanced down the slope in streaming folds of translucent flesh and unfixed symbols. The dwarf fell upon the ground he'd just vacated. Thormud's crystal familiar turned wing and flapped straight away across the plain, pealing a random series of plaintive notes.

It was up to Kiril Duskmourn to quell the threat.

The elf squared her shoulders and pulled Angul free of his sheath.

Clarity flashed over Kiril like a sunrise, its brilliance rolling in all directions, chasing away every shadow, every shade of gray, every doubt, and every worry. Warmth, peace, and freedom from uncertainty and skepticism suffused her. The Blade Cerulean burned triumphantly in her welcoming grip, its color tinged the brilliant blue that only stars could achieve. She wondered anew why she didn't draw the blade more often. It was like coming home.

The distractions that made moral judgments difficult burned away in the glorious certitude that pulsed from Angul. There was right and there was wrong—no extenuating circumstances, no means to an end, and no second chances.

Not even for Angul's wielder.

As always, the blade singed her hands and sent a thread of agony through her mind. The pain was her punishment for the alcohol blurring her brain and thinning her blood. If she were not the wielder and sole gateway through which Angul could affect the world, her punishment would have been harsher. But it was this pain, and the toxic effects of the whisky, that allowed Kiril to retain the least thread of herself when she had Angul in hand.

Sometimes.

Kiril raised the Blade Cerulean, and his white light doubled, then redoubled again, shedding light like the day in all directions. Her lips moved, but Angul's words formed in her mouth. Angul said, "We do not suffer abominations."

In the light of the blade's radiance, the creature was undeterred and continued its advance. One of the intruder's free-floating glyphs flared purple and darted forward, striking Kiril.

It struck her with the force of an iron mallet, then shattered, used up. But Angul helped her bear the pain stoically and without flinching. The creature was wrong, and would be dealt with. Its sorcerous attacks couldn't be allowed to deter justice.

The elf charged, bringing her blade around to slice the creature's head from its shoulders. One of the floating sigils interposed itself and flared on contact with Angul's steel. The sigil shattered, but in so doing, Kiril's blow was blocked.

Kiril counted ten more floating sigils. Her strategy was simple. She would target each sigil individually, until she had destroyed every last one of the intruder's protective glyphs. Then she would slay it, without hindrance.

The elf set to work, hacking at the creature's floating glyphs even as it flowed forward to threaten the insensate dwarf. Each of Kiril's swings smashed another defending sigil, and the air was aglow with violet motes and crunching sounds akin to plates being shattered on the floor, one after another.

A remote voice clamored for Kiril's attention. It was a wisp, a filament, but she was able to discern its message: She would not be able to destroy all the sigils before the creature fell atop Thormud. What of it? The creature was an abomination, and had to be destroyed. To take any other action jeopardized doing what was right. Besides, the dwarf had much to answer for, and in other circumstances might face Angul's wrath. It did not concern anyone . . .

The faint voice yelled, No! Listen, you motherless-son-of-steel! I am the wielder—you are the blade!

Are you sure? Kiril felt like herself, only better, righteous, and perfect in her resolve . . .

The portion of Kiril that was concerned with Thormud's welfare gathered into a knot, then launched itself against Angul's surety of purpose. If Thormud were attacked in his defenseless state—there would be consequences.

Consequences? What of it? Let us not worry. We do what is right, no matter. Too much thinking is an excuse to avoid doing what must be done!

Damn it, consequences matter! Grunting with effort against her own misfiring muscles, she feinted with the blade at a sigil, but at the last moment deflected her thrust so that the shining length of steel sliced deeply into the creature. The Blade Cerulean found solid, yielding flesh in what had seemed a completely immaterial foe.

The creature screeched. Angul had hurt it—the blade's blessed hunger found vulnerable flesh even in ghostly tissue. The intruder trained its fiery eyes on her, forgetting its goal of reaching the dwarf.

All but one of the sigils shot at her, and flensed her skin like tiny knives.

Kiril knew pain, then pain redoubled. The shock jerked Kiril back to her right mind, even as smoke curled up from her skin in numerous spots where she'd been struck. Angul's unwavering holy conviction kept her on her feet, barely. The sword was only as effective as his wielder—he spent some of his hoarded power to send a healing current through her limbs. The intruding creature turned and flowed back toward the bluff top, where inviolate darkness remained. With only a single floating glyph, which looked more like a chunk of purple crystal than a glyph, it was defenseless and declawed.

Kiril stormed up behind it and plunged Angul down upon the trailing edges of the creature's filmy flesh. The blade pierced ectoplasm and earth and pinned the creature in place. Before she could think any more about it, she pulled her hands away from the hilt, breaking contact.

As always, the withdrawal was instant and retributive.

When the spastic pain had eased, Kiril rolled into a sitting position. The intruder was gone. The darkness that had crowned the bluff's summit was gone, too. The last undestroyed glyph that had orbited the creature lay in the earth, a dead piece of crystal. Angul was still stuck in the earth, tip down, a few yards from the dead crystal. Angul smoldered, sending a tendril of pure white smoke skyward—she could imagine his fury at being sheathed in unconsecrated soil, like any common blade.

Kiril allowed herself a small smile of satisfaction.

Thormud snored nearby. His color had returned to his face. Xet, the coward, was curled up like a cat on the dwarf's chest. The destrier, without anyone to command it, had not moved. The plain before them was otherwise empty.

Kiril stood and dusted herself off. She moved to the dwarf's side and shook him. Thormud's eyes shuttered open immediately. His expression was a question. Kiril helped the dwarf to his feet.

The geomancer pointed at Angul. "What is wrong with your sword? I've never seen it smoke like that." He paused, then asked, "What happened?"

"That ghost-bastard you summoned . . ."

"I didn't summon it! It followed me."

"It came because of you, right? It knocked you cold, but I nicked it with Angul. It turned on me and tried to do the same."

Thormud said, his voice low, "It bested me as if I were nothing. Thank you for banishing it where I could not."

"You know how it is when I have my sword drawn. Nothing that sheet-wearing bastard threw at me mattered."

"How exactly did you dispatch it?" Thormud picked up his selenite rod as he spoke.

Kiril shrugged. "Once it expended all its little floating friends, I pinned it to the dirt with Angul." The elf pointed to the simmering sword. "After that, it faded, I guess."

"You guess?"

The elf turned without answering and withdrew a pair of black silk gloves she kept folded in her belt. She pulled on the gloves while studying Angul. With her hands covered, she grasped the sword's hilt and jerked him free of the earth. Kiril studied Angul's inlay—"Keeper of the Cerulean Sign" in star elf script—then jammed him into his white leather sheath.

Kiril didn't like being questioned by Thormud—she didn't know the answers. When she was one with the righteous blade, she was not tormented or put upon. Why not pull him out again and tell Thormud what she thought of his stupid stunt of luring the creature out of the netherworld in the first place?

Her hand reached, but instead of grasping Angul's hilt, she pulled out her flask, spun off the cap, and knocked one back.

Better.

Sighing, the dwarf bent to study the ground where Kiril had pinned their attacker. He ran his fingers through the dirt, scooped up a palmful of grains, and let them fall, one at a time, his expression intent. Thormud shook his head. "The attack was too quick for the earth to recall."

He ascended to the bluff top and repeated his actions, but they proved no more fruitful. Kiril watched, scowling at Xet, who flew intricate, probably meaningless patterns in the air above its master's head.

Thormud paused, scratching his beard. A new thought struck him. "Xet! Bring me the big map!"

"Find something?" Kiril asked him.

"I remember a detail from my divination."

The crystal dragonet winged over to the destrier and dived headfirst into one of Thormud's packs. It emerged several heartbeats later with a leather tube clamped in its mouth. Kiril recognized it as one of the map cases that the dwarf referenced from time to time. She recalled this map as having recognizable names and political borders inscribed on it. Many of the dwarf's other maps depicted topography meaningless to her.

Meanwhile, the dwarf approached the destrier. Xet craned its neck to deliver the map to Thormud's outstretched hand. Kiril ambled over, too. Might as well see what the old dwarf was up to. Better to get the explanation as it developed, rather than ask Thormud to recap later, after he thought too much about it—the dwarf would one day kill her with his mind-numbing explanations.

Or, in order to prevent that, she'd stick her dagger in him. If only, she mused, grinning.

Thormud looked at her enigmatic grin, smiled without understanding the reason for his bodyguard's expression, and unrolled the map on the destrier's back. He grabbed Xet and placed the creature on one side of the curling parchment to hold its edge down, and weighted the other edge with his moon rod. The dwarf had to study it for only a few moments before his finger stabbed down into the lower right corner.

"The Golden Water!" he said, exultant.

Kiril cocked an eyebrow.

"This was in my vision—a swath of water that shone like molten gold. I thought it seemed familiar. North of it was a singular spire, like a wolf's . . ." the dwarf's voice trailed off as his finger traced north across a wide bay labeled "The Golden Water," to the coast near a city called Huorm. Standing just a few miles from the water was some sort of natural rise called Adama's . . .

". . . tooth," finished the dwarf. His finger tapped the landmark. "Adama's Tooth. That's the place the earth first showed me, before I became lost."

Kiril asked him, "So what?"

"We shall discover 'what' when we get there."

Kiril studied the parchment. The map didn't show elevations, but Adama's Tooth looked suspiciously solitary. She rubbed the scar on her hand where lava had burned her during a previous expedition planned by Thormud. "You're certain it's not a volcano?"

The dwarf brightened. "Oh, wouldn't that be just delightful?"

"Right," Kiril said. "Hey, our friend left a small piece of himself behind—see that? One of his sigils."

Thormud stared at the tiny piece of purplish crystal. He produced a leather scarf, dashed over, and quickly wrapped the crystal, completely hiding it.

"Why'd you do that?"

"Whatever sent that creature might be able to see out of the crystal, as if it were a window," murmured the dwarf.

"Is that so?" The hair stood up a little on Kiril's neck. "Maybe we should bury that little package here and now."

Thormud shook his head. "No, I think we can learn more from it before we do that."

Kiril looked at the dwarf and said, "I had better not see that crystal again, understand?"

"We'll see, Kiril. It is for me to decide."

CHAPTER NINE

Why did you follow me?"

The vengeance taker hung in the chamber, his prison a blaze of slowly churning light.

"Release me, and I'll tell you all you want to know, and more."

Ususi shook her head. "Wrong. Tell me, then I decide your fate. I know your kind doesn't like to be dictated to, but you're in no position to insist. Tell me why I shouldn't just leave you to rot."

The man shrugged, unfazed by Ususi's threat. "Then listen. Crisis has reached Deep Imaskar. If you do not return immediately, our hidden stronghold may fall. It may have fallen already."

Ususi blinked. A plea for help was the last thing she anticipated from her tracker. "By the Purple Throne, what are you trying at? You can't trick me with crazy yarns! Why have you come after me now, after so many years? Why can't the Hidden City let me go? You know I'll not betray its secrets!"

The man tried to wipe his brow, but the magical trap prevented him from completing the action.

He shrugged instead, and said, "You expect reprisal for bypassing the Great Seal without permission and leaving behind Deep Imaskar? At any other time, you would be right to fear punishment. But think. You said it yourself—if it had been deemed a worthwhile expenditure of our resources, we would have had you back long ago, Ususi Manaallin."

He fixed her with his large eyes, whose depths were as bleak and colorless as a winter sky. Despite his helplessness, Ususi shivered under that ruthless gaze. Could such eyes even consider lies? She cleared her throat. Despite his abilities, he was her prisoner now and couldn't hurt her.

"What is your name?"

"I am Iahn Qoyllor, and I first heard the Voice of Damos fifteen years ago."

Ususi's eyes flicked to the relic strapped to the man's right hand. She suppressed a shiver.

"All right, Iahn. Tell me your disaster story and why you were sent to find me."

"Darkness hammers against the Great Seal, a supernatural force that we cannot identify. Horror stalks the streets, and even the Hidden City's most stalwart defenders fall before its onslaught. The lord apprehender says we have but one hope: Ususi Manaallin. To this end, I was dispatched."

Ususi couldn't suppress a yelp of protest. "Huh? That's gibberish! What hope? And what do you mean, darkness?"

"The lord apprehender bid me tell you this. 'Retribution seeks the descendents of ancient Imaskar. Something old has awakened, something with no love for the long dead god kings. Since they are long gone, it comes for us. It reaches forth from the lost Celestial Nadir.'"

Ususi felt as if she'd been punched in the stomach. "The Celestial Nadir?"

"The lord apprehender said more. 'This threat arises from where we cannot go—we cannot find access to the Celestial Nadir. We have no knowledge of how the great Imaskari of elder days entered their legendary place behind the world. We can't find our foe. No one can, except Ususi Manaallin. Her life's study is the Celestial Nadir, and she defied the edicts of the Great Seal to expand her research on it. For the sake of all surviving Imaskari, we pray her search has yielded fruit all these years since we let her go.' "

"Riiiiiight." Equal parts praise and threat, mixed with a call for help. It might just be a message from the lord apprehender.

Iahn slowly spun in his prison.

Then again, this was a vengeance taker's story. Ususi knew countless tales of vengeance taker guile. This man's words were no doubt a ploy calculated to make her release him. Vengeance taker deviousness was legendary.

"Here's what I think," offered Ususi. "I think you finally *did* decide to track me down, and here you are. But you got a little too eager when you caught sight of me. And here you linger, caught. A fly in amber."

The man narrowed his eyes. Anger? Probably not the wisest choice, taunting a vengeance taker.

But his talk of darkness reminded her of her unsettling dream. And of the darkness growing at the heart of her keystone, and of the Celestial Nadir crystal she'd found in Two Stars. She reached into her purse and brought out the crystal.

Ususi gasped. The darkness at its heart had grown three-fold since she gazed at it last night. The keystone, on the other hand, seemed unchanged.

Seeing the crystal, Iahn drew in his breath quickly, almost hissing. "Where did you get that?"

"Why do you care?"

"The creatures that I dispatched near your travel coach all wore pendants of the same crystal. They were hunting you."

"Creatures hunting me?" Ususi laughed, almost relieved. "All right, you're really off the cliff edge. Nothing is hunting me—I haven't seen a soul for tendays. I can't believe a word you are saying, can I?"

"Why don't you go out and see for yourself? Perhaps then you'll cut me down from this confinement and apologize for doubting I spoke the truth."

"Why don't I, indeed?" What she would actually do, she told herself as she slipped carefully beneath the floating form, careful not to become entangled in the snaring magic, would be to pack up the travel coach and drive hell-bent for the nearest big city—Assur, probably—where she could charter a ship.

With any luck, the vengeance taker would never free himself. But her luck may have been pushed too far already. By all rights, the vengeance taker should have found her and dealt with her without falling afoul of a trap.

      ✪   ✪   ✪   ✪   ✪

When Ususi returned to the chamber where Iahn still floated, she merely made a slashing gesture and spoke a magical phrase of negation. The white light faded, and Iahn dropped to the floor. He gracefully spun as he fell and landed poised on his hands and feet, then stood to his full height.

Iahn broke the silence. "You see I speak the truth. They were trailing you for days. I saw their sign on your trail as I caught up to you in the wilds."

Ususi nodded. In her hands were three more chunks of Celestial Nadir crystal, each crudely attached to a leather thong. She said, "There was one more pendant, but it was burnt and crumbled. This truly is Celestial Nadir crystal. Or, as it's called in these parts, 'Datharathi crystal.' "

"Are you sure they're safe to touch?"

"Why wouldn't they be?" Ususi wondered.

"These pendants bound the creatures together and provided guidance. Or controlled them. The infernal one drew great strength from his, before it killed him. When I stripped the pendant from one of the still-breathing archers, she died as quickly as if I'd removed her heart."

Ususi involuntarily flinched and thrust the pendants out to arm's length. Yet she didn't drop the crystals. Instead, she quickly stuffed them into her shoulder bag. She coughed, recovered her dignity, and said, "Perhaps they'll yield their secrets to me, then. I can probe their nature more fully when I return to my coach. After I clean up the mess those creatures made." She'd nearly cried when she'd seen what the creatures had done to her home on wheels.

Iahn nodded. "And then we return to Deep Imaskar. We should get started immediately. Even with your travel coach, it will be a journey of many tendays, maybe a month or more."

Ususi swiveled her head and fixed the vengeance taker with a frown. "If things are as dire as you say, then we may not have that much time. I believe I am on the cusp of discovering a new access point into the Celestial Nadir—a local access point."

"Here, in this complex?"

Ususi sighed. "I'm afraid not. But I've been traveling south ever since I purchased the Datharathi crystal in Two Stars. That crystal is from Durpar, and even now we straddle that country's border. It is only a few days' travel to Vaelan, where we can inquire about the crystal. I want to know who mines it and where the mine is located. The mine is an access to the Celestial Nadir. Of this I am certain."

Iahn cocked his head. "If you believe this, why waste time here in this derelict ruin, still dangerous after all these years?"

"I possess a map that reveals ancient Imaskaran sites

such as this one. It seemed reasonable to check out the sites that fell along my path to Durpar. Legends claim that there are twenty gates in all, and I'd like to find every one."

The vengeance taker considered. "A loss of a single day, when measured against the months I've tracked you, is reasonable. However, if your lead proves false, we must turn north and make all haste toward the subterranean entrance that will take us back to Deep Imaskar."

"Of course." Well, she silently appended, it could take two or three days to locate the access point. But short of killing her (which she now knew was not the vengeance taker's goal), he would not be able to force her north until she was satisfied that no access portals survived in Durpar.

Iahn started for the surface. He called over his shoulder, "Even if your fascination for our ancestors' lore blinds you to Deep Imaskar's plight, your sister's continued well-being must concern you. What threatens to breach the Great Seal threatens her equally."

The wizard stood with her mouth agape. What a thing to say!

"What do you know of my sister?" Ususi yelled at Iahn's retreating back, her fists clenched.

He paused, but didn't turn. "I was commanded to find you. Do you think I would leave any stone unturned in that search?"

"Did you talk to her? Did you harm her?" Even as she asked, Ususi knew the answers to her questions were negative. Qari's condition prevented speech, and Ususi would have known if her sister had been harmed, just as her sister would know if harm befell Ususi.

Iahn stopped and turned. His face, if expression were possible for a vengeance taker, seemed slightly rueful. "Of course I didn't harm her. I merely sought her out to see if she could help me find you. Unfortunately, she wouldn't speak to me. I apologize. I didn't realize it was a sensitive topic."

In a small voice, Ususi said, "She doesn't speak to anyone. Not even to me anymore." Her sister Qari, congenitally blind, had never spoken aloud. But Qari and Ususi had spoken to each other when they were children, mind to mind. As they grew older, that ability had dimmed and eventually failed. They still shared a dream at times, or at least they had while Ususi remained in Deep Imaskar, but even that had stopped since Ususi had moved beyond the Great Seal. Unless her dream of darkness was somehow connected to the darkness Iahn claimed had Deep Imaskar under siege . . .

"How did you find her?" Ususi demanded of the vengeance taker.

"The lord apprehender told me where she was."

Ususi clenched her fist. Another promise broken. Qari's condition required special care and solitude. Ususi had acquired both for her sister, paying a steep price for discretion above all else. The lord apprehender's knowledge of secrets held and disclosed in the Hidden City was deep. And apparently, not beyond betrayal.

The travel coach was not wrecked, but the disarray of its contents pained Ususi. As soon as she and Iahn returned, she and her silent uskura set about tidying the clutter. The vengeance taker avoided impatience with steely resolve, but finally murmured something about retrieving his crossbow bolts and searching the bodies for additional clues.

As she cleaned up, Ususi considered the odd assortment of creatures following her. Who had sent them? How had they known about her? Iahn postulated the darkness threatening Deep Imaskar had made enough inroads to discover that he had been sent to look for her, because of her specialized knowledge concerning the Celestial Nadir. If so, perhaps this mysterious force had decided to look for her, too, in hopes of finding her first.

Through the broken coach door, Ususi observed Iahn's return. He sat down outside the coach and began to fit sturdy bolts into the underside of a custom crossbow. She studied him a moment. This man had spoken to Qari. He was an unexpected link to her past.

Ususi stepped out. "Uncover anything else?"

The vengeance taker shrugged and pointed to a few pouches, packs, skins for water, and other oddments typical of travelers.

The wizard pressed him. "Nothing about their identity, who might have sent them, or where they hailed from?"

"You already have the pendants, Ususi. You must have some way to divine their nature."

"There are some spells I might try," she allowed. "Once I get this place ship-shape."

Iahn nodded. Just as Ususi was about to return to the task, he said, "Ususi, I am curious. What exactly is the Celestial Nadir? I hardly feel I understand it. How can I assess the wisdom of anything we do without that knowledge?"

"It is an ancient space. A half-space, where forgotten things litter the void."

"Imaskari-fashioned?"

"It is," replied Ususi. "It is an artificial void created thousands of years ago by our ancestors. They used it to store their secrets, their refuse, and their . . . mistakes."

Iahn leaned forward, waiting for her to continue.

"The ancient Imaskari used their artificial demiplane to conduct their most hazardous arcane experiments. They also used it to store the fruits thereof, hidden safely behind the walls of the world."

"Has one of these walls weakened? Has someone liberated one of these 'mistakes,' seeking to use it against us?"

Ususi nodded slowly. The creature Iahn had faced had seemed to hint along those lines. "That's a possible scenario. Also, the lord apprehender's message seems to imply as much. My research shows that thousands of years without maintenance weakened the once strong boundaries of the Celestial Nadir. Contiguous planes bled together, and pseudo-reality gave the realm a permanence, and unpredictability, never intended."

"Can you identify our attacker? Is it an entity from the Celestial Nadir with which you are familiar?"

"Not at present, but I need to learn more. To be honest, for all my research, the Celestial Nadir is a project of many lifetimes. All I can currently say with any certainty is that whoever or whatever our foe is, it seems capable of using the fabric of the Celestial Nadir against us. This crystal"— Ususi pointed to her satchel—"is a manifestation of the Celestial Nadir's existence. It seems to have been somehow . . . corrupted."

With these words spoken, she decided the time was right. The travel coach was clean enough. She would see what she could see with the clues at hand.

Ususi retrieved the three pendants and placed them on the ground. From the coach, she fetched a yellowish vial from a cupboard where several more glass containers were neatly snugged into a wooden rack. Many of the little vials had been smashed by the intruders, but enough remained for her to seek answers.

She seated herself next to the pendants. Iahn didn't move from his position. She removed the cap from the vial and drank down the citrus-flavored elixir. Ususi didn't believe in brewing foul-tasting potions.

Her lips tingled, her eyes sparked, and her mind quickened. The sky above became a portent of the day and night to come. Odors wafting on the air revealed landforms for many miles in every direction—the scent of a thousand things normally too subtle for human notice. The menhirs on the distant bluff were revealed as the warning markers they'd been constructed to be, meant to scare away intruders, not draw them. The wheels of her travel coach were a history of every rock, every sand pit, and every cool river crossing they had endured since each had been fitted to the axle. Connections between herself and the vengeance taker she had not previously realized suddenly crystallized, and she feared him less—and more. Iahn's eyes were so much like a cloud-scrubbed sky in the dead of winter—but were they capable of reflecting the sun?

Ususi shook her head—the elixir lasted only moments. She concentrated on the three crystals.

At first the pendants seemed mute, scrubbed of all history. But then each revealed that it was not of this world. Instead, they were brought in from a mine—a mundane mine? The crystals had been mined in the Celestial Nadir. How had they come into this world? Vague hints and half-remembered clues gelled in the wizard's mind as she examined the crystals. They spoke of a distance, but compared to how far she'd come, it was negligible. South and east . . . most recently from a city on the edge of a great sea. Assur, she wondered?

No. The signs were clear. It was Vaelan. The mine was not in Vaelan, but those who mined the crystal could be found in that city.

Vaelan was where she and Iahn would go.

CHAPTER TEN

Wake up, Warian! Lost your wits since you left? I asked you what you've got against my squad?"

Warian blinked again. His assessment of the situation in Eined's apartment shifted. It was painful making the mental adjustment to reflect his uncle's appearance.

"Zel? What're you doing here? Are these your men, ransacking Eined's place? I thought they were burglars."

"Eined's missing, Nephew! These fellows are looking for anything we can use to figure out what happened to her. The family thinks she's been kidnapped."

"Kidnapped! By whom?"

"Don't know. Some bastard hoping to claim a ransom. Like I told you, if I knew, I wouldn't be tearing apart your sister's apartment."

Warian took a deep breath. His strength was trickling back. Calling on his arm's hidden reserve was apparently something he shouldn't do lightly. He said, "Sorry. I didn't know what they were doing here. It looked like something I should break up. You have to admit—stumbling upon it, it wouldn't look good."

Zel just grinned his crazy Zel grin. Truth to tell, Warian had never quite trusted his Uncle Zeltaebar. If the Datharathi family had a truism, it was that Zel never told the whole truth.

His uncle scratched his ear. "So, what are you doing back? Did you get some sort of message from Eined? What'd it say?"

Warian realized how his presence must look. He raised his real hand. "No, Uncle, I received no message. I just got into town today, and thought I'd go see Eined. She's my favorite sister."

Zel snorted. "Your only living sister, you mean?"

"Always the sensitive one, Uncle."

"Seems a little strange that you'd come back just when Eined goes missing, though, doesn't it?" Zel fixed Warian with a penetrating stare.

"And the suspicious one. You think I'd hurt my own sister? I want to know what's happened to her, too! You think I know something you don't?"

"I don't think it, I know it. You wouldn't be here otherwise. And I don't mean here in Eined's home. I mean back in Vaelan. You swore you'd never return. Something's made you decide otherwise. What gives, Nephew?"

Warian considered telling his uncle about his arm, but since Zel hadn't mentioned the method by which his nephew had just decimated his crew . . .

"I'd like to call a family meeting—I'll tell everyone at the same time."

Zel whistled. He said, "You don't have the authority to call a meeting. But don't worry!" Zel made a calming gesture at Warian, who'd started protesting. "The next meeting's in two days. Come to that. In fact, your presence will be in my report—it'll be better if you're there to answer the questions that come up."

"All right, then."

Warian looked around the room—it was in complete shambles—then back at Zel. "About Eined—did you find a ransom note?"

Zel shook his head and said, "Nothing like that. She just walked out and never returned—no messages, no preparations—just, gone."

Warian wondered if his sister had merely had enough Datharathi politics and left Vaelan, as he had. Could be the case. On the other hand, he'd received no message from her. If she were leaving the city, he imagined he'd be the first person she would contact.

Aloud, he said, "Well, perhaps she'll turn up. She won't be happy to find what you've done to her place, though."

Zel snorted. "Nothing gold can't fix."

Warian sighed. The classic Datharathi answer.

"Say, Zel—one of your men thought I was a 'plangent.' What was he talking about?" Warian decided to play dumb despite his conversation with the rickshaw driver, who'd told him about the new Datharathi innovation. He was curious about Zel's angle.

A sour smile came from Zel. "The family has opened a new front on trade. We're now in the 'personal improvement' business. My siblings have figured out how to make Datharathi crystal replacements that are better than the limbs folk were born with. Too bad about your prosthesis, Warian—the new ones are better than regular flesh, not worse."

Warian nodded. It seemed clear his uncle hadn't seen him using his own arm to such spectacular effect, or understood what he was seeing. He wondered if his prosthesis had somehow intercepted a power boost meant for Datharathi crystal-wearing plangents. He didn't understand how that could be, but he was no warlock, gemstone engineer, or spell-monger, either.

Warian asked, "If it's better than flesh, why don't I see you sporting the plangent look?"

"Me? No. I prefer the parts I was born with, thank you."

Warian filled the subsequent two days dodging various inquiries from his family. Zel was good to his word—he told the others Warian had returned to town. After getting more than two invitations to meet "just you and me" before the family council meeting, he made himself scarce. Warian didn't want to hear the inevitable side proposals or deals. He wanted to see everyone at once and gauge their reactions to his question. His facility with games of chance was more than just luck, after all—he had a knack for reading people's true motives lurking behind whatever their mouths were saying.

He rented a flat in the upscale but still shabby Vartown district. There, he wiled away his time catching up on the latest underground, counter-culture art craze of Vaelan— libelous plays decrying the members and policies of every major chaka. The Datharathi family was not spared. Warian did himself a favor by not identifying his lineage to the other tenants. Indeed, he enjoyed a particular one-man performance that portrayed his Uncle Xaemar in all his overweening confidence, to great comedic effect.

In this manner, two days slipped past, stung by occasional pangs of guilt. Several times, Warian considered hunting for his missing sister, but he couldn't stand the thought of being cornered by the family. He would look for her after the meeting.

Warian made a conscious decision to arrive after the council meeting was scheduled to begin, and he slipped into a side entrance of the Datharathi family compound, where he was stopped by a servant. Recognizing Warian, the servant told him in a hushed tone that the meeting had already started. Warian nodded and quickly made his way to the boardroom.

All the senior members of the family were already gathered around a marble table. Only five of the ten chairs were filled. Warian walked to his own seat and sat down. Uncle Xaemar was in the midst of one of his cutting diatribes about a competitor. Despite his nephew's absence of five years, Xaemar continued expounding on his obtuse point, ". . . so the bids have been placed, the three-ship fleet is underway, and we have just three tendays . . ."

Warian stopped listening and glanced around the table.

Uncle Xaemar was the ranking family member by virtue of being the oldest of Shaddon's children. But eldest child or not, Xaemar's judgments were rarely questioned by his siblings. Only Grandfather Shaddon ever found fault with Xaemar's directives, and then only to be confrontational, not because Xaemar was wrong.

Warian's senior uncle never made a decision without calculating each and every outcome, moving only when the odds were overwhelmingly in his favor. According to family gossip, Xaemar was celibate, never drank, and on average, got only half a night's sleep each day. The rest of his time was spent at the desk in his study, dreaming up ever more elaborate business ploys. Warian studied him. More wrinkles gouged his face, but the biggest change in Xaemar since Warian had last seen him were several crystal prostheses—Xaemar was a plangent.

As Warian glanced around, he saw that every family member present sported extensive prostheses, save for Zel and himself.

To his right was Aunt Sevaera, and next to her, Zeltaebar. Zeltaebar looked half asleep, but Warian doubted that Zel, despite his slouching posture and lazily shuttered eyelids, missed anything Xaemar said.

Aunt Sevaera, on the other hand, stared directly at Warian, her eyes alight with supposition. Warian waved at her. She smiled, though her plangent crystal half mask turned her expression into more of a grimace.

Eined's seat was empty. No surprise there. But so was Grandfather Shaddon's. When Warian was regularly attending family council meetings five years earlier, Shaddon never missed a meeting. Warian wondered what could be so important that Shaddon would allow Xaemar to have the final word over Datharathi Minerals. Shaddon was a right bastard despite being his grandfather, and would rather be damned than give Xaemar or any other family member carte blanche over the family business, even if Xaemar was a prodigy of business leadership.

Also at the table sat a pair of third cousins that Warian didn't know well, Barden and Corlaen. They seemed fascinated by Xaemar's droning. His uncle was elucidating something about distribution, levies, port fees—Warian tuned him out again.

Two of the empty seats had belonged to Warian's parents. Warian tried to push the memory aside. He'd always wondered about the accident that had taken them. Something never seemed right.

When Xaemar finally wound down, his eyes alighted on Warian and widened slightly, as if seeing his nephew for the first time, even though Warian felt as if he had just sat through an eternity of Xaemar's talk.

"Young Warian!" Xaemar exclaimed. "Reports of your return were accurate, and timely! Don't worry, I've put time in the agenda for you. Please tell us why you've deigned to return. Zel said you had something to ask of the council." Xaemar gave a patently false smile. His uncle couldn't care less if Warian was ever seen again, and in fact, may have preferred it that way.

Warian decided to dispense with pleasantries. Getting quickly to the point was a Datharathi trait his family would appreciate. "I returned because the crystal arm Shaddon gave me has begun to . . . malfunction in a peculiar fashion."

"That's awful!" exclaimed Aunt Sevaera. She looked critically at his arm. "Slow and ugly as ever, but it looks functional."

"Thanks, Aunt. Yes, I know my artificial limb's inelegant lines don't match the latest Datharathi fashion." Warian nodded toward his cousin Barden's svelte, lifelike crystal arm that matched with almost perfect fidelity the arm Barden had been born with. Warian's own fake arm was angular and faceted in comparison.

Xaemar brightened. "That's right—our plangent line has been enormously successful in Vaelan. We can charge outrageous rates. Shaddon says we're ready to begin offering plangent upgrades outside Vaelan—beyond the Durpar region, even, if the price is right."

"How great for you," said Warian. "Now—about my prosthesis . . ."

Xaemar inclined his head but began to tap impatiently on the marble table. Warian knew that his time was running short.

"The thing is, I wonder if your new 'line' of prosthetics isn't having some sort of . . . retroactive effect on my arm."

"How so?" wondered Sevaera.

"Less than a month ago, my prosthesis—became suddenly stronger. It was as if my arm had received . . . a charge of supernatural strength. I nearly killed a man when I accidentally hurled him twenty feet into a wall. I want to know if this is your doing. Something you've done because of your plangent program? How can I get it under control? I don't want to hurt anybody by accident." Warian was fairly sure he knew how to trigger the strength after the incident in Eined's apartment, but perhaps there was a way to call upon its strength in a controlled manner.

Xaemar started to ask a question, then paused, staring blankly ahead. After three or four heartbeats, just as Warian was about to ask his uncle if everything was all right, animation returned to the man's face.

Xaemar questioned him, a new note of authority in his voice. "Twenty feet, you say? Are you making that up?"

"No, Uncle. In fact, it might have been more. And not only that. With the strength came speed. Everyone in that tavern seemed to be moving through molasses, except for me. Is this what it means to be a plangent?"

"No, nothing that extreme," said Sevaera. "I mean, I'm stronger, and a hair faster, but . . ."

Warian's aunt paused as if a new thought intruded. In a more excited tone of voice, she asked, "Faster, too? Come, tell me more, Nephew!"

Warian cocked his head. She never used to call him "nephew." She didn't like the implication of age in that familial term.

"That's all there is to tell. I was faster and stronger."

"Any side effects?"

Warian shrugged.

"Well, well, well," muttered Xaemar. "Can it be your prototype arm has discovered something of the élan that resonates in our own plangent suite of prostheses? Shaddon said that . . ."

Again, the pause. The hairs on Warian's nape prickled when he realized everyone in the room paused as if to ponder the same thing—everyone but him and Zel. He shot Zel a puzzled look. Uncle Zeltaebar looked a little worried.

Breaking out of his thoughts, Xaemar continued speaking as if there had been no pause. "All experimental crystal implants were to be destroyed and replaced with crystal from the newest veins, as Shaddon instructed. He said crystal mined from the older veins was compromised and prone to malfunction. It could be your arm is teetering on the edge of complete malfunction."

Xaemar delivered this dismal news in a manner that seemed . . . greedy. In fact, everyone but Zel looked at him with a simultaneous gleam of hunger suddenly illuminating their features.

Warian shifted uncomfortably in his seat. "So you think the arm is simply giving out, and it's—what? Sputtering on the last dregs of its magical charge?"

"It could be, could be," purred Xaemar, in a very un-Xaemarlike fashion. "There's only one thing to do—you'll have to let your Grandfather Shaddon take a look. It simply wouldn't do for a Datharathi to lose the use of his prosthesis, even if that Datharathi had fled from his responsibility to the family. It would reflect poorly on the plangent enterprise."

Warian sighed. "Plus, I'd sure hate to lose the use of my arm."

"Be that as it may, I'm sure Shaddon would love to examine his original crystal prosthesis after all this time. I have no doubt about it."

"Makes sense. I'd like to see my famous grandfather again," said Warian. If anyone could diagnose the strange new abilities of his artificial limb, it was Shaddon, the man who'd attached it. "Where is he?"

Aunt Sevaera broke in. "Oh, he's out at the site. Right in the middle of some delicate work just now, and he can't even make time for our family meetings. You'll have to travel to the site to see him directly."

"Oh, come on!" protested Warian. He hated "the site"—the peculiar mine where one of the family's many mining tunnels had opened into a bizarre region, the region where Datharathi crystal was mined. Now that he was back in Vaelan, he didn't relish the idea of leaving so soon.

Especially with his sister missing. The more he thought about it, the more concerned he became for Eined's welfare. She was a tough one, certainly, and could probably handle a lot more than Warian himself. Still . . .

"Come, come, don't be like that," said Xaemar. As he spoke, a discomforting tic caused his left eye to flutter spastically.

Warian had never seen Xaemar suffer from such a thing. Warian pretended not to notice—was it a sign of age, or a side effect of the plangent procedure?

Xaemar continued. "Your Grandfather Shaddon isn't far from Vaelan. You can take a sky skiff. It'll be a trip of no time at all."

"All right. Maybe in a few days, after I've had time to see what I've missed in Vaelan in the last five years. And I want to help locate Eined!"

His family stared at him, quiet and considering. Then Aunt Sevaera said, "If you want our help on this, Nephew, you'll abide by the schedules we set."

Warian frowned, then asked, purely for informational purposes, "When's the next skyship leaving?"

"Tonight!" Xaemar rubbed his hands together. Disquietingly, so did Sevaera, Barden, and Corlaen. What the . . . ?

"However, before we make preparations for Warian's trip, we can't forget Zel is due to give a report." Xaemar turned slightly in his chair to fix Zeltaebar with a glare from his single, violet-tinged crystal eye.

Xaemar asked, "Where is Eined?"

CHAPTER ELEVEN

Ususi and Iahn drove the wizard's coach, pulled by two summoned steeds, through the west gate of the city of Vaelan.

The west gate opened on high ground, and the view of the city, as it fell away to the north and east toward the stunning shores of the Golden Water, was broad and expansive. It was easy to see why Vaelan surpassed Assur as the crown jewel of Durpar's trading empire. A central region of proud, tall towers constructed with gold leaf and glass exulted in the midday light. Whitewashed walls separated city districts, and the buildings were of pale stone, or perhaps took plaster and paint particularly well. Terraces, broad flights of stairs, rooftop coffee shops, and bazaars of every description seemed the order of the day in Vaelan.

Just inside the west gate, Ususi paid to have her coach stored indefinitely. She put down a considerable deposit, just in case they found access to the Celestial Nadir within the city. Eventually, she would come back to claim her custom travel coach.

Ususi was accustomed to crowds, but the throngs in Vaelan were something else again. Even Two Stars, a city that prided itself on trade between cultures, had not prepared her for the multitudes surging through Vaelan's streets. The avenue they strolled along was filled on both sides with outdoor restaurants and cafes, all crowded with people. Most of the patrons seemed as interested in consuming the exotic delights before them as watching the continuous parade of passersby.

Courtesans, in scores, more than Ususi had ever seen at once, walked the city streets, clad in diamonds, body paint, and garments spun of the finest silks. Beggars in rags clutched at the robes of passersby, asking for handouts. Unshod children scampered underfoot, absorbed in their youthful games. Sitar players and bards singing strangely nasal ballads were featured along the many rooftop cafes. Half-dressed barbarians with oversized weaponry strapped to their belts pushed arrogantly through the throng. A group of elves in high court dress clustered around a street vendor selling roasted vegetables on sticks. A brave woman wearing red body paint goaded an unshackled ogre to juggle various pieces of crockery. Several halflings perched on an elevated byway, watching the traffic, pointing out oddities, and laughing among themselves.

Ususi even spotted a few eastern-looking men in warrior's dress she recognized as common in Two Stars—merchants and their bodyguards from much farther north and east of Vaelan.

And all of this she saw on a single street!

The people were fascinating, but Ususi's eye was also drawn to the myriad stalls and stands of every stripe, some of which surely straddled the border that separated legal wares from black market merchandise. One hawker claimed his golden eels were the most succulent to be had in west Vaelan, while another described the fragrances available on his cart as exotic samples from "distant Tu'narath, brought only at great risk and expense to delight the senses of the common Vaelanite."

Closing her eyes couldn't shut out the clamor or the smells—the air churned with dueling odors. Fresh bread, eggs, spicy tea, oil, wood smoke from an oven filled with roasting sausages, devil weed, wet wool, exotic perfumes, sweat, and the faint odor of the docks—the countless smells concentrated in Vaelan were overwhelming.

A crush of people pressed upon them at an intersection. A black-haired courtesan pressed against Iahn and ran her fingers down his bare arm. "Such sinewy strength—such exotic pale skin," she purred. "Where ever are you from? I'd love to hear your story. In private."

Ususi shooed the woman away, shaking her head. Iahn looked after the woman as she moved away and was lost again in the crowd. Somewhat foggily, he said, "I've never smelled that particular fragrance before—I wonder from what flower it was distilled."

Ususi had a few notions, but before she could formulate a response, a woman caught her eyes. The woman stood upon a slender white bridge above their path. The skin on her face and bare arms was partially replaced with a thin veneer of Celestial Nadir crystal!

"Iahn, look!" She pointed up at the woman, but Iahn already had her in his sights. With a fluid motion, he caught Ususi's pointing hand and guided it down to her side. He clasped her other hand in his grip and drew her close as if sharing a friendly embrace.

He whispered, "Best not to draw the attention of any who wear the crystal. Something dark looked out from behind the eyes of those who hunted you. The woman on the bridge

. . . and there to the left, that man in the rich robes—see his eyes? If their flesh is infected with the Celestial Nadir crystal, could not the darkness behind the world see out through their eyes, too?"

Ususi gave a slow nod. "Perhaps."

She studied the woman on the bridge as they drew closer. The woman was speaking to an exotic fabric merchant. Nothing could be more natural. Except for her encrustations of crystal.

"No question about it," Ususi whispered. "Someone in Vaelan has found an entry into the Celestial Nadir!"

"You were right," said Iahn, not grudgingly. "We must locate that access. We cannot afford to approach one of these compromised citizens directly. But . . ."

Iahn paused near a confection vendor and motioned Ususi over. The smell of sugary cakes made her mouth water.

"Hungry?" Iahn grunted. He motioned for the vendor's attention. Ususi shrugged. If Iahn wanted to sample the local cuisine, she would be right behind him. Those little cakes smelled good.

Iahn caught the notice of a thin, middle-aged man with curly brown hair streaked with gray. The man's smock was streaked with flour, and he was flanked on all sides by racks of his delicious-looking bakery.

The vengeance taker scanned the merchandise, then pointed. "Two of those," he said in the common trade tongue.

The man nodded curtly. "That'll be one pari, or equivalent in silver, if you please."

Iahn made a show of getting out his pouch and counting out his foreign currency. As he did so, he asked the vendor, "I'm new to Vaelan. A fabulous city. And so strange. Why, my wife and I"—Ususi frowned at Iahn—"my wife and I just saw the oddest thing. A woman on the bridge back there was covered with purple crystal!"

The man's face stretched into what was probably supposed

to be a smile as he watched Iahn painstakingly fumble through his coins. The vengeance taker was putting on a show with a faked lack of dexterity.

The vendor said, "Yes, yes—a plangent."

"A what?" demanded Ususi, moving forward.

"Plangent. Anyone who gets an implant at the Body Shop is called a plangent. If you had the coin to spare"—the man looked critically at the paltry heap of coins in Iahn's hand—"then you could do the same."

The vengeance taker handed the vendor three pieces of silver. As the man weighed them in his hand, Iahn asked, "Why would one want to replace his flesh with inanimate crystal?"

The baker shrugged. "They say plangents are smarter, faster, and stronger than regular folk. I've heard that plangents live longer. Not a bad deal. But it's too expensive for people like you and me." The vendor turned his head and fixed his eyes on new customers standing behind Ususi and Iahn. The vendor was finished with them.

Wizard and taker moved back from the stand, munching on their cakes. They were at least as good as they looked and smelled, Ususi decided.

"All right, then. Let's go find the Body Shop," said Ususi.

"First, allow me to fashion a disguise," replied Iahn.

No placard proclaimed the shop's name. Such advertising was not needed. The structure revealed its nature with a startlingly tall and slender sculpture that thrust up from the building's center, reaching some seventy or eighty feet. The sculpture depicted a smoothly flowing human form with one hand reaching skyward in supplication. Portions of the gray stone sculpture had been seamlessly replaced with violet-tinged crystal—one arm, one leg, one eye.

The architecture of the building was modern and flowing and seemed part of the sculpture itself. The combination was graceful and moving, like a piece of art representing the struggles of mortals who always strive for personal redemption.

Iahn pointed to the crystal and looked at Ususi. The wizard glanced up and shook her head. She whispered, "That's rose quartz, not Celestial Nadir crystal." She strolled casually into the lobby of the Body Shop, with the vengeance taker only a stride behind. Ususi's invisible uskura followed, silent and unknown to all but the two Deep Imaskari. Iahn had warned the wizard against calling upon it—doing so would only draw attention.

He and Ususi wore disguises created with Iahn's expertise, which included small elements of magical glamour. Ususi was unused to wearing illusions, but Iahn had assured her that darkened skin, short hair, and flamboyant dress would fool the eye of any casual observer. Certainly his own long, ragged cloak, wide-brimmed hat, and scraggly, unkempt beard was good enough to baffle even Ususi's eyes had she not seen him assume the guise.

Iahn was her servant, and she the lady of some great merchant house in nearby Assur.

The lobby was a study in smooth, flowing lines, longer than wide, like a great hall in a noble's mansion. Six displays graced the two long walls, three on each side, guaranteed to draw the eye by the simple fact that nothing else was for sale, or even visible to distract attention. A woman waited, a smile on her face, on the far side of the room, beside a single white door. She was dressed elegantly, the lines of her gown plunging down her back. The color of the gown, a pale lavender, almost white, complemented the crystal encrustations of one arm, one leg, and one eye. The woman was a plangent.

"Welcome to the Body Shop, Madam," she said, and flashed a winning smile.

Ususi nodded, but paused to gaze at each of the displays in turn. Iahn shuffled along behind, obedient, his head down, but not so much that he couldn't eye the shop's wares.

Each display was a human-size sculpture of an idealized human, gender unclear. Each sported a different Celestial Nadir crystal prosthesis. The two nearest the entrance had but one implant each—an eye and a hand. The two stone models in the middle of the rows each sported three artificial parts. The final two sculptures, closest to the plangent attendant, seemed more crystal than sculpture.

The attendant continued smiling, seeming perfectly at ease. Ususi coughed and said, "My friends have been telling me for months about the new look coming out of Vaelan. Before I arrived here, I thought they spoke of a new body paint, or piercing, or some combination of the two. But this is a little more extreme!" She waved her hands at the displays.

"Oh, it is more extreme, I can assure you, Madam . . . ?"

"Please call me Urale," said Ususi. "This is my man-servant, Alon."

The plangent glanced at Iahn, dismissed him, and fixed her gaze upon Ususi, her smile growing broader and more friendly, if that were possible.

Iahn continued to stare at the plangent, his eyes missing nothing. He wondered if she would be vulnerable to a death stroke, with her new physiology. He shrugged and watched the woman breathe, noting the way her muscles gathered in her shoulders, legs, and back as she moved toward Ususi.

"Then please call me Tebora!" Tebora's crystal eye flickered to life. Iahn, sensitive to flows of magic, felt his carefully crafted illusory guise waver under the arcane probe, but it held. He saw Ususi stiffen, then relax—Ususi was also sensitive to harsh emanations of magic.

Ususi cleared her throat. "Very well . . . Tebora. Now, please explain to me why I'd want to mar the flesh given me by my fair mother and lordly father by implanting gemstone piercings that are so . . . sizable?"

"The modifications we offer are more than fashion," said Tebora. "They are an improvement. To accept Datharathi crystal is to simply become better!"

"Better?" Iahn detected the note of interest in Ususi's voice—was it feigned or real?

Tebora moved closer, to the display nearest Ususi. "Oh, yes, Madam Urale! For instance, this configuration before you— it's called 'Strong and Tireless!' And why is that? Because once you accept these Datharathi crystal substitutions"—she waved to the display where the sculpture's left arm, right leg, and long strip down the back were artificial—"you'll find yourself with the strength of several men, and with the vigor to hold your own against any normal person!"

"Really? That seems an extraordinary claim," said Ususi.

"Oh, but why would I say so if it weren't true? Perhaps you'd like a demonstration?"

"Maybe," said Ususi, "First tell me—why do you call these crystals Datharathi?"

The woman laughed. "Do you jest? Surely you've heard of Datharathi Minerals, one of the most influential chakas in Vaelan?"

"Oh, of course I have—who hasn't? But where do they mine the crystal?"

The woman paused as if considering the question, but Iahn tensed. Something moved behind that pause—he could feel its enmity. It wasn't the saleswoman. Whatever it was, "it" gazed out at Urale and Alon for a moment through the woman's one living and one crystal eye, then retreated, apparently satisfied.

Oblivious to whatever had just passed through her, Tebora said, "Who knows where the crystal is mined? Who cares? The raw crystal's no good by itself, anyway—it must be custom cut and fitted by our trained staff here at the Body Shop to imbue its spectacular advantages. Raw Datharathi crystal is worthless. But maybe you're looking for something other than our 'Strong and Tireless' configuration? How about 'Quick and Vigorous?' 'Insightful and Spellstrong?' 'Pious and Healing?' 'Cerebral and Ki-strong?' Or, how about the complete package—a whole-body prosthesis with every attribute we offer? Those are too expensive for any but our noblest, richest, highest-class patron—I'm sorry, I shouldn't have brought it up. I'm sure I didn't want to insult your means . . ." The woman trailed off with a long-practiced appraising tone in her voice.

Iahn was amused, seeing the art of the deal in action, but he didn't betray his disguise. He was only a servant. Instead, he continued to watch the plangent, looking for her physical nexus, where one swift blow or slash would collapse her life. Because of all her crystal enhancements, locating her weak points was proving difficult, despite his expertise in detecting such things.

Ususi said, "I don't think I can decide all at once! I mean, the choices! Plus, how do I know what you say is even true?"

Tebora sang out, "The customer asks for a demonstration! Hmm . . . why don't I wrestle your manservant? That should prove something. Certainly a normal woman of my shape would be hard pressed to overcome a man accustomed to hard work?"

Iahn began, "Madam Urale, I don't think . . ."

"Perfect. That, I'd like to see," said Ususi. Iahn sighed. Ususi didn't know his illusory guise might not hold up to rough physical contact. He shambled forward dejectedly, and said with a feigned accent, "What does the lady wish of me?"

"Fabulous!" The woman was obviously delighted to show off her plangent-granted prowess. "Face me. Each of us will attempt to throw the other to the ground. It should be fairly obvious . . . well, you'll see!" The woman laughed.

Iahn stood before the plangent, waiting, watching, looking for the least weakness in the poise and posture of his enemy. Ususi said, "Go!"

The vengeance taker did not sinuously plant his palmed dagger in the woman's kidney, nor did he smash her windpipe with his left elbow, twist her around to choke the blood supply between heart and head, or even sweep her legs from beneath her. He stood and waited for the woman to make the first attack.

The Body Shop attendant stood poised, unmoving. She, too, waited for her adversary's opening.

"Come, sir! Don't let your station keep you from it! Come at me! I assure you, I can take care of myself!"

"By the Voice!" muttered Iahn under his breath, but be nodded. He threw a purposely clumsy punch at the woman. As he expected, she ducked aside. And as he feared, she was impressively fast. As she moved, her artificial limbs lit with diffuse illumination.

Iahn moved to reset, and nearly cried out when the woman's hand snaked forward to capture his retreating fist. So fast! But he was faster, if barely, and he resumed his guard.

The woman frowned. Iahn railed against his stupidity. It simply wasn't like him to make such a mistake. He should have let Tebora grab him. He said, "My pa taught me something of boxing, Miss. He had it tough on the docks."

Tebora chuckled, "Perfect!" and lunged for him. He resisted his reflex to roll away, and she had him. She squeezed him so hard he gasped, then she threw him to the floor. Only his training allowed him to take the fall without breaking an arm or his back. The woman apparently had little regard for others' servants.

Tebora looked back at Ususi, Iahn stretched out at her feet. "See! Despite his boasts, I knocked him down easily, because I'm a plangent. You could be the same as me, or choose some other attribute mix. You could . . ." The woman's voice trailed off as she gazed at Iahn gathering himself on the floor. The illusory facets of his disguise were boiling away like mist in the sun, leaving gaps and fissures through which his true appearance began to wink.

He had but a moment. If the presence he had seen outside the Imaskaran ruin lived in Datharathi crystal, then it probably also lived in the plangent. If the presence within her crystal limbs caught sight of his real shape, he feared every other plangent in Vaelan would also know a Deep Imaskari vengeance taker was in town. He thrust himself from the floor, his legs like great springs. As he rose, he cocked his left hand into a fist and delivered an uppercut, perfectly timed with the assumption of his full height.

The blow, which impacted perfectly on Tebora's most vulnerable bone and nerve plexus, might have taken her head clean off if she were a normal, unenhanced woman. Against Tebora, it was merely sufficient. The saleswoman gasped at the impact, then slumped down, unconscious. The luminosity of the woman's artificial limbs dimmed and went out.

"Well," said Ususi, one hand fumbling inside her disguise, perhaps seeking her wand in a reaction too late in coming, "I . . . I'm relieved to see plangents are no match for a vengeance taker."

Tebora's limbs relit with an electric crackle, and lavender radiance started to pulse anew in the chamber.

"Go!" yelled Iahn. His disguise was in utter tatters.

Ususi went. He raced after her out the door and into the street. As soon as the door closed, they slowed to a regular gait, like others who walked nearby. Iahn surreptitiously stripped away the dregs of his ruined disguise. He followed Ususi, assuming a position as a bodyguard instead of a manservant, especially with his dragonfly blade once more in hand instead of strapped uncomfortably to his back.

"Where to?" the wizard asked him as she walked down the street.

The hairs on Iahn's neck prickled—one of the protective enchantments he cast daily on himself was alerting him he was under unseen observation. The vengeance taker pointed toward the closest alley. He considered telling Ususi how foolish she'd been in agreeing to the saleswoman's suggestion of a fight. But she was a wizard—she could figure it out on her own. The most important thing now was to deal with whomever was following them.

Ususi walked into the alley and Iahn ducked in after her. In Vaelan, alleys were usually small side streets, but in this case, Iahn and Ususi were granted a stroke of luck—the passage was so narrow that relatively little light illuminated it from above. Plus, the alley was jammed with enormous jars and vases belonging to a nearby retailer. He motioned Ususi to continue walking. She shrugged and acquiesced, moving ahead of him. Iahn secreted himself behind a large vat filled with white beans and waited.

Not ten heartbeats later, a shape with a hood drawn low over its face and a blue sash tied around its waist stepped around the corner and into the alley. As the spy passed Iahn, the taker grabbed the hood and pulled it back. "Hold, plangent!" he cried.

"No!" It was a woman, but not the one Iahn was expecting. She wasn't a plangent. Iahn breathed a small sigh of relief.

The woman didn't struggle in his grip. Instead, she pulled her hood down over her face again. She said, "I am not your enemy."

Ususi turned and rushed back.

Iahn said, "I don't know if you are my enemy or not. Why were you following us?"

"I watched you enter and leave the Body Shop, the first people I've seen from outside Vaelan to do so. I wanted to warn you to stay away from there—if you take the crystal, you'll never be the same!"

Ususi interjected. "The same?"

The woman shrugged. "Different . . . not yourself."

"What's your name?" asked Iahn.

"My name is Eined Datharathi."

CHAPTER TWELVE

The door opened, and carts filled with delicacies rolled into the room, pushed by kitchen staff.

As was customary for Datharathi family council meetings, exquisite foods were brought up from the kitchens to fortify the hearts and stomachs of meeting-goers. One cart bore stacks of engraved plates, slender wooden utensils, goblets, and linens. Two more carts were covered with platters of food. Warian was suddenly hungry as he noted sliced clary peppers, salted ham shavings, curried nuts, pale cheeses, and many plates filled with masterfully cut slices of raw fish on rice. More platters bore fried breads, fruits sliced into fanciful shapes, apples in cream, and a tureen of thick fish soup.

Warian recalled that this was an aspect of Datharathi Minerals that he didn't altogether detest. He got up, grabbed a plate, and loaded up on all his old favorites.

His uncles, aunts, and cousins, who hadn't had to go five years without being feted with such a glorious spread, gave the food little notice.

Xaemar asked Zeltaebar, "Zel, please tell me where Eined's run off to! You've pulled enough money out of discretionary funds to find an entire family. One woman hiding in Vaelan shouldn't be able to elude you."

Warian cursed mentally, stuffed a handful of salted ham shavings into his mouth, and interrupted Zeltaebar's explanation. "Wait. Zel told me Eined was kidnapped."

Xaemar looked nonplussed. "I sincerely doubt that. I think the girl absconded."

Warian put down his plate, eyeing it somewhat regretfully. But the conversation demanded his undivided attention. He threw an accusatory glance at Zeltaebar.

Zel spread his hands. "We don't know what happened to her. She could have been kidnapped, whether Xaemar thinks so or not."

"Doubtful," said Xaemar.

"Let me get this straight," Warian said, "You think she ran off on her own? Why would she do that?"

"The girl is ill," said Xaemar. "Not physically. Mentally." He tapped his temple with one finger by way of demonstration. "Over the last few years, she has become more and more unbalanced, more paranoid. I think she finally suffered some sort of nervous breakdown."

"Paranoid about what?" It wasn't like his no-nonsense sister Eined to entertain paranoid fantasies.

"Us!" broke in Aunt Sevaera, her voice incredulous. "The poor thing started making wild claims against her own family. Of course, her claims didn't seem too different from the kinds of things you used to say, Nephew." She fixed him with a reproving glare.

"I used to say you were all cold-hearted gnomes who cared

more about money than anything else. Is that the kind of thing she said?"

"No," answered Zel. "Well, not just that. She thought the crystal was cursed. She liked to tell people that those who exchanged their flesh for Datharathi crystal would never sleep without nightmares again. She thought the crystal threatened the sanity of those who accepted it."

Warian tipped his head back slightly, absorbing Zel's words.

Xaemar continued. "Zel describes the situation accurately. She was fixated on Datharathi crystal and the Body Shop."

"Any truth to what she was saying?" asked Warian. In his own recollection, he couldn't recall an increase in bad dreams since he'd received his artificial arm.

"Of course not," replied Xaemar with a dismissive hand wave. "But truthful or not, her words were beginning to hurt the plangent project. She was talking down our most important new business venture to anyone who would listen. As kindhearted as we are, we couldn't stand for that."

"You couldn't 'stand for it'? What does that mean? What did you do? Is that why she ran?"

Xaemar said, "We did nothing. We merely offered to heal her misconceptions. We told her all infirmities of body and mind are healed for those who become plangents. We told her we had scheduled an appointment for her at the Body Shop."

"The next thing we knew," said Sevaera, "she was gone. Flew the coop."

"You were going to make her?" accused Warian. "With the very thing she most feared? None of you have changed at all, have you? The same old Datharathis, willing to use force if they can't get their way."

"Force? No . . ." objected Xaemar

"You threatened to cut off her stipend if she didn't take the improvement," volunteered Zel in an off-hand tone.

Warian nodded. Sounded just like Xaemar. His uncle did

not have the good grace to look sheepish. He just shrugged as if to say "So? It's just business." Warian recalled when things had reached their worst before he left Vaelan. Xaemar had cut off his own stipend. No big surprise. He'd do it to anyone who didn't tow the Datharathi line.

"Be that as it may," said Xaemar, "where did she go? Enough assigning blame. She's not right in the head, and as family, we owe it to her to find her and help her."

Warian snorted. If his sister were actually sick, then he hoped she was found. But was his family misrepresenting his sister's plight in order to put a better spin on the situation? He'd learned that accepting his family's claims at face value was sometimes risky. But he didn't know why she would vanish into hiding. His family was hardhearted, sure, and stubborn, but Eined was part of the same family. She could hold her own in family politics.

Zel said, "As far as I can tell, she's still in the city. My agents tell me they've sighted her a couple times."

"Tell your agents to bring her in, dear Zel," instructed Sevaera. "The longer she is out and about without taking the crystal to stabilize her mind, the sicker she becomes. The poor thing could hurt herself. Or someone else."

Warian asked, "If being a plangent is so great, why doesn't Zel have to 'take the crystal?' "

"It's like I told you, kid. I say, 'Don't fix what . . .' "

Xaemar interjected. "Zel, Eined, and even you—if you stay—will embrace the family business, Warian. We must display a united family front, after all."

"I've already got a prosthesis." Warian raised his arm.

"A malfunctioning prototype on its last gasp. And you're no plangent—the newest prostheses aid both physical and mental skills. It's a complete solution," explained Xaemar.

Zel gazed at Xaemar, saying nothing. Warian guessed Zel was silently cursing out his brother for being such a high-handed canker.

"Well," said Warian, "let's have that argument later. First,

I want to see Shaddon and find out what's going on with my arm. If my simple one-piece prosthesis can malfunction, who knows what kind of failure all your new 'whole-body prostheses' could undergo." He made a fake shiver. Sevaera glared at him.

"Enough blather." The thoughtful expression returned to Xaemar's face, yet he spoke. "Zeltaebar, find Eined. Restrain her if you must, for her own safety. Bring her here. Warian" —Xaemar turned his distracted gaze on his nephew—"You will go see Shaddon at the site. Leave tonight. Sevaera will accompany you."

Warian sighed. "We'll see."

CHAPTER THIRTEEN

Datharathi!" exclaimed Ususi. Her hand flew up, instinctively preparing to cast a blood ravening bolt or a gout of flame.

Large clay vessels obscured Ususi, Iahn, and the woman who'd followed them into the narrow alley. The woman, Eined Datharathi, was young, with dark hair and eyes and tanned skin. She wore a voluminous cloak, and the blue sash around her waist was fine silk.

"Datharathi—as in the crystal?" inquired the vengeance taker, one arm on the woman's elbow as if casually escorting her. In truth, Ususi knew his hand was as good as an iron manacle.

"Yes, my family is responsible for mining the crystal sold in the Body Shop." She spat, apparently considered a curse in Vaelan. "My grandfather created the plangents!"

"I see," said Ususi, although she did not quite understand what the woman was saying. "You are . . . on the outs with your family. Is that what you're pretending?"

"Pretending!" Eined nearly yelled, a flush blossoming in her cheeks. "I'm here to warn you—to help you—and you accuse me of, of . . . what? Being in cahoots with the Body Shop?"

Iahn looked her in the eye, as if he could gauge truth with vision alone. Perhaps he could. Ususi required more information—her first inclination was to assume Eined represented a trap. After all, they'd just exited the transformation shop with the saleswoman lying senseless in their wake . . .

Ususi said, "I'm just trying to discover the truth. Trust is in short supply—we were attacked in that building. Why should we believe you? You appeared just now, as we were leaving the Body Shop."

"Because I've been watching the shop—I just told you! Your friend here with his hand on my arm was dressed differently when you went in, and obviously was in the middle of removing a disguise on his way out. I'd say you went into that shop expecting some sort of trouble. And by the way you ran from the exit, I could tell you found it."

Iahn broke his silence. "How can we be sure you're not part of that trouble? You've admitted you're of Datharathi blood."

Eined nodded. "Damning, I know. But why would I warn you if I wished you harm?"

"Simple. You're setting a trap," Ususi verbalized her suspicion, then looked up and down the alley for Eined's potential compatriots. She couldn't see anyone huddling in the shadows, but that didn't mean the woman wasn't playing them.

"Look," said Eined, "I don't have any crystal implants—almost everyone in my family does. If I had taken the crystal, you'd be right to distrust me—no one is the same after the procedure. They tried to get me to take a few prostheses. That's why I went into hiding."

"You are a fugitive from your family?" said Iahn.

Eined nodded.

Iahn looked into Eined's eyes a moment longer, then let go of her arm and glanced at Ususi. "I judge we can trust her. Perhaps she can help us, and we can help her."

"You're the vengeance taker," Ususi agreed. Takers were renowned for the ability to discern truth from falsehood. But they'd been known to be wrong. Ususi vowed to keep half an eye on this woman.

Ususi mollified herself by recalling that even those who'd earned a vengeance taker's trust were only under a little less scrutiny than his enemies. It was the nature of the vengeance taker order to view all with some level of suspicion. Or so she'd heard.

"I do need help," allowed Eined. "Since I went into hiding, my family has been looking high and low for me. I've about exhausted my resources."

"And we need help, too," said Iahn. "Perhaps our needs and abilities can be shared."

Ususi said, "We need to find the source of the crystal."

"The source? The shop . . ."

"We need to find out where the crystal is mined," explained Ususi.

"So you can shut down its production?" asked Eined.

"Mayhap. And for other reasons."

Iahn gave a subtle shake of his head, but she had already ceased speaking. Yes, she was aware, no need for Eined to know their deeper purposes.

"Well . . . if you promise to sabotage production, I can tell you where the crystal is mined," said Eined.

Iahn shrugged. "We can do no more than promise to try. Success may or may not follow."

Eined squinted at the vengeance taker uncertainly.

Ususi sighed. "Yes, we'll stop the mining operation, Eined. If we can, we will. Where is the mine?"

"You'll need to charter a boat. The mine is not on this side of the Golden Water."

"Then what?" asked Ususi.

"That'll have to wait for the other side of the gulf."

"Tell us where we need to go," instructed the vengeance taker.

"I will—because I'm going with you. I'll take you to the site personally."

Ususi glanced sidelong at Iahn. Was the woman showing her true colors? Suspicions again scurried through the back of the wizard's mind.

Ususi said, "I don't think that's a good idea."

"Then I won't tell you where to find the mine. If I'm not with you, there's no chance you'll get into the heart of the mine, anyway. You need me."

Iahn said in his no-nonsense manner, "If you come, I can't guarantee you'll survive. You'll be safer here."

"If I don't come with you, how can I be sure you're holding up your end of the deal? Besides, I already told you—my family is leaving no stone unturned in searching for me. If I can get out of the city, they'll never find me—I'll be safer if I'm not here."

Ususi thought the mine was likely a fortified Datharathi holding, where Eined might be more easily recognized than in the thronging streets of Vaelan, but she held her tongue. Regardless of the vengeance taker's ability to discern betrayal, the wizard hoped Eined's appearance wasn't evidence of an elaborate conspiracy meant to snare her and Iahn.

Iahn said "Very well. You're with us."

Ususi frowned, but Eined smiled.

The vengeance taker continued. "We have little time to waste, Eined. Are you ready to leave immediately? I'd like to go straight to the docks."

"Yes. I travel light these days."

The sun glistened on the waves rolling in toward the pier.

Iahn bartered for passage across the Golden Water to Huorm. The smell of fish mingled, not unpleasantly, with the salty tang in the air. Iahn was relatively new to wide bodies of water, but he was coming to enjoy the broad vistas he'd experienced since leaving Deep Imaskar.

Yonald, ship steward for *Smoke and Fire,* named a ridiculous price for passage.

Iahn merely shook his head. He said, "We'll pay you one quarter of the price you've named now, and that amount again when we safely reach the opposite shore."

Eined, in her hood, and Ususi, still in the disguise Iahn had fashioned for her earlier, stood nearby. Dockworkers rushed back and forth, loading and unloading crates and barrels from the holds of the half dozen merchant ships tied up along the pier.

The wizard noticed several people whose backs were not bowed beneath the weight of crates. They were moving along the dock.

"Iahn," Ususi said, stepping to the taker's side, "look!" She gestured down the pier where the stone causeway met the shore. Half a dozen men and women strode purposefully toward them, shoving aside dockworkers with disdain.

The one in the lead, a burly red-haired man, yelled, "Eined Datharathi! We have a writ, signed by Xaemar Datharathi of Datharathi Minerals, that remands you into our care! Surrender yourself!"

Eined gasped and stepped behind Iahn, so that the vengeance taker momentarily occluded her from the approaching group. Eined whispered, "Zel probably stationed men at all the city exits! I should have guessed he'd do that. Damn! I wish we had splurged and chartered an airship!" The vengeance taker said nothing, merely watching the men as they approached, confident their purpose would be revealed shortly.

The redhead halted, facing Iahn and Ususi, and he looked at Eined. "Please come with us, Madam Datharathi. For your own safety. You're sick, and your family wants to help you."

"Help me? I don't need their kind of help!" Eined's voice quickly rose in pitch. Iahn could tell she was scared. She didn't need to be.

The vengeance taker looked the red-haired man in the eye and said, "This woman has secured our services for all her needs. If she is unwell, we will see to her health. If she has other concerns, they will be met. Leave. You are distressing our patron."

The man shook his head. "Sorry. We've got our orders direct from the top man in Vaelan. You have no standing here, outlander."

"I give you one warning," said Iahn. "If you and these others do not vacate this pier immediately, I shall judge your presence to be a threat to our patron, and take appropriate steps to eliminate that threat. Permanently."

The redhead crossed his arms and moved his feet to a wider stance, a clear challenge to Iahn's pronouncement. A woman with a nasty scar that connected her left eye to the corner of her mouth moved to stand at the man's left. An oddly doughty halfling with an oversized club stood at his right. Behind the red-haired man stood three more men in uniforms proclaiming them to be of the watch. Apparently, no one was accustomed to hearing ultimatums made by agents of Deep Imaskar. Then again, they had probably never encountered or even heard of a vengeance taker before.

Too bad, thought Iahn. Their ignorance won't protect them from judgment.

Yonald, the ship steward, took a few paces back. He, in contrast to the newcomers, was a smart man—and more perceptive than the redhead, who had exactly three more heartbeats left in him.

The arts of judgment studied by the protectors of Deep Imaskar were widely varied. They included the ultimate poison (that produced by a damos), intimate knowledge of anatomy and its key weaknesses, weapons, and magic. With so many options, Iahn nearly insulted his profession by simply stepping forward and pushing the red-haired man off the pier.

Ususi made a throwing motion toward the group, releasing a vivid cone of clashing colors that shimmered over the five assailants, giving them a sickly appearance. The three uniformed watchmen instantly slumped to the pier. Iahn could see that they still breathed and were merely unconscious.

The two remaining antagonists, the scarred woman and the halfling, were apparently well paid. They attacked instead of running away. The woman charged Iahn with a dagger in each hand, the snarl on her face distorting her expression into something even more bestial. The greasy, hulking halfling threw his club end over end and struck Ususi in the shoulder. Eined screamed.

Iahn didn't much care if he killed the dagger-wielding woman or the halfling. They had been warned, so their continued defiance could legitimately be answered with extermination. But he suddenly worried that killing a citizen of Vaelan might hurt their chances of securing a ship berth. He leaned forward and left, deftly evading the woman's first knife thrust. As he leaned, he separated his thinblade from the hilt of his dragonfly blade so he had the thinblade in his left and the deadly dragonfly blade in his right. He countered the woman's first dagger thrust with his thinblade, piercing her arm just below her shoulder blade. She shrieked and dropped the dagger. Iahn leaned forward to avoid her second thrust, then sliced the second dagger—and a few fingers—from her grip with a savage flick of his dragonfly blade. The woman collapsed, holding her mauled hand and howling in shock.

Iahn spun and saw the halfling advancing on Ususi. Eined cowered behind the wizard. The halfling wielded a short sword forged of black iron. Red glowing runes swirled on the blade. Not good, Iahn judged. The tempo of his heart increased. He lunged, weapons ready to dispatch Ususi's assailant.

Before the halfling reached her, and before the vengeance taker could confront the halfling, the wizard pointed a finger at her attacker and uttered a sharp incantation. As if discharged from a thunderhead's swollen belly, a jagged electric lance briefly connected Ususi's finger and the halfling's head.

Blinking away the afterimage, Iahn saw Ususi casually blow a slender remnant of smoke from her finger. Of the halfling, all that remained was a charred smear and a few smoking oddments of the little man's equipment. The short sword still gleamed evilly in the sun. Iahn kicked it over the edge of the pier, and heard it splash into the water.

Ususi nodded at the vengeance taker, turned to Yonald, and said, "Sorry about the . . . interruption. If I recall, Iahn quoted you a price we'd be willing to pay." She pointed at the steward with the same finger she'd just used to fell her attacker. "Does that work for you?"

Yonald gulped and nodded.

Iahn rubbed his chin. The wizard knew how to imply a threat nearly as well as someone of his discipline. Of course, as a wizard of Deep Imaskar, Ususi had the power to back up her warnings.

Soon enough, they were aboard. The crew cast off, and the ship sailed northeast across the Golden Water, toward the port city of Huorm. Eined said it was their first stop on the journey to the mine.

Yonald gave Ususi and Eined his cabin for their use. No doubt he booted some lesser crewman from his or her cabin, who in turn booted another sailor. Ususi retreated to the small berth as soon as they boarded. Her invisible uskura followed her, as it always did when left without specific commands.

Yonald's cabin was of the sort Ususi appreciated—neat and tidy, with every article stowed efficiently. She found a slender drawer that contained a few sticks of incense, and she lit one. The glow of the small taper soothed her. The blanket on the cot was clean, too. She massaged her temples and sat down. The passage would take a little less than a day, but she was tired from the recent excitement. What she really wanted was a nap. Her head felt heavy and full—a sign that a headache might rise up to torment her. Sleep sometimes quelled the pain before it came home to roost.

Sleep claimed her almost instantly, but lightly. She dozed, aware of the gentle rocking of the boat and the shouts and calls of a crew seeing to the ship's needs. As sometimes happens on the edge of wakefulness and sleep, Ususi imagined she could see what was going on outside her room. No doubt her imagination painted the scene from the sounds she heard, but nevertheless the vision seemed real. She saw two crewmen in the stern repairing a sail with thick thread. Four men crawled in the rigging, cursing and tying stays and furling sails. Another, the lookout, sat higher yet, calling out landmarks. Two officers smoked pipes on the main deck as they discussed their route, supplies, and crew schedules. Ususi saw Iahn at the prow, gazing across the water with his icy, penetrating, but impenetrable eyes.

What was the vengeance taker looking at? A cloud hovered on the horizon, dark with rain. Ususi realized the cloud might be the vanguard of a savage storm, for it quickly swelled and billowed forward, blotting out more and more of the heavens. The cloud was like an eclipse, but of the entire sky. Iahn continued to stare forward, as unresponsive to the sight as a statue. The lookout did not cry a warning; the officers did not cease their smoking. What was wrong with them? Couldn't they see the danger to the ship? Shouldn't they be striking the sails, battening hatches, or something?

The darkness rushed forward, accelerating and growing as if some death god were pulling a grave shroud across the firmament. Darkness, absolute, thundered down on the wizard, and all sound and light were instantly quenched. Ususi cried out, but her voice was mute and her limbs apparently shorn from her. The more she struggled, the less she could feel her own presence. She was drowning in night.

As the formless, churning void clutched her, a slight sensation trickled back into her extremities. Some new force drew her, accelerating her through the nothingness.

The silence was shattered by awful sounds that smashed at her eardrums, followed by a vague, grim hum that promised an unutterable fate. Screaming, she plunged toward a blot of even more concentrated void.

Before Ususi could be pulled into the bizarre singularity, she saw a flicker of light. Like a flood victim finds temporary deliverance from the torrent by grasping a passing branch, Ususi caught herself by focusing on the glow.

Within the glow was a woman who looked like Ususi. But the woman's eyes were empty, hollow orbits.

It was her sister, Qari.

Qari reached out from the glow into the darkness where Ususi trod and said, "Take my hand, Sister. You shouldn't be so afraid of the dark, you know. Darkness is my constant companion. It doesn't terrify me. I've learned to make a friend of it."

Ususi strained toward the hand. She struggled to rediscover her missing limbs. Or should she just will herself forward? She yelled, "Qari, where are we? What's going on?"

Qari swiveled her head so that the shocking emptiness of her missing eyes was indisputable. Qari said, "You need to embrace the darkness, as I have." So saying, she reached up with her other hand and pointed at the sunken, cavernous pits where eyes should have looked out.

"No!" Ususi screamed, and she woke.

Sun streamed in through the edges of the small porthole. No storm of darkness thundered outside. She heard once more the yells of the crewmen as they went about their duties.

Nothing but a dream . . . but the taper she'd lit before lying down was dead, its tiny glow snuffed.

CHAPTER FOURTEEN

Kiril Duskmourn's legs ached as if she'd ridden the stone destrier for days. Because she had.

Thormud insisted they always travel at night, avoiding villages and cities. They'd just passed a sizable town that Thormud had called Sezilinta. Normally, the fewer people Kiril saw, the better. And traveling in the dark usually suited her just fine, given her star elf heritage. But not tonight.

Tonight the sky was uncharacteristically heavy with clouds that veiled both moonlight and starlight. A constant spit of fine rain fell, slowly wetting every surface and penetrating every covering. After just a quarter day's travel, Kiril's hair was matted with moisture, and water continually dripped into her eyes. Her sodden clothes were cold and clammy, even in the desert. She could hardly see more than a few yards ahead through the misty rain. And the stone seats that at first had seemed reasonably comfortable now worked at rubbing her skin raw. Plus, the seats were cold. Once, she mentally compared the seats to tombstones, then she couldn't banish the image.

She was more miserable than usual. And given her normal demeanor of low-grade irritability, that was a feat.

Worse yet, the old dwarf was in a talkative mood and kept badgering her with questions about her past. He should know enough not to pry, she thought. But maybe he was feeling the effects of the cold rain, too, if he was willing to rouse her ire by questioning her—and she'd given him clear signals that she'd rather be left alone. Was Thormud actually trying to get a rise out of her, just for some diversion on the long journey?

"So tell me again," Thormud asked Kiril from his seat ahead of her, "how old did you say your sword instructor was? Seven hundred? That's old even for an elf, I hear."

Perversely, she decided not to give in to the geomancer's pestering with her usual stream of invectives. She merely grunted.

"And what about the human you were working for right before I employed you—he looked like he was ninety if he was a day. For humans, that's standing with one foot in the grave."

Kiril shrugged, knowing the dwarf couldn't see her. Her silence was answer enough. Another drop of water splashed into her left eye, and she roughly wiped it out.

"And me—I'm no dwarf lad in my first hundred. In fact, I'm probably in the last fifty years of my career."

"So?" Kiril finally asked.

"It's just that I wonder if you know anyone who isn't old."

Kiril grunted again. She said, "You know how I hate most people?"

"Yes . . ."

"I pick all my acquaintances old so they don't live long."

Thormud paused for a moment, then, "Ho ho! I've discovered my companion has secret aspirations to entertain, after all these years! She's bitter, no doubt about it, but witty, too."

"Why don't we pass the time with you telling me about all the different layers of sediment below us, like usual?" asked Kiril. "That way, you get to yammer on and on about something you care about, and I get a nap."

"That's more like the elf I know."

Kiril restrained herself from reaching forward and throttling the dwarf's thick neck. Instead she said, "Let's rest. You said we might reach Adama's Tooth tonight. My muscles are all cramped with the cold. I can protect you better if I can get the blood moving in my arms and legs again. If we face any more of the creatures like we fought a few nights ago . . ."

Thormud made several gravelly noises as if he were gargling pebbles. He was speaking Terran, commanding the stone destrier. The great creature's pace slackened to a trot, a walk, then ceased. It squatted down, allowing its riders easy egress.

Kiril stood and nearly slipped on the rain-soaked stone of the destrier's back. Thormud, despite his graceless manner, walked sure-footed off the destrier to the ground below. Anytime the geomancer walked on stone or earth, his footing was assured. He carried an earthlamp, whose normally warm glow was rendered pale and cheerless in the sleet. Xet rode on the dwarf's shoulder, unconcerned with the endless spray.

Thormud looked around the desolate landscape—what was visible through the mist—and said, "You broach an excellent point. That which faced us earlier was potent. I think it's time I call in a few favors for additional aid."

"Favors?"

"The elemental lords of the earth may hear my entreaty, and may respond with aid."

"Calling in the big swords, eh? Good idea."

The dwarf went about his preparations, which to Kiril looked identical to the preparations Thormud made before every geomantic endeavor. In other words, utterly monotonous. But what else was there to do?

First Thormud used the butt of his selenite rod to scratch an intricate circle into the earth. Then he poured colored powders into the four outer quadrants of the circle—red, blue, white, and brown—and finally black and white at the center, in a commingled pile. He had once told her that the powders represented the elements, but she had always believed only four elements built all of reality. Fearful of an overlong explanation, Kiril never asked why he used six colors.

Next the dwarf usually began mumbling in Terran. Not this time, Kiril noticed. Instead, he reached into his robe and brought forth a small package wrapped in leather. The package looked suspiciously familiar.

Kiril stopped her pacing and cleared her throat, trying to get the dwarf's attention. No luck—or he was ignoring her.

At the center of his circle, the dwarf unwrapped the package and revealed the purple crystal within. It was the remnant of the creature they had faced down a few nights ago.

"Thormud, you phlegm-brained flea haven, what are you doing with that?"

The dwarf, accustomed to Kiril's cursing, had the grace to look somewhat guilty as he said, "If I'm going to entreat the elemental lords of the earth for aid, I need to show them exactly the sort of threat I'm anticipating. Don't worry, I'm not going to . . ."

The crystal in Thormud's hand suddenly blinked on, shedding a haunting purple glow over the misty ground.

"Blood!" swore Kiril. "Cover it, or break it!"

The dwarf hurled the crystal away. It flew thirty or so feet and shattered on a rock. Its light stuttered and failed.

For a few heartbeats, Kiril gazed intently at the point where the crystal had shattered, waiting for any repercussions. She already clutched her long elven dagger in one hand. Nothing. Nothing in that instant, anyway.

The swordswoman turned her head to curse Thormud. But the geomancer was already involved in a new summons—he was lying stretched out in the center of his circle, mumbling. He'd better hide! It wouldn't save him from the tongue-lashing that brewed within her. The dwarf was the one who instructed her to keep that crystal covered!

Slight tremors and groaning rock gave signals that Thormud's summoning ceremony was working . He was calling something big up from the earth, Kiril judged.

A crack and flash snagged her attention back to where the crystal had shattered.

"Stuff it!" she swore, eyes wildly scanning for the source of the noise and light. Nothing—just darkness. She didn't believe it. Something had looked out through that crystal when the dwarf had stupidly uncovered it so close to their goal. And like last time, something had been sent back to deal with the curious geomancer. Whatever it was, it would be dangerous.

She walked slowly forward, dagger in one hand, her other hand poised to grab Angul. The sleet continued unabated, and the hollow tightness waking in her belly intensified the cold.

Another few steps . . . she paused. Kiril was moving too far beyond the light of the dwarf's lamp. If something had found them, its view of her, silhouetted against the light, made her a perfect target. Great.

"I'm going to feed that dwarf his rod," Kiril promised aloud. She wove the dagger around, keeping it moving and fluid, but felt foolish without seeing a target to intimidate with her blade work.

She wondered, again, if she should acquire an enchanted blade in addition to Angul. A capable sword with no agenda.

Her dagger seemed so insufficient these days.

Yeah, no more stinking debate. Next time the opportunity arose, she'd procure something—maybe a flaming sword, or a starblade like Nangulis wielded before he'd sacrificed himself . . .

Something blurred out of the darkness toward her. She stabbed the dagger wildly, hitting a greenish shoulder as it smashed into her gut. A massive foot slammed down on the instep of her left leg, trapping her foot. She tipped over like a felled tree and lost her grip on the dagger, which still jutted from her attacker's shoulder.

Standing over her, its right foot still pinning her left, stood a massive, demonic humanoid. It was almost twice her height! Green skin glistened under black leather armor, and a pair of short ivory horns protruded from its forehead. A jagged splinter of purplish crystal protruded from its chest. Half-dried blood slicked the armor around the wound where the crystal protruded. The crystal flashed, pulsing violet light into the rain-soaked night.

It growled and ground her trapped foot painfully into the dirt with its tremendous weight.

Her right hand fumbled at Angul's sheath. The creature kicked with its other leg, connecting with her hand as she grasped at Angul's hilt.

Angul spun across the dirt, and her hand flared with pain. The moment of connection with the Blade Cerulean enlivened her enough to wrench her foot free. But the touch had been too brief. She hadn't gotten a real grip on the hilt. If she had, no force in the world could have broken her grasp.

She scrambled forward through the enormous creature's legs and stood up behind it, weaponless. The damned starblade she'd wished for moments earlier . . . she shrugged.

Nausea suddenly clawed at her stomach. Something about its presence . . . Her energy and will to resist trickled away as if the creature were a vortex and her health were seawater. She jumped back as the monster whirled around, ebony claws scything the air. Even that small distance helped—the leaching of her strength faded, perhaps ended.

"Thormud, you bluntnub! Help me!" she screamed. The creature blocked her view of the dwarf and his summoning circle. She couldn't see what the geomancer was doing, and the dwarf did not respond. Her eyes darted left—there lay Angul, glistening with its cerulean-tinged luminosity. Thirty feet too far.

Her attacker spoke, using accented Common. "I have been instructed to make certain you never hold that weapon again." The crystal in its chest flashed and gleamed, sending disconcerting shadows across its monstrous visage.

"I'm going to rip your spine out through your mouth, you blood-baiting pimple," Kiril told the demon.

She feinted forward, but ran for her sword, a full-out sprint.

She glanced back. The creature opened its mouth and exhaled winter.

The falling rain between her and the creature froze into hail, and the water slicking her skin froze into a painful crust. The cold burned first, then numbed, and she fell, gasping. She was a half-dozen paces short of Angul.

"F-fu-blood!" she gasped. Kiril was as chilled as if she'd stood a half day unclothed in a blizzard.

The horned giant laughed and pointed an ebony-tipped claw at her. A thin black ray etched the air, but she heaved out of the way . . . even farther from the Blade Cerulean. Where the ray touched, the sickly sweet odor of rot bloomed.

The ground shuddered, and the booming clatter of falling rock pealed into the rain-soaked night. The ground shuddered again, and again. *Boom-boom, boom-boom, boom-boom.* Something very heavy rapidly approached.

Both swordswoman and demon glanced toward the geomancer and his circle. The silhouette of a humanoid creature, larger even than the horned attacker, blocked Thormud's lamplight. The moving heap of earth and rock, about the size of a small tower, lumbered forward in a clumsy run. Its fingers were curled into clublike weapons. Jagged stones studded its upper arms, shoulder blades, and head, which was a blunt, nearly featureless lump of stone. High on its head protruded a natural mineral crown of uncut diamonds, rubies, and other flashing gemstones.

The creature, pounding the earth with each step, rapidly closed on the horned demon. This was who had answered Thormud's call—a creature the geomancer called "Prince Monolith." The dwarf had many friends and pacts with entities of the earth, though his relationship with Prince Monolith and the others was nothing like a master and servant relationship.

The ivory-horned assassin whirled to face the earthen elemental lord, forgetting Kiril. It shamed her that her muscles were so chilled that she could barely crawl toward the Blade Cerulean.

The dark monster again exhaled a swath of limb-numbing cold. Frost bloomed across Prince Monolith, riming its face, chest, and upper arms, but the elemental's charge was true.

The earth lord smashed a fist down on Kiril's attacker. It squealed and rocked with the blow, but remained on its feet. Instead of retreating, it lunged at Monolith and embraced the earth lord within the grasp of its night-dark claws. Prince Monolith attempted to peel the horned creature off its chest, but its claws bit deeply and held.

Kiril crawled another few feet, gasping and cursing . . . and suddenly Thormud was beside her. The dwarf helped her stand and proffered an open vial. The elf grasped it and drank. Healing warmth exploded in her stomach and radiated outward into all of her extremities, easing the worst of her chill and stalling the frostbite that numbed her fingers and toes. She mumbled thanks, but the dwarf was already running toward the altercation that raged between the two towering creatures.

The horned beast continued to gouge and score Monolith's chest and sides with its claws. Monolith staggered. Kiril had seen the earth noble take stronger blows with less effect. How . . . ? She realized the demon's life-draining miasma was potent enough to affect even an elemental noble.

Prince Monolith thundered several harsh syllables, speaking the language of the earth Kiril couldn't comprehend.

Thormud replied in Common, answering Monolith's question. "No, you don't need to preserve it—destroy it if you can! The longer it survives, the more our enemy perceives! Be careful of the crystal in its chest—it is some sort of infection!"

The snarling demon, still gripping the elemental in its raking claws, growled in Common, "Meddle not in affairs beyond your ability, geomancer. You're—argk!"

Prince Monolith clamped his grip onto his tormentor and raised the creature high, each massive hand wrapped around one of the demon's arms. The creature's legs kicked violently in the air. Monolith boomed, "I free you from your bondage." So saying, he pulled. The creature came apart with a sound like burlap ripping. The elemental flung the two pieces to either side.

Kiril swallowed and focused on the remaining threat amidst the shower of gore.

The purple crystal that had been in the demon's chest rolled free, glaring a sickly violet light. Thormud raised his rod to smash the crystal, but the earth lord reached one gargantuan hand down and touched it. Immediately, the glow was doused. "I have power enough to suppress whatever infection hides in this fleck of stone," the elemental proclaimed.

Thormud lowered his rod and nodded, but eyed the apparently quiescent crystal. He addressed the earth lord. "Prince Monolith, you have my heartfelt thanks for honoring the accord we made so many years ago. You came to my summons quicker than ever before, and your unexpected celerity is appreciated."

"I sensed something wrong in the vacuous spaces above the mantle," replied the prince. "I came to see what you knew of it, and found your elf embattled with a seed of the very trouble I detected."

Kiril interrupted, shaking her head. "Still one for impressive-sounding words. What're you a prince of, anyway? I've always wondered."

Prince Monolith rotated his body to face Kiril. "You've grown crueler over the years," he observed.

She shrugged. "The world's a tough place when your flesh is mortal."

"The world tries those whose flesh is mineral, too."

She snorted and turned to retrieve Angul. She carefully avoided touching the blade's hilt as she slid him into his sheath. The blade steamed and hummed in frustration. So like a child in his unwavering, uncompromising desires. The old heartsickness welled up as she accidentally recalled what Angul had been.

"Tell me, then, Thormud Horn—what do you know about the poison shard controlling the flesh of your attacker?" As the elemental noble spoke, Xet winged in from the rain-shrouded darkness and alit on Monolith's shoulder.

"Prince, it is a long story."

The elemental nodded.

Thormud continued. "We've traced twisted telluric currents and a disturbance I can't describe. That disturbance is related to these crystals. We've seen crystal of this sort before, integrated into a monstrosity different from what you just defeated. It seemed infected with an evil presence. I don't know if each crystal holds a separate evil, or if each stone is a portal through which a single presence can reach out and influence the world around it. I summoned you because we are near a potential nexus for this crystal, although perhaps not the true source of our troubles. I was hoping to ask for your aid when we arrived there."

Monolith gazed down at the crystal with the empty caves

of his mineral eyes. "I can tell you this. The mineral is not native to our earthly orb . . ."

"Where's it from?" asked Kiril.

Thormud motioned for her to be quiet, but the elemental lord took no notice. He continued to stare intently at the dark, blood-slicked shard.

Kiril muttered, "I'm thirsty," and reached for the flask of the verdigris god. She was still a little shaky after being so overpowered by the horned interloper. A couple of sips was just the thing to lift her spirits.

"It is a mineral whose nature is quite strange," Prince Monolith finally stated. "It appears to be the sort of encrustation that might occur along the edges of an . . . expanding demiplane."

"Demiplane!" exclaimed Kiril. She wiped her mouth with her sleeve, the contents of her flask still bitter in her mouth.

"Yes," said Monolith. The earth lord pivoted to face east, the direction they'd been traveling, toward Adama's Tooth. "I sense some resonance with the crystal in that direction.

"But . . ." Monolith slowly pivoted again until he faced north, toward the line of mountains whose foothills they were already traversing. ". . . the largest, most malignant intrusion of this putrid crystal into the orb lies on the surface, that way."

"East is the way to Adama's Tooth, not north!" exclaimed Kiril.

Monolith shrugged his mountainous shoulders. "I believe you should reconsider your destination, lest you fail to find the true author of your misfortune and it instead eliminates you."

"North lies Raurin, the Dust Desert. Certain death for any who are not desert-born. Or so I've heard," observed Thormud.

"That may well be. But the infection has its true source to the north."

The dwarf nodded. "North it is."

Kiril said, "Thormud, we're so close to Adama's Tooth. We should mop up whatever's brewing there, then head north afterward."

"I can lead you directly to the infection's source in Raurin," interjected Prince Monolith. "If you follow me, I will overstay the limits of our original pact. I will aid you until the infection is cut away from the orb, or until my ultimate destruction."

Kiril paused in her protest, considering. In her experience, the amount of time that elementals even half as powerful as Prince Monolith persisted was usually counted in heartbeats, never days.

"Prince Monolith," responded Thormud, "your generosity, as usual, is without bound. We accept your kind offer. Please lead us north and help us heal the earth of this wound."

"I will."

"Great," muttered Kiril. "Let's head blindly north, into the desert. Sounds like a dripping great idea."

Being a practical elf, she knew that investigating the nearer Adama's Tooth was still a better idea, all else being equal. Even if it wasn't the primary source of these blood-damned crystals, discovering whatever lay within the rock could provide clues about the nature of the disturbance in Raurin—clues that might help them prepare to meet a completely unknown threat. Perhaps even the kind of clue that would prove the difference between their success or ultimate failure.

She shrugged. "What about this crystal? Is it dead now?" wondered the swordswoman.

Thormud stepped closer, pointed his selenite rod at it, and uttered a sharp word. The crystal began to tremble as if it convulsed with a shiver of ever-increasing frequency. A heartbeat later, it shattered into ineffectual dust.

"Yes," said the dwarf.

Kiril smiled. That smile faded as she observed the old

dwarf walking away, his steps unsteady, and perspiration on his brow.

Her employer wasn't well.

CHAPTER FIFTEEN

After the rest of the family departed from the meeting, Warian's eyes were drawn to the carts stacked with delicacies. He hated to see good food go to waste. Time for an impromptu feast.

Warian was poking away at a plate of pickled mushrooms when Zel popped into the room. His uncle began to heap a plate with delicacies. Warian ignored him.

Zel reached for the platter of pickled mushrooms. Without turning his head, he whispered, "Eined got out of Vaelan earlier today."

"What?"

"I had agents watching the docks. Turns out Xaemar has people searching for Eined, too, but she's got herself some allies. They took ship and departed. A regular seafaring ship. Anyway, she's safe."

"Where'd she go? Who was with her?"

Zel shrugged. "Sounds like she may be heading out to see Shaddon."

Warian paused. He'd decided to refuse a trip to the mine site, despite Xaemar's order—or rather, because of it. But if Eined was headed for the Tooth, then he would follow. In the skyship, he'd probably get there ahead of her. He grinned. Relief flooded him. He couldn't wait to see his sister again and catch up on family gossip.

The mountain-bounded wizard state far to the west called Halruaa was famous for its gold mines, its fiery wine, and most of all, its vessels that sailed on air instead of water.

The wizards of Halruaa jealously guarded the secret of skyship manufacture, keeping the advantages of air travel for Halruaa alone. But like all national treasures, an adequate sum of cash deposited into the proper pocket was sufficient to temporarily suspend Halruaan law, long enough for wealthy entrepreneurs across the Shining South to pay for and receive one or more custom-built Halruaan skyships.

The Datharathi family was nothing if not wealthy. It secured three skyships for its personal use.

The Datharathis used their precious skyships only for urgent business, and then only if a family member was aboard. Warian had ridden a family skyship on several occasions before he'd fled Vaelan. Of all the things he'd left behind, he most missed the thrill of sailing the sky.

Despite Warian's protests at leaving Vaelan so soon after arriving, he was excited to be aloft again. Only one thing soured the trip—Warian wished for one less Datharathi passenger.

Aunt Sevaera had boarded at the last moment. He disliked the woman at least as much as he disliked the rest of the family elders. No, he realized, he had a particular dislike for Sevaera. He hated the way she sometimes slathered him with her unearned motherly-but-paper-thin concern. He saw right through her façade. She did it hoping to find one more lever to influence him.

Warian stood at the skyship's railing as it lifted up and away from the broad platter of twinkling lights below. He'd been in Vaelan for only a few days. But he was certain that Shaddon had the answers he sought concerning his arm. His grandfather would know how to regulate the newfound power that Warian could sometimes trigger. He hoped he could enjoy the arm's heightened ability at a moderate, steady level rather than the all-or-nothing explosion of energy he had experienced, an expenditure that left him so drained he feared death would follow overuse.

A cool wind, comfortable after the day's heat, brushed his face as he watched Vaelan fall away. The vast, dark gulf of the Golden Water was not so golden after the sun had fallen well below the horizon. They'd reach the mine by morning—Adama's Tooth. That was where Warian had been fitted with his prosthesis.

Warian shifted his gaze away from the vista and back toward the deck. He'd ridden this skyship, called *Stormsailer,* before. *Stormsailer's* architecture was like a standard sailing vessel, and her crew was similar. Three masts, square sailed, rose above him, reaching for the stars. The main difference between the skyship and a regular watercraft were the plates affixed beneath the ship, carved from the shells of Halruaan sea turtles and invested with Halruaan spells that produced extraordinary lift.

The crew saw to the needs of the ship under the direction of Captain Darsson, a Halruaan native with experience in wizardry—enough experience to control the ship.

The deck was quiet, and Sevaera was nowhere to be seen. She'd apparently slipped off to her cabin while Warian had engrossed himself with the ship's launch. Good.

He turned back to the bow and watched the receding lights along the coast of the Golden Water. The stars were bright, but washed out by a bright moon to port. Ahead, moonlight was smothered in a layer of roiling thunderheads. He'd seen the great clouds on the horizon before the sun sank. Somewhere ahead, a mighty storm raged.

The wind picked up abruptly, slapping Warian's face. Cool and refreshing earlier, it turned cruel and biting.

Warian stepped away from the bow and headed for his cabin on the port.

The cabins on *Stormsailer* set aside for Datharathi family members were fitted with great glass portholes that offered a spectacular exterior view—nearly as good as the view from the deck railing. The cabins had the added advantage of being heated.

Warian's cabin was directly across from Sevaera's. Her door was closed, but he saw light leaking beneath it and heard the tinkling notes of her harp. His aunt loved to play, but had never been as good as she supposed. Warian was surprised at the proficiency and grace of the music he heard. His aunt had improved a lot in five years. He wondered if it was due to practice or her plangent upgrade. Probably the latter.

Strange. His own door was closed, as he'd left it, but no light spilled beneath it. When he'd dropped off his pack, he'd lit a lantern and left it burning precisely so he wouldn't have to return to a dark cabin. At least, he thought he had. Maybe the oil was used up?

Warian pushed the door open and entered. Moonlight streamed in through the wide porthole, giving him more than enough light to maneuver through the tight space. Even though he had just been on deck, he walked directly to the porthole and gazed out.

The moonlight rippled across the otherwise dark plane of water below. From this vantage, he couldn't see the shoreline at all. In fact . . .

The door creaked behind him and gently snicked shut. Warian swung around and saw someone standing inside his cabin.

"Hey!" Warian yelled, startled.

"Shush!" whispered the figure urgently. Warian saw a moonlit hand touch the intruder's lips, urging quiet.

"You'd better . . ."

"I said keep quiet, Nephew," the voice said, louder. It was a familiar voice.

"Zel?" asked Warian, incredulity prodding him off-balance.

"None other. I'll thank you if you don't say that again so loudly."

"Why?"

"Has your absence made you thick?" his uncle whispered. "No one knows I'm on board. I aim to keep it that way."

"You outrank her—Sevaera, I mean—in the family council. I don't understand. Surely you don't have to hide from her." Disdain curdled Warian's voice as he said his aunt's name.

"You've been gone a long time, Nephew. New ways for new days—things have changed in the family council. I occupy a rung only one up from your missing sister Eined. Come to think of it, you're probably higher than me."

"That's crazy." Warian moved forward and pulled a burning coal from an iron pot below the lamp to relight the wick. Only the finest accoutrements for House Datharathi's private skyship, after all.

"Is it? You have a crystal prosthesis. You're no plangent, true enough, but in the eyes of the others, you're more like them than not."

"Only plangents can wield power in the family business?"

Zeltaebar nodded.

"Then why don't you take the implant?"

"Because something's wrong. I wouldn't take that crystal into my body if you paid me my life trust in one payment."

Warian was surprised. For Zel to walk away from money and power, the reason would have to be spectacular. Warian had left behind his own trust for ideological reasons, but in his experience, Zel was less principled. In fact, he had always felt that his uncle was motivated primarily by money. Personal danger was only one more calculation in Zel's balance sheet of life.

"Wait. If you think something's wrong with the plangents, why were you hunting Eined to force her into the procedure?" Warian demanded.

Zel's hands went up in a placatory gesture. "Hold on, hold on. I wasn't going to turn her in, you numbskull!"

"Is that so?"

"Yes! When I found her, I planned on fleeing the city with her. I wouldn't force the crystal on my own blood kin, for doom's sake!"

"But she's going to the site, right? That's what you told me at the meeting today," Warian accused.

Zel smirked and nodded, but held up a hand again. "You're a smart kid, Warian. I know you have more going on up there than the rest of the family gives you credit for. Plus, you seem to be half plangent. You have their strength and speed, maybe even more than they do, from what my boys said . . ."

"Only when it's triggered, and then it drains me near to death," Warian interrupted.

"Sure, sure—but you get to access the good stuff, without the downsides I've noticed." Zel cast his eyes to the floor.

Warian waited a moment, then said, "Please, go on. I know you love center stage, Uncle."

Zel smiled his agreement and continued. "It's nothing definite—just circumstantial events, and weird feelings I sometimes get when I talk to my brother or sister. We all were pretty close growing up. Of course, we grew apart as adults—we each fell into the role that best suited us in Datharathi Minerals. But I've known Xaemar and Sevaera since we all toddled to nursery school together. And ever since they've taken the crystal, they've been different."

"Better, you mean?"

"Yes, but also . . ." he cleared his throat. "Every so often, I'll be talking to one of them, and out of the blue I feel like I'm talking to someone else. The *same* someone else—every time, and with both of them. And I tell you what. Whoever that someone is, he seems a right bastard."

"Have you ever called this 'other' out on its supposed presence—told it you knew it was there?" wondered Warian.

"Almost. Right after the family meeting today. I found Xaemar to get his signature on a requisition. As we spoke, he changed. I looked up and saw a darkness—a hunger behind his eyes that made my skin crawl. It seemed unholy. I said, 'Brother, what's got you so excited?' He just laughed. I pretty much ran out of there. His laughter chased me.

"When I got that report about Eined's escape, I sneaked up to the roof and stowed aboard. I never want to see what lives inside my brother again."

"Sounds sort of crazy, Uncle. But now that you mention it, I did notice everyone acted a little strange at the meeting—more thoughtful than their usual charge-ahead style. Maybe it's just another malfunction, like my arm, but psychological."

"Maybe," said Zel, doubtfully.

"Well, we'll talk to Shaddon about this tomorrow. He's the lead on the plangent project. He'll help me repair my arm, and maybe he can calm your fears about your siblings."

"Or confirm them."

"Maybe Shaddon needs to tweak his crystal implantation technique," Warian conceded.

"There's another possibility," said Zel. "He could be contaminated, too. After all, he's subjected himself to the same plangent treatment. Actually, he's taken more crystal than any other plangent. He could be as mad as a Veldorn monkey all alone in his sanctum under Adama's Tooth."

Warian looked away, worry suddenly creasing his brow. Then he said, "I'm not contaminated, or at least I don't feel any different. If I'm free of this hypothetical taint, perhaps Shaddon is, too. I doubt he'd allow himself to come to any harm. He's the most accomplished mage this family has ever produced, if you can believe his claims."

Zel looked at Warian, calculation narrowing his eyes. "Yes, but if you were contaminated, would you know it? Would he?"

"Come on, you're just trying to spook me! Of course we'd know it. This could all be a minor glitch in the plangent program that you've blown up into your own personal conspiracy theory. It could be nothing."

"Or we could be going to face the man from whom all the contamination flows."

CHAPTER SIXTEEN

Shaddon gazed into a massive crystalline boulder suspended on an iron chain.

It was the largest uncut stone his miners had ever discovered. His first thought was to use it as another crystal for his prosthesis project. But this particular globe of purple mineral proved far more significant than every earlier specimen he'd prized from the great dark.

Shaddon grinned so fiercely his face nearly split.

In this piece of mute stone, he had found untapped energy—energy eager to jump into all the previous mineral he'd cut to such exacting standards. The arrival of this massive sphere marked the transition where his prosthetics research graduated from sub-par replacements to superhuman relics. With this orb, he was able to fashion plangents.

The limbs, organs, senses, and even reasoning faculties he installed in plangents were superior to anything mortals were born with. He could truthfully claim the ability to make people better!

True, he had a few bad nights when the energy source fueling his plangents proved itself sentient. What had he unleashed?

Those fears had passed. This entity showed him advantages he'd never dreamed possible. With the great orb, he could seize absolute control over everyone who accepted a plangent implant.

In the two years since this great discovery, Shaddon's attitude had slowly migrated from vague unease to glorious satisfaction with his newfound power, despite a single downside. He pushed his mind away from that topic. His was the power of absolute mastery over a growing number of better-than-normal wealthy merchants, nobles, and other people of note.

Shaddon Datharathi reached out his artificial hand to change the focus of the colossal globe. Each rough facet glowed with an image, as if from a different viewpoint. Each image was, in truth, from the perspective of someone who had submitted to Body Shop improvements.

The plangents, who came to the Body Shop as rich, powerful elites, thought they were gaining membership in an exclusive club. It was true—in submitting to the implant, they gained the powers of a super-normal human, as promised. What they didn't know was that wearing a Datharathi prosthesis of recent manufacture put the wearer's soul in thrall.

Shaddon grinned even wider. He was the thrall master.

The project had exceeded his wildest hopes. His subjects of control continued to proliferate. Each offered him a new window on the world—and a new vessel that would accede to his utter bidding. Why not smile?

He giggled, the tone high and tittering. He watched from the eyes of a nobleman of the Kant family as he sneaked away to a tryst with a secret lover. Shaddon shifted his focus, and with only a twinge of pain, mentally propelled his senses into his thrall.

The next instant, he was the noble. He could feel the man's breath, feel his crystalline heart, move his hands, twirl his body, whatever he desired. He let out a hoot in the man's deep voice, then retreated back into his own body, leaving the nobleman turned around and confused about the moment of lost time.

Shaddon would have time enough for idle fun later. At the moment, he needed to ponder a recent development—his grandson Warian had returned to Vaelan. And with such an interesting story. His prosthesis was acting up, surging with a strength it had never before possessed.

How could that be? None of the pre-plangent prostheses were linked to the orb. Had some sort of spontaneous linkage occurred? Possibly, except no matter how he tried, he couldn't find his grandson on the great orb. Did he have a plangent's strength without the bondage? He needed to get a look at that arm.

It had been simplicity itself to puppet his son, Xaemar, into sending Warian directly to Adama's Tooth. He seized control of Xaemar so often these days it was like putting on an old glove. Shaddon wondered how much of Xaemar's original mind remained. He had pushed it aside so often— there could be permanent damage. He resolved to look into it. Later.

If Warian's original prosthesis had gained some of the power generated by the entity, or from a source other than the entity, then Shaddon needed to know. Shaddon couldn't slide his senses into his nephew, which galled him. But if Warian's particular investiture of crystal represented a way to avoid control, this was knowledge Shaddon needed!

Could he free himself from the influence of the entity,

without giving up his own control? Could he cut Pandorym out of . . .

Darkness doused a quarter of the facets on the great crystal orb. Shaddon's grin collapsed.

"No," he whimpered. Guilt blazed like a bonfire through his consciousness. "I didn't mean it! I was just wondering—I did not plan on taking any action. You don't have to come forward. I promise, I promise! Please . . ."

The darkness multiplied until every facet was as black as a vein of coal—and then grew darker. The void crept over the faces of the crystal orb, until all the chamber was dark.

The only remaining light glowed from a point in Shaddon's frenzied mind. A purplish radiance lived there, but even that light was shot through with darkness, black worms infesting the core.

"Pandorym, no . . ." pleaded Shaddon, his desperation a deluge of sick terror.

His supplications were worthless. Just as Shaddon could look out from the eyes of those who wore Datharathi crystal, the entity could look out from Shaddon. He, alone of all plangents, was able to retain the memory of being pushed aside while the other looked out; such was the price he paid for his ability to control others.

The pain couldn't have been worse if his innards had pushed out through his skin to make room for the cold intrusion.

Through his retching, Shaddon began to scream as the darkness took him.

CHAPTER SEVENTEEN

Ususi discovered a few tins of dried fish in Yonald's cabin after she and Eined had made a casual investigation of every compartment and closet.

She couldn't sleep after her nightmare. She was haunted by the darkness and Qari's pronouncement that she should "embrace darkness." Ususi shuddered as she imagined again the hollow orbits of her sister's vacant face.

The wizard consumed the contents of a tin of snapper as eagerly as if it were a fabled mithridate concocted by healing alchemists. Of course, she knew it wasn't really an antidote for nightmares, and it could not insulate her against future recurrences. A little oily, but salty, as she liked it. Perhaps the simple act of eating it gave her comfort.

The Datharathi woman quickly ate a similar

portion of fish then fell asleep. Night ruled outside the cabin, but sleep eluded Ususi. They'd reach Huorm in the morning, maybe before first light. If she was to be worth anything at all the next day, she needed her sleep. The anxiety of not sleeping drove slumber further away.

"To the dooms with it."

Ususi slipped on her shoes and went up on deck. Her uskura followed after, carrying a lantern. She hadn't unpacked her delver's orb—she didn't want to take the time to look for it in her pack.

Light rain fell, but it wasn't cold, and it wasn't falling hard enough to drench her hair or clothing—it was more of a mist, and it was bracing. The sea was black in all directions, but lanterns shimmering around the perimeter of the craft illuminated small areas of dark water. She saw only a single crewman high above, mucking with ropes. The impenetrable blackness all around reminded her uneasily of her dream.

A spot of warmth on her left hip caught her attention—her pouch. She had many pouches, but this one held the three pieces of Celestial Nadir crystal Iahn had retrieved from the creatures in front of the ancient Imaskaran complex.

She reached her hand into the pouch—the stones, in their leather wrapping, were hot to the touch! She drew the wrapping forth and emptied one of the stones into her hand to get a better look at it. The moment it was free of the leather, the crystal flashed a brilliant ray of purple light. The flash speared into the dark waters around the ship. Then the stone went dark and cooled down.

"Oh, dooms and damnation!" Ususi spat. The crewman in the rigging rewarded her with a startled look. She ignored him.

Unless it was her imagination, a faint violet radiance lingered in the sea where the light from the crystal had touched the water's surface. But the radiance fell behind as the ship plowed forward.

She threw the dark stone into the sea. She paused,

grabbed the pouch that contained the remaining two Celestial Nadir amulets, and threw the whole thing in. She turned and rushed toward the prow, looking for Iahn.

The vengeance taker was wrapped in a light blanket, lying under a stanchion. When she was still ten paces from him, Iahn slipped free of his roll and bounded up on his feet, so quickly that Ususi almost didn't see him move.

"Yes?" he inquired.

"Iahn," she breathed, "We might have a problem."

He waited, saying nothing, merely studying her with his pale, incurious eyes.

"Some . . . I don't know . . . magical probe found the three Celestial Nadir crystals I've been carrying. I felt the contact as it was made. I threw the stones overboard, but we may be marked, nevertheless. We'd best be ready."

The taker said, "I'm always ready, Ususi."

She sighed. Not everyone could be as thoroughly competent as vengeance takers were—or pretended to be. "My mistake. I didn't mean to imply otherwise."

She mumbled a quick protective enchantment, a minor ward of stone. Her skin grew a mineral sheen that was unmistakable.

"Do you mind walking with me along the deck?" the wizard asked Iahn. "I thought I saw something in the water, but it fell behind."

"We move swiftly through the water," observed Iahn. "But let's be sure we remain ahead of what you saw. Which was . . . ?"

"A glow."

"Hmm."

Ususi followed the vengeance taker down the deck toward the stern, stepping around coils of rope, barrels lashed to the railing, and other stowed supplies. At the stern, a short ladder led up to a rear-facing platform perfectly positioned for staring aft. Beyond the glimmer of the ship's lanterns in the foaming water, all was dark. The shushing sound of the vessel's passage through the sea wasn't as reassuring as Ususi had found it earlier.

"We'll wait here a while," counseled Iahn, peering into their wave-tossed wake.

Ususi nodded.

A noise like tearing fabric caught Ususi's attention. She touched Iahn's shoulder but saw his head was already cocked, listening.

Ususi whispered, "Was that a sail?"

Brilliant purple light flashed in the ship's wake. She was answered.

"Be ready," mumbled Iahn. The vengeance taker held out his damos. A light touch from his other hand opened an orifice in the disk. Ususi shuddered as she glimpsed the oily, resinous liquid quivering within. Iahn smoothly removed three bolts from the bottom of his crossbow and dipped their points into the well.

Ususi moved back a pace from the vengeance taker—she didn't want to be nicked by accident. She rehearsed a few spells in her mind—Ususi was adept at producing blasts of fire and arcs of lightning, energies sufficient to deal with most threats. She preferred lightning . . .

Something squirmed in the darkness behind the ship, coming closer.

An awful shape oozed out of the night to stand before them on the edge of the platform. It was a creature formed half of bone and half of blackness so dense it possessed actual substance. In silhouette, it was a faceless, wingless demon. Its bony claws were long and tipped with the void. A needle-thin shard of Celestial Nadir crystal poked from a hollow in its forehead.

"Shadow eft!" said Ususi in surprise.

Iahn fired one of his poison-tipped bolts, which caught the creature squarely in the chest. It threw back its head, opened its mouth in a silent scream, and toppled off the back of the ship.

"What is a shadow eft?" asked the vengeance taker, nonchalantly cocking his crossbow with the second poisoned bolt.

After getting her breath back, she said, "Shadow efts were assassins for the ancient Imaskari. Efts were kept in suspended animation until some noble needed to eliminate a rival. Then an eft was programmed and decanted. An eft assassin, being part shadow, could find and kill most creatures before they even knew they were being stalked."

"I've never seen one before."

"Shadow efts haven't been in the world since the Imaskari Empire failed," said Ususi, a note of wonder in her voice.

"What about that crystal in its head?"

Ususi shook her head. "Nothing in my studies connects shadow efts with Celestial Nadir crystal—although now that I think of it," she said, "maybe the old Imaskari stored shadow efts in the Celestial Nadir when they were in stasis. If . . ."

Iahn's shadow suddenly revealed itself as a monstrosity of bone and darkness. Night-dark claws plunged into the vengeance taker's back, and he stiffened with pain and surprise.

Iahn's blood dribbled onto the deck as he struggled in the monster's grip. The shadow eft rose straight into the night, its feet dangling, as if being reeled upward by an unseen rope. The retreating eft was taking Iahn with it.

"No!" yelled Ususi.

The wizard uttered the triggering syllables for a difficult spell. Then she commanded, in the language of Imaskar, "You are dismissed; desist and return to your plane of birth!" Magic unfurled from her mind and fingers, discharged through the air, and connected with the rising shadow eft.

The eft melted into the darkness. Ususi sucked in a breath. Gone? Or merely unseen? Then Iahn dropped hard onto the deck. The impact knocked the crossbow from the vengeance taker's grip. With a single clatter and bounce, it bounded over the railing and was swallowed by the water with nary a splash.

"Effective," coughed Iahn, a hint of strain in his voice. He stood, slightly unsteady.

"I'm sorry about your crossbow, Iahn."

He shook his head and raised a hand.

"And I'm sorry I dropped you, too."

The vengeance taker nodded. Blood seeped down his right arm, but he was already reaching into his kit. He pulled out a tiny vial. Ususi recognized the vial's design—before she'd left Deep Imaskar, she'd purchased elixirs in similar containers. Its fluid was charged with a spell of minor healing.

Iahn unstoppered the vial and tossed down the contents. A flush passed across his features and his posture straightened, though the rents in his clothing remained. The vengeance taker dropped the empty vial back into his kit.

"Do you think we've seen the last of them, Iahn?"

He shrugged. "Can't say. I doubt it. You tossed three crystals overboard? We'd best assume one more eft, at least."

Ususi looked around, trying to see into every hollow and shadow, squinting hard. A bad strategy—her imagination tried to convince her that each pool of darkness hid a lurking eft. Could she banish the shadows as she had the last eft? Well, she could do better than that, now that she thought about it.

"I've got something that might work," she murmured, and fumbled with the various scrolls at her belt. She had six leather tubes affixed, and in each were three or more fine parchments on which were penned active spells encoded in magical glyphs. While she kept many spells mentally prepared, the scrolls served her for emergencies, bearing effects she might want on rare occasions. She also had a few spells of unique potency given to her by powerful friends, or looted from ancient tombs.

"This one, I think," Ususi said, and pulled out a brownish, crumbling parchment on which yellow symbols glimmered with their own internal glow. "Ready yourself for an early sunrise, Iahn," she warned the vengeance taker, and she began reading.

The words were merely the keystones of the magical structure already imbued in the fabric of the ink and parchment. As she spoke each word, the fiery yellow writing faded, and a brilliant charge grew on the edge of her consciousness.

With the last word uttered, light as bright and unforgiving as the sun blossomed overhead. She'd grown accustomed to the daystar over Faerûn in the years since she'd left Deep Imaskar, but the transition from night to day sent a jolt through her eyes, dazing her for a moment. She saw one of Iahn's hands jerk up to shade his eyes, and simultaneously heard a terrible screech from behind the closest mast.

The spectacular burst blossomed across the wave-tossed water and illuminated half the deck in bright sunlight. A shadow eft tumbled out from behind the mast, scrabbling for a hold with clawed fingers. Its form grew ragged and pocked as daylight ate at the shadows that served as the eft's flesh.

Despite the creature's agony, the faux sunlight wasn't enough to kill it, or even stop it from charging straight for Ususi. The wizard unconsciously backpedaled, but the thing was on her in a moment. She raised an arm, ready to unleash another spell. Ususi saw a sweeping claw waver in the air, becoming paper-thin, as if shedding the dimension of width, enhancing its sharpness to a supernatural degree. She shrieked and threw herself back, but the shadow claw caught her across her face, left arm, and side.

Searing pain shattered her thoughts, and the strength seemed to pour out of her legs. The wizard sprawled onto the deck, her head lolling.

Iahn, exquisitely illuminated in the fading sunburst, crossed into Ususi's dwindling field of vision. With a quick step, the vengeance taker pivoted his upper body and lunged, punching with a right cross. His hand, instead of being balled into a fist, was open, and the damos strapped to his palm gaped.

As if stopping himself from a fall, Iahn's hand lashed out and caught the shadow eft on its broad back, connecting the open mouth of the damos to the shadow eft's body with incredible force.

The shadow eft arched its back and spasmed. Already made partly of darkness, the eft's body darkened further, beginning at the point where Iahn's hand clamped down on the creature's back, then spreading across the entire figure. The eft tried to scream but remained mute unto its last breath, which Ususi witnessed—the creature was utterly consumed by its own shadow, the virulence of its form suddenly undone by the poison of the vengeance taker's damos.

Or was her vision dimming? A warm stream of blood tickled her neck as she lay, unmoving, on her left side. Her blood pooled on the deck beneath her, ominous for the speed at which the diameter expanded.

Yet Ususi was strangely incurious. It wasn't as if her strength were deserting her—her will to care about her situation was simply leaking into the floorboards. Even breathing was a chore. It'd be so much easier to simply quit worrying about it all.

Hands rolled her over onto her back. Iahn's face hovered above her. It wore an expression she'd never seen before. Worry?

"Ususi, hold on. I've run through my healing drafts," he said. "Where do you keep yours?" Iahn quickly searched the many pouches on her belt. She could feel the tug and pull as he opened each pocket and pulled out the contents. But she didn't really care. It seemed sort of funny. Too much effort to laugh, though.

Where were her healing elixirs? Her expeditioner's pack had a little rectangular case filled with ten or so curative drafts, she recalled. It was a struggle to focus enough to speak, but Iahn looked so touchingly concerned.

"My cabin . . . in my pack," Ususi finally breathed.

"Wait," the vengeance taker commanded, and raced away, leaving Ususi bleeding on the deck.

Alone. Just as she preferred. She looked straight up through the invisible glass of night and saw that the clouds had pulled back. The tiny sparks of a million stars twinkled, calling her. Their still, calm majesty stole down upon her, overwhelming her. Ususi wondered if she could will herself forward and upward, into final, beautiful oblivion. The sound of the waves breaking along the side of the ship, with their timeless certitude and obstinacy, urged her on.

And why not? She had so many questions she knew would never be answered. What was she accomplishing in the day-to-day existence she endured—what greater good was being served? Her dream of rediscovering ancient Imaskaran sites seemed childish, and its appeal faded as she turned over that desire in her graying thoughts. She mentally reached back toward her youth, trying to find the spark of excitement that usually accompanied thoughts of her search, and failed to find any. Was that dream just a convenient fiction she told herself? Was she actually laboring through each day to "get by, get through?"

If she survived this night, all that lay ahead of her was day after plodding day of more of the same, a hollow husk of what her hopes had promised.

The magnificence of the sparkling stars called to her more insistently.

Tears formed in the corners of her eyes. It was a blunt, harsh, banal life she lived. Now was her chance to end the strife, the uncertainty, the little defeats and pains that so plagued and disillusioned her. And she was suddenly so cold.

"Drink this," a voice urged. Liquid poured into her mouth. Ususi coughed, turned her head, and spit it up. She wasn't going to give in to salvation that easily. The liquid tasted like tangerine, light, clean, and fresh. It was a pleasant taste, but she fought the urge to enjoy it. She wanted the lonely stars back.

A strong hand held her chin, and another infusion of liquid trickled down her throat. This time, when she tried to spit it up, a hand massaged her neck and she involuntarily swallowed the potion.

The call of oblivion faded slightly. Strength grew in her arms, legs, and core. The cool splendor of the night transformed into a cloudy, rainy evening on the rough planking of a sea-tossed ship. Where were the tiny points of light that offered her their cosmic embrace?

Sorrow clutched her, and tears began streaming down the wizard's cheeks.

"Don't cry," said the vengeance taker, misunderstanding her tears. "You'll be all right."

She nodded. Her raveled will began to reassemble as the mortality of her grievous wound receded. Her emotional transcendence had been a physical response to death's nearness—her body had foreseen finality, and attempted to ready her for the end. So she supposed . . .

Life had been poured rudely back into her, but her memory of death's acceptance lurked. The knowledge that she did not fear death stood in the shadows of her consciousness, like a lover she would miss, but whom she was certain to meet again one day. Until then, though . . .

Ususi grabbed one of her rescuer's hands, squeezed, and said, "Thank you, Iahn. You've saved me." She wondered if her words were true.

CHAPTER EIGHTEEN

Warian couldn't sleep. His mind kept returning to Uncle Zel revealing himself as a stowaway. His uncle's words buzzed and rattled around his brain, enhancing his anxiety the longer he considered them. His uncle's terrific snores weren't helping. Only Warian knew Zel rode *Stormsailer,* so of course, his uncle stayed hidden in his cabin.

The snores had been light and breathy at first, soundless enough that Warian could almost ignore them. Before long, the snores began to thunder. On more than one occasion, Warian rose from his bed to glare down at his uncle who lay on his back, mouth ajar. When he pushed Zel onto his side, the snoring eased. But the relief was temporary. A short time later, a snorting cough woke Warian from a drowse. Zel had rolled back to his preferred position. It was no wonder the man had never taken a wife.

Eventually, Warian constructed a tent of three pillows across his head. With two standing on edge on either side of his head, and one lying across the pair, the down stuffing helped deaden the noise of Zel's obstructed breathing. By the time he found himself staring up into the underside of a pillow, sleep's promise had wholly deserted him.

What if Shaddon was contaminated with the same strange presence Zel noticed plaguing Xaemar? Warian couldn't laugh off the possibility—he'd noted something strange at the family meeting, that was sure. And the change in his own arm must be somehow connected. What if Shaddon was the actual source of the contamination? It seemed a reasonable guess. Shaddon was a Datharathi, and that meant finding opportunities for business and advancement whenever possible.

And his arm—would he, too, fall under the influence of the contamination? Would he find that his wishes were being suborned by a will not his own? And most disturbingly—would he even know it? His relatives gave no sign of being aware that their personalities were under assault. Either they didn't know, didn't care, or didn't remember. Or Zel was wrong.

Either way, Warian cared. Maybe he was stupid for not immediately taking the drastic step that would safeguard him from potential influence. Maybe he should chop off the arm and be done with it.

The trauma he'd experienced upon first losing his natural arm came and sat on his chest. Or, the influence that potentially controlled him tugged on those memories—what was free will? Bugger.

Warian turned onto his side, but his movement upset the balance of his pillow dolmen, and two pillows toppled to the floor.

"Damn it all!"

Warian sat up and looked to the porthole. Orange and

pink hues highlighted the dark line of the horizon below. Dawn wasn't far off.

Warian rose from his bed and stood directly before the porthole. At least the view he had so admired last night had returned. Sometime toward morning, the ship had broken through the storm and ominous cloud cover. Now the skyship pressed ahead, just below fantastic masses of white and gray. Looking out the window, Warian felt like a minnow swimming in an unbounded ocean among leviathans of mist. A fluke thrash of any of these mythical swimmers could smash *Stormsailer* and send the debris flittering down into the sea.

Another sawing snore pierced through Warian's imagery. He reminded himself once again that Zel, as an apparent ally, probably shouldn't be choked awake.

The skyship reached Adama's Tooth right after dawn.

Warian watched from the upper deck as the flying craft made its approach. Zel remained in the cabin. With luck, no one would find the stowaway until after Warian and Sevaera disembarked. But Zel had other plans—he began preparing a disguise. Warian left him to his task.

Adama's Tooth was a nearly vertical natural monolith with deeply cleft, striated sides. Warian knew it rose at least two thousand feet above the meandering coastline of the Golden Water. Many stories circulated about Adama's Tooth—according to some accounts, the spire was not natural at all, but artificially raised by the effort of a great wizard, long dead, though Warian couldn't recall the supposed wizard's name.

The less civilized Durpari tribes of the region called the spire Dragon Lodge. In fact, it had been a sacred site of worship for many locals before the Datharathis had bought the rights to open a mine in the tower's side. Those same locals had launched a number of raids against the mine over the years. The first few times, the mining equipment, brought in at great expense, had been destroyed.

Datharathi Minerals learned its lesson, and radically increased security.

One of their first efforts was to cut off road traffic. Most access into and out of Adama's Tooth was changed to airship traffic. Gates and other security measures were installed along the slender, steep road that spiraled up the outer skin of Adama's Tooth.

Stormsailer made for the skydock set deep in one of the shadowy vertical canyons near the summit of the spire. The floating ship slid gracefully between the bulwarks of stone on either side, and halted in midair. A stone pier jutted from one side of the inner cleft, resembling half of an arched bridge. An overhang blocked direct morning sun. The dimness was brightened by brilliant magical torches set along the pier and along a carved platform.

As soon as a crewman tied the skyship with stays and guy ropes, Sevaera appeared at Warian's side. His aunt touched his shoulder and said, "We're expected. Don't dawdle, Nephew."

"But I need my bag . . ." Warian trailed off when he saw a uniformed porter wheeling Aunt Sevaera's luggage, with Warian's own traveling bag atop the pile, after his aunt. Trust her to be efficient.

His aunt and the porter moved down the gangway and confidently onto the pier. Warian followed, more cautiously. He looked down as he traveled along the gangway. Vertigo clawed his spine as his eyes traced the vertical side of the tooth all the way down to the rocky ground far below.

Once they reached the sturdy stone ledge, they quickly moved into the main tunnel, heading toward the heart of Datharathi Minerals's enterprise in Adama's Tooth. The porter paused, allowing Warian to precede him. As Warian passed the man, the porter winked. A heartbeat's confusion gave way to recognition. Zel's really was a master of disguise.

The corridor walls were smooth and polished. Redstone squares tiled the floor. Smokeless torches alternated on either side, about every ten paces. Nothing but the finest for the Datharathis. Of course, this was the executive entrance to the mining headquarters—the lower shafts sunk through Adama's Tooth were as rough and crude, but workable, as might be found in any mine.

They reached the nexus, where several wide, well-lit passages met. Warian expected his aunt to take the passage that led toward family quarters, but she turned toward the lift tunnel.

"We're going down into the mine?" Warian questioned.

"Yes. Shaddon has moved his staging area closer to the location where the crystal is extracted. He's waiting for us."

Warian scratched his nose and said, "Porter, come with us, please. I have some items in my bag that I may want to ask my uncle about."

"Yes, sir," said the porter, his accent and tone completely unlike Zel's normal speech.

Sevaera cocked her head, but wasn't curious enough to say anything. Instead, she moved to the edge of the lift and addressed the lift operator, a burly half-orc.

"Drop us to the Fifth Deep."

The lift operator nodded and grasped a great wheel set into the wall. Warian knew the lift was raised and lowered through a series of counterweighted chains, and that the wheel didn't require much strength to turn. Those who traveled up and down the mine shafts were heartened to see a burly lift operator, nonetheless.

As the shaft's gray walls flowed past on all sides, to the accompaniment of clanking chains and creaking pulleys, Warian asked, "Fifth Deep? I thought there were only four—and the lowest was where Shaddon first found the

crystal we're all so happy with." Warian pumped his prosthesis to demonstrate.

"We opened a new face on the dig."

"Really? I don't know how that's possible, unless you're
actually digging below the base of Adama's Tooth. If that's
the case, wouldn't it be easier to sink a new shaft from
outside?"

"You'll see, Nephew. The Fifth Deep doesn't obey all the
rules you're accustomed to."

"What?"

Sevaera merely smirked. She was too smug by half.

The long descent ended. A wide tunnel through the naked
rock beckoned. They moved forward and, almost immediately, the nature of the tunnel changed. The lift shaft and
all the tunnels above shared traits of recently excavated
stone, with sharp edges, exposed facets, scratches, and blast
marks. But the tunnel they now traversed was smooth, as
if worn by extreme age or perhaps the passage of water.
Stalactites reached down from above, white with calcite,
and the left wall was thick with delicate boxwork, something
normally found only in unworked caves.

"You've found a natural cavity!" exclaimed Warian.

"True, as far as it goes," replied Sevaera.

The passage opened into a wide, domed cavern.

"What's this? Is that a building?" asked Warian.

Ancient structures, half excavated, stood revealed in the
light of brilliant mining torches. The ruins were so ancient,
they nearly seemed natural formations of the cavern. Worn
and skewed by unknown ages, half walls emerged from the
grasp of the stone. The visible structures were composed of
purple stones, but they reached up from the detritus of millennia, tracing a broken, unknowable floor plan below the
earth. The recent excavation ranged over the entire cavern,
but even to Warian's inexpert eye, it was clear that more still
lay buried than had been pried free by the work of pickaxe
and rock knife.

Several natural passages meandered off the wide cavern, some lit, others dark.

"We think this was an old Imaskaran compound," said Sevaera, "hidden here for thousands of years."

Warian nodded, studying the cavern. He could see small outcrops of the very crystal from which his arm was fashioned, and from which all the plangents drew their greater-than-human abilities. The bits of raw crystal he could see from where he stood had to be worth a fortune.

"Seems kind of wasteful to let all this crystal lie about, unless . . ."

Sevaera nodded. "Yes, we've found a much purer, concentrated source. Shaddon says we no longer need to sift through the dirt and blast through rock—we have access to as much pure crystal as we'll ever need. This pure vein was what allowed the plangent project to move forward."

"Hmm."

Warian cocked his head sharply toward one of the darkened tunnels. Had that been a scream? His aunt hadn't reacted—but the porter also looked curiously at the dark tunnel entrance.

"Aunt, did you hear that?"

"Nothing for you to worry about—we're late, and Shaddon is waiting." So saying, the woman moved purposefully toward another tunnel. Warian shrugged and followed. The porter brought up the rear, still hauling the baggage.

They passed a few dozen side passages, heard a few more worrying noises, and once passed through a mass of air so putrid that Warian had to pull his shirt up across his nose and mouth to filter it. Eventually, they reached another chamber.

Unlike the previous excavation, this one was divided into two areas. One section had been extended by miners, or his grandfather's magic. The newly carved space was expansive and contained numerous wooden workbenches. About half the benches were neatly arrayed with tools of various types that resembled jeweler's and sculptor's adzes, hammers, and carving tools. The other benches contained the same, plus chunks of crystal mounted in vises, each partly carved to resemble some portion of human anatomy.

Warian saw a preponderance of hands, arms, and legs, but also strangely sinuous crystal sculptures. These seemed uncomfortably organic, like something one might confine inside a human body. Looking at them made him feel faintly sick, because he knew that they were probably meant to replace natural organs. It struck him as insanely dangerous now that he saw these raw, unfinished prostheses. A doorway stood open at the far end of the work area.

Warian turned to look at his aunt. How many of these internal implants did Sevaera carry? How much living tissue had she sacrificed to become a plangent? His aunt, watching him, misinterpreted his stare and said, "Soon you'll be updated, Warian, and become fully plangent, like me." Her smile was absolutely predatory.

He swung around and looked at the natural portion of the cavern. It was bare but for a ring of ancient standing stones. Each menhir rose between ten and fifteen feet in height. A gap of perhaps five to ten feet between stones allowed access to the interior, which was empty. But . . .

Dimness inhabited the ring's center, despite several brightly burning torches mounted just beyond its periphery. It was as if the light were having trouble reaching past the stones to illuminate the center.

"Is that some sort of ongoing spell?" Warian asked.

Several steel carts with wide metal wheels stood lined up along one wall. Ruts in the floor revealed that the carts had entered and exited the ring many times. But there was just enough room for one cart inside the ring. Most of the carts were coated with crystalline dust.

Sevaera said, "I suppose it's a spell of a sort. It's a permanent source of magic that opens a door to somewhere else! The portal is a trade secret of Datharathi Minerals. We're mining extraplanar material, crafting it into prostheses of various types, and selling it in Vaelan to rich nobles and merchants. We're making a fortune, and we've only just started."

"Where does it lead?" asked Warian.

"Where do you think?" snorted Sevaera. "Somewhere strange, somewhere odd—someplace no one else has access to. We've cornered the market on the crystal."

Warian squinted at the stone circle, trying to catch some hint of the realm beyond it.

"Not now," said his aunt. "We're late for a meeting." She turned to the right and walked past the workbenches and the prostheses, toward an open door.

Warian wondered where all the miners had gone, as well as all the artisans that must have been diligently carving the crystal displayed on the workbenches. Perhaps the mine was between shifts.

Through the doorway was a small corridor that emptied into a decorated chamber. Book-filled cases, leather stools, warm magical lamps, and wall hangings concealed the fact that the room was far below the earth. But a thick coating of webs covered most of the ceiling and the corners of the room. This feature seemed ominously out of place to Warian.

A high-backed leather chair commanded the room's center, facing away from the door but toward a great, multifaceted orb. The orb was carved of crystal, and it hung suspended on an iron chain. Warian gasped when he saw that each facet glowed with a separate image, as if from a different viewpoint. It was a riot of moving pictures, impossible for him to look at for long.

"What is that?" he asked.

The chair turned from the orb, and a figure rose from where it had been seated.

It was his grandfather, Shaddon Datharathi, of course.

But a much-altered Shaddon since Warian had seen him

last. Warian gaped at the changes, unable to take his eyes from the glittering crystal facets of his uncle's new flesh.

"Welcome, Warian," said Shaddon. "You and I have much to discuss."

CHAPTER NINETEEN

Thormud was sick, but wouldn't admit it.

He could be such a witless, obstinate knob, reflected Kiril.

Sometimes he acted just like a . . . a dwarf!

She shook her head and spat. Kiril didn't share an automatic dislike of the only other populous, long-lived mortal race of Faerûn, as did some elves she could name, but sometimes you had to call it like you saw it.

The bitter taste of whisky from her last mouthful sustained her, but it didn't wipe away the darkening flush on her employer's face, or dry the perspiration from his brow.

The jouncing stride of their mineral destrier added to the dwarf's discomfort. They ascended a winding, narrow pass between the Giant's Belt mountains on their right and the Dustwall on their left. But worse than the summoned destrier's gait was the unrelenting sun.

Kiril mopped the dwarf's brow again and adjusted the impromptu shade she'd erected over his seat. Thormud was sweating so much, she could hardly keep him from dying of thirst.

"Tell me again why you've decided we should travel by day instead of night as you were previously so fond of?" she asked the dwarf.

"Prince Monolith thinks it best," was all the dwarf had the strength to say.

"Stuff Monolith," she muttered, but acquiesced without further argument, as she had on the previous two instances when she'd brought up the same point. Because of the shadowy, voidlike power of whatever lay beyond or through the crystals, Prince Monolith thought it better to travel by day, when that influence might be weaker.

Prince Monolith stalked ahead of the destrier, following the narrow rut that served as the trail over the pass. They had not yet met another traveler. Given the steepness of the trail and the sheer drops to either side of the switchbacks they zigzagged up, Kiril wasn't surprised.

The rut traced a crevice between a wooded slope on their left and an open drop to their right. The drop fell away into a vast gorge—far at the bottom, a river snaked and foamed in its bed. Beyond the river valley, another mountainous rampart rose, equaling and exceeding their current height. The jagged range taunted time itself, and the slow, eroding winds and water plied their work upon it.

Straight ahead, across the river valley, rose the slopes of an even taller, broader peak. Its base was hidden in forested foothills, but most of the mountain rose skyward, free of any covering of greenery. Instead, the highest portions of the peak were clothed in the white of eternal ice.

The sun on the snow dazzled Kiril's eyes, and she dropped

her gaze away from the miles of towering rock. She'd see it a lot closer soon enough.

Despite their pledge of daylight travel, clouds blew in from the west and caught them at the highest point on the pass the next day, just as they moved beyond the last of the scattered, skeletal trunks bearing needles on only one side that hardly qualified as trees. Whiteness enveloped their vision—the belly of a cloud blanketed the world, snow swirled, and the temperature plummeted.

"You can't catch a break, can you?" Kiril asked the sleeping form of her employer. She'd strapped the dwarf into his seat, and his bearded head lolled with each footstep of the destrier. Wind lashed across the destrier's back, stinging the elf's eyes with sharp snow. She noticed that new droplets of ice caked Thormud's hair and skin, so Kiril wrapped the dwarf in another blanket, the last.

"How much farther?" she called ahead at the dark shape of Prince Monolith. The elemental thumped through the gathering snow without the least difficulty. Great furrows trailed behind Monolith on either side of his path, which made the way easier for their mineral destrier.

"We must move forward until we get off the highest portion of the pass. The cold does not concern me, but your flesh will prove less resistant."

Kiril nodded "You're quick on the uptake. Pick up the pace, will you? Thormud's almost frozen solid."

Monolith didn't respond, nor did his pace vary from the steady, ground-eating lope he'd first adopted. The destrier continued to follow in the prince's trail, but even with the furrow, its gait began to deteriorate as the dwarf's health flagged. Kiril hoped their mount's ability to carry passengers wasn't contingent on Thormud's health.

The swordswoman shivered, then struck her forehead

with the heel of her palm as an idea occurred. What a moron! She'd had the means to warm the dwarf all along.

She plucked the flask from her hip, twirled off the metal cap, and tipped the opening to Thormud's lips. He unconsciously swallowed the few tiny sips that Kiril allowed him. She had a pull herself. The warmth hit her belly and immediately spread to her extremities. That was better! She gave the dwarf another small sip.

Kiril laughed. After all the times the dwarf had given her his sour look for drinking too much and too often. It was a small revenge, but necessary if the dwarf were to pull through. If he did, she'd tell him how she'd been forced to give him spirits enough to warm his blood.

The elf shrugged. She knew drinking from the flask was only a temporary measure. Alcohol didn't generate warmth—it merely allowed the reservoir of warmth stored in the core to be liberated. By drinking the hard stuff, you'd warm up your fingers and toes in the short term, but freeze to death all the sooner.

She hoped Prince Monolith hurried. She didn't want to have to bury the dwarf at the top of the world, under a drift of icy snow.

Flakes swirled across her eyes, obscuring her vision.

The dwarf's health improved markedly after getting down off the top of the pass. Thormud sat in his seat, blinking at the harsh sun and drinking frequently from his waterskin.

The destrier's pace was steadier as it followed the thudding steps of Prince Monolith down the dry path of a prehistoric, nameless river. The mountains on this side of the pass were nearly empty of vegetation, unlike the southward face they had ascended.

Ahead and below lay the flat face of Raurin. They were

so high above its empty reaches that Kiril spied a distant dust storm of incredible ferocity. Swelling and towering like a genie loosed from its bottle, the gargantuan wind devil suffused with sand danced westward. It strode above the dead plain, promising stinging death to any at its feet. Kiril couldn't gauge the column's true size, but she didn't doubt it was supernaturally large. Such storms were one of the reasons travelers rarely chose to chance the briny sand seas of the Dust Desert.

"I hope that storm passes before we get down to the edge," Kiril told Thormud.

"Mmm."

She'd been trying to engage the geomancer in conversation all morning, with limited success.

Prince Monolith plodded onward and downward.

They continued to follow the parched course of the ancient river down from the foothills. Day passed into midafternoon. The river's dead path wound among hills rounded and degraded by eons. Kiril saw nothing but worn boulders, pebbles, and fine rusty sand. Nothing moved on the river bottom, whose stones were bare even of dead lichen.

The malignant wind devil with the sandstorm shrouding its base hadn't passed over the horizon as they'd descended the pass. Instead, it twisted and swelled toward them, as if it were a sentient guardian come to bar their passage into Raurin. Perhaps it was.

"We'd better find shelter before it gets here," Kiril told Thormud as she pointed toward the approaching storm.

"Mmm."

"Damn it."

Kiril yelled ahead, "Monolith, Thormud's still not himself. Don't expect any direction from him, if you're waiting for it."

The deep voice of the elemental noble resonated back, "Why should I? I am the guide, not he."

"All right, rock head, if you're so smart, maybe you should think about that approaching wind devil. We won't survive its outskirts, let alone the column at the center."

The elemental stalked down the empty path, but one of its stone arms rose and pointed ahead. Kiril followed the direction of his gesture and saw a tiny cavern mouth, perhaps five hundred paces distant, gaping from the side of the empty stream bed.

She shrugged, saying nothing. Truth was, she was slightly embarrassed she hadn't descried the cave mouth herself. She was an elf, after all, and had a reputation to maintain.

The storm stifled the sun as they reached the aperture. They moved through a baleful twilight stained with bloody light. The cave opened out of the flat, eroded face of an ancient riverbank. The cave's sides were crumbled into heaps of crusted dust, but Kiril immediately noticed a suspiciously clean avenue down the center of the cavern floor. More suspicious yet—the flickering illumination of lantern light emerging from what should have been a lonely, black hole.

Someone lived in the cave—perhaps several someones.

Prince Monolith reached out and touched the rock above the cave entrance. He held the position briefly, then stepped to the side of the cave entrance and ceased all movement.

"Not coming in?"

He replied, "I doubt I would fit. Plus, I might frighten the natives."

"What kind of natives?" asked Kiril.

"Environs as harsh as Raurin are extreme, but mortal flesh, for all its frailty, is surprisingly adaptable. The rock has led me to a colony of dervishes, despite an enchantment of misdirection attempting to lead me astray. But I have a closer association with the world than most."

"I hope they're friendly."

"Enter and ask for shelter. I have observed that cultures

perched on the edge of wastelands often prize hospitality above all other values."

The storm was sweeping down upon them and beginning to sting Kiril with windblown grit. "I don't see what choice I have."

Monolith stood silent as stone.

The elf wrestled Thormud down from his seat and bodily carried him into the cave entrance. She'd worry about their equipment and supplies, still lashed to the destrier's back, later. Xet fluttered around unhelpfully.

The lantern hung from the ceiling some thirty feet down the cavern's throat, rusted and battered, but burning a half-full reservoir of oil that smelled pleasantly of cloves. The lantern light revealed the edge of a chamber that widened gradually toward a great wooden gate blocking the mouth of a deeper tunnel. The floor was worn smooth, as if by vanished waters . . . or by years of busy feet. Dust from the storm outside began to swirl across the stone surface. She set Thormud down with his back against the cavern wall.

With the storm howling at the cave mouth, Kiril pounded on the wooden gate, carved with abstract designs.

After a short wait, too brief for Kiril to consider pounding a second time, a small panel high on the door slid open. An amber glow and tinkling music streamed from the grilled opening.

"Hello?" said Kiril.

A man's voice replied from the other side of the door. "What do you want?" The language was Elvish, with something like a Yuirwood accent, but more liquid.

Kiril was too surprised by the language and what it implied to immediately respond.

"Well," said the voice again, in its strangely accented Elvish, "I can see you are not djinn; perhaps you were chased by a djinn to the safety of our doorstep?"

"Perhaps," said Kiril, not actually sure what the voice was asking her. "A storm came, and we saw the cave. We hoped it would give shelter—we didn't know we'd find someone living here."

"No? You weren't looking for the hidden city of Al Qahera or its people? But only those of elf blood could hope to locate Al Qahera—it is an ancient enchantment we preserve."

"I am an elf, that's true, but I hail from the north, from . . ." she almost said Stardeep, but finally said, "from the Yuirwood forest. I am not of the Al Qaheran clan. Elves hidden in the Yuirwood call themselves 'people of the star.' But I am not really part of their society any longer, either. I am a traveler."

"You've traveled far, and to one of the most inhospitable places in the world. I see no children with you, just a mountain carver. Are you carrying contraband?"

"I don't understand."

"Sometimes oathless smugglers make *haddrum* runs between Huorm and the oasis towns."

"I don't know what *haddrum* is, but, no, we're not carrying dangerous substances, if that's what you're implying."

"Then what?"

"It's a long story. I'd be happy to tell you if you let us in. My friend here is sick."

"Mmmm, hmm, yes, so I see," said the voice, and paused. "Very well. I'm a good judge of character, so I tell my sons and daughters." The sound of a bolt being drawn back momentarily drowned out the sound of the blowing sand. "Be welcome in Al Qahera! Bring with you no deceit, and you shall find none here."

The great carved door swung wide, and standing in its gap was an elf wearing a long, heavy gown of spun white cloth, over which he wore a larger, looser garment stitched with intricate script Kiril didn't recognize. His face, while certainly that of an elf, was strangely weathered. Despite his fey blood, his skin marked him as one who'd spent a lifetime in the sun.

"My name," said the man, "is Essam. Enter." He moved

to the side and gestured inward. Behind him Kiril saw the heart of the dervish community of Al Qahera.

The entrance, wide as it was, opened onto a far larger and deeper plaza, enclosed on all sides by stone balconies, galleries, and square tunnels leading to hidden rooms. The entire plaza was brilliantly lit by hundreds of clove oil lanterns. Great bronze plaques with calligraphic script hung from every surface that didn't sport a tapestry of intricate weave. A beautiful mosaic design was laid out in tiles that paved the entire floor of the plaza. A high-walled stone well protruded from the plaza's center. From where she stood at the entrance, Kiril scented the cool tang of deep water.

People moved everywhere—men, women, and children. All were elves, and all were weathered like Essam. The adults wore flowing, colorful gowns, but the children wore loose pants and simple tunics.

One edge of the wide plaza, which was well over a hundred paces in diameter, hosted a bazaar with several semipermanent stands. The elves of Al Qahera were thickly gathered there. But the appearance of strangers had apparently distracted the Qaherans from the merits of their transactions. Everyone in the subterranean, lanternlit plaza looked in her direction.

Essam clapped his hands and yelled, "Call the healer—we have visitors, and one is ill. Come! Do not stare, my friends—we shall have time to make their acquaintance when our visitors have rested and washed away the burdens of their journey." Essam paused and smiled openly at Kiril. "Perhaps we might hope for a story from our guests, describing how they found themselves on our porch, running before a *gowaan* storm."

Several children rushed forward, curious, along with a young elf woman in a blue caftan, hardly older than a child herself. She nodded at Kiril and said, "My name is Fadheela. You and your friend can stay in our guestroom. My father is a healer."

Kiril blinked, taking in the comfort of the round chamber. A covering stitched with desert stars hung from the ceiling. Soft sheepskin lay across the floor. A fire in a tiny side alcove burned away the subterranean chill. No smoke lingered in the room—the fireplace was apparently well vented. Kiril wondered briefly how fresh air was drawn in, then shrugged. The elves of Al Qahera had obviously worked it out.

"I *do* feel much better, Kiril," said Thormud in an irritated tone. The dwarf sat propped up on the small bed, his back against a wooden headboard carved with still more elaborate designs. "I'd like to go down to the plaza tonight to talk with the Qaherans."

"You heard Fadheela's father. You've caught some sort of dolor, and you need bed rest if you want to shake it off."

"But . . ."

"Tonight, you sleep."

The geomancer sighed. "Perhaps that would be best. I am strangely fatigued."

Kiril didn't tell the dwarf the entire diagnosis. Fadheela's father felt that the dwarf might be suffering from some sort of magical curse. It was a potential explanation for Thormud's lack of response to the healer's spell of purification.

"Damn right, it's for the best. Don't worry. I'll tell you everything that happens. Maybe they know something about what we're looking for. Maybe they've seen something strange out in the desert."

The dwarf nodded but was already blinking his eyes. He fell asleep a moment later.

Kiril pulled up his blanket, strapped Angul to her belt, and departed the small chamber.

Fadheela waited for her in the foyer of the apartment, one of many similar apartments on both sides, above, and below. The best apartments faced the central plaza of Al Qahera, and as a healer, Fadheela's father enjoyed some privilege.

"How is your friend?" Fadheela asked.

"Better. He's asleep. Maybe I'll take him something to eat later."

"Good—that sounds good!" Fadheela clapped happily, then reached forward to grasp one of Kiril's hands. The swords-woman, out of surprise, allowed the desert elf to complete the motion without losing a limb.

Fadheela said, "Come with me, then. Everyone's down in the plaza. You'll just love meeting everyone, I promise!" The girl pulled, and Kiril consciously forced herself not to resist the tug out of the apartment. They walked onto the wide balcony two stories above the tiled floor of the central courtyard and looked down.

Since she'd rested in Fadheela's rooms, answered her father's questions, and washed off several days of travel, the lamps in the courtyard had been turned down, dousing the corners of the chamber in warm shadow. A large bonfire blazed in a stone-lined firepit. Kiril traced the smoke as it rose up past their balcony and floated up a few more stories before exiting through a large cavity in the ceiling.

The odor of something succulent roasting over the flames pulled her gaze back down to the fire, where young Qaherans slowly turned several spits. Others were setting up large plank tables and stools. A group of elves tuned up flutes, sitars, drums, and other instruments. Well over a hundred people gathered in the plaza—and perhaps double that number.

"What's all this?" Kiril asked, an anxious note creeping into her voice.

Her enthusiastic guide smiled and said, "We do this every night—don't worry, you needn't fear being singled out."

Kiril nodded, still suspicious.

Fadheela pulled her along the balcony toward a stair-way that spiraled down to the plaza, and whispered as they neared the bottom, "But your presence is unique, and we'd all love to hear something of your journey!"

Kiril muttered, "Blood, I'm sure you would."

Essam met them at the bottom of the stairs.

"How is your stout friend? In Mas'ud's able hands he must be doing better, yes?"

"Much better," Kiril assured him. No need to discuss curses in polite company, she thought.

"How joyous!" her host enthused. "Now come, I've reserved a place of honor for you by the fire. It is always cold down here in Al Qahera, despite the desert above, and you'll be glad to sit close."

Kiril just nodded. She drew most of the eyes in the plaza as Essam and Fadheela led her through the throng. Her neck and cheeks warmed. She did not enjoy being the center of attention.

They made their way to several stools near the fire, as Essam promised. She dropped onto her stool immediately, then saw that everyone else remained standing. She yearned for a pull from her flask. With steely determination, she kept her hands at her sides, but the flush of embarrassment blossomed visibly across her checks.

The Qaherans bowed their heads in a moment of silence. Once concluded, the stillness was shattered by laughter, loud cheers, a cacophony of instruments, and a few songs. Various spirited discussions picked up where they'd left off before the hush. Most everyone sat down at the tables, Kiril was relieved to see.

And so the evening progressed. Portions of burned meat, burned vegetables, and burned fungus were pulled off the spits and sent circulating around the tables. "Burned" was apparently the preferred style of cooking in Al Qahera. Between courses came musical interludes, stories, and acts of skill that included a knife juggler and a puppeteer. Large jugs of water were sent around, cold and fresh, apparently just pulled up from the central well. To Kiril's jaded throat, the water went down like the finest Sildëyuir vintage. It wasn't long before she found herself listening happily to the music, hanging on the words of the storytellers, and laughing uproariously at several extemporaneous acts put on by the desert dwellers.

Essam turned to her and said loudly, "Tell us a story, Kiril!" She stood up, and with uncharacteristic openness, began to relate to the elves of Al Qahera the story of her most recent trip with her employer, Thormud Horn.

Kiril spoke in generalities, without specifying what worried the geomancer so much that he had initiated a trip into the desert. Kiril wasn't even completely clear on what they were chasing. She glossed over certain details, such as Prince Monolith joining them. She didn't want to explain that an earth elemental lord was camped out in front of the dervish community.

When she reached the point in her travelogue where Thormud determined that the true nexus of their quest lay in the Raurin desert, her listeners' interest intensified.

Essam cleared his throat and interrupted Kiril. "Forgive me, but please allow me to ask—what is the nature of this evil that lies out in our desert?"

Kiril shrugged. "I don't know for certain. Thormud called it a 'splinter' that infected the earth. It has something to do with the purple crystal—every threat we've faced has borne a purple crystal."

Exclamations broke out among her audience.

"What is it? What do you know?" demanded Kiril.

Essam calmed the Qaherans' outburst and told her, "Perhaps we know something of the thing you seek in the deep desert. It is new, and it is dangerous. We call it the Storm Spike."

CHAPTER TWENTY

The vengeance taker, wizard, and Datharathi fugitive disembarked at Huorm.

Eined scanned the docks for agents hired by her family, but saw nothing suspicious. To hide her identity, she tied her blue sash around her head like a great scarf.

"We'd best keep an eye out, anyway," Eined cautioned, her voice uncertain.

"Datharathi agents aren't as ubiquitous as you'd feared," suggested Ususi.

"Perhaps," allowed Eined.

Iahn led them into the city. They located a horse breeder willing to rent a secondhand travel coach. It was a crude, dirty version of the custom coach the wizard had left behind in Vaelan, but Ususi supposed it would serve.

As the sun reached its zenith, the coach pulled out of Huorm's north gate. A little-used dirt road led north, toward rolling foothills crowned by the Dustwalls. A broader road led east and west. They turned west, directly toward the lone spire of Adama's Tooth, easily visible among the lower foothills as a lone peak, strangely tall and slender.

Ususi drove, using her magically summoned steeds to pull the coach. Iahn sat on the bench at her side. Eined rode inside the carriage, hidden from casual observers. No need to tempt Datharathi sympathizers or sycophants with glimpses of a lone family member traveling without her normal retinue.

The wizard drove at a brisk pace, but not so swiftly as to draw attention. Outside the city, carriages were rare. Foot traffic ruled the road, though most folk moved to the side rather than face down an oncoming horse and wagon. After traveling a quarter of the afternoon, Eined called from a side window, "There! Take that road!"

The main road, heading west, veered to the north. Eined pointed to the south, to a narrow, slightly overgrown trail. Eined's head poked fully out of the carriage window as she said, "That leads directly to Adama's Tooth. It used to be the route for low-grade ores to be transported out of the mines below the peak, before Shaddon moved in permanently and established an air link."

"What kind of traffic are we likely to see on it?" Iahn asked.

"Hardly any. Shaddon's got Adama's Tooth sewn up pretty tight. Housing and meals are provided internally, and outside supplies are brought in from Vaelan via airship."

Iahn nodded, satisfied. Ususi turned the carriage down the narrow track. The vengeance taker noted a few stares from nearby travelers, but nothing beyond typical curiosity.

The new trail, despite being narrow, was in excellent condition, and they practically raced down it. The thin spire of Adama's Tooth grew to become the dominant feature of the surrounding landscape. Sunlight failed as they drove into the shadow of the slender mountain.

"Why is it called Adama's Tooth?" asked Iahn, leaning over to direct his question into the open carriage window. "Was Adama some ancient hero of your people?"

"No. The Adama is what passes for religion around here."

"Truly?"

Instead of replying, Eined opened the side door of the still moving carriage, climbed the side ladder, and seated herself behind Iahn and Ususi.

"Now that we're so close to Adama's Tooth, it's probably better if I can see what's coming. There—we want to turn right here." The woman pointed toward an even narrower path off the trail they'd been following. "It looks steep now, and it'll get steeper. I hope your summoned steed is up to it, or we'll be walking before we get to the top."

Ususi nodded and turned the carriage down the path. As promised, the angle pulled all the riders back in their seats.

"This will get us to a side door halfway up the peak. Unless Shaddon changed the locks, I can get us in without attracting any notice."

Their speed dropped to about half their earlier clip—the summoned beast struggled with the grade, but persevered.

Eined touched Iahn's shoulder. "Sorry—you were asking about the Adama? Adama is not a person, but a belief system and a code of conduct. To the average Durpari, the Adama is the one true force guiding their lives. It encompasses all the deities of what some call the lesser beliefs." She shook her head and smiled sardonically.

"You do not follow the path of the Adama," Iahn concluded.

"I did, once. But if you are part of a merchant family long enough, you either learn to lie to yourself—a mind sickness I'd prefer to avoid—or recognize the Adama as just another in a string of half truths the merchant elites feed the lesser classes to keep themselves on top."

Iahn said, "How so?"

"Think about it. The Adama teaches that only through honest business practices and mutual respect can one find peace and happiness. The key word is 'honest.' Sitting on the council of any of the big chakas in Vaelan quickly teaches that larger profits are possible the further a merchant stretches the concept of honesty."

"Mmmm," agreed Iahn noncommittally, seeing that Eined was expressing pent-up hostility. She might be correct, but he had little common experience as a basis for comparison.

"But," continued Eined, warming to her argument, "the Durpari people get their sense of truth, fairness, and racial tolerance from the conviction that everything and everyone is a manifestation of the Adama. It's the foundation by which they conduct themselves. In fact, word of the Adama has spread to other lands, giving all of us a reputation for evenhandedness and fairness—which only enhances business prospects."

"Eined," Ususi said quietly, "we're being hailed. What should I do?"

While Eined lectured Iahn on the Adama, the road had begun to switch back and forth at an alarmingly precipitous angle. In a short time, they ascended a few hundred feet on a path that zigged and zagged upward.

An iron gate blocked access to the roadway ahead. On the left side of the gate was an impassable vertical wall. On the right side, a drop of a few hundred feet emptied onto a reddish-brown boulder field. Two men stood on the road in front of the gate, near a small guard cave hollowed into the side of the mountain. One had his hand on the pommel of his sheathed sword. The other, a pace behind the first and standing in the mouth of the cave, had a bow in hand and a shaft resting lightly on the string. Although the arrow was not yet drawn, the threat was implicit in the man's stance.

The guard with the sword moved a step closer and yelled,

"Stop! Turn around. This route is closed."

Eined stood immediately and raised her hand in greeting. "Captain Alberik, don't you remember me?"

The captain blinked his eyes, then a grin spread wide over his face. "Mistress Eined!" The guard stopped, at a loss for words.

"How long has it been—five years?—since last you opened the side gate for me, Captain?"

The guard nodded. A smile flirted with his lips. "Too long. I've missed you."

"Yes, yes, and I you," said Eined hastily. "I'm back now—I must run up and talk with my uncle. Be a prince and open the way for me, won't you?"

Alberik asked, "Why didn't you come by airship? This access is closed."

"If I had come by airship, how would you know I'd returned?"

The captain blushed, then said, "I thank the lady's kindness." Alberik turned to the other guard, who stood puzzling over his captain's apparent familiarity with the intruder. "Open the gate. It's all right—this is Eined Datharathi!"

The other guard jumped, retreated into the cave mouth, and in moments the sound of a metal crank was audible. The gate slowly slid into a recess in the cliff wall. As it did, Alberik moved to the side of the carriage. He reached up and grasped one of Eined's hands, asking, "Will you come back to see me?"

Eined smiled and said, "I hope so." Ususi drove the coach forward. In moments, they left behind the open gate and hopeful guard captain. Eined smiled fondly and said, "The fruits of a misspent youth sometimes work in your favor."

The increasingly angled path terminated in a dark tunnel mouth. Adama's Tooth still soared higher into the air. Even the efforts of dwarven engineering had limits—no mundane road could hope to reach Adama's Tooth's apex.

Eined pointed out the airship port—two great wings of stone high above them. They could see the silhouette of a ship hanging at a pier within the torchlit cavity.

"Someone from Vaelan is here. Probably just a routine visit." Eined's voice betrayed uncertainty.

"No doubt," said Iahn. He was sure he'd have noticed any magical scrutiny of their approach. He'd felt none. The vengeance taker doubted that anyone expected Eined to appear at the family mine site.

Ususi drove the coach to the edge of the tunnel mouth and stopped. "We're too wide," she said, comparing the width of the tunnel to their carriage.

"This high passage is rarely used, and never by conveyances as large as this. We'll have to walk from here."

Ususi nodded. She tied off the reins, pulled the handbrake, and pointed at the steed tied into its harnesses. With a small pop, the creature vanished.

After dismounting, the trio gathered in front of the tunnel. Ususi snapped her fingers and said, "Bring me my pack!"

Eined glanced at the wizard, then at Iahn, uncertain if Ususi were talking to her. She gave a small jump of surprise when the coach door opened of its own accord and Ususi's large pack floated out and into the wizard's hands.

"Don't worry. My uskura is always with us," said Ususi, as she reached into the pack. She pulled forth a tiny orb of pale stone.

Eined peered around, trying to discern the invisible helper, with no luck.

"It's perfectly natural. Where we're from, they're common aides."

"Where you're from . . . where is that?" asked Eined. "I've noticed how pale you both seem. And the streaks that run through your skin."

"Our home is far from here," broke in Iahn. "Now, let's enter and find what we came for."

Eined nodded and dropped the subject.

Ususi released the orb to orbit her brow, and a bright light broke from it. Following the wizard, Eined and Iahn entered the tunnel mouth.

CHAPTER TWENTY-ONE

What's wrong, Grandson?" asked Shaddon. "Are you not happy to see the excellent fashion in which your grandfather has preserved himself against time's insult?"

The living flesh of the elder Datharathi, if any remained, was lost in glittering, glassy facets. His face was a crystalline mask, but beneath it, veins pulsed with blood, raw muscle moved, and bone gleamed. One eye socket was replaced completely with a crystal orb, but the other remained real—a watery blue orb that rolled and fluttered as if caught in a trap. The man was clothed head to toe in ornate golden robes complete with a stiff collar, cape, and silken gauntlets, so Warian was unable to determine the extent of Shaddon's self-transformation. Warian feared the worst.

"I'm . . . glad to see you again after so long, Grandfather," he finally managed. Warian unconsciously tried to catch the porter's eye—had Uncle Zel known the extent of Shaddon's transformation? The consummate professional, Zel didn't react to Warian's glance. Instead, he moved to one side as if looking for a place to set down the baggage.

Shaddon grinned. Somehow, the crystal of his face was able to flow and move almost like real flesh. Seeing the naked sinew beneath the mask made the expression too much like a skull's rictus for Warian's comfort. He partially averted his gaze.

"And it is good to see you, too, Warian. Very, very good indeed." If possible, his grandfather's grin seemed to stretch wider. Warian's earlier concern that Shaddon might harbor the same taint as the other plangents returned and perched on his heart.

"Because you miss your grandchildren?"

"Certainly, always. But also because of what you represent, Warian. You're the first, you know. Your arm is what led to all this." Warian's grandfather gestured to his own face and toward Sevaera, who stood nearby.

"I'm here because I've been having trouble with it. It is malfunctioning of late, and I'd like to learn to control it."

Shaddon nodded. "Yes, I've heard. Let me take a look," he commanded, approaching Warian.

"You've heard? But we've only just arrived."

"You don't think my communication with Datharathi Minerals is limited to the speed of an airship, do you? Of course not. I have my ways. Now, let me see your arm."

Warian held out his prosthesis, palm upward. His grandfather reached out with his gloved hands and ran them along the crystal.

"Interesting," said his grandfather in a distracted manner. "You may not know it, Warian, but your prosthesis is cut from a portion of the lode not connected with the pure vein we found recently. It is not part of the crystal node that has brought the family so much wealth and influence."

"I saw the new mine—and some sort of magical portal. Where in the name of the four dooms does that thing lead?" Warian imagined some sort of fiery hellscape, the typical destination of such ancient gates, according to popular tales and tavern songs.

Shaddon chuckled. "Time enough for full explanations later. Let's see . . ." Shaddon gazed intently at Warian's prosthesis. Shaddon's crystal eye glowed, hinting at some sort of magical analysis beyond Warian's ken.

"What's the verdict?" asked Warian.

"Impossible to say for sure," said Shaddon, releasing Warian's arm. "One thing is certain. Your arm is not part of the new crystalworks. That may be why you're losing control over it, as you say—though I suspect there's more to it than that."

Warian shrugged.

"In any event, if I'm to reach a definite conclusion, I'll have to remove it."

Warian's jaw dropped. "Remove . . . no. Out of the question."

Shaddon laughed. "Your error is your belief that you have any option other than what I want. The arm will come off. By Pandorym's voice, you will . . ."

The porter brained Shaddon with an iron bar he'd apparently pilfered from a workbench in the neighboring chamber.

The light in Shaddon's crystal eye winked out, and he dropped heavily to the floor.

"Let's get out of here, kid," the porter said, his voice returning to the timber and Vaelanic accent of his Uncle Zel.

"You'll go nowhere," said Sevaera. She stood in the doorway, blocking their exit. Her voice was oddly deep and throaty—but familiar. All too horribly familiar. Shaddon's voice issued from Sevaera's mouth.

Warian and Zel blinked, stunned. Sevaera yelled, "Aid me, my pets!"

Zel looked around nervously, then advanced toward the exit, the iron bar gripped solidly in his pale hands. He said, his voice slightly shaky, "You saw me strike down dear old Dad. I'll do the same to you, Sis. Get out of my way."

Sevaera said, "Your father is more resilient than you think. Open your ears, fool—who do you think is talking to you?" The voice was unquestionably Shaddon's scratchy tone. Zel merely shook his head, refusing to consider the truth.

A spider the size of a dog dropped onto Zel's back. Zeltaebar uttered an oath and began to beat at his back ineffectually with his pry bar. Sevaera tittered in Shaddon's heavy tones.

Warian turned and knocked the spider away with his prosthesis. The arm was still slow, slower than flesh, but he caught the creature squarely on the torso. As it fell, it snapped overlarge mandibles at Warian. Its mandibles were crystalline, through and through, and glowing with violet malevolence.

"Watch it, Zel. These things are enhanced with crystal!"

Zel whirled and struck at the spider. It caught the iron bar in its mandibles. Zel cursed and tried to pull the tool free. The spider flexed its fangs, and the iron bar began to bend. While the spider was occupied, Warian moved forward and delivered a terrific kick directly to the spider's head. Something crunched, and sticky fluid spurted. A moment later, the spider's legs curled up beneath it and it ceased moving.

Three more spiders dropped from the ceiling. One had crystalline mandibles as large as the first spider's, another had legs of slender violet stalks, and the last spider's spinnerets, protruding obscenely from its posterior, were composed of humming purple crystal.

The three arachnids dropped so they were roughly equidistant from each other, with Warian and Zel penned in at the center of the triangle they formed. Warian couldn't decide—should he trigger his arm, or wait? The weakness that would follow would make him worthless.

"We've got trouble, Nephew," Zel breathed, sizing up the spiders.

"Indeed," said Shaddon's voice.

Warian's grandfather stood up from where he lay, apparently no worse for wear. His voice again emanated from his own throat. Sevaera blinked and shook her head.

"What happened?" she asked.

The spiders held their distance, taut with expectation. Warian supposed they waited for a signal from Shaddon—perhaps a signal as ethereal as desire. His grandfather was demonstrating the danger of taking a prosthesis. He could send more than a signal—he could send his entire consciousness, like a possessing spirit. The evidence was incontrovertible. Except Warian was certain he'd never been possessed by any outside consciousness.

Warian exclaimed, "You can't reach me, can you? That's why you want to remove my arm. I'm outside your control!"

Shaddon laughed, but it was strangely nervous. Both eyes, the flesh and the crystal, darted about as if searching for something, then focused again on Warian. He said, "Something like that. Just as I can command those who are outfitted with my advanced prostheses, I myself am susceptible to influence by a . . . disagreeable entity I'd rather avoid. Your prosthesis harbors the secret of erecting that barrier. And, by all accounts, it grants you some of the benefits a plangent enjoys."

"If you want my help, I'll give it," said Warian, trying to look into his grandfather's eyes and discern if the man spoke truth. "If you're afraid of something beyond you, let's work together. You don't need to . . ."

"No. It's far beyond that now. There are other players in this little drama, and they're making a nuisance of themselves. Events have advanced too quickly."

"But . . ."

"Sevaera! Restrain these two. The arachnids will help. More visitors have arrived!" So saying, Shaddon blurred out of the chamber, moving with the enhanced speed only a plangent could muster.

Warian pleaded, "Aunt, let us go—can't you see Shaddon's corrupted? We need to flee!"

His aunt, still confused and perhaps a bit scared, nevertheless stood her ground. She said, "Don't take me for a fool, youngster. Stay where you are, or . . ." she trailed off, gesturing to the spiders.

Taking her wave as a cue, two of the monsters rushed forward. The one with the crystal legs jumped at Warian. Before he could do more than widen his eyes, it was on him, sticking to his body with its prosthetic legs. The spider with the crystal mandibles skittered toward Zel, who raised his bent iron bar and called, "Warian—if you can use your arm, do it!"

Sevaera squawked, "Stop! I command it! You spiders—I did not tell you to attack! You stupid, stupid creatures!" The woman stamped her foot, and her crystal implants began to glow. Instead of taking action, she continued to shout at the spiders. The one on Warian responded by squeezing him. The arachnid closing on Zel continued its advance. The final spider turned and began to exude slender strands of crystal webbing.

Warian realized that events had spiraled beyond his aunt's control. He didn't trust her anyway, since she was susceptible to Shaddon's control—or perhaps some deeper, more corrupt entity, if Shaddon could be believed.

Warian focused his mind on his prosthesis.

Violet light took fire in Warian. A miniature sun burned a circuit down his forged arm, awaking it to something better than mere life. Warian grinned, and with the merest flick of his prosthetic finger, propelled his eight-legged attacker off his body and out the open doorway.

He turned. The light in his energized arm was bright—brighter than it had been on the two occasions he'd called its power. He laughed, drunk on the feeling—he was faster and stronger than ever! His power was mounting, not diminishing.

Another theory immediately vied for his attention. Could it be that he was simply draining his life-force more completely each time he called on the artificial limb's hidden gift? Intuition told him that the less agreeable and more deadly explanation was the likely one.

Could he control the effect, he wondered? Could he moderate how much energy his arm pulled from his body and mind? The previous times he'd triggered his ability, he'd been desperate, as he was now. But then, as now, the arm brimmed with so much more strength than he needed. And when the implant dimmed, he felt so horribly drained.

Warian concentrated on dimming the light in his arm, imagining its brilliance damping but not failing completely.

A green and purple haze swirled before him, and a sharp nausea dug into his bowels. His breath heaved, but the radiance of his arm faded without going out.

Immediately, the sounds and movements around him returned to a normal speed.

His Uncle Zel yelled, in a voice barely distorted, "Warian, get this thing away from me! What are you doing standing there?" The crystal-mandibled spider snapped at Zel, but Warian's uncle fought it off, just barely, by swinging his iron bar.

Warian moved to aid Zel, but fell down instead. Had he drained himself anyway? No—something tugged at his foot—he was caught! Glistening purple strands of crystal stretched between the floor and his left leg, anchoring him in place. The spider with the prosthetic spinnerets had been busy. To Warian's horror, it spun yet another crystal strand, one end of which caught him on his crystal arm.

He flexed his dimmed prosthesis, trying to break the hair-thin strand. The web was tougher than it looked, but with a bell-like pop, the strand broke.

An instant later, two more webs landed on him from the busily spinning weaver. "Damned beast," he cursed. So much for conserving his energy.

Consciously, he increased the arm's radiance. Enhanced strength was his again. With a light tug, he pulled free of the strands holding his arm, then climbed to his feet. He reached down and snapped the strands still attached to his foot. Simultaneously, he tamped the radiance down to the barest glimmer. A hollow feeling was beginning to blossom in his chest, but the moment he cooled down the brilliance, the empty feeling stopped growing. Warian knew he was fast approaching the limit of the usable energy of his body.

Without pausing, he charged at the web-spinning spider. It worked its spinnerets with great speed, ready to release another entangling salvo. The spider skittered away from Warian's charge, but he grabbed hold of its fat, hairy body. It writhed and snapped, and he nearly dropped it. Instead, he whirled in a half circle. Warian released the spider at the terminus of the circle's arc with a hard snap. It flew like a ballista bolt into the wall, making a satisfyingly loud crunch as both its carapace and crystal shattered.

"Warian!"

He turned and saw a spider bite Zel. His uncle dropped the iron bar and clutched the bloody wound on his leg. The spider, its crystal mandibles stained red, moved in for another bite. Warian was too far from his uncle to do anything but stare with sick horror.

Both Warian and Zel yelped in surprise when Sevaera dashed forward and stomped on the spider with her artificial leg. The woman kicked the creature flat until little remained but a sparkling, bloody smear.

Sevaera tried to put a hand on Zel, but her brother flinched away.

She asked, "Zel, what's going on? I know Father said to hold you, but . . . plangent spiders?"

Still clutching his leg, Zel said, "Thank you for coming to my rescue. But it doesn't mean I trust you. You're compromised." He limped toward Warian and the exit.

"Aunt Sevaera," Warian began, but stopped. He wanted to invite his aunt to join them—but as Zel said, she was a plangent. How could he depend on her to control her own actions? Shaddon demonstrated that he could possess her at any time, and implied even more frightening aspects of the entity in the crystal.

He decided on a different tactic. "Aunt, you must get those crystal implants removed. Shaddon has gone mad, or he's been possessed, or maybe both. He's able to commandeer the body of every plangent he creates."

"Commandeer?"

"Possess and control every action."

Sevaera gasped and asked, "Did he do it . . . to me? Just a little while ago?"

Warian nodded.

The woman, already pale, paled further. She said, "I've suspected something wasn't quite right, you know. Too much lost time. And every so often I'd find myself somewhere strange with no memory of how I'd gotten there, or why I wanted to go there."

"Shaddon was testing out his new toys," said Zel, somewhat maliciously.

"I don't . . . I don't know what to do." Her last words spiraled up in pitch. Tears welled in her eyes. Sudden sympathy for his normally cruel, self-assured aunt took Warian by surprise, and he took a step toward her.

What happened next would haunt his dreams for years to come.

Sevaera's eyes widened in sudden panic, as if she spied

something utterly abominable. He'd never seen such naked fear in anyone's expression. She gasped, "Run!"

"Sevaera?" questioned Zel. But a black film glazed the woman's eyes. Humanity leaked away, and what stared out at them was the soul of the void. A grave-cold wind blew up, and Warian's hair streamed toward his aunt. She had become a deep, dark well, and a monstrosity lurked at the bottom.

Her mouth opened wide as if she were about to scream. Instead, without any visible articulation, an awful voice rumbled, "Come to me."

Sevaera's mouth gaped even wider, but Warian saw nothing within but darkness. As her mouth widened, the wind redoubled. Warian had to lean away from his aunt, and Zel grabbed hold of his arm. Fragments of broken crystal from the spiders slid along the floor, accelerating as they neared her. They were sucked without a trace into her mouth.

"Come to me," said the appalling voice once more, louder.

The high-backed chair slid toward the woman. Books flew from the shelves like a converging swarm of bats. Each one disappeared down her maw, getting stuck only momentarily on the edges of her lips. The great crystal hanging from its chain strained toward her. The bodies of the dead spiders, slick with blood, tumbled into the epicenter of her influence, then were sucked down into the metaphysical cavity.

Zel shook Warian. "We have to get out of here, kid!" Warian broke free of his horror trance, grabbed his uncle's arm, and dashed through the exit, skimming past Sevaera. He ran down the short corridor and into the workroom beyond. The radiance in his arm intensified, as did the force pulling him backward. Loose objects in the workroom began to pelt and bounce off him as they arrowed through the air toward Sevaera.

"Ouch!" A sealed glass jar filled with greenish fluid knocked his uncle down. Warian didn't stop—he just pulled his uncle forward. He had to bat away panels ripped from the wall, sidestep sliding benches, and duck candles as lethal as crossbow bolts. Only the enhanced strength granted by his arm saved Warian, again and again, plus lent him enough power to pull his groaning, protesting uncle.

The telltale tingle of his arm's imminent failure began to grow in his chest—a cavernous, dead feeling. If he allowed the prosthesis to fail now, they'd be pulled in. Warian glanced back and saw Sevaera walking after him with an awkward, stiff-legged gait. A rain of tools, crystals, papers, lamps, and candles gathered in a whirlwind around her before being pulled in.

Warian lost all restraint and pumped the power of his arm to its brightest glow yet. He dashed through the work area, his uncle in tow. Objects seemed to hang suspended as he moved at superhuman speed, almost beyond mortality. But his strength guttered all too soon. He didn't dare swerve toward the side entrance—if he did, they wouldn't make it.

His uncle screamed something. He was struggling to get to his feet despite Warian's grip on his arm, but the man's voice was too warped by speed for Warian to understand.

Warian couldn't answer, anyway. All his concentration was required to continue on toward the ring of ancient standing stones. He gasped and nearly passed out, but pulled himself through a gap between two of the stones, into the interior of the ring.

He ended up someplace quite different.

CHAPTER TWENTY-TWO

Essam of the desert-dwelling elves addressed Kiril and the throng gathered in the plaza of subterranean Al Qahera. "The great rock appeared in the wake of a tempest fiercer than most that stalk Raurin. If you knew the wildness of Raurin's storms, you'd know that this event was singular in its violence. Thus, we call it the Storm Spike."

Kiril gave a heartfelt nod, remembering the wind devil that had pursued them onto the dervishes' doorstep.

"So sudden did the storm hit that several of our people went missing, including two of Al Qahera's best archers. We never did learn their fate." A sigh escaped many throats. "They are missed."

"When the storm subsided," Essam continued, "we sent foragers to see if the winds had uncovered anything of interest. Every so often, a big storm uncovers some likely artifact, fossilized creature, or other curiosity we can sell for a good measure of grain, cloth, or spice down in Huorm."

The swordswoman nodded. She supposed the desert was rife with interesting relics—she vaguely recalled that some old human civilization once claimed the desert as its own—before destroying itself. Faerûn had a way of eating civilizations, especially those that overreached themselves. In other words, human civilizations.

"Three foragers—Feraih, Ghanim, and Haleem—walked north. The dusts subsided, and a bright dawn, clear of flying sand, lured them onward. Something new glistened on the horizon, flashing prettily in the sun. A day's gallop on camelback brought the foragers to the desert newcomer."

"The Storm Spike? What did it look like?"

"At first glance, it seemed like a splinter of purplish stone and dark crystal that reached for the sky. But Feraih was the first to realize that what had really appeared in the desert was a tall, slender tower—a made thing. Made by whom, though, she couldn't begin to guess."

Was this the epicenter of darkness Thormud detected, and the destination of their tendays-long quest?

"What did they do next?" Kiril asked.

"Ghanim and Haleem spied an entrance, and they went inside. Feraih waited outside, in the tower's shadow. When half a day had passed, she went to the entrance and found it sealed. It looked as if it had always been sealed. She knew that couldn't possibly be true—her friends were within. She tried her rock hammers, minor enchantments of opening, and even prayer—nothing sufficed. The entrance was closed.

"After two days, Feraih returned to Al Qahera. That night, she slept again in her own bed. In the morning, her brothers found her dead. Mas'ud the healer was unable to find anything wrong—he suspected she had fallen into a curse."

Mas'ud believed Thormud was suffering from a curse—might they be the same? Anxiety wrapped its prickly cloak around Kiril's shoulders.

"So we call the Storm Spike a cursed thing, an intruder in Raurin, and something to steer clear of. Since Feraih returned, no Qaheran has journeyed north to again gaze upon the dark tower, the mere sight of which can curse an observer to her death."

After recounting Essam's story about the Storm Spike to Thormud, it was all Kiril could do to restrain the dwarf from leaving immediately. By the next morning, there was no arguing with him. Despite the night's rest, the dwarf remained pale and shaky in the reddish light of the new day. He'd lost weight, and his hair had noticeably whitened since they'd set off from their home in the Mulhorand scrublands.

"You're still too sick, Thormud. We should wait a few more days until you're better," pleaded Kiril.

The dwarf patted her hand. "I might not have the luxury of a few more days."

"Don't be so god-cursed dramatic," the swordswoman huffed, but an uncharacteristic quaver in her tone belied her anger. She didn't know how to end the mysterious curse sapping the geomancer's life. Perhaps the best choice was to race to the Storm Spike and deal with whatever inhabited it. In so doing, perhaps the curse could be dissolved.

Many Qaherans, including Essam and Fadheela, followed Kiril, the geomancer, and the annoyingly underfoot Xet into the ravine that housed their hidden city. The Qaherans were impressed when Thormud spoke a word and the mineral destrier stirred. It rose from beneath the great sand dune that covered it during the evening's storm, shaking away the grit to reveal its strong lines. Kiril was relieved to see their supplies still lashed to the destrier's back.

After the excitement over the destrier, Prince Monolith showed himself. Unlike the destrier, he had submerged himself in the stone of the ravine wall. Without warning, he simply walked out of it, much to the Qaherans' consternation. A few Qaherans cried out in alarm.

"Don't worry—he's our friend," said Kiril.

The elemental noble bowed low to the dumbfounded elves, then walked down the ravine, eager to be off.

As they said their good-byes, Essam produced a wide, curved scabbard from his cloak. He said, "Kiril, please accept this, a gift from the Al Qahera."

"A sword? But I already . . ." the swordswoman trailed off. Not too long ago she'd wished for another weapon, one she could draw forth without imperiling her mind and soul, as was the case with Angul.

"This was Feraih's blade, and it carries a minor enchantment. Please use it to strike against whatever killed Feraih, and presumably, Ghanim and Haleem. In this way, Feraih's soul can rest easy."

Kiril, unaccustomed to ceremonial politeness, said, "Thanks." She took the scabbard, and with her other hand pulled out the blade. As she did so, she distinctly felt Angul shift in his scabbard. He wasn't happy about her hand on another sword's hilt, that was clear. She smiled. Too bad.

Essam said, "This blade is called Sadrul, and it is the sharpest blade in the city—so sharp, Feraih once used it to divide a man's dignity from his self-esteem."

"What?"

Essam laughed, "A joke! Heh! But all the same, Sadrul is very sharp. Be careful."

"I will," promised Kiril, "and thank you again. If I can use it to get vengeance for Feraih, I will."

Essam nodded, slapped the side of the destrier in farewell, and turned toward the cave mouth of Al Qahera.

Thormud guided the destrier down the ravine and toward Prince Monolith. Kiril looked back and saw the small group waving at them. Moisture caught in her eyes. What the blood? She was tougher than this. But despite her short stay among the desert elves, she had become, briefly, part of their community. The feeling had been outside her experience for more years than she cared to count—since before Stardeep, really.

She strapped Sadrul to her belt. Angul shifted again and rumbled a note of displeasure.

"Don't worry, lover," she said, reaching back to pat the larger blade's scabbard. "You're still my number-one killer." Angul stirred and grumbled anew, probably objecting to the label "killer" she'd chosen.

Despite her praise, Kiril knew that the next time she needed to solve a problem with sharpened steel, she'd draw Sadrul. If the blade measured up to Essam's claim, it might see more time out of the scabbard than the Blade Cerulean. Until she required Angul's exceptionally potent abilities, he would remain unhappily sheathed.

They topped the ravine. Morning sun blazed across Raurin's wasted plain. Striated dunes stretched away to the north, east, and west. The heat hugged the swordswoman, and fine beads of perspiration immediately broke on her brow.

Monolith thundered forward, his great feet sending up sprays of sand. At the limit of Kiril's perception, on the northern horizon, something flashed and twinkled with reflected light. Something purple.

CHAPTER TWENTY-THREE

Eined Datharathi motioned for the vengeance taker and wizard to pause. They'd already traveled several abandoned, unlighted tunnels, but Eined guided them without indecision, relying on Ususi's light. She whispered, "The new excavation is just ahead, down this passage. Not far beyond is the extraction area for the crystal. You must help me destroy it."

Ususi looked at Iahn. They owed this woman, but they needed "the source of the crystal" to travel back to Deep Imaskar. Iahn gave a slight shrug.

Ususi said, "We'll do what we can, Eined." She hadn't quite lain aside her initial distrust of Eined. While events had done nothing to paint the Datharathi defector as anything but what she claimed, the possibility lurked that she was leading the two Deep Imaskari into a fiendishly designed trap.

Eined nodded and moved forward. They rounded a bend, and Ususi saw ruins. Imaskaran ruins, without a doubt, but older even than the empty outpost where Iahn had first found her.

Crumbling, half-excavated walls of purple stone cast dark shadows in the light of several dazzling magical lanterns. Small outcrops of Nadir crystal glinted here and there, somehow obscene in their excess. Stepped excavations revealed deeper structures in three locations across the cavern floor. One of these was so deep that iron scaffolding fortified the sides of the earthen pit.

"Is this it?" Ususi asked, looking for a sign of the portal. No excavation tools were evident, and indeed, the entire dig gave the impression of having been abandoned months or even years earlier.

"No," said Eined. "If we take that tunnel . . ." her voice faltered as she pointed to one of the many tunnels that branched off the cavern.

A man stood in the shadows, his arms crossed. Ususi blinked—she hadn't seen him arrive. Was this Eined's trap?

"Grandfather," Eined managed before terror smothered her voice.

"Hello. My name is Shaddon Datharathi. You've intruded into my sanctum, my place of business. In the process, you've apparently corrupted the mind of my poor, misguided granddaughter," spoke the man in a dry, piercing tone. His features were shrouded in darkness.

Iahn subtly shifted his weight, preparing to deliver a vicious strike if needed. In a rush, hoping to forestall the vengeance taker for a moment, Ususi said, "We apologize for our sudden appearance. We don't want trouble. We'd like a little help. And we want to help you, too . . ."

"Indeed? You want to help me? In what fashion?" Shaddon sounded amused.

The wizard forged ahead. "I have some bad news to deliver. I'm afraid the crystal you've been retrieving from . . . wherever you've been getting it . . . is infected with something terrible. It has the ability to take over the minds of those who wear it. Even people who simply remain in contact with unworked crystal too long may be at risk." Ususi shivered, thinking back to the Celestial Nadir shards embedded in the shadow efts on the ship.

"Really?" The man sounded surprised, then stepped forward into the brightness of the chamber.

The light of a dozen torches flashed and twinkled off his crystalline face. For all Ususi could guess, Shaddon was completely sheathed in the stuff.

Shaddon said, "That doesn't bode well for my health, does it?"

Eined gasped. Ususi put a hand to her mouth. Even Iahn seemed taken aback. In his stoic fashion, he blinked.

"Don't worry, you strangers who've appeared out of the blue to kindheartedly warn me of the shortfalls of the plangent program. I know something of the 'infection' of which you speak."

"Then why haven't you closed the mine—and with it, the Body Shop?" demanded Eined.

Shaddon laughed.

"Because," guessed Ususi, "Shaddon himself is the source of the infection. He can influence the minds of those closely associated with the crystal." But even as she said it, she wondered.

Ususi continued. "Which means you've been aware of us for days, as we approached Vaelan, then took the ship across the Golden Water—you've been attacking us!"

The man appeared genuinely surprised. "You think I've been attacking you?"

"You deny you can influence those with prostheses you install?"

"Can't deny it," said Shaddon, grinning, his crystal face

deforming as if flesh. "I know the secret of branding each crystal I make so it serves as a conduit for persuasion. My influence is strong with everyone who possesses the enhanced abilities of a plangent. In fact, I can do more than merely influence. But, sadly, I'm not the only one who can access the crystal conduits I've fashioned."

"Who else? Xaemar? Zeltaebar?" demanded Eined.

"No. Unless you're lying," he told Ususi, "the creature that watched you, for reasons I'd like to discover, is called Pandorym." Shaddon shuddered slightly when he said the name.

The vengeance taker shot a look at the wizard and said, "That name was used by one of the creatures that hunted you before I slew it. I forgot it spoke that name until just now."

Ususi cocked her head. Pandorym . . . Pandorym. The name was familiar. Something she'd read about long ago, something to do with ancient Imaskar. Then she had it. Her eyes widened. Of course, Pandorym was one of the first subjects she'd studied before she bypassed the Great Seal of her hidden city. Like many ancient, fell magics, Pandorym was supposedly stored safely in the Celestial Nadir. It was one of the things she'd researched so she could steer clear of the creature's cage, should she stumble upon it during her quest.

"Ususi," pressed Iahn, "do you recognize the name?"

"Yes," she replied.

Shaddon took a step forward, strangely intent on the wizard. He said, "I could be destroyed for even asking this—but tell me more. Quick!" He glanced back down the cavern he had come through. Ususi caught some faint sounds, like glass shattering and distant yells, but perhaps she was mistaken. She let her memory of the tome she'd found in the Purple Library swim before her eyes.

"Pandorym is the name of a doomsday weapon of sorts, a prototype entity conscripted out of desperation by the ancient Imaskari," said Ususi. "At least, so the records indicate in the Purple Library. It was designed solely as a deterrent, but a deterrent so potent it would give pause even to deities bent on vengeance."

"Why vengeance?" wondered Eined.

"Nothing stirs the gods' wrath like the wholesale enslavement of their believers. Which is exactly what the ancient Imaskari were guilty of. They needed labor to support their expanding civilization. The wronged gods' world-shaking anger exposed the Imaskari Empire to divine retribution. Thus, the Imaskari prepared their deterrent—Pandorym."

"What is Pandorym?" demanded Shaddon, moving a step forward. The crystal on his face, as well as more crystal apparently hidden under his clothes, began to gleam.

"I don't know exactly what it was. Is. Like I said, the records, what I can remember of them, claimed Pandorym was a deterrent. Like all deterrents, they believed Pandorym would never be used. Or possibly—I'm not sure—he was too potent to be controlled."

"But they eventually unleashed Pandorym, is that right?" said Shaddon, his crystal eye blazing with intensity.

"No. They didn't have the opportunity. True, Imaskar's ruins litter the empty places of the world. However, it was not Pandorym that brought them low—the Imaskari were never given the chance to offer détente. The raging gods and their empowered champions among the enslaved ended the Imaskari reign before the threat of the Pandorym doomsday entity was ever made. All their plans, weapons, and desperate schemes came to naught."

"But Pandorym is loose now," insisted Shaddon. "It is in the crystal. It reaches out through the new crystal I use for artificial limbs and organs!"

Ususi looked at him. "How did you find the crystal?"

"I found bits of it here in these caves. But a while back, I found an inactive portal to a nether space. After a few years of examination, I forced open the portal and discovered a demiplane of great age. In this space was a massive tower of ancient construction, cold and dead. I also discovered a mother lode of the purest crystal, which I've been putting to use ever since."

A great crash and the faint sound of a distant, roaring wind issued from the tunnel behind Shaddon.

Ignoring these noises, Ususi addressed the elder Datharathi. "You fool! The portal to this 'nether space' of yours—where is it? You have unstoppered Pandorym, who was held safely for millennia!"

The crystal-faced man only muttered, "I wonder . . ."

"Grandfather, is it true? Is all this your fault? Have you done this willingly?" yelled Eined. She rushed forward, one hand raised in either accusation or anger.

Shaddon pointed a gloved finger at his granddaughter, as if to gainsay her question. Instead, a slender ribbon of darkness burst from it and struck Eined in the chest. She gasped, surprise turning to horror. She fell, sprawling to the ground.

The vengeance taker rushed forward and swung his dragonfly blade at Shaddon. The crystal-covered man swayed back, just beyond the arc traced through the air by the blade's tip. Shaddon pointed his finger again, this time at Iahn. The vengeance taker simultaneously raised his own hand, and with a mumbled syllable of warding, shredded another dark ribbon into so many threads.

The sound of the wind escalated in the corridor beyond, then suddenly fell to nothing.

"Shaddon," yelled the wizard into the sudden quiet, "why must we fight? We . . ."

An icy breeze froze the words in Ususi's mouth. The crystal that sheathed Shaddon's face no longer glowed violet—it became a mask of utter night. Black vapor streamed away from Shaddon's body like the sun's corona, if the sun had been a source of darkness instead of light.

A lifeless voice rumbled, "I recognize you, Imaskari scions. I will be revenged upon you." The words were an archaic form of the Imaskaran tongue that Ususi had assumed was remembered only behind the Great Seal.

The wizard stumbled back, her hands already tracing the outlines of a powerful ward. As she did so, she asked, "Why?"

"It must be so," thundered the terrible voice. The blot of darkness that obscured Shaddon's form swelled. "Your bloodline is Imaskaran. Imaskari remnants will be expunged first. Imaskar will fall. I will take the keystone you carry."

Ususi finished her spell, and a blue glow took up residence on her skin and garments—the telltale sign of protective magic. She edged over to where Eined lay and touched the woman. She could pass the protective glamour to any living creature.

The glow did not pass from the wizard's finger into Eined.

Shaddon, or Pandorym, had killed her.

Ususi stood and said, "I won't give a monster like you anything!"

"I do not ask."

The possessed form of Shaddon stretched its arms to both sides. From every finger, dozens of umbral ribbons burst and swirled through the air at Ususi.

The strands, in the hundreds, fell upon her glittering blue aura and broke. But her aura's potency was halved, as shown by the weakening of its glow. Where each ribbon had grazed the ward and shattered beyond its radius, lingering coolness pressed on Ususi's skin, promising worse with Shaddon's next salvo.

Iahn appeared behind Shaddon. The vengeance taker stabbed his drawn blade deep into the darkness shrouding the elder Datharathi. The form in the center of the thickening cloud jittered, then spun around with blinding speed, one arm extended wide. As Shaddon completed his spin, one hand lashed out like a scything blade, trying to catch the vengeance taker across the throat. Iahn deflected the blow along the flat of his dragonfly blade, but the force of the blow knocked the vengeance taker's weapon spinning away.

Shaddon's other hand, closed in a fist, and jabbed with the speed of an adder. Iahn evaded it with an economical head bob, just as quick. Shaddon's sinews were enhanced with the power summoned by his Celestial Nadir prostheses, but a vengeance taker's abilities drew from years of hard training and sorcery.

Ususi whispered words of ineptitude and hurled them at Shaddon, who absorbed them without flinching. The wizard next traced a sign in the air, but Shaddon evaded the small, whirling vortex that tried to pull him up. She spoke the dark syllables of the Decomposition of Umyatin, but before she could finish, another barrage of wavering black rays fell upon her from one of Shaddon's hands. His other hand connected in a particularly vicious cross to Iahn's left shoulder, just missing his head. The wizard cried out as her protective screen failed, and several thin ribbons chewed through her flesh, thankfully still hardened from the ward she'd erected upon first entering Adama's Tooth. Blood flowed, and she hoped the pain meant only a superficial wound.

Iahn continued to circle and jab with his bare hands, attempting to prevent Shaddon from matching each of the wizard's attacks with a salvo of his own. The elder Datharathi managed to release another barrage against Ususi, but the vengeance taker took advantage of his split attention and assayed a vicious, low-leg sweep. The blow knocked Shaddon's feet from under him, and he clattered to the floor.

Shaddon bounded back to his feet, tangible claws of darkness growing from his fingers, and a mane of ebony fire rimming his brow.

Iahn backpedaled, spoke a single resonant word, and faded from view.

Shaddon intoned, "I see you." The possessed Datharathi waved its burgeoning claws of darkness through empty air and knocked the vengeance taker into view from the mystical angle of space in which he'd hidden. Iahn rolled away from the claws in a smooth tumble toward Ususi. Simultaneous with his roll, the wizard saw the taker deftly open and plunge a finger into his damos. Shaddon turned and advanced upon Ususi, claws clacking and ebony mane dripping malevolent fire. As Iahn finished his roll, she erected a semi-solid wall of ice, hoping to hold Shaddon back long enough for her to devise a better strategy.

She glanced at Iahn. The vengeance taker popped the finger he'd dipped in the damos into his mouth. Ususi gasped, "By the Great Seal!"

Iahn's eyes glazed, his vision fixing on some distant horizon. His head lolled, and he slurred, "One whose flesh is partly crystalline is yet thrall to his mind—and his mind is in thrall to Pandorym. Sever the first connection, and the second connection is for naught. Sever the second connection, and we . . ."

Even as he uttered the last of his warning, his diction improved. Ususi realized the vengeance taker's body was throwing off the poison.

Ice fragments exploded outward as Shaddon clawed through the magical barrier. He spoke. "The keystone will be taken. The keystone . . ."

Ususi uttered a spell to freeze Shaddon's will, its sharp consonants and long vowels buzzing in her throat. The spell took shape and descended upon Shaddon like a stooping hawk. For a heartbeat, then two, Shaddon stood transfixed, his body refusing to act as his mind, or Pandorym's will, directed him.

The reprieve gave Iahn enough time to snatch up his fallen dragonfly blade.

Ususi shouted to the vengeance taker, "Use your damos on him!"

Without answering, Iahn took his blade and shoved it unceremoniously into the unmoving Datharathi's chest, but it failed to penetrate.

The vengeance taker said, "His flesh is completely encased in crystal."

Ususi yelled, "He's struggling against the bonds of my spell—kill him! Use your damos."

Darkness scythed around the transfixed body of Shaddon, swooping and whirling like a murder of crows.

Iahn explained, "I emptied the damos reservoir to see ahead to a future that contained both of us. It'll take a day for the damos to refill. The Voice is not something called on lightly, and doing so has consequences."

"Then forget Shaddon—by the time Pandorym breaks down my spell, we'll be gone. The portal must be this way!" Ususi made a dash toward the tunnel Shaddon had appeared from, but paused.

The still form of Eined lay sprawled in her path. The Datharathi woman's spirit had fled the world, to a place of final freedom Ususi herself had nearly reached when the efts had mauled her. The stars had been so bright. . . .

Iahn saw Ususi's hesitation and sheathed his dragonfly blade on his left hip. He stooped, grabbed the girl, and threw her limp body over his shoulder. Without visible effort, he ran past Ususi down the corridor. Wiping a tear from her cheek, Ususi followed.

The vengeance taker ignored the side passages. Unearthly screeches pealed from one dark opening, and a venomous glow leaked from another. But the main passage was clear, and soon enough emptied into another large cavern. This grotto was the site of some sort of recent disaster. A pile of broken wooden tables, the wreckage of expensive equipment, and a variety of other debris left a whorled trail of destruction across the floor. A woman lay at the spiral's epicenter, unmoving. Crystal implants were visible on her body. Some creature or force had apparently removed the woman's head.

Ususi turned and saw the menhir ring. Her heart leaped! The ring was a duplicate of the Mucklestones of the Lethyr Forest, which meant . . .

"There! A portal into the Celestial Nadir," the wizard breathed.

The bright, unwavering lights on the cavern's periphery failed to illuminate the ring's interior.

"Careful," the wizard told Iahn as he moved toward a gap between two stones, "it's open. Even without a keystone, they've managed to access the Celestial Nadir."

The vengeance taker nodded and stepped through. Ususi followed.

CHAPTER TWENTY-FOUR

The sun burned a hole in the sky. Whisky burned Kiril's throat and warmed a path to her stomach.

A slender tower reached toward the heavens as they galloped across the scorched dunes, raising a line of dust in their wake.

Sweat stung the elf's eyes, but she resisted rubbing them. She could clearly see the splinter for the first time. The shard towered a mile or more into the sand-hazed sky.

"Blood!" she cursed. Kiril took another swig, then holstered her flask.

The stone destrier ate up the wasteland miles, swelling the tower's silhouette to an improbable height. The geomancer dozed at Kiril's side. He was strapped into place, lest he roll off in his daze. He woke now and then to look at the splinter, mumble something half lucidly, then fall back into a fitful sleep. His curse-born illness had resurged. The dwarf's energy failed by the moment. Ahead, the booming sound of Prince Monolith's strides seemed to count the heartbeats remaining to the dwarf.

"Hells and blood," muttered the elf.

They reached the base of the splinter in the late afternoon. Vast and imposing, many-windowed and sprouting hundreds of secondary spires, Kiril could see for herself that the edifice was not an unworked fragment carved off some larger chunk of purplish stone. It was an enormous artifact of some previous era, worked by hands and minds informed with skill now unrivaled in the world. Hundreds of balconies, balustrades, verandas, spiraling stairs, and sealed doorways dotted the great tower's sides, all empty and silent. Drifts of sand and rust stains spoke of metal fixtures that had entirely dissolved.

The lowest visible balcony was a good two or three hundred paces above the desert floor. Below it were sheer-sided tower walls as seamless and slick as an ice cliff. Kiril knew some dwarves and humans possessed great skill in climbing sheer rock or ice, but they weren't along, nor was any of the elaborate equipment such a climb required.

The prince raised one hand and pressed it against the side of the purplish stone. "It rebuffs me," reported Prince Monolith. "I cannot force an entry."

"Do you know who built it?" blurted Kiril. She recalled the fantastic glassy architecture of her own star elf heritage. This stone tower rivaled even the most fantastic glass fortresses of Sildëyuir in its size and imposing impregnability.

"Thormud could answer that question." Monolith turned and strode back to the destrier. The elemental lord removed the dwarf from the destrier's back. He held Thormud in his massive hands. He exhaled long and hard, and golden motes of light danced from the elemental lord's open mouth to settle on the geomancer's beard and face.

The dwarf opened his eyes. They were clear again. Thormud looked up at the prince, "Thanks for that, old friend."

"It is only a reprieve, I'm afraid," said Monolith.

The dwarf nodded. "Then you'd better set me down."

The elemental obliged. Thormud pulled from his belt his selenite rod, and smiled. He nearly seemed his old self in that instant.

The swordswoman asked, "A reprieve? What does that mean?"

Thormud ignored her and approached the vast tower. In a manner not dissimilar to Prince Monolith's earlier pose, the dwarf pressed his palm flat against the stone.

"The stone was worked over five thousand years ago," Monolith offered.

Thormud nodded and closed his eyes. In his hand, the moon rod began to shed its silvery radiance. The geomancer worked his slow, telluric magic.

The sun began sinking. The tower's shadow stretched across the barren plain, farther than Kiril's eyes could follow. Jagged peaks reached up well beyond the horizon—the Giant's Belt, of course. She marveled at the distance they'd covered in just a few days.

She looked at the dwarf's stocky figure. She doubted anything could keep the plucky geomancer down for long. Whatever malaise or curse he'd picked up tracking the tower's location, she was confident they'd find an antidote once they gained the tower's interior.

A grumbling tremble from Angul's sheath suddenly reminded her that not all stories have such happy endings. She groped for her flask.

Before long, Thormud's eyes popped open and he stepped back from the tower's base. "It's Imaskari built, if anyone had any doubts. If my ability to speak to stone has not failed me altogether, it is the Palace of the Purple Emperor itself."

"Truly?" spoke Monolith, impressed for the first time Kiril could recall.

"Yes. Back from a long, profound slumber in a dark space, the stone tells me."

"Hold on," interrupted Kiril. "What's the Palace of the Purple Emperor?"

"It marks . . . marked . . . the Imaskaran capital, Inupras."

Kiril looked around. "Seems out of place here."

"It hasn't been here for thousands of years. Inupras may well be buried in the sands of time below us, but the palace has spent the centuries elsewhere."

"Where?"

Thormud shrugged. "Some phantom space engineered by the absent Imaskari, no doubt. The Imaskari excelled at such things. Indeed, the palace itself was said to be ten times bigger inside than on the outside, hiding hundreds of dimensional halls, vaults, and arcane chambers. Including the Great Imperial Library."

"It's already so big."

"Stories are sometimes exaggerated," said the dwarf. He shrugged again. "What is most important for us right now is to get inside and make our way to the Imperial Weapons Cache. Something dark has been disturbed in the heart of the palace."

"What are we looking for?"

"That which has seen and cursed me. A weapon left over from the last Imaskaran war, the stone says. Something never used, thankfully."

The dwarf stepped back a pace from the blank surface of the palace wall. "What ever disturbed the weapon has partially deployed it."

Kiril asked, "How can a weapon be partially deployed?"

The geomancer began tracing a great circle on the face of the palace wall with the tip of his moon rod. As he did so he said, "The weapon isn't an object—it is an entity. An entity with power approaching that of a god, with both a physical and mental presence. Even when held in physical captivity, the psychic component may roam. Given the chance, it may infect surrounding matter. Some portion of the psychic component of this entity has been freed."

A frisson of familiarity jolted Kiril. She was familiar with something like this. She'd spent years as a keeper in Stardeep, where the heinous traitor was guarded. A conspirator whose overweening ambitions threatened all the star elf race, and more. A bastard who'd taken from her the only thing she'd ever loved, and left her with nothing but a cruel burden to bear. That was the reason she carried Angul.

Thormud continued. "The stone of the palace is enchanted to rebuff just this sort of contamination—the Imaskari performed a lot of dangerous experiments here. But the space where the palace spent these last millennia is not so impregnable."

"I know of this space," interjected Monolith. "It is a demiplane that grows without bound. Full of mischief. My brethren seek to close the portals that open in the earth. Yet portals persist."

The dwarf nodded. "Somewhere, somehow, a portal has been accessed. The Imaskaran Imperial Weapons Cache was disturbed. A vile cognizance was awakened. That cognizance instigated the palace's fall back into reality. Hold on."

The dwarf finished tracing his circle and began to elaborate on the design with quickly scribed sigils beyond the radius of the ring.

Thormud continued. "I infer from the stone's description that the entity was able to return the palace to reality because of the introduction and spread of infected crystal into our realm."

"The crystal that infused the creatures we fought!" exclaimed Kiril.

"Yes. Whoever holds a piece of infected crystal serves

as an eye—and worse—a conduit to the entity's power and desires."

"This entity—what is its name and origin?" rumbled Prince Monolith.

"Pandorym," replied the dwarf. As he spoke the name, the glow surrounding Thormud's selenite rod dimmed and the geomancer clutched his side.

Kiril rushed to support him, but the dwarf waved her away. "Don't worry about me. Just listen. The mineral memory does not know the entity's origin—I imagine it was plucked from some chaotic prototype reality by the Imaskari. Or perhaps it is the result of risky arcanological research. In any event . . ."

The dwarf made one final inscription with the butt of his rod, then stood back. "I can open a passage into the tower. The opening will persist only a few moments. Once inside, I recommend you both head upward. My connection with the palace stone informs me of a central stair. At the top of the stair is the Imperial Weapons Cache."

"What do you mean, 'you both'? What about you?" questioned Kiril.

The geomancer looked at the elf and shook his head. "Listen to me, Kiril. I've got only a few moments of consciousness left. Some influence of Pandor—"

The dwarf flinched, then continued. "The entity's curse has got its claws into me. I carried an infected crystal for too long, and during my previous divination, it saw me. If I enter, it will know instantly and send all the servitors it is assembling throughout the tower to contest my presence. I must wait here."

"But you're sick," protested the elf. She knew better than to argue. Thormud had that look. When the dwarf's eyes glinted so stubbornly, there was no quarreling. Kiril knew from long experience that even venomous cursing wouldn't dissuade him when he'd set his mind to something.

"I'd be struck down within moments if I were to enter.

Better I take my chances out here than suffer the certainty of my fate in there. It falls to you, Kiril. You and Prince Monolith." The earth lord nodded.

"Enter the cache and secure the weapon. If you don't, I'm afraid that its influence will continue to grow. When its influence waxes through enough intermediaries, it'll free more than its mind. Then it won't have to rely on servants any longer."

"What shape will its body take, I wonder?" growled Monolith.

"Nothing we would want to see," answered Thormud. "Ready yourselves. I am opening the passage . . . *now!*"

The geomancer threw his moon rod at the circle he'd scribed on the wall. The milky jewel on the rod's tip struck the rock head on and exploded in a dazzling flash of iridescent light. Cool, stale air rushed from the gap.

Thormud fell to the sand, unmoving.

Prince Monolith scooped up Kiril as she bent to check on Thormud. She blistered his ears, "Let me down, you bastard of a pebble! You bloody dust mote, I'll hew you down to size! I'll . . ."

The elemental, uncaring, bore her and itself through the opening. A moment later, the passage sealed behind them and all light was extinguished. The prince lowered her to the floor. She managed to keep her feet as he placed her on solid ground.

Kiril railed at the earth lord. "He could be dead! Why didn't you let me help him?"

Monolith didn't respond. Kiril couldn't see him in the utter dark, but she could sense his presence. She pounded a balled fist onto his stone-hard chest.

The elemental rumbled, "His fate isn't decided yet. But if we don't win, he'll certainly die."

"You heartless rock!"

Monolith's deep voice descended further. "I've known Thormud far longer than you. Stop acting the child."

"Blood!" she cursed, then subsided. "Just bloody fine." Kiril blinked away red stars of anger, leaving darkness so complete it bored into her eyes. "I can't see," she mumbled. She knew Monolith was right. A tantrum wouldn't do anything but make her feel better for a few loud moments.

Faint light seeped into the air. Xet was emanating a dim glow.

"Why aren't you with Thormud?" Kiril screamed at the creature.

"Thormud sent Xet with us, to guide us to the chamber where we'll find the source of his affliction. Xet comes along, maybe to save its master's life."

Xet cawed a series of forlorn chimes.

The swordswoman fumed impotently.

The crystalline dragonet glittered no more brightly than a star set high in the night sky. The gleam was more than sufficient for Kiril's eyes—she preferred starlight to daylight. But Xet's illumination was unsettling. It meant the geomancer was all alone.

The light revealed a bare space shod in rusted iron. The floor and walls were dull and bare, and the high ceiling and narrow passage reminded Kiril of some long-deserted catacomb. Waterlines were visible on the powdery red walls at just about the tip of Kiril's reach. She bent down and touched the floor. It was bone dry. Whatever liquid had once passed this way hadn't flowed in eons. She hoped their presence wouldn't change that.

The passage sloped upward to her left, but the grade was almost undetectable.

"This way?" she asked, pointing up the gradual slope. "Not really a stairwell, but it slopes up."

Xet pealed in the affirmative and flew ahead.

Kiril unsheathed Sadrul, the gift of Al Qahera. The razor-sharp blade glittered in Xet's glow. Angul, still in his sheath, groused.

Kiril paused and said, "I ask the gods of Sildëyuir to

watch over my friend Thormud. See him through to safety."

See to it, if my past service and sacrifice meant anything at all, she silently added.

A long journey in the dark was thus begun.

CHAPTER TWENTY-FIVE

Chill air brushed Warian Datharathi. He cried out and fell on his face. His prosthesis went dead and its light failed. He gasped for breath. He felt as if he'd just finished a sprint where he pushed himself too hard. Yet his arm hadn't killed him . . .

Coughing and shaking, he pushed himself onto his hands and knees. Where was he?

Darkness was all he saw . . . and a broad ribbon of stone knifing through it. Stars settled into focus above him . . . and below? Vertigo tumbled his stomach.

He blinked. Unconsciously, his fingers tried to work themselves into the hard rock, abrading the fingertips of his natural hand. It was the stone of a great obelisk, similar to one of the menhirs that ringed the portal through which he'd plunged. But this menhir was wider. And much, much longer, like a path. Or a bridge, over nothingness.

The stone path traced an unwavering line as far as he could see—which was unnaturally far. Illumination leaked onto the path from an undefinable source, making a road of light through a sea of blackness scattered with tiny glimmers.

Warian crawled forward and peered over the side. Void beckoned in all directions. From what he could see, if he fell, he'd never find the ground, only endless, vacant space.

Wait. No, it wasn't quite empty. He spied a mote of radiance below. The mote . . . it was actually a dimly lit chunk of stone dozens of paces across—an island in a sea of night. Demolished walls of a templelike ruin gaped up at him from the isle. Light leaked from the temple walls, twinkling with witchlight. The entire edifice receded as he watched it. Gazing around the vast space, he noted tiny flickers of light in every direction, all moving along seemingly random paths.

"What is this place?" he asked aloud. He was having difficulty processing a vista so far outside his experience.

Too tired to stand, he shambled on hands and knees to see what might lie behind him.

He was at a nexus of three paths. The one he'd first gazed down apparently had no end. The second was long, miles long maybe, and seemed to plunge into a wavering, colored curtain.

But the third path seized his attention. The third stone road ran for only a few hundred paces, then connected to a massive, irregular boulder. Crystal encrusted the third path in a lattice of purplish mineral. Warian was reminded of the inside of a geode. He held out his false arm and compared. It was a match.

The encrustations gradually thickened along the third path as it approached the massive chunk of strangely shaped stone. The path was a gradient leading toward the heart of the lode, he supposed. The encrusted surface of the path had been half cleared, mined away.

The crystal that remained on the road's surface was scarred, broken, and littered with sparkling dust and debris. A battered wagon was parked a dozen or so paces down the path. Shovels, tamping poles, pickaxes, and other mining tools lay haphazardly scattered on the road.

Where were the miners? Did they fall?

His eyes narrowed as he studied the irregular shape at the path's end. It looked like a giant egg that someone had cracked. The glint of pure crystal sparkled along the seams.

No doubt about it—this was Shaddon's new lode.

Screaming, Zel fell out of nowhere and landed on the stone path. His iron pry bar clattered nearby, almost bouncing off the road.

Had Warian been standing, he probably would have fallen from the path. As it was, his heart jolted and doubled its rate.

Zel landed on the path, yelling, and scrabbled along the stone as if he couldn't figure out which direction was down. Just like Warian had fumbled and groped before he got his bearings.

"Hey! Uncle, calm down!" He suppressed a chuckle and grabbed for one of Zel's hands. "If you keep this up, you'll knock us both off. Stop it!"

"Warian!" Zel ceased his mad antics, blinked, then grabbed his nephew by the shoulders. "By the four dooms, I'm glad to see you!"

"What happened? I had your arm. Why didn't we appear in this crazy place at the same time?

"Don't know. You were pulling me along against the . . . the . . . Sevaera's whirlwind. Then you disappeared as you passed into the ring. I almost got sucked back into Sevaera's damned maw. But after you disappeared, she let up. I followed you."

Warian nodded. "Sorry I left you behind. I've never been through one of these before. I don't really understand it. Speaking of which, I don't see a way to go back through from this side."

"Who'd want to? She's waiting back there. Hey," Zel looked closely at Warian. "How're you? You look beat."

Warian was bone tired, true. But not as exhausted as he'd feared after using his arm. Figuring out how to ration the prosthesis's energy had saved his life, he was sure. "I've been worse."

Assisting each other, they both stood.

"Why did she stop after I went through the ring?" wondered Warian.

"She, or whatever was in her, doesn't care one whit about me. You seem to be the prize, Nephew."

Warian rubbed his forehead. "My arm. It's immune to the control that Shaddon has over everyone else with Datharathi prosthetics."

"Shaddon, and that thing that had Sevaera."

Warian nodded.

"Another thing I don't understand," said Zel, "is this place. Isn't this where the controlling entity comes from? We might have gone from the cauldron straight into the fire, but it really doesn't seem too bad here. Yet. . . ."

Zel's eyes widened as he took the time to gaze around the emptiness that stretched without limit in every direction.

The air was sharp and cold, like the air just before dawn, but not damp. A faint odor tickled Warian's nose, like the smell after a thunderstorm. But mixed in was the smell of something rotten, closer. Something had died near them, and recently.

Warian pointed out floating motes of earth and stone as they drifted all around. Most contained disintegrating constructions.

"Amazing! Isn't this amazing? I've never seen anything like this. It's incredible!" Zel forgot about their predicament as the floating ruinscapes captured his imagination.

"See that one?" Zel pointed. A perfect cube, each face a mirror, tumbled through the darkness, tracking a path from nowhere to oblivion. "I wonder what's inside? Treasure of some sort, eh?" Zel chuckled.

"Now that's an odd one." Warian's uncle jabbed his finger into the void. Distant lights reflected on the shimmering, fluctuating surface of a misplaced lake. Lapping, splashing waves on the surface were faintly audible as the globule sailed high overhead and away again.

"Zel—"

"Better not mess with *that* one!" crowed Zel, his finger finding yet another object. A slab of transparent glass about twenty paces long and half as wide tumbled below them. As it spun, Warian caught a sudden whiff of carrion, different from the rotten odor he'd smelled earlier. Caught in the slab's center, like a fly in amber, was a monstrous humanoid creature apparently formed of moist earth. Its legs were short and thick, and its arms tapered to bony claws. Teeth, rotting scraps of cloth, and bone shards protruded here and there from the muddy flesh. A dirt-encrusted skull provided the creature with a leering grin. The slab whirled away into the dark.

Warian grabbed his uncle's shoulder to get his attention. "We should get out of here before Sevaera, or whatever's riding her, decides to come through."

"Aye, I suppose. Hey, look!" Zel pointed along the path in the direction of the wavering curtain Warian had seen when he'd first arrived.

"Uncle!" Warian recalled that Zeltaebar's reputation for exasperating dillydallying was well earned.

Zel said, "No, no . . . I see something, something important. Sort of looks like a spire. A tower, maybe? But it's all hazy, like I'm seeing it through water."

Warian followed his uncle's gaze down the path. He suddenly realized that the wavering curtain wasn't completely opaque.

A grand tower wavered and danced as if behind a heat shimmer, as if it were a mirage. The stone road arrowed for miles across the dark, directly into an elegantly arched gallery that protruded from the half-real structure.

Hundreds of secondary spires rose from the enormous, many-windowed edifice. Terraces, outside galleries, open stairs, and sealed doorways studded the structure's sides, barely visible through the shimmering veil. The base of the tower fell into invisibility far below.

"Do you think that's where the chief puppeteer lives?" wondered Zel.

"Yeah."

"Maybe Sevaera didn't follow because she didn't have to. Whatever possessed her lives there." Zel pointed at the shimmering behemoth.

"Possibly."

They gazed at the vast structure and the narrow path that led toward it.

Warian looked the other way, hoping to spy something that would offer better hope. In one direction, the stone path plunged onward, span after span, narrowing across the leagues to a single point—a point that appeared to promise eternity.

The other route, encrusted with crystal, led only to the nearby blob of dark stone, with its cracks revealing the crystal riches inside.

"Maybe we should check out the jumbo geode first." Zel rubbed his hands and picked up the iron bar he'd carried with him through the portal. After a moment's consideration, he dropped the bar and took up an abandoned pickaxe instead.

"This stuff is pretty valuable. We wouldn't have to make artificial parts out of it," he said, and walked toward the cart and scattering of tools. "Phew, something really stinks over . . . oh."

Warian walked cautiously down the path, across the mined-out crystal.

The source of the rotting odor lay in the mining cart.

A half-orc was stuffed into the cart, obviously dead. The half-orc wore miner's dungarees, and its hoary skin was filthy with dirt and crystal dust. Warian was startled when he saw a crystal pendant hanging around the orc's neck. Burn marks scorched the flesh around the crystal, as if it had overheated and cooked the orc completely through. Then Warian realized that the crystal itself seemed charred, and was obviously cracked. He gazed intently at it, but could detect no glimmer of light swimming in the pendant's depths.

"I can't figure what killed him," Zel said, his hands on his hips as he gazed into the open cart.

"His amulet."

"Aye, that's obvious. I mean, why?"

Warian shrugged, at a loss. "Maybe the 'puppeteer,' as you put it, couldn't control the miner well enough without a prosthesis, and just killed him with some sort of magical overload."

"Is that possible?"

"How should I know?" Warian kicked at the cart. "I don't know how Shaddon—or the puppeteer—is able to control people through Datharathi crystal." Warian froze for a moment. A worrying thought struck him as his eyes skimmed the fields of mined and virgin crystal that encrusted the stone road.

"Uncle, why aren't we dead?"

"Because we're smart, we're quick, and . . ."

"No, look! Crystal everywhere—the perfect vessel for controlling minds, right? We've seen that it only manifests in this damned stuff." Warian waved his hand down the stone lane, thickly encrusted with the pernicious material.

Zel rubbed his chin. "Well, you have an arm made of it, and so far you seem to be immune to its influence . . ."

"Yes. Shaddon made it before he found the portal. I just assumed that all the crystal on this side of the portal was corrupt."

Zel shook his head. "Maybe only if it's brought into the real world?"

"I wonder."

He thought about Shaddon's claims. "Or, maybe the crystal must be prepared in a particular fashion—and my arm wasn't. Nor is this raw crystal. It hasn't been mined and worked by Shaddon, who made it susceptible to outside influence so he could serve his own purposes."

"Could be. Or perhaps the puppeteer is just toying with us." Zel peered down the path where the crystal gradually thickened to form the irregular bulb of cracked stone.

Warian looked back and forth between the irregular boulder and the wavering tower. Out of nowhere, a searing flash dazzled his eyes.

" . . . *eretu dmaadar grethalsa od favara!*" a loathsome voice broke upon them.

Blinking, Warian looked ahead, behind—and then up.

Sevaera's head, sans body, floated above them, dripping blood. It was nestled in a penumbra of writhing shadow. The puppeteer had killed Sevaera and was using her head as a malefic vehicle.

"No . . ." pleaded Zel, his jaw dropping open.

The despicable voice repeated its imperative in a language unfamiliar to Warian, then swooped.

Warian lifted his crystal arm to cover his face. He tried desperately to trigger its latent power. And he failed. He was too drained—he couldn't forge the link!

The disembodied head swooped and butted Warian in the chest. A sledgehammer couldn't have struck harder. Warian pitched sideways off the path, his body twisting in midair, his arms flailing for a grip. He caught himself on the edge, the crystal digits on his right hand more hindrance than help. The flesh and blood of his left hand absorbed the cruel sharpness of the ledge. The weight of his body threatened to peel his fingers from their purchase.

He looked up, but the stone path blocked his view of what

was happening above him. But he could hear.

Zel cursed, repeating "bastard!" over and over in a crazed voice. He heard the sound of metal on bone—had his uncle connected with his pickaxe?

"Draka ni dornu dmaadar!" screamed the vile voice, just out of sight.

"Bastard!" his uncle yelled again. His pinched, manic tone implied a break with sanity that wouldn't come as much of a surprise.

Warian strained, trying to pull himself up.

A finger slipped. It was all he could do to hold on.

"Zel," he cried. "Kill it!" And "Help, I'm slipping!"

Another flash dazzled Warian. Something else had come through the portal.

CHAPTER TWENTY-SIX

The eternal, mote-littered dark welcomed Ususi after a long absence. The Celestial Nadir once again accepted her into its twilight vastness.

The wizard fell a few paces through an awkwardly defined portal focus. She nearly tripped on Eined's limp form. Iahn must have dropped her. She saw him streaking toward a small flying creature wreathed in darkness. Another man she didn't recognize stood near the flying creature, swinging wildly at it with a pickaxe.

She was thankful that the misdirected focus was displaced upward, not left or right, off the path. Otherwise, instead of standing at the center of a three-way nexus, she might be flailing her way through a tour of the abyssal spaces of the Celestial Nadir.

Ususi pulled out the keystone and issued a word

of command. It lit with a violet radiance. For the first time in a long time, the wizard smiled.

Here in the Celestial Nadir, keystone in hand, she possessed a measure of authority over the crystal denied her outside the artificial space. This was a good time to measure her control against that flying creature, which had turned its back on the man with the pickaxe to deal with the charging vengeance taker. The flying creature looked like . . . a severed head! Ususi gasped.

It was the missing head from the woman on the other side of the portal! The head was partly sheathed in Celestial Nadir crystal. Ususi raised the thong on which the keystone dangled, and concentrated.

The keystone pulsed once, twice, thrice. A single flash burst in the crystal sheathing of the head. It screeched and shot straight upward at least fifty paces. In the Imaskaran tongue, it screamed, "Use not the keystone against what I have claimed!"

Ususi called up, "Try to stop me!"

It swooped down at her, leaving a meteor green streak across the dark. A corona like flowing hair, shadows given fell substance, writhed with soul-shearing hunger.

She concentrated again upon the keystone, and gazed with enhanced insight upon her attacker. She blanched. Pandorym's influence was a slimy tentacle of putrid will that reached from far away to grasp and hold up the head, and empower it. It was a stain of something that should not exist, reaching from somewhere not far along one of the paths of the nearby nexus.

Nausea accompanied her recognition of the psychic pseudopod, but she tried to force the tentacle to release its grip on the head. It was like trying to peel an orange made of granite. She concentrated harder. A trickle of blood dripped from Ususi's left eye.

To no avail. The grip of the tentaclelike thread of influence had its roots too deep in the crystal-sheathed head.

"By the Seal Broken!" she cursed. Pandorym had greater control over the crystal than she supposed. She cried out and dived to one side, but was too slow. A slashing ribbon of darkness grazed her shoulder. Pain blazed through her arm and neck.

The wizard retained her hold on the keystone, despite the pain. She concentrated through the ache, determined to prevail. A pulse of clean violet light discharged from the keystone, traced an erratic, dancing path through the air, and buried itself in the severed head. Pandorym's influence prevented her from gaining control over the crystal of the Celestial Nadir, as was her right as holder of the keystone. But she could burn out the crystal implanted in the woman's head.

The head screeched and again shot straight upward. The mane of dark tendrils surrounding it wavered and flailed about. The head's trajectory wobbled and dipped, then steadied itself.

Ususi lanced her will into the keystone and hurled yet another bolt at the head. The blazing energy arc struck true. The limbs of darkness entwining the head winked out.

Her attacker fell out of the air and bounced on the path, coming to rest at Ususi's feet. In an unnerving death spasm, the eyes in the head tracked around, then locked Ususi in their gaze. The mouth worked, and the voice spoke again, diminishing as it uttered its last, "Your hidden city burns. All those dear to you feed the flame . . ."

"What?" screamed the wizard.

Pandorym's presence fled. All that remained was the severed head of a woman unknown to Ususi. She kicked it. "Tell me what you mean!" In her mind's eye, she saw her blind twin, Qari, quailing before the heat of purple flames she couldn't see.

Iahn's hand restrained her from booting the head off the path. He said, "We must go. We've reached the Celestial Nadir. Take us to Deep Imaskar, so we may save our city."

"Indeed. But who's that with the pickaxe? What's he doing?"

A tall, white-haired man who had been brandishing a pickaxe when Iahn and Ususi burst through the portal was now lying on his stomach, his head and arms hanging off the path, straining to reach something Ususi couldn't see.

The man hauled himself backward, and the wizard gasped. A younger man slid upward from where he must have been dangling below the path. She gasped because the newcomer's left arm was pure Celestial Nadir crystal.

"Iahn!" she warned. She raised the keystone again. She could burn the arm out, too, before Pandorym jumped into another vessel.

The vengeance taker was already in motion, moving with a speed no mortal limb could match.

The older man turned, saw the charging vengeance taker, and scrambled for his pickaxe, yelling something Ususi couldn't decipher.

Ususi gazed at the young man with the crystal arm through the lens of the keystone, looking for any clues.

The wizard yelled, "Iahn! Stop!"

She sensed no evidence that the young man's crystal arm had ever been influenced the way the animated head had been. In fact, the prosthetic arm was intangibly linked to the Celestial Nadir in a fashion similar to what she enjoyed through the keystone. But his linkage was more . . . organic. She saw the possibility that the young man might be able to draw strength from the Celestial Nadir, like the plangents could.

"I said stop, Iahn!"

Scowling, the vengeance taker slid to a halt before the two strangers, dragonfly blade in hand. He didn't sink the blade into either of the men's heads, so Ususi considered her command a success.

The younger man yelled, "Are you more servitors of the crystal?" He squinted guardedly at Ususi's keystone and pumped his fist, as if readying himself for some great effort.

"No," Iahn responded.

"No?"

"We are not agents of evil," confirmed Ususi, walking near to them, though she didn't put down the keystone. "We are here to oppose that which has awakened here. I must ask—who are you? Why are you trespassing in the Celestial Nadir?"

"Trespassing?" asked the older man. "This site is under the control of Datharathi Minerals. We've established a mine claim here, no matter the outré landscape. Up until a moment ago, Madam, we were running for our lives." He paused. "I'm Zel. Zel Datharathi. Thank you for dealing with our pursuer."

"You are welcome. But as to your claim—it is invalid. This location isn't open to mineral exploration. This entire realm"—Ususi gestured around at the mote-littered darkness—"is a relic of the ancient Imaskari. As such, it is the property of Imaskar's inheritors. Besides, it's terribly dangerous."

"Yes, we've come to understand that," said the young man, "to our sorrow."

"Did you get your prosthesis at the Body Shop?" asked Ususi, pointing to the crystal arm.

"No. It predates the Body Shop by four or five years. Don't worry—I'm free of the taint these plangents seem to carry."

Ususi nodded. It fit. Only the crystal worked specifically by Shaddon, or touched by Pandorym prior to implantation, seemed to carry the taint. While both her keystone and the young man's arm showed dark filaments in the core, the discoloration appeared to be only an indicator of Pandorym's awakening in the Celestial Nadir, not a sign of influence from that malign entity.

"And who are you?" Ususi asked.

"I'm Warian Datharathi. This is my Uncle Zeltaebar. The

opening into this terrible dimension is my grandfather's fault."

"Is Shaddon your grandfather?" Ususi asked.

Warian nodded. "Did you meet him? He's been . . . subverted by some malignant creature he found in this dark realm. He sold his soul for the sake of gold long ago, but his aspirations for complete power finally consumed him in this enterprise. I've . . . I've never been close to him, not since I was too young to know better."

Zel said, "Actually, no one in our family was particularly close to him. Except for poor Sevaera." He pointed at the head at Ususi's feet. "Her trust in Shaddon led her down a terrible path." His voice caught as he spoke, and he wiped at one eye.

Warian gave a small shake of his head as if attempting to push away an unpleasant thought, then looked back at Ususi. "Who are you? I've traveled the Shining South widely over the last few years, and neither of you are from around there, that's obvious."

"We have a connection to the Imaskari who built this space," responded Ususi. "Whatever your grandfather awoke here, it is a vengeful force that now moves against a refugee population of Imaskar that secreted itself away long ago. Unless we can stop it, that population will be eradicated."

Warian's eyes grew wide. "How's that possible? The Imaskari are long dead. No offense," he finished, looking slightly sheepish.

"We've maintained the secret of our survival for protection," said Ususi, and gestured at herself and Iahn. "Our forebears made many enemies, and we, the children of that great empire, have renounced the imperial dreams that proved only a path to destruction."

Iahn had fixed her with an unflinching glare. The wizard knew why. She'd revealed the existence of surviving Imaskari. But this young man wore a crystal graft embedded in his flesh that wasn't susceptible to Pandorym's manipulation. He could help them, and Deep Imaskar, too.

"Now that Pandorym has attacked us, our existence is no longer a secret. Thankfully, my arrival here in the Celestial Nadir means I can take direct action against the threat."

"Pandorym?" wondered Zel.

"The evil woken by your grandfather is called Pandorym. It is a powerful entity, kept safe and sealed away by the ancient Imaskari for good reason. And . . ."

A far more unpleasant revelation had to be made, and she didn't want to do it. But speed was important, and she felt obligated to tell them before she could ask Warian for aid. Her stomach fluttered as she prepared herself.

"I, um . . ." Ususi stammered, her voice nearly breaking, "what is your relation to Eined Datharathi?"

"She's my sister," said Warian. "Why? Have you seen her?"

Ususi cast down her eyes. She said, "I knew her briefly."

Warian looked past Ususi, to the nexus of the three paths. His hand went to his mouth as he stared, and recognition of what he saw penetrated his soul. He made no sound, but his quivering shoulders communicated a terrible grief.

Iahn helped Warian and Zeltaebar Datharathi prepare Eined for burial.

The boy, Warian, wept quietly as he worked. Zel's eyes were bright with restrained tears and his fingers shook. Neither quailed from what had to be done. The vengeance taker respected them for that stability of character. They'd obviously both been close to the girl, in their own ways. For his part, Iahn was impressed with the strength of personality that had propelled Eined as far as she'd gone, even without martial skill or magical aid. Without her, he and the fugitive wizard would still be casting about for a way to regain Deep Imaskar.

That was their destination, and they needed to move quickly. Ususi had glared at him when he demanded she take them straight to Deep Imaskar. Apparently he'd failed, once again, to observe protocol. He sighed. He recognized that she knew more about Pandorym and what to do about it than he, a strong-arm vengeance taker. She was a wizard, Imaskar-trained. She said they needed Warian's help, and therefore, his good will.

So they aided the young man in paying final respects to his sister. Ususi magically produced rolls of fine white linen for funerary wrapping, along with fragrant oils and a tome titled *The Writ of Adama* the wizard somehow managed to draw from the sunlit world into the lightless artificial void. Ususi's Celestial Nadir expertise, plus her knowledge of spells and sorceries, made her a potent force. Potent enough to deal with Pandorym? The vengeance taker shrugged. Time would tell.

Before long, Eined was fully wrapped and prepared according to the Vaelanites' wishes.

Ususi lit a brilliant magical light over the three paths. They stood around the tiny form that lay at the nexus's center, their heads bowed. Many moments passed.

Warian bent down on one knee. "Good-bye, Sis," he breathed. "I'm . . . I'll miss you . . ." He couldn't finish. In one hand he clutched Eined's blue sash.

Zel stepped forward and laid his hands on Warian's shoulders. He said nothing.

Ususi swallowed. Her eyes glistened. With a taut voice, she said, "The Celestial Nadir has seen its share of burials. The remains of powerful emperors drift within this great dark, in grand mausoleums of granite and crystal. But it is not the style in which our loved ones are given over to the great gulf that matters. It is our memory of the departed and the esteem in which we hold them that lets them live on."

Ususi coughed slightly and continued. "In the short time I knew Eined Datharathi, I found that her character was among the finest and strongest I've known. She was willing to endanger herself to accomplish what she thought was right, and for that willingness, she made the ultimate sacrifice, despite our best efforts to guard her."

Ususi paused, leaned down, and laid her hand on the wrapped figure's forehead for a moment. She straightened, and a tear traced a sudden line down her cheek. She said, "Eined Datharathi's sacrifice in bringing us here, to the Celestial Nadir, could be the difference between the extinction of the rest of her family and its survival. Moreover, had she not risked all to guide us here, Deep Imaskar would have no chance at all for salvation. If we survive to record it, Eined Datharathi's name will be remembered among the greatest heroes of our people."

Iahn squinted slightly, the only outward sign of his consternation. Ususi had broken the law of the Great Seal again by speaking of Deep Imaskar to those who did not dwell there. He hoped he would not bear the burden of imposing discipline on her.

"And," added Zel, "If we survive this, those of us untainted by Shaddon's folly will raise her to the status of family saint, and put her likeness in stone in our hall." Zel squeezed Warian's shoulder again, and the young man bent down to tie Eined's blue sash around her wrapped wrist.

With a gesture from Ususi, the body slid toward the edge of the path. Instead of dropping, it drifted gently into the dark. Iahn noted that the wizard had the keystone clutched in one hand. Ususi's mastery of the Nadir uplifted the wrapped body.

The white form slowly receded. As Eined dwindled, she flared with illumination, taking on the same glow as all the other objects that drifted within the artificial space. The body receeded, growing smaller and smaller, until Eined's light was indistinguishable from the other motes that wafted through the darkness.

She was gone.

With a subtle swing of her head, Ususi gestured Iahn to follow, and they walked a few paces down the stone path. Warian and Zel remained together, gazing into the dark.

The vengeance taker said in a low voice, "A good sendoff."

Ususi said, "Thanks. That was one of the harder things I've had to do." She rubbed her lower lip. Then, "Let's give them a few more moments. Besides, I want to tell you something."

He cocked his head, disliking drama.

"Iahn, I know you want me to create some route that'll connect us immediately to Deep Imaskar. But listen. The source of the attack on our city is close. And unless I miss my guess, it comes from . . ." the wizard pointed down the path that was blocked by a shimmering screen, blurring the image of an incredibly tall fortress tower, ". . . there."

"That fantastic structure, my friend," explained Ususi, "exactly matches a painting hanging in the audience chamber of the lord apprehender."

"I've seen that painting. What is it?"

"The Purple Palace. The ancient seat of the Imaskari Empire."

Iahn blinked. "Incredible."

"A paragon of understatement. Do they train you for such subtlety?" asked Ususi. "Apparently, the entire palace was stored in the Celestial Nadir before the end of the empire. The records in Deep Imaskar assume that the palace remained in the world, buried below the shifting sands of Raurin. Turns out, it's been here all along."

"It does not quite look 'here,' though," commented the vengeance taker.

Ususi's brow furrowed, and she gazed at the structure through the keystone.

Still gazing through the translucent stone, she said, "You're right. It's not. How strange!"

"What?"

"It has slipped into our world! It has returned . . ." Ususi continued to observe the structure through the lens of her keystone, apparently learning additional information through its tiny aperture, ". . . can it be? Yes! It has found its original foundation. But it retains a tenuous link with the Celestial Nadir. The link is Pandorym's influence. Its psyche is entangled with something still here."

"Let me take a stab—is it entangled with that?" Iahn pointed down the path to the great misshapen boulder.

"Difficult to say."

"Then let's find out." The vengeance taker gripped his dragonfly blade, wondering what sort of violence he could bring to bear on such a large rock. Ususi followed him. She said, "Whatever the link, Pandorym remains rooted in the palace. Which makes sense. Some of the creatures it threw at us, like the shadow eft, are remnants of a race that now exists only in the Imperial Weapons Cache. Pandorym must have released and subverted them to its own power. I wonder what else it's released."

Iahn nodded as he studied the great rock, more concerned with it than Ususi's musing for the moment.

The vengeance taker looked to the wizard and saw she was standing some paces back, inspecting the boulder through her keystone. After a few moments, he grew impatient and sheathed his weapon. Then he pulled himself up onto the stone.

With skill acquired during a childhood spent in a gargantuan cavern, he free-climbed the overhanging, bulging rock surface. He easily reached the lowest jagged crack in the boulder's mostly smooth surface.

Iahn was somewhat familiar with geology, thanks to Deep Imaskar's location, and therefore knew a geode was a hollow, spherical rock whose cavity was lined with crystals. Some geodes were completely filled with crystals. Those were called nodules.

Gazing into the crack, Iahn thought this great boulder was completely filled with Celestial Nadir crystal, making it a nodule. But something glimmered at the nodule's center. A palely glowing blot like a luminiferous fungus, or subterranean sea shape . . .

Then . . .

Darkness.

Blowing, howling, damp gloom. Shadows reaching like fingers . . . grasping. Stretching closer. Screaming . . .

Iahn's eyes snapped open. He lay on the path, at the nexus of the three ways. Ususi bent over him, patting his cheek and looking concerned. The two Vaelanites stood nearby, looking useless.

He demanded, "Tell me what happened. I recall . . . a nodule?" Darkness clawed at his brain and was gone again in a flash. He clutched his head.

Ususi said, "You tell us. One moment you were describing how the cavity was filled with agate. Then you screamed and fell fifteen paces without trying to catch yourself. I thought you'd been struck dead, or petrified. Then I heard you mumble about fingers. We dragged you back here. What did you see?"

"Something we need to destroy."

The vengeance taker tottered to his feet. Pain lanced his left shin, and his right shoulder and arm—souvenirs from the fall he couldn't remember, he supposed.

He told them, "Something terrible is caught in that nodule . . . Pandorym, you called it? If we destroy it, we destroy the threat reaching into the world, and into Deep Imaskar." Now who was the loose-lipped one? Didn't matter. His conviction made him reckless.

The one with the crystal arm stepped forward. His eyes were red, and his face tear-streaked. "Yes, let's destroy it!"

"Iahn, Warian, wait. You're only partly right. That husk of stone may—*may*—imprison Pandorym's body, whatever shape it truly possesses. Or it could be some other entity completely unrelated to Pandorym. The Celestial Nadir is filled with such dangerous detritus. Either way, it's important to remember that the body and mind of Pandorym were never kept in the same place—too dangerous."

"Explain," he ordered.

"I described before how Pandorym was a doomsday weapon the Imaskari didn't dare release. They only wanted to threaten Pandorym's release, and thus the entity's psyche was extracted from its physical shell and stored in the Imperial Weapons Cache of the Purple Palace."

Ususi turned to point at the wavering façade of the palace. "Now the psyche has partly freed itself, with Shaddon's help. The mind is the only vulnerable portion of Pandorym. The body, even if that is it, is beyond my ability to affect, even if I use the keystone to scrape away the Celestial Nadir crystal that has scabbed over it. We must go to the palace, find the vessel that once contained Pandorym's psyche, and close it again."

Warian asked, his face flushed, "Since Pandorym has all these servitors, why doesn't it just coerce one into fully releasing it?"

Ususi said, "I'm sure Pandorym's tried that many times. The longer we fail to contain its growing influence, the sooner it will be successful in freeing its mind from the arcane constraints that yet tether it."

Iahn asked, "My duty is to return you to Deep Imaskar so you can stem the incursion. Yet you say our best hope is to enter the Weapons Cache of the Purple Palace instead of returning first to our imperiled city. Will you stake the safety of Deep Imaskar on this course of action?"

"I don't see any other option. If we go to Deep Imaskar to fight whatever else Pandorym has corrupted and freed from the Weapons Cache, we'll be attacking only the symptoms. We must get to the root of the problem and restopper Pandorym's mentality before it does find a way to free its mind and reunite with its physical shell."

The vengeance taker considered Ususi's words. Her assessment was probably correct. He glanced at the irregular nodule.

Darkness flashed again through his thoughts and skittered away. He'd seen something that he'd not soon forget.

"Very well, Ususi," agreed Iahn. "Let's go."

CHAPTER TWENTY-SEVEN

The dragonet's glimmer preceded Kiril and Prince Monolith through the narrow stone corridor. They circled up, up, and up in a gyre whose eventual termination seemed unlikely. The slope was shallow at first, but progressively steepened. Every hundred paces brought them past a sealed arch. Kiril supposed these opened to the tower's core, but each was bricked over with purplish stone. Like the corridor, the sealing stones were scarred and stained by some great drowning years ago.

The monotony was eventually broken by a scattering of cracked bricks that spilled into the corridor. The stones sealed an arch that had partially collapsed—centuries ago, by the look of it. Xet fluttered past the gap in the corridor without slowing.

Kiril paused a moment to peer through the broken masonry.

"Hey, I see light!"

Monolith, bringing up the rear, said, "This tower is too large for us to explore every room, or even every floor. Nor need we, because Thormud provided Xet with a route to our objective."

"What if we stumble on something useful?"

"Leave it be—we have a long way to go."

Kiril sniffed and lingered in the breach to see what she could. The space past the arch was a great foyer, high-beamed and supported by massive columns. Twelve or thirteen pits, each as wide as a human was tall, marred the otherwise smooth floor. Rusted, egglike metallic objects, partly crumpled, dented, or otherwise damaged, plugged all but one of the pits. The open pit was covered with a metallic oval, but it hovered just above the pit, slowly rotating. A pale lavender light shone up from the hole, bathing the rotating egg and glinting off silvery highlights.

"Xet, come here a moment," Kiril instructed. Thormud's familiar chided her with a series of high-pitched bell tones, but flew to her and perched on her shoulder. Thormud must have also commanded the familiar to listen to her orders. Xet wasn't happy about it. Too bad.

With the additional light provided by the dragonet, she could make out the ceiling of the chamber, some forty or fifty paces above the pitted floor. Cavities in the ceiling exactly mirrored those in the floor. A thin streamer of smoke or moisture rose from the top of the single rotating egg, swirling and spiraling toward the ceiling, where it was sucked into an opening. Was each ceiling cavity a chimney?

"What do you suppose . . . ?" began Kiril.

"Come." Monolith put a huge hand on her back, but refrained from pulling her back.

"All right, you damn rock," she consented. She knew he was right: Thormud depended on their swiftness.

Onward.

Walking up the spiraling slope in the darting, flickering light given off by Xet took its toll on Kiril before long. The wavering shadows, unexpected flashes of illumination, and stretches of unrelieved blackness were enough to give Kiril a splitting headache. With her head pounding, she called a rest.

"Hold on," the swordswoman said. "My eyes are throbbing. I need a moment."

Xet bleated, circled in the air twice, and settled to the floor of the passage. Behind her, Monolith said, "Very well."

Kiril sat, leaning her back against the cool wall of the corridor. She held her forehead, then rubbed at her eyes with the heels of her palms, stopping only after she had induced phantom stars. She rested for a while in soothing darkness. As a torch, the swerving, erratic Xet was a failure. The choice was either to stop for a rest from its frenzied illumination, or smash the little dragonet into so many pretty shards. A few moments of darkness and a sip from the verdigris god took the edge off.

She sensed Prince Monolith's disapproval even without opening her eyes. The big rock was too much of a purist. She barked, eyes still closed, "Leave off. Trust me, you'd like me far less without my flask."

The elemental lord's silence felt like further condemnation. She swore, "Blood and fire!" She opened her eyes. Prince Monolith was gone. She'd constructed the entire exchange. Was it guilt? Disgusted, she threw the enchanted flask as hard as she could. It clanged against the opposite wall and toppled to the floor. A thin stream of whisky poured into the corridor. She felt shame at how far she'd tumbled, at how much she depended on that flask. There had been too many drunken nights. And days. Had she held too tightly to the Cerulean Blade? Angul should have remained where he was forged.

She shook away the phantoms and asked, "Where has

that rock gotten to?"

Xet, thinking she commanded it, launched into the air and shot up the corridor in the direction they'd been traveling.

Kiril snatched up the leaking verdigris god and screwed on the top before Xet's light was completely gone. The inexhaustible contents could easily be the genesis of another deluge in the ancient corridor, and she preferred to keep the spirits for herself. She dashed after the retreating light and carefully clipped the flask to her belt as she jogged.

Ahead, Xet's light paled before a new source of illumination. A dim gray glow leaked down the corridor. Kiril pulled Sadrul from its sheath and chased Xet to the corridor's end.

She entered a chamber whose dimensions measured at least a hundred paces in all directions. Slender five-story windows punctured the wall to her right. The wan, gray light pushed into the tower through them. She supposed the windows pierced the tower's exterior, and therefore looked out over the Raurin, but a gauzy haze filled each narrow enclosure, smothering most of the light.

Pillars scribed with glyphs, unfamiliar to Kiril, held up the beamed ceiling. Great slabs of stone made up the walls opposite the windows, each bearing line after line of unreadable script. A massive humanoid sculpture stood on the left side of the chamber, near the wall glyphs. Its arms were extended so that its hands rested against a convex glass wall perhaps as high as an ancient oak. Its posture suggested that it sought to push the circle of glass farther into the wall—or to hold back the wide circle from moving into the chamber. Whatever its intention, the threat of action was proved hollow by the centuries it had stood. Kiril could make out some sort of fluid languidly churning and turning behind the dusty glass.

The sculpture was three times as tall as Prince Monolith, but the earth elemental ignored his stony kin. He gazed with some agitation at the glass wall. The tiny dragonet lit on Monolith's shoulder.

"Thanks for leaving me in the dark," said Kiril as she reached the elemental lord.

"Xet was with you," replied Monolith, distracted. "I heard something . . . splashing . . . and moved to investigate while you rested. Kiril, look at this barrier—can you sense what lies behind it?"

"I can see that it—"

"It is a terrible threat. It is water, elemental and potent! Something beyond even my power, perhaps, caught here in a vast glass globe. This stone sculpture holds it in place, else it would roll forth. Even outside the glass, I can feel its enmity, its will to drown, dissolve, and erode all that it encounters. I don't think I've ever experienced such raw hatred before. The animating spirit that suffuses it—it is asleep! Perhaps I should vanquish this aqueous insult. . . ." The elemental lord ran its great hand across the glassy wall, as if feeling for a seam.

"Monolith!" yelled Kiril. "You really irk me sometimes, you know? Who told me to leave off prying into things that don't concern us? Leave it alone, unless this sphere is the evil influence that Thormud tracked across half of Faerûn."

The crystal dragonet chimed.

The earth elemental paused, then lowered its massive limb. "No, it has nothing to do with what we seek. Xet says we must ascend still higher."

"Then step away."

Prince Monolith complied, but said, "When we finish, I will return to determine the nature of the entity trapped in this chamber, and dispose of it permanently."

"Great. I'm happy for you," Kiril snorted.

Xet, sensing resolution, launched itself into the air. The dragonet arrowed toward the far side of the chamber, toward a great door, slightly ajar.

A flicker of darkness flashed from the dimness behind the door and struck Xet.

Thormud's familiar rang like a chapel bell as it dropped

from the air, its light quenched.

"What the . . . ?" Kiril hunkered down and raised Sadrul. Something behind the door was shooting at them. In the light from the covered windows, she spied the fletched shaft that had brought down the dragonet. The arrowhead was carved of bone and bore the inscription "AQ" in the elven alphabet.

Two humanoids swathed in cloaks and hoods entered through the door. One had an arrow nocked in a long bow, and the other was pulling a new arrow from a quiver.

"Wait," yelled Kiril. The newcomers were Al Qaherans—she recognized their dress. Perhaps even Ghanim and Haleem, the compatriots of Feraih whose blade she bore. Kiril raised Sadrul higher and yelled, "We're friends! See? I bear the blade of your friend Feraih! I was given it by—"

Both newcomers let fly their arrows. One shaft flew wide, but the other pierced a hole in her shirt and scraped painfully on the fine silver mail she wore beneath.

"Gods blast you!" she screamed.

Lavender fire bloomed within the amulets each wore. Virulent flame limned them.

Kiril recognized that hue, and charged.

One of the corrupted Al Qaherans dropped its bow and pulled a great falchion from the sash around his waist. The edges of the falchion glittered with purple fire.

The other figure turned to face Prince Monolith. His hand reached up and, with a swift jerk, broke the cord that bound the amulet around his neck. Drawing forth a new arrow, he wound the arrowhead through a knot in the cord of the glowing amulet.

Monolith lumbered forward.

As the flames limning his body began to sputter and fail, the corrupted elf fired the arrow toward the elemental noble, rending the air with an amethyst tail. Separated from his amulet, the elf toppled forward, his animation spent.

Monolith ducked, but the arrow wasn't aimed at him.

The missile arced across the chamber and punched straight through the glass wall at the earth elemental's back. Liquid spewed from the puncture. More disturbing, the amulet, floating within the fluid, pulsed back to life. The water draining from the transparent enclosure boiled, bubbling up in a wine-dark hue.

Kiril's attention was snatched away from the wall when a falchion nearly ended her. The other Al Qaheran hacked at her with fire literally burning in his eyes. She countered with Sadrul and groaned in surprise—the elf was incredibly strong! Her new blade absorbed the blow but was nearly knocked from her grip.

Worse, the corrupted dervish was quick. She staved off a slash, a jab, and another slash, all in less than a heartbeat. Stumbling back, she sought an advantage.

She decided to gamble on Sadrul's supernatural sharpness, which Essam had asserted was the sword's claim to fame.

Instead of deflecting the dervish's next swing against the side of her own blade, she fully rotated Sadrul, so its edge was bared to the falchion. Kiril hardly noticed the tug on Sadrul's hilt when the falchion's steel was cut in half. Kiril grinned and moved in.

Without his falchion, the Al Qaheran couldn't protect himself from Kiril's salvo of razor-sharp blows. The elf dervish was dispatched. The Qaheran's amulet tumbled away from his bleeding form and lay pulsing on the floor. Remembering the danger of naked crystal, Kiril aimed Sadrul for one more blow and shattered the amulet's jewel into powder. She hoped it was enough to sever the evil influence and prevent other threats from being sent through it to contest her.

Things were not going as well for Prince Monolith.

The prince of elemental earth battled his nemesis, a great pillar of turbulent, chaotic water. The fury of the water elemental, held for ages since its last opportunity to drown the lower halls of the palace, was multiplied many times over from a crystal seed that pulsed in its depths like a fiery coal, goading it and feeding it with a supernatural strength far beyond its already potent abilities.

Prince Monolith was held aloft in a column of freestanding water. The column swirled with the fury and speed of a deep ocean vortex. Held transfixed within it, the elemental lord began to dissolve. Muddy clumps spattered the walls of the chamber, out of reach of the elemental who might have used the material to heal himself.

Through the watery roar, Kiril heard Prince Monolith screaming. The swordswoman dashed forward, Sadrul in hand. The blade was sharp—sharp enough to disrupt a water elemental? She slashed, penetrating the column at its base, scoring a wide incision in the fluid.

A pseudopod of water lashed from the column. Despite her attempt to parry, it slid over her sharp blade and her body without pause. She drew in a quick breath.

A fierce jerk sent her to join Monolith in the vortex, unanchored and spinning wildly. She flailed with the Qaheran blade, sending trails of bubbles flitting madly through the turbulent water. As the chamber spun round and round, she spied Xet as it ducked back down the corridor through which they'd first entered. Bastard familiar.

Her quick breath had been too shallow—already her lungs burned. Worse, the gyration forced more and more blood to her extremities. She'd be pulled apart before she drowned. She relaxed her hand, and Sadrul flew from her grip and was expelled.

Straining against the spinning water, Kiril retracted her arm and got a hand on Angul's hilt.

The Blade Cerulean slipped free of the bondage of his sheath.

Lucidity seared her consciousness. Doubts, worries, and pains of mind and body faded as new certainty was born in her right hand and quickly spread to engulf her. The Blade Cerulean flamed triumphantly in her welcoming grip, its star blue fire burning and boiling the tissue of the watery creature that held her.

The star elf was spat from the vortex with the velocity of a ballista bolt. She windmilled through the air, but a pillar came up too fast. Agony jolted across her shoulder and back. Robbed of velocity, she fell a full story to the floor. Her left ankle twisted, and she heard something snap.

Through it all, she retained a grip on her sword. For her perseverance, she was rewarded. Kiril stood, her breath coming in ragged gasps. Angul took from her the pain in her back and arm. Her ankle supported her weight as if whole.

Kiril raised the blade, and his blue-white light doubled, then redoubled again, shedding light like the day in all directions. Together, she and Angul said, "All abominations will be vanquished."

The vortex towered over her, and at its apex it held a madly spinning blot of earth—Prince Monolith. The column suddenly doubled over, like a striking snake, and attempted to smash her down, using Monolith's body as the hammer.

Kiril rolled to her left and was clipped on her right hip by one of the earth elemental's thrashing arms. She kept her feet, and the vortex reared back, pulling itself out of reach and the muddy body of Monolith back into the air.

The swordswoman took a step to close the distance, and her hip buckled. She fell on her face. The corrupted water elemental's blow had been mightier than she'd supposed.

If not for my shelter, Angul spoke into her conscious mind, *that blow would have smashed every bone of your fleshy frame.*

Kiril understood the Blade Cerulean was apologizing for failing to fully protect and heal her from the last savage blow. It was the first time the elf could recall her blade not meeting a challenge. For some reason, the thought was a welcome one.

"Blood!" she screamed, forcing herself to her feet despite the wrenching flare in her right side. The blade darkened as it registered her curse, but forwent retaliation for her impious word. The water elemental was aiming another blow, using Monolith as the weapon.

Instead of allowing her to jump away, Angul pulled himself up like a spike to meet the mallet. For the blade, friendships and alliances mattered not. For Angul, overcoming the unrighteous and the abominable came first and last, damn every consequence. Angul was intent on sacrificing Monolith, if he still lived, to deprive the watery scourge of its weapon.

"I'm the wielder!" hissed Kiril. As the blow descended, she crumbled and rolled back and to her left, slapping the damp stone with her left hand to absorb the fall instead of her hip and back. She maintained her grip on Angul with her right hand, despite its flare of displeasure. She was ruining its strategy!

Kiril sprang to her feet as she exited the roll, anticipating the vortex's reaction. She charged the vortex's base even as its muddy crown coiled up and back.

Angul's blue-white fire burned hot as she lunged forward and plunged the blade directly into the vortex.

Cerulean battled sapphire, fire contested water.

The ensuing steam explosion threw Kiril back across the wet floor. Angul's fire sputtered, but the water elemental's vortex was unraveled. The column of water collapsed, deluging the floor of the chamber. Prince Monolith crashed to the floor, and stone shrapnel from his fall scored Kiril's face. What remained seemed more a mound of mud than anything else.

Kiril's will reunited with Angul's as she spied the tiny amulet that still pulsed with venomous luminescence. She dived at the glimmering shard.

As a phantom, wine-colored tentacle reached from an interstitial space focused by the amulet, the Blade Cerulean smashed the malign talisman into a thousand burning, guttering splinters.

CHAPTER TWENTY-EIGHT

The pale-skinned wizard said Eined was dead. Even after the funeral, he couldn't grasp it.

Ususi said his sister perished nobly. Nobly or shamefully, the horrifying, dawning realization that his sister was gone occluded everything else. A gasping emptiness inhabited Warian's chest. It was an echoing hollow nothing could fill, but his thoughts swirled around it like water circling an abyss.

He clenched his crystal fist, ready to vent his sudden fury. Violet light leaped dangerously in his prosthesis. What would he smash? He saw nothing but the path below his feet. No railway or embankment separated him from the gulfs of darkness that Ususi and Iahn's ancestors had constructed.

With a strangled sob, Warian dropped to his knees and struck the path with his flashing prosthetic. His fist punched a small crater, and cracks in the stone raced ahead and behind him. The path shuddered, and he heard his uncle cry out behind him.

A hand touched his shoulder. He turned his head, saw Zel. "Why?" Warian asked. "Why'd she have to die?"

His uncle squeezed his shoulder and said, "More than your sister is dead this day, Nephew."

Warian realized Zel's own sister had also died, Sevaera. And perhaps Zel's own father was, if not dead, compromised to such an extreme degree that he might as well have perished.

"I'm sorry, Uncle. I just . . ."

"You'll have your chance to exact vengeance when we get into that tower, if the Imaskari are right. Unless you exhaust yourself out here battering the stone, or send us all screaming into the dark."

Warian nodded and allowed the lavender radiance flickering in his arm to lapse. Zel helped him to his feet as he weathered the momentary wave of faintness following his arm's surge. The weakness was not nearly as bad as before, since he'd started to practice accessing the arm's strength in controlled bursts. It was a triumph he would have enjoyed sharing with Eined.

Up the path, Iahn paused where he walked with Ususi. The wizard looked ahead to the wavering walls of the tower, now only a few hundred paces ahead. The vengeance taker turned and fixed Warian with his ice-cold eyes. He said, "The paths are not indestructible."

Warian nodded, blood rushing to his cheeks. Damn. He briefly felt much younger than his twenty-two years.

Iahn turned and conferred with the wizard, who was pointing ahead. Feeling the pressure of Zel's hands on his shoulders encouraging him to proceed, Warian walked ahead.

" . . . some sort of broad interface with the Celestial Nadir and the world," Ususi was saying. The wizard had her key-stone out and was studying the wavering façade of the tower through it.

"Yes," she continued. "It's a magical mechanism the Imaskari put in place in case the Purple Palace ever returned to the world. This path maintains a connection with some chamber inside the palace. If we walk the path to its end, through the interface, we should be injected back into our world, safely inside the tower."

"And not far from the weapons cache?" asked the vengeance taker.

"Only a floor or two below, from what I remember of the floor plans."

Iahn nodded and increased his pace. He threw over his back, "Time is precious."

Ususi turned to Warian and Zel. "Once we get into the palace, we could go up against Pandorym, plus whatever else Pandorym has released from the weapons cache to defend it. Be ready for anything." She looked dubiously at Zel, then turned and moved quickly to catch up with Iahn.

"Do you think that look implied something?" wondered Zel.

"She wants you to be careful, Uncle."

"And you?

"I've got my arm. You've got . . . a pickaxe."

Zel chuckled and slung the haft of the pickaxe over his shoulder.

Stepping through the wavering interface was like walking beneath a waterfall—icy, and just as shocking.

Warian stiffened, but the cold faded. He wasn't actually wet. And the gulfs of the Celestial Nadir were gone. Instead, the glimmer of Ususi's head-orbiting light revealed the confines of a cylindrical stone corridor. Inscribed glyphs spiraled endlessly around the passageway. He jumped when the glyphs pulsed, sending a whirl of white light corkscrewing down the passage a hundred paces or more. Zel suddenly blinked into the space next to Warian.

The wizard said, "We stand at the endpoint of a more sophisticated version of the stone circles, which are the usual means to access the Celestial Nadir. This is probably one of the twenty gates."

"Twenty . . . are you saying there are twenty gates into the Celestial Nadir?" asked Warian.

"Yes. Prior to this journey, it was my goal to find and catalogue all of them. I suspected the Purple Palace contained at least one gate, but figured it would be years before I learned whether I was right or wrong. Funny. Until recently, this gate wasn't even accessible from our world."

"You're sure we're back in the world?" asked Zel. He cast a suspicious gaze down the narrow, circular corridor.

"If not the world, then at least the Purple Palace," said the wizard. "Soon, we'll encounter Pandorym."

"And defeat it," added Iahn. The vengeance taker muttered a few words in a language unknown to Warian and trudged ahead.

Ususi nodded, apparently agreeing with Iahn's statement, and followed.

Warian and Zel brought up the rear.

The long, spiraling corridor opened into a wider space. Iahn and Ususi entered, and Warian moved just inside the new chamber. The wizard's light flickered around, revealing a wide, empty room with a single exit opposite the corridor. It was shuttered by a rusted slab of iron.

"If I recall correctly . . ." Ususi began, then a shudder rumbled below Warian's feet. He tried to retreat the way he'd come, but he bumped against his uncle.

"Get back!" Warian cried.

The floor dropped away. He fell, as did Zel and Ususi. The vengeance taker performed a desperate and impressive leap toward the far door, where an iron handle glinted invitingly, but he came up several feet short and plunged like the rest of them. He tumbled through a series of braking maneuvers against the wall.

Warian smashed hard onto stone. Thuds, cries, and gasps peppered the darkness around him, and he knew he wasn't alone. Ususi's light flicked back on.

The stone pit that enclosed them was perhaps fifteen paces across. Putrid, slimy water pooled in the corners. Disintegrating bones lay scattered across the room. The walls rose on all sides about twenty or thirty paces, to a ceiling of rusted iron.

"It closed?" groaned Zel, who lay next to Warian. "It closed us in!"

Iahn, who'd somehow managed to land on his feet, helped Ususi to stand.

Breathing hard, the wizard said, "An automatic trap, meant to apprehend intruders. How stupid of me not to foresee such a possibility. I know better."

"Then you should have warned us," accused Zel. A thin line of blood trickled from the older man's brow.

"Cease!" snapped Iahn. "Is anyone hurt badly?"

"I think my leg's broke," grimaced Zel. "I can't move it, and it hurts like a devil's got his teeth in me."

Ususi said, "I'll be fine when I get my breath back. Tend them, please, Iahn?" The wizard rooted around in her satchel and withdrew a vial she pressed into the vengeance taker's hand.

Iahn inspected Warian first and helped him to his feet. Other than having his breath knocked out of him, Warian was healthier than he expected after falling such a distance. He'd sport some terrific bruises later, though.

Next, Iahn knelt at Zel's side and probed Zel's left leg, which was splayed too far to one side just below the knee.

"Fractured," Iahn concluded. The vengeance taker unstopped the vial Ususi had given him and administered a portion of it to Zel.

Zel attempted to drink down all the fizzing fluid, but Iahn drew back. "Not all at once. We must conserve. Your leg should be mending already."

As Warian watched, his uncle's leg slowly straightened to true, and the lines of pain in his face eased. "I do feel better," Zel said.

"You'll walk with a limp for a while," said Iahn as he rose and turned to Ususi.

The wizard approached one of the walls, which wasn't as bare as Warian had first assumed. Subtle characters were reflected in Ususi's light, forming a script unfamiliar to him. A moment later, each strange letter began to glow with a cool blue radiance.

Warian joined the wizard and vengeance taker at the wall. "What is it?"

"Instructions for getting clear of the containment," said Ususi. "Any Imaskari who resided in the palace would know the answer to this riddle, so if accidentally caught in the automated trap after coming through from the Celestial Nadir, he could regain freedom in short order."

"It's a riddle? And you know the answer?"

"Yes. Yes, it's a riddle, but I don't know the answer. For certain. But perhaps we can think of the answer together," said Ususi.

As Warian studied the lighted inscriptions, those in the center swam and changed before his eyes, forming words he could easily read. Symbols on the periphery remained incomprehensible, but they didn't seem important.

Warian asked, "Couldn't someone not authorized to know the answer, like us, work it out, too? That would negate the entire point of the trap, right?"

"You would be correct, of course—however, if any but an Imaskari attempts to answer the riddle, the walls of this room will close down upon us and squeeze us dead. Or so promise these glyphs." The wizard pointed to the upper right corner of the wall at an inscription that remained meaningless to Warian.

"Oh. A trap within a trap."

"How efficient," said the vengeance taker.

Warian nodded and said, "Maybe I'd better not even read it. Zel, you look away, too."

Zel shrugged and turned away, as did Warian. Ususi read.

"The Thirty-Eighth Law of Veracity holds that a magical elixir can never be entirely drunk. A residue always remains behind. A miser mage who collects empty elixir vials can make a new elixir to drink from the residue of every five empty vials found. When he has collected twenty-five elixir vials, how many new elixirs will he be able to drink?"

Warian's uncle guffawed. "Ridiculously easy! Twenty-five vials can be arranged into five groups—so the elixir-grubbing mage could drink five more potions."

Warian flinched and whispered, "Only an Imaskari can answer!"

"Don't worry, Warian," said Ususi. "To formally answer this riddle, the changeable script now instructs me to answer aloud in the language of Imaskar."

"Say five, then," Zel said, rubbing his hands in anticipation.

"No," interrupted the vengeance taker. "Five is incorrect."

Ususi looked at Iahn. "Why so? Seems straightforward enough."

"That should be your first warning—too straightforward. A real riddle hides an answer in an answer. Otherwise, it's only a child's calculation. But a riddle has been posed, because the true answer is six, not five."

Zel said, "How do you figure?"

"The mage makes five new elixirs from the twenty-five empties he has, and after he drinks them, he has five more empties left for one more elixir. Thus the answer is six."

"Seems a little slippery."

Warian nudged Zel and said in an undertone, "Reminds me of the kind of merchant deals I've seen you put together."

"Fair enough," Zel allowed.

Ususi stiffened and said a word in a language Warian didn't know.

The cool blue radiance of the glyphs heated, transforming into an angry, scathing red. The sound of stone grating on stone vibrated up through Warian's feet.

"It *was* five!" crowed Zel. He was thrown to the ground when the floor gave a great lurch.

Doom bellowed a fell promise as stone scraped over stone. The walls began to close in.

"No, it was six," asserted Iahn, his voice calm as he began to trace his hands through a constellation of arcane movements.

The wizard, looking stunned, said, "The trap triggered with my answer. The choice was correct. Am I not Imaskari enough to qualify as one of the ancients? Has the bloodline diverged so widely?"

Warian concentrated, and his arm flared with violet potential. He strode toward one of the approaching walls and landed a terrific hammer fist. A great shower of stones exploded from the wall, but the stone was so thick that it actually absorbed little of the blow. The greater part of the force rebounded into Warian's prosthesis. The impact was so potent, it jolted him out of his Celestial Nadir mastery. He fell to his knees. Tiny points of light prickled his vision, and nausea grasped at his stomach. The light in his arm went out.

Iahn stepped forward, snatched Ususi around the waist with one free arm, and finished his somatic gesture with the other. When nothing happened, he noted, "Magical escape is blocked."

Zel tried to force his pickaxe blade into the advancing seam where an approaching wall met the floor. "The crack's too small—I can't get any purchase!" he yelped.

The wizard conquered her shock and yelled, "Stand next to me. Quickly!" Without waiting for Warian or Zel to comply, she rushed through a spell, sputtering over some of the syllables. The Vaelanites stumbled toward her.

On a rising note, Ususi finished speaking, making a warding, circular motion with her hand above her head. Marble crystallized from the air, encasing the four delvers in a dome of solid stone. The harsh, scarlet light was gone, and Ususi's free-flying light bounced around the too-small enclosure. The sound of the approaching walls diminished, but did not cease.

"This will protect us?" asked Zel.

"I hope so. Long enough for the trap to reset . . ."

Either Ususi's summoned wall would block the crushing walls, or it wouldn't. Warian whispered, "Come on, come on," over and over, but he wasn't sure who he was urging to what end.

The air splintered with the sound of the advancing walls' contact with the marble dome.

"It's holding!" yelled Zel.

A deep whine became audible, then began to ascend in pitch.

"The walls still attempt to crush us," Ususi said.

A hairline crack appeared on the dome's surface and raced a jagged path down one side. Another appeared, then another. The whine was becoming the shriek of a harpy, and a fine dust of disintegrating stone began to rain down inside the dome.

"The dome is failing," said Iahn.

"Thanks for the news!" yelled Zel, his eyes darting around the tiny space, looking for some miraculous opportunity.

But there was no escape.

The whine, threatening to rise in pitch beyond Warian's hearing, stuttered. The floor shook with the report of something like distant thunder. The whine regained its strength and ratcheted upward again. Another detonation rattled through the dome, closer than before. A basso succession of sounds penetrated the damaged dome. The new noises almost resembled speech in their regularity and cadence.

"Is someone out there?" Warian asked. "That sounded like someone speaking!"

Needing no further encouragement, Zel yelled at the top of his lungs, "Hey! We're in here! Help!"

With one final boom, the whine failed completely. The cracks in the protective marble dome ceased multiplying. The deep-pitched noises sounded again, and comprehension dawned on Warian. He heard, ". . . ruined the crushing plates. Something is caught inside."

Another voice, this one much harder to hear through the stone, yelled, "Blast, blood, and rot! What do you care? It's probably another crystal puppet."

The first voice said, "I can travel as easily through the stone of the structure as through the passageways in between. If you feel that my choices are not perfect, perhaps you should consider . . ."

Ususi pointed to the dome, and with a flash and a pop, it disappeared.

Standing over them, amidst the rubble of shattered walls, was a massive animate sculpture. The creature was like a man made of fused boulders. It wore, or more accurately, sprouted from its head, a crown of uncut rubies and diamonds. It stood nearly three times Zell's height, the tallest of the group.

The silhouette of a mail-clad elf looked down at them from the lip of the pit. This one said, "Now, look! I told you to ignore it, but you had to mess with it. Just like before!"

A tiny creature flew down into the pit to alight on the shoulder of the great earthen being. Warian realized it was another animate sculpture, this one like a tiny dragon carved of reddish glass. It opened its mouth and pealed a series of tiny, bell-like chirps. The sound was reminiscent of laughter.

Ususi stepped toward the great earthen entity and said in Common, "Greetings. I am Ususi Manaallin. Thank you for disrupting these encroaching walls. We would have been crushed. We are in your debt. But who are you? You don't seem to be in thrall to Pandorym . . ."

Warian tensed.

"I am Prince Monolith. I am in no one's thrall. The question is, what are you doing in this ancient tower of malignancy?" Iahn moved as quickly as a snake to stand protectively next to Ususi, one hand on his dragonfly blade, still sheathed.

Ususi replied, "That was my question for you. We are here because this structure was built by my ancestors."

The figure from above yelled, "So this is all your fault!" Warian now recognized the one above to be a woman, though he'd never seen an elf, male or female, quite so broad of forearm and rough of voice and manner.

"What blame do you place on us?" inquired Iahn, his voice ice. Warian judged the vengeance taker was only a jibe or two away from launching a physical attack against the newcomers.

The elf pointed at Ususi. "She just said your ancestors built this place. You must be Imaskari, hiding all these centuries when everyone thought you were dead. I've spent the better part of two months tracking down this tower because of the fell influence it released into the earth! Did you release it? My friend Thormud lies sorely wounded, or dead, because if it!"

Iahn bristled, but Ususi said, "Pandorym is what we call the evil you speak of. It is even now using the greater part of its strength to destroy my homeland, and may have already done so. We have not released it. We are here to destroy it."

His face suddenly hot, Warian interjected, "My sister died to bring these opponents of Pandorym here! Don't suggest they're in league with the master of this tower, or you dishonor Eined's name!"

The elemental called Monolith raised both of its giant hands, palms outward, and said, "You are not of this tower,

I sense, but are newly come to it, like us. I have saved your lives, I think, from these crushing walls. That should prove our good intentions. For now, my friend and I will have to trust yours. Perhaps we should join our strength to overcome this Pandorym?"

"You believe them?" snorted the elf woman. "I want to know who released Pandorym if these relics of the empire didn't do it." She glared at Ususi.

"It was my grandfather," said Warian. "Shaddon Datharathi. He found his way into a forbidden plane where this tower, until recently, slept through the centuries. Greed drove him. We're here to help put right his mistake."

"Sounds good enough for a trial partnership," interjected Monolith. "What do you say, descendents of Imaskar?"

Ususi considered, nodded, and said, "Help us out of this pit, and we'll compare strategies."

CHAPTER TWENTY-NINE

Another set of circling stairs. It wasn't far now. The Imperial Weapons Cache was ahead. And, presumably, Pandorym.

The stained corridors, translucent stairs, sealed chambers, and dozens of fascinating but ultimately unimportant features of the Purple Palace were behind them. As were the most vicious protests of the elf woman who called herself Kiril. She'd finally accepted Prince Monolith's opinion, but distrust still lay openly across her face whenever Ususi looked back.

Of course, Iahn wasn't much better. Because Ususi was of his lineage and knew something of his ways, the wizard saw the vengeance taker's behavior for what it was. She could see Iahn's distrust in the way he carried himself, how he kept his hand always ready on the hilt of his weapon, and how he consistently checked the behavior of the elf and elemental as they traversed the dark corridors of the tower. He was on knife-edge alert, ready to assassinate the rough-speaking elf and at least damage the elemental lord at the first hint of betrayal. To everyone else, he probably seemed stiff and unfriendly.

The two Vaelanites were likewise quiet, or perhaps merely tired, and at the very least, emotionally drained. The one with the prosthesis was running on willpower alone. Ususi hoped the slow walk would help renew the young man's energy. Iahn had offered him some morsels from his pack to keep his strength up. Warian's facility with his arm could prove pivotal in dealing with Pandorym. His sister's death colored all Warian's utterances, or lack thereof. Ususi knew she would suffer the same way if Qari were to come to harm. Perhaps Ususi's sister was in danger even now, back in Deep Imaskar. If only she could see what was happening there!

But dealing with Pandorym in the palace was the quickest, surest method of stopping the entity's forces . . . she fervently hoped. No. No, she *knew* her course was the right one, but would they be quick enough? Would they even be successful? It was all she could do to force herself ahead instead of back to the gate into the Celestial Nadir, and from there directly back to the foot of the Great Seal, using her keystone to forge a way.

"Explain again what this Pandorym is, and what your great-to-the-gills grandparents did to anger it," insisted the hard voice of the elf swordswoman, continuing a conversation Ususi thought was complete.

Ususi took a deep breath and said, "It is an entity too powerful to be controlled or even destroyed. The ancient Imaskari were under siege from their slaves' avenging deities. They were desperate. A powerful Imaskaran imperial faction lured Pandorym from a distant dimension beyond the local cosmology. In a fashion I do not understand, they caged Pandorym and threatened its release in this world as a way to dissuade the gods from destroying the Imaskari Empire. Apparently, the threat wasn't taken seriously, or the Imaskari were destroyed before their threat was issued. Either way, Pandorym remained forgotten and confined for millennia. Until miners from Vaelan found a gate into the Celestial Nadir, found the palace, and partially released Pandorym. Pandorym, once released, dropped the palace back into the world, onto its original foundation."

"These miners . . ." began Kiril, but the wizard snapped up a hand to deflect the elf's question. Ususi wasn't about to reveal the relationship between Warian, Zel, and Datharathi Minerals to this revenge-obsessed elf warrior, especially one who carried a blade of considerable potency. Ususi's magic-sensitive eyes watered whenever she looked directly at it.

The wizard said, "What's important now is to bind Pandorym anew into whatever cage it slipped from. The fact that we still walk freely in these halls should be assurance enough that it has reclaimed only a fraction of its potential power."

Kiril replied, "Sounds like a familiar tale. I know something of binding wickedness."

"Really? What?" asked Zel.

"Let's just say that well-meaning accomplishments rarely go unpunished."

Zel waited for more, but seemed unwilling to press. Kiril lapsed back into silence.

They curved around another bend in the corridor and faced darkness.

Ususi's hand went to her mouth. "No . . ."

Night blocked the passage ahead.

So complete was the blackness that the magical radiance of Ususi's orb dimmed as its farthest rays fell into the dark chasm. A cold breeze cooled her flesh, and the howl of a distant wind conjured the image of desolation. Shadows rippled, and tendrils of darkness emerged, dissolved, and reappeared, as if attempting to cross the intervening space and pull all of them into its insatiable void.

"I dreamed . . . I have dreamed this!" the wizard insisted.

She backed up. Iahn's sudden hands upon her shoulders turned her about so she faced away from the unnerving abyss. "What do you see?" he asked, his tone conveying worry, even if his eyes retained their usual pristine clarity. "Is it more than an enchantment of shadow?"

She croaked, cleared her throat, and tried to speak. "It . . . it is something I've faced in my dreams for . . . more years than I can name." She stole another peek at the apparition at her back and shuddered. "It's my nightmare, here now, alive in the world."

"How can that be?" demanded Kiril. The swordswoman pushed forward to stand alongside Iahn. She was as tall as the taker, and perhaps broader of shoulder.

"I don't know," Ususi responded. But she did know. It was the doom she and her sister Qari had shared since they were children. They would one day face darkness, irredeemable and absolute.

And here it was.

"Ususi, we must press forward if we are to breach the weapons cache," Iahn said, taking one of her hands in both of his own. "Dissolve this magical gloom and reveal the threat Pandorym truly poses. Are you truly so afraid of the dark?"

"It's not the dark—it's what the darkness hides!" she yelled in the vengeance taker's face. But as she spoke, she wondered if it were true. Her lifelong nightmares had conditioned her to quail in the face of utter gloom. Pandorym's mind and essence were things of darkness made manifest, and it blocked her way forward.

She took a deep breath, fighting to impose calm. She could flee, true, and let Deep Imaskar fall by allowing Pandorym to go unopposed. Or she could deal with the murk that blocked their way. It couldn't hurt to try to dissolve the gloom in greater light, could it?

Ususi reached up and tapped the jewel that hovered overhead, muttering encouraging thaunemes of amplification. Responding to her magical plea, the illumination of her orb waxed.

Ususi swiveled to face her nemesis. Radiance poured from her free-floating light, meeting the darkness like an ocean wave meets a rocky coast. The gloom splintered and fell back . . . then drank down the light entirely.

The distant wind suddenly screamed in Ususi's ear, and the darkness pounced.

Light guttered and failed. Ususi's voice choked up, and her limbs were swaddled in oblivion. Her lifelong nightmare was back, this time all too real. The darkness, after these long, empty years, finally got her.

When the wizard was snatched away, Iahn yelled "Ususi!" and plunged into the blackness.

Warian moved forward, but his uncle held him back. "What can you smash if you can't see?"

The elemental lord thundered at the swordswoman, "It obeys the rules of darkness, I deem, even if it is possessed of something more nefarious. Burn it away with Angul!"

Kiril's hand went for the lesser blade she carried on her belt.

Monolith cried, "It must be Angul. No time for half-measures!" The elf's hand wavered, then diverted to Angul's sheath.

Kiril pulled Angul forth and gasped. Runes on the unclothed blade burned with blinding intensity and blue flame. The advancing margin of darkness reversed itself. With a posture forged from blade-given surety, the elf stepped forward a pace, then two. The darkness roiled and flailed against the perimeter of Angul's glow, and Kiril moved forward another step.

Here and there, the sphere of brilliance surrounding Kiril dimmed, and lightless tendrils slid inward along invisible fractures. Another step forward and the sphere shrank to half its size. Undaunted, Kiril advanced.

The roused dusk swallowed her.

As if energized by enclosing Angul's brilliance, the face of the black wall swelled. Zel, Warian, and even Prince Monolith fell back, but too slowly. All were engulfed.

When the perimeter receded to its original position, the hall was empty. No evidence of intruders remained to mar the ancient stone floor of the Purple Palace.

Ususi rolled over and over, impelled by a force with no substance. She spun through a screaming void of spiritual emptiness. How had she escaped the darkness during her last dream, when wakefulness had been denied her?

Qari! Her sister had come into her dream, saving her. Would a memory of her sister offer aid now? She fastened upon the idea of Qari and tried to shout her name, though the use of her voice was denied her.

A glimmer of cool, blue radiance broke upon her mind. It wasn't true light—it seemed more like a species of understanding. Spiritual illumination, perhaps. In its glow, she grasped the vague, ill-defined connection that she and her twin sister shared since childhood, and retained still.

Following the connection down its ill-defined, looping path, she found at its end a silhouette. It was Qari.

Qari spoke. "Years have piled on years since last we talked, Ususi. I'm glad, even as this focal event of your life, and mine, overtakes us, that we have this brief moment to talk once more." Her sister smiled and held out her hands.

"What . . . are you here with me, in the darkness of Pandorym's veil?" Ususi strode forward, her arms and legs suddenly resolved in Qari's aura. Qari grasped Ususi's hands. Warm and vital, her flesh seemed real.

"In a way. My mind is with you—my percipience. My physical form, despite its faded claim on reality, remains in besieged Deep Imaskar, where the fires of Pandorym's vengeance have breached the Great Seal. Slaughter walks the streets. Our chat must be short."

Too much information, too many implications—even the nature of their connection. Nausea threatened to overcome the wizard, the result of understanding her sister's words. She had so many questions for Qari. "Your 'faded claim' on reality—what are you talking about? And the 'focal point' of our lives—you mean Pandorym?"

Qari laughed, but sadly. "All these are connected. The dreams that plagued us since we were children were more than a presentiment of what you would one day face, and fail to overcome. You see, my very existence is a direct consequence of Pandorym's meddling in its future, our past."

Ususi feared her sister had slipped into insanity. Or she had herself and merely dreamed all this. But she said, "Time is sacrosanct. No one may alter its flow, everyone knows this. The mage-researchers of the Arcanum spent enough time proving it . . ."

"Mortal rules do not apply to beings that exist outside of the world, and so outside of time. Pandorym is such a creature. Even as it was caged, it saw ahead to the moment of its release. In that chance for freedom, it recognized a possibility that, along a minor timeline, one would be born who might find herself in the right place at the right time to stem its reemergence. That person was you."

Qari forestalled Ususi's next question, speaking over her. "Hush, let me finish. Time is not so elastic for you and I."

Ususi reluctantly nodded.

"Pandorym took steps to prevent you from overcoming it. It reached forward, imparting what influence it could, hoping to create deterrence enough to prevent she who would one day threaten its bid for freedom. But the mere act of its temporal reach forged two competing possibilities. In one case, it succeeded, and Ususi was born to dread the darkness. But every coin has two sides. Pandorym's meddling also caused Qari to be born, whose congenital blindness limited her world, but gave her an ability to pierce any darkness and to see even where no light may ever shine."

"Two timelines? But we exist together—you are my sister!"

"I am your twin to a greater degree than you have ever imagined. I am an alternate you."

"This *is* a dream! Or you are crazy. Or I am. Has darkness driven me insane with fear? How can you be an alternate version of me, yet have grown up with me in Deep Imaskar?"

Qari cocked her head and said, "How could I not? But moments are precious right now. We've come to that crossroads—you must accept my gift. You must accept my percipience. With it, no darkness will ever blind you again."

"But you need it . . ."

"Everyone in Deep Imaskar will be dead soon, and me with them, if you do not press forward now. If I give up my vision through the darkness, I may perish, true. But listen. Everything—hopes, worries, fears—all these pale in the face of death. Only that which is important remains."

Qari released Ususi's hands and held hers up before Ususi's face. She put her palms over the wizard's eyes and said, "See, as I have seen."

At long last, Ususi saw again the high, hard celestial lights that haunted her days and nights since she nearly perished on the ship. Beneath their elysian clarity, Ususi's perception would never again be impeded.

Immersed in nothingness, Iahn's consciousness slowly leached away. He had no limbs to flail, no voice to protest, and no magic to dispense. He was an insect in pitch, and soon he'd be extinguished.

A touch jolted the vengeance taker. The single sensation was sufficient for him to find a focus. The sensation grew more pronounced. Something touched his open eyes. He blinked, or he thought he did. Yes . . . he was on his feet, moving in a daze over some hard surface, but he couldn't see what.

Despite his stubborn nature, he allowed himself to be guided forward, into a sudden, blinding light.

Before him, in a broad hallway lit with Kiril's blazing sword, stood the swordswoman, the elemental with a tiny dragonet perched on one shoulder, and Warian and his uncle. Ususi pushed him forward.

Of the darkness, he saw no sign.

Ahead, a bronze-colored iris stood partially dialed open, and additional light streamed through the crack.

He turned to look at Ususi and blinked. Her eyes were like twin stars, blue-white and twinkling as if at some great distance.

Warian said, "Thank you for saving us from that . . . that awful blot." The young man's voice was strained and his features pale, as were Zel's, and probably the vengeance taker's as well.

The wizard responded as if to some different statement. "My uskura is lost."

"You pushed us clear of the darkness," Warian insisted, waving behind him. No evidence of the veil of life-sucking night remained, except in memory.

"I didn't push us clear. I saw through the darkness and helped you all do the same. But at what cost, I wonder? My sister may have given up her special sight . . ." Ususi's eyes, glittering cold and hard, drifted out of focus.

"Your sister?" asked Iahn. "You have news of Deep Imaskar?"

"Slaughter walks the streets, she said . . ."

The bronze iris at the end of the hallway spun open. Beyond was a spacious, moon-bright hall, but a human figure just inside the opening partially blocked the view.

An icy breeze flowed from the figure, and a black vapor streamed away from its body, tinged with violet light. Iahn recognized the aura of a Pandorym agent.

The figure spoke in the vengeance taker's native tongue. "Imaskari scions, if the dark won't have you, I shall."

It was Shaddon. Before the figure could unleash its lashing ribbons of murderous darkness, the earth lord's long arm delivered a terrific punch, smashing Shaddon back into the glaring white chamber beyond.

Iahn rushed in.

Monolith's blow was mighty, and Shaddon's form smashed against the far side of a great chamber. Many creatures moved about the edges of the room.

He understood then why the chamber was called the weapons cache. The vengeance taker's eyes widened. He ran, aiming neither for Shaddon nor the clot of creatures milling through the chamber. He saw something that his training called out for him to seize for himself.

CHAPTER THIRTY

Zel watched the naturally pale, dangerous vengeance taker charge ahead. Zel tightened his grip on the pickaxe and whispered, "So much for common sense." Then Zel ran into the Imperial Weapons Cache.

Others barreled ahead of him. The pallid foreigner had gone first, and the wizard woman dashed after her compatriot. The foul-mouthed elf with the burning sword was only a step behind her.

Even his own nephew beat him through the door. Zel's checks flushed, and he asserted, "I'm not afraid!"

He yelped when a great stone hand grabbed him.

The elemental lord pulled him back and turned him around, looking Zel in the eye. "Stay back, and remember what happens here today. And please guard my little friend." The crystal dragonet on

Prince Monolith's shoulder hopped from the elemental to Zel. Zel was surprised to find that the creature weighed practically nothing.

The earth lord turned and dashed after the others. The dragonet belled loud and long, but the sounds emerging from the chamber were earsplitting. Zel moved forward tentatively to watch, relieved and ashamed that he had an excuse to remain out of the conflict.

The fabled Imaskaran Imperial Weapons Cache was essentially a fat, egg-shaped cavity seemingly wider than the tower's dimension could contain. Ususi's first impression was a cloud-swaddled sky, but the lines of the floor and curving walls and ceiling quickly resolved. Thousands of circles of every size were set into the floor. All were at least three or four feet in diameter, though many were much larger.

The circles capped thousands of inset storage cylinders sunk below floor level. The capacity of the chamber's thousands of hidden silos took away Ususi's breath.

The caps along the periphery of the great chamber were plain metallic bands, unadorned but for a simple symbol—sword blade, spear, bow, quiver, and so on. The wizard was no tactician, but she supposed there were enough of these mundanely-stamped silos to equip a small army with arms and ammunition, presuming each sunken locker contained what its stamp promised.

Toward the middle, intricate mechanical locks adorned the caps. At the hub of the great chamber, elaborate warding glyphs of inlaid Celestial Nadir crystal inscribed the sunken storage cylinders. Hundreds of protective warding circles were inscribed across the tops of all the innermost silos, some layered over one another, forming a diagram of staggering complexity, not dissimilar to the designs inscribed on the Great Seal back in Deep Imaskar.

But a great swath of the interlocking wards and circles was tangled and uneven. Here and there, cylinders stood raised from their compartments, their contents revealed. The wizard saw glittering black swords, slender steel wands, smooth-stocked crossbows, glassy darts filled with phosphorescent pink liquid, scarlet goggles, beetle-black gauntlets, dragonfly blades like the one Iahn carried, and other equipment that reminded Ususi of scuttling insect limbs and carapaces. But most disturbing were the raised cylinders that resembled sarcophagi more than equipment chests.

The sarcophagi were faced with glass. Creatures hung within, in a pale green briny solution, preserved against the long, slow grind of time. Ususi saw trolls behind the glass windows, demonic hoof-footed humanoids, human-sized eggs the color of flesh, bony shadow efts, mantis-headed insectoids, human-dragon hybrids, and at least one tentacle-faced humanoid with soulless white eyes frozen open in its captivity: a mind flayer of ancient vintage.

Several dozen unjacketed canisters yawned, open and drained. The creatures once contained therein, clustered near the room's center, were decanted and active. Thankfully, the wizard saw no mind flayer lords.

Those freed were bad enough. Some were monstrosities she had faced in the caverns below the world. A few she knew through her studies. She recognized trolls, a dozen or more mantis-men. One figure towered over all the others, human in shape, but at least twenty paces tall! This giant's skin was light green, as were its eyes and glittering hair, though it bore a purple crystal on its chest. A storm lord? Here was Shaddon, too, staggering back to his feet, though he seemed damaged from Monolith's bold strike. Her arcane studies were unable to identify all of the monsters.

She spotted a free shadow eft! She shuddered, remembering again the sea passage across the Golden Water.

Each of the loosed creatures bore a violet-flaring Celestial

Nadir crystal, some on cords, others pierced directly into loathsome flesh.

The cluster of Pandorym-controlled monsters stood poised and dangerous, guarding that which lay at the cache's center.

The top edge of a canister ten paces in diameter peeked just above the floor's surface, like a dais. The canister was only partially unjacketed from its silo. Ususi saw that the mechanical locks that once kept the container secured were only partly engaged. Worse, several lines of protection inlaid with Celestial Nadir crystal across the canister's lid were chipped and broken. The canister wasn't entirely free of its storage silo, and the bulk of it still languished in its cavity.

But for the thing sealed within, the slender gap in its cage was enough.

A whirling scab of lightlessness, as perfectly black as Ususi's most terrifying childhood dream of the dark, streamed from the narrow gap in the floor. The darkness hovered, straining and pulling, but didn't move more than a few feet from the canister from which it emerged, as if tethered.

Ususi called upon her borrowed percipience and gazed into the dark.

Pandorym was there.

If not in body, at least in purpose. It saw her and saw that its dark hid no secrets from her. In unison, every servitor intoned, "I require the keystone. Relinquish it, and I may spare your home."

Ususi's percipience pierced even to the center of Pandorym's darkness. There, a circular gateway yawned, suspended several feet in the air. Ususi gasped when she recognized the streets of Deep Imaskar visible through the opening. The wide avenues, the tenement pillars, library spires . . . burning. Silhouetted in the flames, dark creatures moved to and fro, limned with violet malevolence.

The wizard of Deep Imaskar began uttering her most potent spells, suspecting they wouldn't be enough.

Kiril advanced into the milk white chamber. Angul burned in her grip. A gruesome multitude opposed her, each suffused with a trickle of power from the demi-entity Pandorym. To her left, the young man with the crystal arm matched her stride, his arm shining with its own light.

The blade spoke in her mind. *These creatures, and their master, are kin to the horrors we are pledged to destroy.*

The swordswoman ground her teeth and took a practice swipe with the Cerulean Blade. Angul scattered radiant fire in his arc.

The blade instructed her. *Whether they are abolethic horrors or evil unaligned, here lie abominations, and thus their existence is forfeit.*

The sword's anger burned brighter, and the certitude of his purpose steeled Kiril's posture. More powerful than any drunken dream or induced high, Angul engulfed her in absolute conviction. She didn't understand Pandorym's origin, but with Angul's influence pounding through her, she knew beyond certainty that it and its servitors deserved no mercy, nor quarter, nor even promise of redemption.

Kiril smiled, advancing.

Running into the chamber, Warian quickly evaluated what opposed them. Each bore the element of the Datharathis' claim to fame—the damned crystal. Here was where Shaddon's quest for wealth had taken him, and despite every warning, here he'd allowed his desire for power to subvert his reason. This damned chamber was where Warian's grandfather had given up his soul.

The Imaskari wizard, chanting and gesticulating, stood to Warian's left. Farther in and ahead of her, the vengeance taker jerked an ancient weapon from a container. Nearing

Warian on his right, the elf with the burning blade advanced. A glance back showed him the earth elemental at the rear. He saw Zel peeking from around the bronze iris. Good. He didn't want to see any more of his family . . . fall. His eyes welled with moisture.

Time to make Eined's death mean something!

He summoned the full power of his arm and walked stride for stride with Kiril and her Cerulean Blade toward the room's center.

Iahn reached an open canister. He crouched behind the stumplike protrusion, hiding from his adversaries, as he studied several pearl-stocked crossbows that hung within. He yanked the nearest from its mount and marveled. As finely fashioned as his other crossbow had been, before he'd lost it during the sea passage, this one was superior. Even more thrilling, the lower section of the unjacketed container held hundreds of bolt clips, each bolt lightly runed with magical vigor. He snatched a clip and worked the crank to load the crossbow. Smooth as silk. If he . . .

A four-armed, human-sized insectoid with a mantis head hopped into view from around the canister. With its amulet shining malevolently on its chest, it directed a ribbon of darkness at Iahn.

The vengeance taker screamed a syllable of warding, too late, and the ribbon found him. Pain seared his right leg. Iahn sighted along the crossbow at the creature's amulet and pulled the trigger.

When the bolt struck the crystal, bolt and amulet were vaporized. The insectoid squealed and dropped, its legs and too many arms flailing madly before losing animation forever.

The vengeance taker allowed himself a nod of self-congratulation as he loaded another bolt.

Prince Monolith charged into the fray. His great strides propelled him past his slowly advancing smaller allies, through the forestlike maze of storage cylinders. Two mantismen launched themselves at his legs, but he bowled through them without stopping, despite their speed and crystal-given strength.

The earth lord ran at the emerald-skinned giant. It was the creature most likely to match its strength against his own elemental power. The prince had always wanted to test his strength against a storm . . .

The giant's eyes sparked, and lightning sprouted from every nearby surface, each bolt skewering Prince Monolith. The electricity seared through his mineral nerves, locking him in place. He strained, threatened with his booming voice, and tried to call upon his power to move through stone, but the electricity held him caged.

The pain crept toward intolerable.

Ususi spoke the words of a protective spell, and her sense of touch dulled as her skin protectively hardened. Monolith obscured her vision of Pandorym for a moment as he charged, but then her view was clear again. As terrifying as the force assembled before them was, her percipience allowed her to see that Pandorym's true strength lay beyond the portal it maintained in Deep Imaskar. Destroying the creature would cut the puppet strings of all the servitors it had transferred there.

She saw Iahn take up a position on top of an unjacketed canister and fire his newfound weapon, one bolt after another. The others also advanced, but she couldn't take time to watch their progress.

The wizard spoke a spell of wind, hoping to disperse or at

least disturb Pandorym's cloudlike form, and so disrupt the portal into Deep Imaskar, but the entity held its form.

If she couldn't close the portal, could she block it? Ususi spoke the short, sharp syllables that beckoned a solid magical wall. Before she could finish, a hail of serpentine, night-dark rays emerged from the creatures at the room's hub. Her eyes narrowed with concern as the shafts fell against her hardened skin . . . then she sighed. Her protective magic was diminished, but it held.

The wizard finished her utterance. She felt nothingness coalesce toward solidity. Though normally invisible, this time she saw her wall take shape in her star-bright gaze. She thrust it into the portal Pandorym hid at its core. The plane of force slapped into place.

Pandorym's vaporous emanation writhed and bucked. The entity didn't like the obstruction. Immediately, she sensed her blockade come under attack. Pandorym sought to eject it. The wizard gasped and tightened the clamps of her arcane will more securely about her magical construction. Her spellcraft was tested nearly beyond its limit as she struggled to hold the wall in place.

The portal at Pandorym's heart hazed, warped, and wavered, but held. She had hit on a workable strategy! If she could maintain the blockade, Pandorym's portal into Deep Imaskar would fail.

Then she saw crystal-faced Shaddon Datharathi, back on his feet, running at her with the speed of a zephyr.

The pathetic man, utterly encased in his own folly, was Pandorym's perfect avatar. Bleeding cracks fractured his human carapace, and the radiance emanating from his mineral skin was dimmer than before. Prince Monolith's initial strike had seen to that. Unfortunately, the man was still very much in the fight.

Shaddon loosed a barrage of pitch-black tendrils from one outspread hand. Ususi sidestepped a handful, but several chewed into her stony skin, nearly exhausting its protection.

She dared not relinquish her wall . . . but Shaddon advanced on her!

Ususi muttered a prayer of thanks when the elf swordswoman intersected Shaddon's path. Kiril slashed with her sentient blade with a power equal to Shaddon's malevolent vitality. Shaddon's left hand and forearm sailed through the air, leaving a spray of blood and darkness. The Datharathi elder screamed, his voice suddenly quite human.

Ususi sidled to the left, trying to maintain her line of sight with Pandorym and the gap in its defense. She sensed the intradimensional portal weakening. All she had to do was maintain her plug of force, and Deep Imaskar . . . what remained of it . . . would be saved.

Kiril maintained her two-handed grip on Angul's hilt as her foe's severed hand and forearm spun away. The crystal-encased human partially freed himself from Pandorym's control, enough to emit a pitiful scream. Too bad. Kiril took advantage of the distraction to plunge Angul directly into Shaddon's chest. Most opponents would have perished immediately upon receiving such a mortal blow.

Violet light flared anew in Shaddon's eyes, and scything ribbons of darkness spewed from his mouth. Where the darkness touched the elf's flesh, they burned like ice and burrowed in.

Angul shored up her will to ignore the pain. It was only skin deep, as yet. Mere pain couldn't hinder her righteous power. She pulled the Blade Cerulean free of Shaddon's chest, then swung it around in a neck-high arc. Shaddon's inhuman speed saved him from her first slash, and her second. Ribbons of darkness cut into her arm and leg. She felt nothing.

Pain was a luxury. So was injury. Blood loss, shock, and dismemberment couldn't prevent her from accomplishing what Angul demanded.

With her third swing, she decapitated the man. The body fell.

Shaddon's head, free of its body, remained aloft, its virulent hate undiminished.

Warian's hair stood on end in response to the electrical storm near him. Blue-white bolts burned through the advancing earth lord . . . over and over. Prince Monolith was caught in a chain of lightning that pinned him for painful moments. Charred, smoking rubble blasted from the earth elemental's form like shrapnel, and Monolith yelled out, furious and hurt.

The green-skinned giant was . . . some sort of titan? A storm giant? Something nearly godlike, Warian's subconscious gibbered. They couldn't face something like that!

Could they?

Could he? Warian clenched his prosthesis, and time floated down a slower path. Even the lightning encircling Monolith seemed to linger in its smoking trails.

Warian moved toward the giant, dodging mantis-men and other horrors. Most did not see him, barely noticing his passing, while others tried to track what must have been a crazy blur.

His dash ended with a magnificent punch to the giant's shin. He rotated his hips and shoulder into the punch as Zel had once taught him, transferring all the power of his arm into the knuckles of his prosthesis.

Nothing happened. Warian allowed himself to fall back to normal speed.

The giant's electrical cage winked out, and it grunted as its leg collapsed. The creature went down on one knee. Warian jumped away, nearly evading the giant's grasp. Greenish fingers closed around him, holding him, then squeezed. Even with the power of his prosthetic girding his strength and endurance, Warian gasped in pain.

Thankfully, the momentary release from the lightning was all Monolith needed.

The elemental noble crashed into the giant and grasped the bigger humanoid with his huge, earthen hands.

Warian fell several feet as the giant dropped him. It needed both hands to resist Monolith's elemental hug.

The vengeance taker aimed, fired, loaded, and cranked the mechanism. Again. And again.

The mantis-men were especially vulnerable to Iahn's deadly aim. As soon as Iahn saw a servitor's amulet, it was as good as out of the fight. If the way each creature screamed and collapsed was any indication, a servitor severed from Pandorym's control was dealt with permanently.

An insectoid broke cover, dashing from behind a canister. It hurled a spear, its aim perfect, and its speed lethal. Iahn slipped left, and the spear whispered its regrets in his right ear as it flew past. He wondered if the creature's speed was the result of its own skill or was an enhancement of Pandorym's power. No matter.

"Got you," he grunted as the mantis-man's amulet shattered, speared by an answering bolt from Iahn's new crossbow.

His was a winning strategy. "Break their amulets!" he yelled to the others, trying to project his voice above the din. "It's their connection to Pandorym. Break—"

A gray-skinned creature appeared from behind a large canister and loped forward, much larger than the mantis-men he'd so far eliminated. A mountain troll, like the one he'd faced days earlier. Iahn took aim . . . where in the name of the Great Seal was its amulet? He spied a chain, but no crystal.

He fired a bolt directly into the charging creature's

forehead. The troll's head rocked back, then forward, a grin on its face. Blood trickled toward its mouth, but the troll roared and accelerated.

The vengeance taker shot one of the creature's eyes before it reached him and snatched at his legs. He skipped left, then right, careful to keep his footing on top of the tall cylinder. The creature was so big, it easily looked over the top the cylinder on which Iahn stood.

The vengeance taker holstered his crossbow in his thigh sheath. When the creature lunged at him again, he launched himself into the air.

He jumped up and forward, rotating into a somersault so that as the troll moved below him, the vengeance taker's legs flew high and his hands were free to grab the troll by its filthy black hair.

Before the creature realized where its target had gone, Iahn was on its back, securing his position with one arm snaked around the creature's thick neck. He squeezed.

The troll's rubbery flesh was resilient. That didn't prevent the vengeance taker from crushing its trachea. The troll squeaked and started to stagger. But Iahn knew the troll's body would repair itself in an instant. He kept squeezing, making certain that the troll couldn't get a breath. Nor could it roar, scream, beg, or even gasp.

The vengeance taker rode the troll down as it collapsed first to its knees, then onto its face. Even then, Iahn didn't relinquish his hold. Instead he yelled, "Ususi! Give me fire!"

Ususi heard the vengeance taker's command, but she couldn't afford to break her concentration. The wizard didn't turn or even process his words. All her energy was necessary to maintain the blockage she'd thrown down Pandorym's throat. The shimmering portal through which

Deep Imaskar's plight was visible hazed further. Its wide diameter fluctuated, and the surrounding void black vapor whipped and lashed as if struggling to maintain its shape in a stiff wind.

Something punctured a small hole in her barrier. Her spell didn't collapse, but she spied something moving from the opposite side of it into the weapons cache.

An Imaskari man appeared in the gloom of Pandorym's form, stepping out of the portal. Had an ally arrived? Ususi didn't recognize him, but her eyes widened when she saw a bloody, oozing object impaled through the palm of the man's hand. A Celestial Nadir crystal was punched all the way through. Was Pandorym overwhelming Deep Imaskar by forcibly converting citizens to be its servitors? The wizard nearly lost her concentration in horror.

The newly arrived Imaskari focused on Ususi. In his hand he clutched a sliver of Celestial Nadir crystal, carved like a small throwing dagger. He raised the sliver high, its needle-sharp end aimed at her head. Did the man mean to launch the crystal at her from across the room? Worry pinched Ususi's forehead.

What would happen if she were infected by a Pandorym-controlled crystal?

The giant was strong—as strong as many of Monolith's noble brothers and sisters who cavorted yet, uncaring of the fleshy creatures that haunted the earth above the mantle. But Monolith was renowned in the wide Earth Court for his strength and solidity.

Monolith grappled the giant around the legs in a great hug. He powered the legs together even as the green-skinned storm lord smashed at the back of Monolith's head. Uncaring, the prince pushed the giant over on his back.

A pale-skinned servitor of Pandorym, one hand pierced

with crystal, the other holding a crystal dagger, appeared in exactly the wrong spot. The falling giant crashed down directly upon the man, smashing him flat just as he tried to hurl his dagger across the chamber.

The giant's fall cratered the floor, and Monolith was on his adversary even before the shock of the impact vibrated through the giant's full length. He had to keep his weight on the giant's torso.

The giant was down, but not out. The earth lord fended off a staggering blow and took a few directly in the head and face. Fortunately, his body was more resistant to pummeling than living flesh. And as mighty as the storm giant was, it was still a creature more like a man than an elemental.

The giant turned on its side, trying to get away from the prince's grapple—a fatal mistake. Though the giant was stronger than the elemental, Monolith was practiced in centuries of contests with his heavy-limbed kin. As soon as the giant gave the prince his back, the earth lord straddled the giant, grabbed him around the neck, and pulled. The giant's lower back was pinned under Monolith's boulderlike weight.

With a savage jerk, Monolith broke the giant's back.

Warian danced away from the titanic figures, barely avoiding the same fate bestowed on Pandorym's newly summoned stooge. Four or five mantis-men remained near the core, not to mention the great smudge of steaming evil that seeped from the cracked silo—was that Pandorym itself? Kiril Duskmourn had just cut down Shaddon, but the Datharathi's head still threatened her. And . . .

A creature, half bone and half void, stepped out of Pandorym's shrouded portal. Blood slicked its shadow-tipped claws, and gore crusted its body in horrible textures.

The creature was fresh from a slaughter. Warian moved, and the world around him slowed again, though not as dramatically as before. He was tiring.

The creature whirled, not as befuddled by Warian's speed as he would have hoped. It clawed at him, each hand like a fistful of swords. Warian ducked right. His left shoulder was scored, but his prosthesis withstood the cuts.

His crystal hand formed a fist, and he slammed it with all the force he could muster into the creature's eyeless, bony face.

The monstrosity exploded under Warian's phenomenal strike, blasting motes of shadow and splinters of bone in every direction.

Warian gasped. The radiance of his arm failed. He'd used all his reserve, holding none back. Exhaustion curled into his limbs, and haze narrowed his vision. Nausea took him to his knees. He didn't have the strength to be sick. He didn't have the . . .

Warian reeled into oblivion.

The Cerulean Blade tore through several razor-sharp, soul-burrowing strands that spewed from Shaddon's mouth. Turning those strands into so much dust, Kiril tried to plunge Angul into the decapitated head, but Shaddon darted outside her arc.

She missed a few strands from Shaddon's next volley. Angul refused to let her feel the pain.

Without consequences, anything was possible—any feat, any good work.

And any atrocity.

Her sword bristled in her hands at this wayward thought, and some of the pain of Shaddon's blows touched Kiril. She gritted her teeth and muttered, "Let me fail here, and these abominations survive."

She deflected another burst of night-black tendrils. Her hands wavered on Angul's hilt, but his fire flickered brightly. Shaddon's dead eyes glinted, uncaring, as he vomited up another torrent of darkness.

A ribbon cut her cheek, and pain flared.

"Damn you, Angul, help me now without messing with my head, or lose your last tie to the humanity your forsook!"

The blade flared—in anger? Doubtful Angul could feel that emotion. Shaddon's head, sensing weakness, darted forward, its mouth eagerly wide, its crystal flesh oozing inky death. The head moved close to deliver an awful coup de grace that only physical contact could allow.

Angul didn't let her down. Shards of Shaddon's skull and crystal rained across the chamber.

Now . . . what was the vengeance taker bellowing for? Fire? The blade flared its blue flame anew. Kiril yelled a battle cry and ran to the Imaskari's aid. Her blade hadn't abandoned her. Besides, igniting trolls was something she and Angul could both agree on.

The murk of Pandorym's form strained and quivered. The portal at Pandorym's heart wavered, narrowing further.

Ususi didn't falter. She imagined the wall she held blocking the passage to Deep Imaskar as a gag—a gag she continued to cram down the throat of a desperately struggling assassin on whom the tables had suddenly turned.

With the ragged edges of her percipience, she noted Shaddon was no more. Zel summoned the courage to enter the room and tend to his fallen nephew. The elf swordswoman torched the body of a gray troll. Iahn stood nearby, firing crossbow bolts at the mantis-men if they dared to poke their heads from cover. The earth lord, Prince Monolith, stood over the body of a fallen giant, near the gap where Pandorym's influence seeped from its jacketed silo.

Pandorym's influence . . . something nagged her. She turned the full attention of her star-bright eyes, Qari's gift, on the boiling darkness of Pandorym and saw the façade for what it was.

What she perceived as Pandorym was only the entity's evil nimbus—the true mentality of the creature still lay entrapped in the partly disengaged canister, thick with the entangling magic of an ancient era. The nimbus wasn't Pandorym—it was Pandorym's herald. But left to fester, it would eventually leverage enough power to pull itself free of its containment. On the other hand, if Pandorym's canister could be resealed in its silo, the nimbus that leaked from the gap would cease.

"Prince Monolith, seal the gap!" Ususi yelled, straining to maintain her spell.

Hearing her, Pandorym redoubled its struggle. Her barrier nearly skittered from her mental grasp. She sensed dozens of powerful presences gathered just on the other side of Pandorym's portal—Deep Imaskar's attackers had returned to the edge of the bridge through which they'd arrived. Trolls, mantis-men, shadow efts, and other creatures pressed against the wall. And an illithid! All were trying to cross the gap and defend their master. Ususi was determined they would fail.

She wouldn't let them through.

"The gap?" The earth lord took a tentative step toward the raised circle in the floor, through which Pandorym's influence streamed. "This?"

"Yes! Close it! Quick!"

Ususi stumbled, one hand out, the other on her forehead as her spell came under even more violent attack. "There are dozens, maybe hundreds of servitors on the other side of the portal, in Deep Imaskar—they're trying to return here. And they will if they break through my containment!"

The earth elemental shook his head, not understanding what the wizard was saying. But he squatted next to the gap to study it. Iahn ran forward, as did Kiril, though Ususi doubted either's strength would matter. From wherever it had been hiding, the crystal dragonet darted down to land on the earth elemental's shoulders. It chimed encouraging tones into Monolith's ear.

The prince put one great hand on the edge of the raised canister and clutched the lip of the silo with the other.

The wide canister, partially unjacketed, with its mechanical locks only half engaged, resisted the earth lord's attempt to close it. The inlaid Nadir crystal lines across the top of the canister lit up, but the radiance wasn't purple—it was yellow. The entangling magic wasn't dead—it sought to reengage.

The citrine radiance penetrated the cloud of blackness. Pandorym's nimbus roiled and boiled, and tendrils of night snaked out to point threateningly at Prince Monolith. But without its servitors to do its bidding, Pandorym's aura was toothless. It would remain so if Ususi could continue to hold the portal.

"Try again!" the wizard commanded.

"Help me!" yelled Prince Monolith.

Iahn and the elf took up positions along the edges of Pandorym's prison vessel.

The elemental's mineral thews contracted with a sound like a rock fall in a ravine. Kiril and the vengeance taker cursed and grunted with effort.

With a lurch and click, the canister popped back into place, sealed.

The portal into Deep Imaskar slammed shut. Ususi staggered as her spell collapsed. The lines of yellow Nadir crystal that inlaid the surface of the canister surged as if living things, knitting and extending themselves in racing lines of arcane fire until they completely covered the silo, their severed ends rejoining to form a perfect circle of warding.

The spiral of void and destruction came untethered. It

whirled faster and faster, wild streams of violet midnight, a vortex of dust and dark, draining away into the ultimate spaces beyond the worlds. With a last furious scream, Pandorym's shadow faded into history's depths.

CHAPTER THIRTY-ONE

Clouds gathered, white on ivory, on the horizon. The day's last blinding rays infused the storm with ominous highlights.

Ususi looked across the trackless Raurin Desert from a balcony high on the Palace of the Purple Emperor.

"Iahn is late," Zel fretted.

Ususi turned to regard Zeltaebar Datharathi.

"Vengeance takers follow their own schedules. They are not so much late as . . . deliberate," Ususi responded.

"He said he'd return today. Here comes day's end. I don't see how we can get a trade covenant brokered between Deep Imaskar and Vaelan if timetables can't be—"

"Uncle!" broke in Warian. The young man with

the crystal arm was seated on a comfortable bench on the balcony. The bench, one of several, and other items of comfort, had been delivered several days ago by Datharathi skyship. They represented sample merchandise that Deep Imaskar might wish to trade for, according to Zel. On a small table next to Warian, playing cards were arranged in several small stacks. Brightly painted dragons of various hues were visible on each card.

The Datharathis—those few who survived destruction by Pandorym—had been quick to see an untapped trade opportunity in Deep Imaskar. Even Warian seemed interested in his family business, now that it tottered close to dissolution. Of all the senior family members, only he and Zel survived—he because his prosthesis predated Pandorym's release, and Zel because the man had been too paranoid to accept the implants.

Seated next to Warian was the elf, Kiril Duskmourn. Ususi watched her curiously. She was surprised that the swordswoman lingered in the palace, especially with the duty she proclaimed, on a daily basis, she had to fulfill. Prince Monolith had departed soon after their victory, taking with him a sorely wounded dwarf geomancer named Thormud Horn. The dwarf's peculiar dragonet familiar, Xet, remained with Kiril, much to the elf's apparent displeasure. Ususi had exchanged only a few words with the geomancer before he left, but she'd thanked him for bringing such potent allies as Monolith and Kiril to their aid. The dwarf had been gracious but sickly. The earth lord had rushed him away to administer healing and rest, possibly far below the mantle, where the elementals reigned.

"Are you even listening to me?" Zel asked her.

Ususi shook her head. "Iahn will return soon enough. Probably with an artificer or planner in tow with whom you can make your deals. In the aftermath of all the destruction and chaos in Deep Imaskar, they'll be desperate to trade for food and goods. But see to it you don't take advantage of Deep Imaskar's problems . . ."

Zel held up his hands and nearly spluttered.

" . . . because I doubt Iahn would look kindly on that sort of profiteering."

"Don't worry, Ususi," said Warian from his seat. "The items we've provided so far are gifts, to show our good intentions. Once your city has had time to get back on its feet, we can begin to talk in earnest."

Ususi nodded. "All in good time."

Zel turned from badgering the wizard and focused his attention on the swordswoman.

"What about you, Kiril? Given any more thought to my proposal? Perhaps this Sildëyuir realm of yours would also like to trade with Vaelan. I could work a deal that would greatly benefit both parties."

Warian sighed, but didn't interrupt. Instead, he returned to fiddling with his cards.

The elf raised a single eyebrow as she regarded Zeltaebar. "You weren't really listening to me, if you think I have enough influence to open the hidden realm to trade. Or if you think I give a damn about trade in the first place."

Zel reddened, but pressed on. "Right. You were saying something about a citadel—that it was time you returned? I'm sorry, what was it called? Deeprock? No? Understar?"

"Stardeep," corrected Kiril. The elf reached for the flask on her hip, spun off the top, and sipped. Even from where the wizard stood at the balustrade, she smelled the bitter tang of hard spirits.

The elf returned the flask to her hip and said, "It's not the kind of place that is interested in barter or luxuries. It's a prison. The less said, the better. Catch my meaning, tradesman?" Kiril fixed Zel with an ominous scowl.

"Hey, I can take a hint!" Zel backed away and dropped onto the cushioned bench next to his nephew, muttering.

The wizard was curious about the swordswoman's bitterness and veiled references. Kiril was adept at saying just enough to rouse interest about her past, before the span when she worked for Thormud. Then she'd invariably clam up, curse, and threaten anyone who asked questions. A story was hidden in her evasions, but not one Ususi had the energy to pursue.

Not when she had her own newly minted dream to follow.

Ususi looked back across the darkening sky.

Since Pandorym's entrapment, she'd explored the palace a little. What she'd found amazed her. The entire edifice was a powerful relic of her vanished ancestors. Some of its chambers seemed bigger on the inside than out. She'd sealed the weapons cache, but other chambers and vaults within the palace promised to reveal less dire secrets. Truth be told, with her discovery of the palace, her impetus to continue her original quest—locating each of the twenty gates into the Celestial Nadir—had waned. The palace alone would take years to fully plumb.

Plus, its size and peculiar qualities offered unique opportunities.

The seed of an idea, rooted days earlier, continued to grow in her imagination. She wondered again—was it time for Imaskar to expand? The city behind the Great Seal would be rebuilt, of course. But perhaps the attack signaled the need for another colony of Imaskari to establish itself. Perhaps even on the surface from which they'd fled nearly four thousand years earlier.

She chuckled. She considered the Palace of the Purple Emperor as the location of her imagined colony. Her exploration of the palace had unearthed startling revelations. She'd discovered how to move the entire structure! Using magical controls in the emperor's suite, she could shift the palace to a kinder location in Faerûn than the center of an inhospitable desert.

But, before Ususi allowed such grand dreams to sweep her away on a new quest, she had unfinished business to attend.

Each day she spent exploring the palace was another day she put off going home.

She had to return to Deep Imaskar. She owed it to her people; she owed it to herself. She owed her sister Qari for her life. Without Qari's gift, when she'd flailed in Pandorym's gulf of darkness, they'd all have perished, or worse. But the price for accepting her sister's gift was steep. Ususi suspected Qari was utterly severed from the world, blind and perhaps suffering.

Ususi had run long enough. She would return to Deep Imaskar and help Qari as she was able. She would return her special perception to her sister, if possible.

After that, she would reveal her grand plans to the lord apprehender. With or without his blessing, Ususi resolved to bring a kernel of Imaskar back to the surface.

In that moment, High Imaskar was born. Whether in folly or in grace, only the future would disclose.

The gray clouds reared above the boundary separating day and night, in whose shadow grew a restful twilight of cooling desert sand.

R.A. SALVATORE
ROAD OF THE PATRIARCH
THE SELLSWORDS, BOOK III

Jarlaxle and Entreri have found a home in the
monster-haunted steppes of the Bloodstone Lands,
and have even managed to make a few new friends.
But in a place as cruel as this, none of those friends are
naive enough to trust a drow mercenary and a shadowy
assassin to be anything but what they are: as dangerous
as the monsters they hunt.

OCTOBER 2006

SERVANT OF THE SHARD
THE SELLSWORDS, BOOK I

Powerful assassin Artemis Entreri tightens his grip on the streets
of Calimport, driven by the power of his hidden drow supporters.
His sponsor Jarlaxle grows more ambitious, and Entreri struggles to
remain cautious and in control. The power of the Crystal Shard grows
greater than them both, threatening to draw them into a vast web of
treachery from which there will be no escape.

PROMISE OF THE WITCH-KING
THE SELLSWORDS, BOOK II

Entreri and Jarlaxle might be strangers in the rugged, unforgiving
mountains of the Bloodstone Lands, but they have been in difficult places
before. Caught between the ghost of a power-mad lich, and the righteous
fury of an oath-bound knight, they have never felt more at home.

NOW AVAILABLE

For more information visit **www.wizards.com**

R.A. Salvatore's War
of the Spider Queen

The New York Times best-selling saga of the dark elves

Dissolution Book I
Richard Lee Byers

While their whole world is changing around them, four dark elves struggle against different enemies. Yet their paths will lead them all to the most terrifying discovery in the long history of the drow.

Insurrection Book II
Thomas M. Reid

A hand-picked team of drow adventurers begin a journey through the treacherous Underdark, all the while surrounded by the chaos of war. Their path will take them through the heart of darkness and shake the Underdark to its core.

Condemnation Book III
Richard Baker

The search for answers to Lloth's silence uncovers only more complex questions, allowing doubt and frustration to test the boundaries of already tenuous relationships.

Extinction Book IV
Lisa Smedman

For even a small group of drow, trust is the rarest commodity of all. When the expedition prepares for a return to the Abyss, what little trust there is crumbles under a rival goddess's hand.

Annihilation Book V
Philip Athans

Old alliances have been broken and new bonds have been formed. While some finally embark for the Abyss itself, others stay behind to serve a new mistress – a goddess with plans of her own.

Resurrection Book VI
Paul S. Kemp

The Spider Queen has been asleep for a long time, leaving the Underdark to suffer war and ruin. But if she finally returns, will things get better... or worse?

For more information visit **www.wizards.com**

THE CITY OF SPLENDORS
A WATERDEEP NOVEL
ED GREENWOOD AND ELAINE CUNNINGHAM

In the streets of Waterdeep, conspiracies run like water
through the gutters, bubbling beneath the seeming calm
of the city's life. As a band of young lords discovers there
is a dark side to the city they all love, a sinister mage and
his son seek to create perverted creatures to further their
twisted ends.

And across it all sprawls the great city itself: brawling,
drinking, laughing, living life to the fullest.

Even in the face of death.

Other titles available in The Cities series:

THE CITY OF RAVENS
RICHARD BAKER

TEMPLE HILL
DREW KARPYSHYN

THE JEWEL OF TURMISH
MEL ODOM

For more information visit **www.wizards.com**